BIRTH OF RESILIENCE

STEFANIE CHU

CANARI PUBLISHING

BIRTH OF
RESILIENCE

*To the person who inspired the character, Gaven, Happy Birthday.
Meeting you was a privilege I never thought I would have, and
your acceptance of this narrative is a heartfelt thank you in itself.*

*And to my bread-loving friend, who would be thrilled to know
that "bread" was mentioned 15 times in this book.*

The Alliance
of Althaea, Minetta, and Valenia
Candela Sea
Morenta
Narvi
Soli
Agna
Avon
Knights Estate
Venne
Akoun
Solarin
Bay o Mine
Saon
Malino
Oban
Oo
Kestrel Bay
Fauna
Falum
Mersa Tribe
Tribe of Aegises
Tribe of Umbras
Viscarian Tribe

ALTHAEAN SEA
ALTHA HILLS
AlthaCity
Allete
Elegen
EVALEEN
Kishnin
Ekvelt
Rhea
Namani
Desdemona
Aias
Yountilla River
Althaea Main
ALTHAEA MAIN
Endine
NANAKA
Naiad
Ganmali
OLINA
OPHALLEN
Gulf of Oris
E URABE
AXILLAIRE
Xeran
Tribe of Celtas
Belligmn Tribe
Alyssi
AN IBE
THE HEARTH
Tribe of Paragons
N
W
E
S

THE ALLIANCE

Empire of
ALTHAEA

Councilors
ADDER & SUZAN

ALTHAEA MAIN
Leader: Gaven

AXILLAIRE
Leader: Yoah

EVALEEN
Leader: Landon

ALTHA HILLS
Leader: High Priest

NANAKA
Leader: Noire

OPHALLEN
Leader: Cole

Empire of
MINETTA

Councilors
DAREH & NOVINHA

AVON
Leader: Shiba

SAON
Leader: Ryland

OBAN
Leader: Hilda

Empire of
VALENIA

Councilors
TAREK & JULIE

Tribe of
PARAGONS

Tribe of
AEGISES

Tribe of
UMBRAS

Tribe of
CELTAS

PROLOGUE

There was a middle-aged woman, one of those worn and broken mothers who looked like she never knew rest. Her hair was tied in a braid underneath a wool blanket with patches of fabric covering what were once holes. She stood still, her transparent silhouette a beacon in the dark forest. She stared back at me, but not a word came out of her mouth; she simply turned and faded into the dark.

You're going to leave us like she left you?

I heard a familiar male voice, one that annoyed me beyond words. I turned to my left and saw his scrawny figure. His face was in the shadows – for the better – but I would recognize that mischievous noble anywhere. He was once my sword and shield, though a butter knife and pan would've done a better job. I trusted him unconditionally, and it was one of the greatest mistakes of my life.

Think about all those people you could've helped, all those soldiers you threw out as bait. You think they'll ever forgive you for that, Gaven?

I didn't want to engage with him, but I couldn't let him get away with saying that. I wasn't going to become a victim to his ploys again. I curled my hand into a fist, ready to knock the wind out of him. But as I pulled my arm back, a pair of small hands gripped my arm. Her strength compared to mine was nothing but a brush of wind, but her sweet, harmonic melody rekindled a faint memory that extinguished the anger coursing through my body.

Was it worth it?, she asked.

I peered down and saw a young girl, half my height. She caressed a purple stone in her palms and showed it to me. It had been so long. I was relieved to see she was well, gleeful to meet her again – but did she feel the same way?

The man she was looking at wasn't the same child she once knew. I had become a liar, a man with no honor, a traitor to my people, comrades, and family. She granted me an opportunity, a second life.

You used us. You said you would return my stone and you lied. How could you?

She was right. I should've never left home. Going to Althaea was a selfish act, but my younger self didn't know better. Even now, I had every opportunity to return home. Why didn't I? Was I ashamed to face her? Afraid to admit my blood had Minettan origins?

My voice was silenced by a knot in my throat as tight as the clot in my heart. I felt the guilt eating away at my mind. My soul ached, twisted and jabbed, and I wanted to scream for help.

The male figure stepped forward, offering me a gold-trimmed dagger in his palm.

You know what you have to do, he said. *It's the only way for you to be forgiven.*

I stared at the weapon with an uneasy temptation. Was it the only way to end this pain? My sense of reasoning spiraled away as I heard more and more voices creeping into my mind.

Then it occurred to me that I had seen and felt this before.

This pain – as much as it hurt – wasn't real, and neither were the people around me. I had to be stronger than my dark past. I searched for something to wake me up from this nightmare, and my eyes were drawn to the man's dagger. I snatched it, and without a second thought, jabbed it into my chest with both hands.

But as blood seeped down my chest, there was no pain. The dagger was replaced with a warm glow under my hands. I fastened my hands around this feeling, not wanting to let it go.

"Hey, snap out of it."

I followed her voice. All was quiet as my eyes shot open, heart racing as my chest heaved labored breaths. The first thing I saw was the lumastōne in her hand, a soft blue glow gently lighting her face. Slowly, I recognized the faint, vintage pattern of the ceiling behind her, and the shadows cast from the nooks. I sighed in heavy relief when I saw a full moon peeking from the window – I knew where I was – and my hands began to release the warm object over my heart.

She pulled her hand back with a troubled look on her face.

"You sure you don't want to talk about it?" she asked.

The last thing I wanted was to place my burden on others. I wish she didn't have to see me like this, or feel the pain that I felt, but who knows where I would be if she was not there to pull me back into this world.

I shook my head and gave her a gentle smile. "Sorry to wake you again."

I pulled the cover over my bare chest and turned to the side, admiring the calm of the night, the moonlight casting a bright barrier over the rooftops of the fortress.

How many times did I have to relive this nightmare? Was this the power of the Blessed – the ability to haunt their victims beyond the grave – or was I not brave enough to befriend the voices in my head?

All I knew for certain was that there was an organization out there planning their next attack, one possibly bigger than we had ever faced. We would be daft to wait until they struck again. Provoking the Blessed was dangerous, but I was convinced that until we put an end to them, my past would continue to haunt me. I couldn't allow them to take more victims. To protect my people and the future balance of the Alliance, every last member of the Blessed must fall, and I would see it done.

Even if I had to do it alone.

PART I

CHAPTER ONE

At the new kōnvoy station in Avon, a conductor reached out his hand to help a lady up the steps, then directed his attention to the family behind her. The station was bustling with nobles, and for the first time since she was a child, Mirari looked like one too. The laced dress that Lucan had picked out for her was not much to her liking, but she had to look her best.

To her left, Kylah was handing a green pebble to young Sarkan. He was five years old now, and brilliant for his age. His parents watched with joy as the little boy grasped it with glee, his eyes following its amber pattern as he turned it in all directions.

Mirari was fixated on a wooden signpost behind them that read: *To Althaea.* It swayed lightly as the next kōnvoy rumbled into the station. Underneath the sign, a couple stepped forward to the side of the tracks, their daughter linked in their arms. They were the very picture of a perfect family — an educated, highly-respected clan of nobles.

Much like the Hale family. They were the nobles who had paved the way for innovation. Most people knew the name; few knew of dark secrets under the surface.

Mirari pictured herself as the little girl. After all, that was the last time she rode a kōnvoy, with her parents and her retainer, Joachim. Back then, she went by the name Roselyn Hale.

She remembered her arms swaying back and forth dramatically with a polished oak-crafted bow and vielle in her hands, mimicking the signpost above her that read: *To Valenia*. She was ready to catapult her instrument over the railing when Joachim seized the vielle and bow from her hands.

Joachim stood as still as the instrument itself. Roselyn wondered several times if he had mastered the art of living without breathing. She had never seen him smile. Not once. He always seemed to be on the watch, listening to the heartbeat of every passerby. She was sure he was waiting to snatch his daggers from the insides of his gold-trimmed, brown coat. All it would take was one clumsy gesture, one suspicious move, and Joachim would end them.

Roselyn wanted to be like that – someone who could fend for themselves and make every assailant beg for their life. But according to her mother, she was a lady, and the only thing she was allowed to hold was a cup of tea, knitting books, and the vielle.

"How much longer?" Roselyn whined. Her parents were steps ahead, conversing with her relatives from Valenia. She had no interest in whatever they were talking about. Neither did her chalk-white cousin standing between his parents with his face glued to a three-hundred-page tome of classical literature about the traditions of the Belligmn Tribe. A tribe that was now extinct.

"Patience, Roselyn," Joachim said, holding her gaze before glancing at the sea of nobles cloaked in feathered coats and hats boarding the kōnvoy headed for Avon. He nodded toward a neon stone behind one of the conductors on the kōnvoy. "You see that kinastōne? It will soon be replaced with the improved version your father made."

Roselyn knew what he was implying. Soon she too would be inventing with hāstals, and assuming her father's role as the next heir to House Hale in Minetta.

But her mother wanted to raise her to be a lady, a woman confined to grace and elegance. Business was for men.

Roselyn was thankful that everything she did – the vielle, choir, embroidery, horse riding – came naturally to her. But she never enjoyed any of it. Her eyes were always fixed on the children outside her window – some her age and others twice as tall – who hopped down streets and threw stones over gates they could not climb. Their laughter echoed from dawn to dusk. She could hear all of it from her study – a carefree melody that stirred as much curiosity as it did jealousy.

Mother scorned them as useless tykes. She was right, in a way, for they didn't have any of Roselyn's talents. But from Roselyn's perspective they had everything she wanted. The knowledge she wanted was outside in the hands of those children. She tried to approach them, but Mother forbade her from interacting with anyone who wasn't a noble. Even when she begged for a little air, to feel the sun on her face, she was only permitted to go out after she was done with her lessons.

But Roselyn was never done with her lessons. Mother made sure of that.

"Roselyn," her father said, his eyes shielded from the sunlight hitting his thin glasses, "say goodbye to Lucan."

Roselyn snapped out of her daydream and turned to her cousin. He said nothing, his eyes stuck in the thick book. He had two pages remaining, and Roselyn didn't want to interrupt him.

She turned to her parents and saw her whole family, including her aunt and uncle, waiting for her to say something.

Their kōnvoy pulled up in front of them, and the adults

started to crowd over the edge of the tracks. Her aunt and uncle were still waiting for the next kōnvoy that would go directly to Valenia.

"Thank you for coming to my performance." Roselyn curtsied to her aunt and uncle. They smiled.

Lucan closed the book and finally lifted his head. He gave a curt nod to Roselyn. "Here. Take this." Lucan handed Roselyn the book. "I think you'll like it."

Roselyn took one glance at the size of the book and immediately doubted her ability to read it. She still appreciated the gift, because Lucan gave it to her. She thanked him.

Her family boarded the kōnvoy and waved one last farewell to Lucan and his parents. They stepped into a spacious, private compartment on the kōnvoy, one filled with velvet furniture and crimson-patterned rugs. Two large windows opened up onto the view of the bright forests of Soli. Joachim stood outside, guarding the door to ensure their privacy.

Her father, Keith Hale, took off his navy coat and hung it by the door. A purple brooch, tightened between a golden rim, shone on his tailored vest. It matched the gem Roselyn had around her neck, and the pin in her mother's waves of raspberry hair. It was a special hāstal manufactured only for the Hale family. They called it a kirinvā stone, allegedly infused with the protective powers of the Gods. But the Hales didn't wear it for protection; it was a statement of power.

On the oak-carved table rested a tray of gold-rimmed tea cups and a plump kettle with rising steam. For just a minute, Roselyn set down her book and hovered over the kettle. She took a whiff and identified the strong, earthly aroma as narcissus tea, a delicacy that wasn't commonly available, but her parents could obtain it whenever they wanted. Her two delicate fingers pressed down the lid as she tilted the kettle, and a stream of smooth amber flowed into the teacups in a circular motion. She nudged two full cups to the edge of the table, for her parents.

As her father took a seat, Roselyn moved toward him. But her mother, Sabrina Hale, patted the seat next to her, and ordered, "Here, child. We have things to discuss."

Things meant Roselyn's current failings, whatever they were. She caressed Lucan's book in her hand as she moved to sit next to her mother.

"Didn't Lucan buy that book this morning?" her mother asked, combing Roselyn's wavy locks of violet hair, a shade darker than her own, with delicate hands that were wrapped in white silk gloves.

"That boy has read every book in the Grand Minettan Library," her father snorted. "Shouldn't come as a surprise that he finished it already."

"It's a shame that Roselyn can't do the same," her mother said, as if Roselyn wasn't directly under her breath.

Roselyn kept her head low.

"Well, then it's a good sign she wants to read more."

"She would have more time to read if you didn't make her take lessons for all those frivolous, useless things." Her nose turned up. "Like horse riding."

"How is horse riding useless?"

"Why in the world would a lady need to ride a filthy animal? We have kōnvoys and carriages. Horses are for soldiers."

Roselyn could sense another quarrel. She couldn't recall a moment when her parents were happy together. They kept their distance from each other back at the estate, each living their own self-absorbed life. If they were forced into the same room, they were almost guaranteed to start a war over – well, anything.

"It wouldn't surprise me if you decided to teach her how to fence."

"Everyone should be able to hold a sword," Keith said, even though he could barely wield one himself.

"I… want to learn how to fight, Mother," Roselyn said. It was the one thing that her father approved of that she had even the slightest interest in. But she knew her mother hated the idea.

"Be quiet, Roselyn," her mother said. She turned back to her husband. "I will not let you ruin the lady I am trying to raise. Have you not embarrassed the Hale name enough?"

"What is that supposed to mean?"

"Don't tell me you aren't aware you practically licked the Region Leader's boots."

"And you think I didn't notice the way you flirted and teased with every noble personage at the reception?"

"Well, somebody has to charm the right people. The Gods know you have all the social graces of a shaved ape."

"At least I don't stuff my chest and toss my money at everything that glistens. Don't flatter yourself. Joachim spends more time with our child than you do."

"You have no idea what's going on in our household. You've been spending all the time you can abroad, probably in brothels with your flatty of a half-brother!"

Roselyn covered her ears and put her head between her arms. She hated the cruelty they tossed so casually, as if constant hostility was the natural marital state. She could feel her eardrums vibrating with their hatred.

Her mother snatched the book in Roselyn's lap and waved it around. Roselyn reached up and tried to take back the book, but she was too short.

"That's mine! Lucan gave it to—"

"Shut your mouth, child!" her mother commanded. "Lucan. Just like his father. That conceited brother of yours is always throwing the boy in our face, taunting us."

"What's wrong with taking pride in your child?"

"He knows Lucan will have a better future than Roselyn."

"You're delusional, woman! Now put her book down."

Her mother threw it. Her father ducked, and the book crashed into the wall behind him. He fumed like a bull, and rushed to her, grabbing his wife by the hair.

"Father, stop!" Roselyn begged. She saw him raise his hand, but Roselyn turned away and squinted, not wanting to watch what was unfolding.

She heard them both tumble onto the wooden floor, followed by grunts and profanities. She heard the sharp impact of a slap, and that's when she had enough.

"Joachim!" Roselyn yelled. Joachim burst into the compartment not a second later. He watched his master and mistress wrestling each other on the ground. As usual, nothing fazed him.

"Stop them!" Roselyn said. Joachim sighed, grabbed her father and pried them apart. Their clothes were wrinkled and torn. Blood dripped from her father's nose onto his once crisp, ruffled white shirt.

"This is all your fault." Her mother jabbed her finger at Roselyn. "Why can't you be better? We should've given you away to the help years ago."

Roselyn's heart felt another blow, as if her mother fired a bolt with her voice. She should have been used to it, but no matter how many times her mother berated her, it always hurt.

Rushing towards her, her mother raised her hand and slapped Roselyn across her cheek. The loud impact echoed even above the racket of the churring kinastōne.

"Sabrina, quit making a scene!" her father said.

"Get up." she scowled, staring down at her daughter.

Roselyn looked away, terrified her mother would hit her again. She couldn't stop trembling. Her mother grabbed Roselyn by one of her ponytails and forced her up.

"No!" Roselyn screamed and struggled to resist. Her mother

slapped her face again. She lifted the helpless girl by her neck. Roselyn choked and struggled to breathe.

"A savage child is no child of mine," her mother said. Roselyn pleaded with her eyes for her mother to stop. When she knew her mother wasn't going to stop, she turned to her father and Joachim for help. The chances of them intervening were close to none.

"Wait outside," her father said to Joachim, nudging to the open door. "Make sure no one hears us." Joachim glanced at Roselyn, and she could see his stern eyes brewing with reluctance. Joachim gave a curt bow, then made for the door.

Roselyn floundered as her mother's grip tightened around her throat. She fought her mother's hands, her mind reeling to stay afloat, to stay alive, but she couldn't keep up. As the door clicked shut, her last drop of hope faded away. The seductive claws of darkness gnawed at her consciousness, and her eyes drooped, her muscles went stiff. Everything faded.

"Mirari." Lucan called again. This time, Mirari managed to blink out of her daze. It didn't matter that her thoughts were interrupted. The details of what happened next would always be a mystery to her.

Fangbane was conversing with Kylah as they were making their way onto the kōnvoy. From behind, Starlight guided young Sarkan up the steps.

Lucan darted his eyes between her and the kōnvoy, realizing something dire. "I'm sorry," he said. "I should've asked if this was okay with you. We can go by carriage, if you'd like."

Mirari shook her head. The past didn't bother her, it just rekindled mysteries that she believed would forever remain unsolved. She was okay with that. The life she had now – the new memories gifted by the friends she made – overshadowed her painful past.

But as she took her first step onto the kōnvoy, she thought maybe, just for this ride, it would be nice to honor the life of Roselyn.

CHAPTER TWO

Morning birds sang in the treetops, stirring Roselyn from her slumber. The sun was barely peeking over the horizon, but it was bright enough to see the trees and bushes.

She could also see clearly the dirt on her lacey purple dress. This was the dress she had worn to her performance for the Region Leader in Soli. She assumed that was yesterday, or maybe the day before. What happened since or what she was doing in a forest, she couldn't remember.

As pretty as the dress was, it felt tight, even itchy at times. But it was her mother's favorite, and she could already see the fumes coming out from her ears once she saw Roselyn like this. She tried to rub off the dirt, but realized it was not dirt, but a burn. She noticed several of them on her dress. She looked at the rest of her body. There were no blisters or injuries on her arms or legs. She felt around her face; nothing seemed out of place there either.

Roselyn looked around again. She was lost and had no idea which direction she came from, but she knew she would get nowhere staying in one place. She didn't have an excuse – the light was on her side.

Besides, the longer she was gone, the worse her parents were going to punish her.

Roselyn picked a direction – out of instinct – and started walking.

Minutes could've passed. Hours? She had no sense of time. She could only follow the direction of the sun, her only reassurance that she hadn't been walking in a circle the entire time.

Her stomach stung like needles. She was so thirsty that her dry mouth begged like a stray dog desperate for food. There was nothing in this forest, that she knew of, that she could eat. She passed by bushes of orange berries and patches of tiny fungi, no taller than the length of her polished nails.

Joachim once told her that Taurin, the God of Land, sowed fake plants to tempt and punish misbehaving children. She'd heard stories of wanderers being poisoned by wild berries all the time, so she knew it was true. She decided not to risk eating anything in this forest.

She took plenty of breaks, sitting on the endless acres of fallen leaves and dried mud that seemed to have no end or beginning. Each time she got back up, her legs wobbled. Roselyn didn't want to go on, but she couldn't stop in the middle of nowhere. Regrets flooded into her mind.

Did walking in an unknown direction make rescue less likely? Was she going in the right direction?

Did she want to be rescued?

The last thing she remembered was her parents arguing over what a disgrace of a child she was. She could still hear their voices stabbing her eardrums, her eyes darting away and pretending none of it was real.

She wasn't sure she was ready to return to that. If she never returned, she wouldn't have to face them.

The sun went down, and her body grew cold. The hunger made it worse. She rubbed her hands up and down her arms to warm herself, but it did nothing. She didn't know how to start a fire. She didn't know how to look for food.

Was anyone looking for her?

This was what she got for not listening to her parents. She always thought she wanted freedom. Now she had it, only to realize she couldn't live outside their captivity.

Tears blurred her vision. She wiped them with her muddied hands, and buried her face in her arms. She didn't want the orange glow of the sun to disappear, but it was fleeing beyond the mountains, ignorant of her wishes.

She begged to be found.

SHE WOKE up against a warm surface. It was comfortable, and she didn't want to move. Whenever she fell asleep in public, Joachim would carry her back home in his arms. Sometimes she pretended to be asleep just to be carried.

But this person didn't feel like Joachim. He was so thin that his sharp shoulder blades were the most unsuitable pillow she'd ever slept on, and he was gripping her legs in an uncomfortable clutch. So, who was holding her now?

Her eyes shot open as she looked up at the stranger who had saddled her on his back. She couldn't figure out who he was based only on his trimmed dark hair. At the slightest movement from her, he turned his head back.

"Who are you?" Roselyn said, squirming to get him to let go. She noticed a younger boy was accompanying him. He didn't help her; he stared blankly as she went into hysteria.

"By the blessed healers of fecundity, calm down!" The stranger tried to keep his grip on her so she wouldn't fall.

"You'll be sorry for kidnapping me!" She screamed, hoping someone nearby would hear. Roselyn had no quit in her. She punched his back, even slapped his arms as hard as one would to test a ripe melon. The firmness in his arms told her he did heavy labor. Getting out wouldn't be easy. When nothing worked, she bit him.

That got him to let go. She tilted backward – in a seemingly endless fall – onto the rigid ground. Now she could run, but her back was in far too much pain. Roselyn groaned as she rubbed her bruised bottom.

She could see that her captors were a stout teenage boy, and the other was about her age. They both had dark hair and alluring cyan eyes, though the older one had a tint of green in his. Their stained shirts reminded her of the rags that potato farmers wore in the field. The boy who was carrying her was only a foot taller, but he had broad shoulders and a touch of peach fuzz. He would need to shave not too long from now.

"We should've just left her," the younger one said with a blank expression.

"Gav," the other boy hushed him before turning back to Roselyn. "Do you have any idea where you are?"

Roselyn looked around. They were on a dirt path that stretched along the edge of the forest. The same forest she had been trapped in for the past day or two, she assumed. The trail went on as far as she could see, across grasslands, and over distant hilltops. Blood drained from her face when she realized she truly was in the middle of nowhere. Even if she ran, she had higher chances of pleasing her parents than arriving at any civilization.

"We found you sleeping in the woods," the older boy said, reaching out a hand to her. "It's not a place you want to take a nap. We were trying to do you a favor and bring you back to town."

She was thankful to be out of the woods, but she didn't know where to go from here. It would be unwise to decline help from the locals.

"Well?" The boy named Gav nagged her. "Do you want us to leave you here?"

She stood up and brushed the dirt off her already soiled dress. "I'll follow you, but I'm walking on my own."

"What a pain."

"Cut it out," the bigger lad scolded, and gave his fellow gremlin a gentle punch on the shoulder. "Our house is not far from here. You can rest there before we go to the nearest town."

Roselyn followed them to a small farm house surrounded by fields of crops, hidden among the trees in a grove. It was the only house in the area. The wooden planks of the siding were weathered gray, and not much seemed to be holding up the crudely thatched roof. Roselyn found it hard to believe anyone would be living in it. She saw a wisp of smoke rising from the chimney, and noticed a plump, fair woman rocking on the porch.

"Salathiel, Gaven, you made a new friend?" The woman said. There was sincerity in the way she spoke.

"We found her in the woods," said Salathiel. "I told her she could rest here for a bit before we take her to town."

The woman smiled at Roselyn. "Well, aren't you a little miracle." Then she furrowed her brow. "You're all dirty. Let's get you cleaned up. I'll warm a bath for you."

"That won't be necessary, Ma'am," Roselyn said. She managed a smile, embarrassed.

"Oh, pish posh. Come," She waved her hand, beckoning Roselyn to go inside the house. "We can't let you go around looking like that. Make yourself comfortable, and I'll bring you some clean clothes. I reckon you wouldn't say no to some fresh bread I baked this morning."

Her stomach roared at the suggestion. She was drooling just thinking about it.

<hr>

ROSELYN FELT herself returning to peace after soaking in a warm bath and indulging in homemade food. Despite the appearance of the ramshackle house, she felt comforted by the hospitality of the family.

She learned that the couple who lived here were named Misa and Marlo Zanette.

Misa watched Roselyn stuff her mouth with bread. She tried to tease as much information as she could out of the girl. But Roselyn only gave away her first name.

"You don't remember how you ended up in the woods, Roselyn?" Misa said. Roselyn recalled leaving the kōnvoy station in Soli, but nothing beyond that. "The nearest station is quite far from here. It's a miracle you made it all the way here by yourself." Roselyn yawned as if just now realizing how far she had come. "How about you stay the night? It won't be long before dark."

Roselyn couldn't object to the idea. She was comfortable where she was, tucked in a warm bed and free to do whatever she wanted. Right now, that was to sleep.

Salathiel and Gaven were secretly listening to their conversation from the other side of the thin wall, taking turns peeking inside.

"She's pretty," Gaven said.

"You like her!" Salathiel said, nearly snorting.

"No! I mean, the way she was all dressed up when we found her."

"I bet she's a noble."

"Go ask."

"Why don't you?"

"None of my business." Gaven turned around and went back to their room. He had already lost all interest in their new guest.

CHAPTER THREE

Roselyn stayed in bed until the next morning. Out of habit, she was up bright and early. To her surprise, so was the rest of the family. The mother and father were in the kitchen, making breakfast. She didn't want to disturb them, so she stayed in her room.

The squeaky floor signaled someone approaching her room. She waited until the figure appeared in her line of sight. It was – Salathiel, was it?

"How old are you?" was the first thing that came out of his mouth.

"How rude." Roselyn scoffed.

"I'm just asking your age."

"You don't ask a lady her age."

"Geez, sorry." Salathiel looked away, but he wasn't leaving. Roselyn could tell her haughty tone upset him a little.

"Well then, what town are you from? I've never seen someone dressed like that around here."

"Fauna."

"Fauna. I guess people who live there really are rich."

"Do I stand out?"

"Like a whole hog in a feast. If you were found by anyone else, I can't guarantee they'd give you the same royal treatment."

"I'm lucky, I guess. Your family is kind."

"Well, you're welcome to join us in the other room." He gestured down the hall. "And whatever Gaven says or doesn't, don't take it personally. That's just how he is."

Roselyn got up from the squeaky bed and followed Salathiel into the other room. Gaven was playing with oddly shaped rocks and wooden carvings. He briefly looked up at her, then continued fiddling with the stones.

"Do you know how to hunt?" Salathiel asked.

"My parents never let me hold weapons," she said.

"Let me teach you some basics with the bow." Salathiel turned to Gaven. "Unless you want to."

As if something had clicked in him, Gaven dropped the rocks and helped himself up. "If she learns from you, it'll take weeks."

Roselyn saw the corner of Salathiel's lip perk into a small grin as Gaven ran down the hall into another room.

"That's how you get him to move," Salathiel said. "He won't miss a single hunting session."

"Isn't it… dangerous to be handling sharp objects?"

"You do what needs to be done. Whether it's to fend off thieves or hunt for supper, you need to learn how to use some kind of weapon if you're going to live here."

"If I what?" she asked. Did she hear him right?

Gaven came back with a flimsy wooden bow and arrow in his hand. The squirt ran past them and out the door as if a whole kingdom was waiting to be claimed. Salathiel guided her in the same direction.

"My parents think it's better for you to stay with us a few more days," Salathiel said. "Do you still not remember what happened?"

"I don't."

"While you were asleep yesterday, I went to town. Everyone's talking about a kōnvoy accident that happened three days ago – some kind of fire or explosion. No one really knows. Could have been those rowdy Althaean pricks. You said you were on a kōnvoy, right? It adds up."

Roselyn thought about this accident. She didn't recall seeing any fire. All she remembered was that her parents were angry with her, and struggling to catch her breath in her mother's choke hold. Or was it all a dream? She wasn't sure of anything at this point.

Salathiel continued, "Rich and lost child doesn't mix well in unknown territories. Better stay low. We'll take you back to Fauna ourselves."

"Where are we exactly?"

"The nearest town is Malino."

"I've never heard of it."

"I don't expect you to. It's small. We never get travelers. You said you were coming from Soli? Malino is about the midpoint between Soli and Fauna. The border to Oban and Avon isn't that far from here."

Roselyn could visualize where they were on a map, and it would be quite a journey. This family didn't seem to own a carriage. Would they have to walk?

This wasn't a concern to Roselyn. She was in no rush to return home. After all, This was the only vacation she was ever going to get.

***

THAT EVENING, Salathiel's mother prepared a marvelous supper with the choicest cuts of the fawn they had brought in. After supper, they played games in the room Salathiel and Gaven shared. They started with playing cards, and moved to one with dice and a piece of paper. Roselyn's favorite game – the same game she had watched her neighbors play – was called Healer's Catcher, a game that involved catching stones with one hand. She had what Gaven called "beginner's luck" and she giddied with delight.

A frustrated Gaven set down the dice and dashed into the kitchen for snacks. As soon as he was out of sight, Salathiel said, "I've never seen Gaven interact with anyone this much. When he first got here, it took him two months before he would look at me."

"Isn't he your brother?"

"Cousin. Mother says he was about to be thrown into an orphanage. He's a bastard child, and my aunt didn't want him anymore."

"Is that… common? For mothers to abandon their children like that?"

Salathiel shrugged. "When you're not a noble, a loaf of bread is worth more than your life."

Roselyn was quiet for a moment. She wondered how much her life was worth.

"That's a good idea," Gaven said as he came bouncing back into the room. "We can sell her for a lot of bread."

"You wish." Roselyn stuck her tongue out at him.

"That would be unfortunate," Salathiel said. "I thought you wanted to marry her."

"Shut up!" Gaven scowled as he took a dive at his cousin. Young and full of adrenaline, he had no fear of pouncing on someone twice his size. Salathiel could push away the feral child with a single hand, but he gave into the thrill of Gaven's challenge. They grappled and laughed, kicked and swatted like two kittens in good fun.

Their play was interrupted by a knock coming from the front

door. All became still and silent in the children's room, in fear that the slightest movement would cause the board beneath them to creak. They communicated only with the shifts of their eyes.

Visitors at this time of night were very unusual – and seldom good news. Were they bandits? Soldiers?

The children stuck their heads out into the hallway, exchanging glances among each other and to their parents, who had tiptoed out of the bedroom next to theirs. No one was in any hurry to answer the door. Anxiety radiated from the adults, which only amplified the children's wariness. At a second louder knock, the children shrank back out of sight. But Marlo, being the man of the house, swallowed his nerves, puffed his chest, and headed for the door.

A noble man was standing at the edge of the porch. His tough-looking face was covered in patches, something Marlo didn't want to question. The man had his attention fixed on someone else – a young boy in finely tailored formal attire at Marlo's feet, barely half the height of the door itself. His skin seemed odd, Marlo noticed, the fairest he'd ever seen. And although the sun had been down for hours, his eyes were concealed behind dark glasses.

It was clear that this young noble was the one in-charge, the man likely his retainer, even though the boy did not seem much older than Roselyn. Whoever this boy was, Marlo knew he must be important.

"Good evening, sir," the boy said, his elocution polite and formal. "I apologize for disturbing you this late. I am Lucan Hale, from the House Hale of Valenia."

Marlo swallowed, and managed to mutter, "M-Marlo Zanette, young Lord. How can I be of service?"

The young man got straight to the point. "You may have heard that a couple of days ago, there was an accident involving a kōnvoy not far from here. Unfortunately, there were casualties,"

As poised as the young fellow was, the loss was clear in his face; he struggled bravely to restrain his emotions.

It was clear to Marlo now that the man who came along with this boy must've been involved in the accident.

"My Lord has the deepest sympathy of my humble self, and all my family." Marlo tried to look as somber as possible – but what did this youngster care about him and his family?

Lucan cleared his throat and reined in his emotions. "With the passing of Keith and Sabrina Hale, their daughter, Roselyn Hale, is now the successor to House Hale of Minetta. Her body was not found, and I have reason to believe she may still be alive."

Marlo instantly knew he was housing the girl Lucan was looking for. His throat was dry, but those countless nights of playing Gotchen had helped him master the art of holding a deadpan expression.

"She's a little taller than me, and her hair and eyes are like lavender. Have you seen anyone resembling the description around here?"

Marlo stroked his chin as he tried to decide what to say. The boy was exceptionally young to be dealing with such matters. Still, he spoke with such grace, it was hard to not take him seriously.

"Well, your Lordship, I wish I could..." Marlo faltered, pondering why the girl had failed to tell them she was from the Hale family. And yet, if the girl had any desire to be reunited, wouldn't she rush out to greet this young family member of hers? Marlo took only a moment to make up his mind. "Let me ask my family. My sons are in bed already, but I will ask them. They hunt regularly, and might have seen something that would help you..." He gently shut the door, leaving the noble boy standing in the doorway.

"What should I tell him?" Marlo asked in a whisper to his

wife. He nudged to the children's bedroom where three small heads cowered behind a half-closed door. They heard everything.

"I don't know… but there must be a reason why she never told us," Misa said. She looked Roselyn in the eye. "Roselyn? Is it true? You're a Hale?" she whispered.

Roselyn was relieved to see Joachim and Lucan alive and well, but they would have little control over what happened to her now. She held back her desire to scream. No sound came out through her clenched teeth, and her voice trembled as she fought to contain her obvious dread. Instead, she shuddered and closed her eyes, fearful of the consequences to come.

Was Misa about to raise her hand? Or would she leave that to whichever Hale was about to take custody of her? She was cornered, unable to come up with a lie to save herself. Her silence gave away the answer to Misa's question, and her hands clasped the edges of her dress as she waited for her caretaker's response.

"You can go home now, sweetie." Misa's soothing voice brought calm to the petrified child. Roselyn opened her eyes and saw the corner of Misa's mouth perking into a smile. Her scowl never came. Beyond that smile, Roselyn saw pure kindness, an inviting warmth that she never knew she desired.

"Please. I…" Roselyn choked as a silent tear escaped. She reached for Misa's hand, and clutched it. "I don't want to go back. I want to stay here with you."

Misa frowned with pity as she tightened her grip around Roselyn's tiny fingers. "But your cousin is here, sweetie. He's worried. Your parents—"

It was a poor choice of words and Misa froze with guilt.

Her parents had passed. That's what Lucan said. Roselyn knew what that word meant, in theory.

Though her face was drained white, there was not a hint of sorrow in Roselyn's eyes. It was news she didn't quite believe, but it wasn't so hard to imagine an empty house without her parents. They were rarely around. Her life would've been the same whether or not they returned.

And if they didn't, joining Lucan's side of the family was even less attractive. He lived a life similar to Roselyn's. But despite only being a couple of months older, Lucan was heaps smarter than Roselyn. Everything he touched, he could remember. Everything he did was beyond perfect. The two were contenders in a race to see who could outperform the other, and their parents were the bettors. Living together? She didn't want to imagine it. Every moment would be a competition, and any friendship she had with her cousin would be destroyed.

Roselyn repeated herself. "I don't want to go back."

Misa couldn't begin to understand why any child born of such privilege would prefer to live with farmers. Then it dawned on her that Roselyn was but a child after all, and children were not worried about things like wealth — only good and evil, and the fate of this child was in her hands.

Misa sighed, and returned to her husband. "She doesn't want to go home."

He shrugged, eyes wide. "She says no, and you decide to keep her, just like that?"

"You always wanted a daughter, didn't you?"

"She's a *Hale*," Marlo reminded his wife. "Not just any noble, a Hale! If they find out that we've stolen their daughter, they'll have our heads."

"People will assume she died in the accident. No one's going to look for her."

"Except that kid," Marlo indicated to the shut door.

"He's a kid, a Valenian one for that matter," Misa countered. "Once this passes, they won't care about the Minettan family. I think we should respect Roselyn's choice."

"She's a kid too. She doesn't know any better. And we barely have enough to feed two children."

"I could use a hand around the house," Misa said. "And the boys favor her so…"

"Well… she's a novelty for now, but—"

"She helped catch the fawn you said was so scrumptious." She lowered her voice even more. "And she's the first person Gaven has taken a liking to."

That sealed the deal. Marlo did acknowledge that his nephew was finally starting to come out of his shell. He had begun to think that the negligence from Gaven's parents had caused irreversible damage, but Roselyn's entry into their lives proved otherwise. She was good for their family, but all good things came at a high price.

Marlo sighed and gave in with a defeated shrug. His wife had made up her mind, and he knew what the children wanted. Misa went to the door, opening it wide to see the small, determined boy.

"Good evening, ma'am," Lucan said.

"Good evening, your Lordship," Misa responded with a smile and curtsey. "I'm so sorry to hear about your loss. We haven't seen anyone like the girl you mentioned around these parts. Best you check in Malino. That's the closest town, only a couple miles north from here."

Lucan's head drooped and there was a heartbroken frown on his face. But he carried on, saying, "Thank you. You have a good night, ma'am."

Lucan left with the retainer and they headed in the direction Misa had suggested. Misa watched from the doorway, making sure that they didn't turn back, before she closed the door and returned to the children's bedroom.

The room was silent. Roselyn stood as still as prey, eyes fixed on the closed door. Her mind dwindled on the goodbye she never said. The thought of never returning to her cozy bedroom, or seeing her favorite cousin again brought a bittersweet feeling. Yet, those memories were not far from the dark ones full of pain, yelling, and isolation.

She locked those dark memories away, convinced that it was the sacrifice she had to make. Immense joy began to radiate from her. It was time to focus on the present. She was free.

CHAPTER FOUR

Mirari's face was inches from a mirror, gazing into her eyes and waiting for... what? The last time she saw something happen to her eyes was years ago. Who was to say it wasn't a hallucination or a trick of the sun? But now she was glued to her reflection.

When ten years passed without an incident, she thought that mysterious ability of hers was gone. But Fangbane saw her fight with fire during the Althaean Siege, and Shiba saw the glow in her eyes when they defeated Laikos.

"Are you ready?" Kylah called from the door with Lucan by her side. Fangbane, Starlight, and young Sarkan had already left the compartment, and Mirari felt the kōnvoy beginning to slow down.

"Give me a moment," Mirari said, grabbing her fur coat and glancing at the mirror one last time as she put it on. Mirari's habit of checking a mirror whenever she had the chance didn't go unnoticed. They probably thought she had become narcissistic for whatever reason.

She didn't know how to tell them, *if* she should tell them.

Why it all happened and what triggered it was still beyond her knowledge. Still, she waited, hoping to catch that glimmer of magenta one more time.

———

SHE WAS ten years old when it happened. In an especially thick part of the forest, miles away from home, Salathiel, Gaven, and Roselyn tiptoed between skyscraping trees, ignoring the singing aviaries above and focusing only on the dirt under their soles. Round seedspikes stuck onto their clothes as they swiped through the bushes. Gaven saw that Roselyn was covered in twigs and pulled a branch out of her hair, even though he knew it didn't bother her. She had racked up dozens of game animals by now and knew that getting dirty was part of the fun. Besides, it helped set the mood and allowed them to blend in with nature, a skill much needed for the hunt.

They had ventured off a little farther than usual, but they were sure, from the tracks and fresh scat, that the boar was somewhere close. As the eldest, Salathiel always played the leader. Gaven and Roselyn waited for his instructions. The trio mastered their own language… in silence.

Salathiel knelt down and began scattering a pile of galuchi seeds, a generous amount that would make any animal's mouth water.

Gaven knew that meant they were going to set up there and wait. He peered over shrubs and low branches, searching for the larger leaves and sturdy twigs they could use as a simple blind. As soon as he got his hands on some, he turned back to Roselyn, who was waiting in between two bushes. She had found their spot.

Behind the bushes and the blind they had constructed, they stayed silent for a while, waiting for the boar to show up on the path. Half an hour passed before it trailed into their sight – a medium-sized young male.

Salathiel whispered to Roselyn, "He's not more than a yearling. Know why that's good?"

She took a guess. "Easier to kill?"

"Not really. He's lean and fast."

Gaven was quick to join the conversation. "It's because the young ones are so tender and tasty."

Salathiel waved his hand in the air – two fingers stuck together. Gaven and Roselyn nodded and waited for his next signal.

Never taking his eyes off the boar, Salathiel carefully pulled out two throwing daggers from the belt along his waist. They were made of heavy metal and he was careful to not let them clang together. His hand slowly rose up, waiting for the boar to come closer.

The young animal hustled nearer, snorting as it followed the scent of the seeds. It came closer to their hiding spot, stopping in front of the small pile of fragrant galuchi seeds. It sniffed the pile cautiously, then began snarfing it down with all the manners of a – well, of a pig.

Salathiel took his aim and flicked his wrist. Two daggers whirled toward the wild hog, one hitting the ground and the other stabbing deep into the meat of its hind leg. The boar dropped to the ground, thrashing around and squealing in pain. It would be dangerous to approach the wounded animal in this state. It may be young, but it still had sharp tusks, and it was maddened by pain.

Despite the danger, Gaven and Roselyn jumped out of the bushes and surrounded the boar from both sides. The blades of their spears hovered inches away from the frightened hog.

The dagger stuck in the boar's hind leg came loose from all the thrashing. It tried to regain its balance, staggering up to defend itself. Its eyes locked on Gaven, charging toward him head first.

Gaven side-stepped, avoiding the hog's gleaming tusks, and the boar's charge went straight past him. He was agile like a wild animal himself. He could tell how they moved. To him, animals were predictable.

But the furious hog turned around and stubbornly charged him again. Gaven held his spear out in front of him, crouching low for leverage, not giving an inch as the boar lunged again. With all his strength, Gaven dug his heels into the soil and caught the boar's charge. As the point buried itself in the animal's shoulder, he let the momentum flex his spear, then flipped the boar like he was shoveling coal. The beast flew several feet in the air, then bashed into the trunk of an oak tree.

The squealing yearling flailed wildly on its side. Roselyn sprinted up to the creature. She lifted her own spear above her head, then jammed it straight down into its neck. It let out one last squeal before all movement stopped, signaling its death.

"Too easy," Gaven said.

"If it was so easy, why didn't you kill it?" she teased back.

They were both huffing from effort, but smiled at each other. Gaven grinned at their teamwork, and their affection, as he unfolded a large black canvas from his bag. The canvas lay flat on the ground and Roselyn helped him lift the boar on top of it before tying the corners into straps for Salathiel to carry over his back. The boar was heavy – Salathiel estimated that it was enough to feed the whole family for at least two days – and he called it a successful hunt.

With the boar over Salathiel's back, they began the hike back home. Gaven and Roselyn trailed behind, exchanging banter as they always did. Gaven didn't want to admit he enjoyed the company of a noble girl, but to him Roselyn was anything but that. She was a partner in crime during their hunts, and the only person who never asked him to tone down his wild side.

Gaven glanced at a diverted road, where some dry grass was flattened, creating a faint trail left by previous adventurers. He had never taken that path before, but it was in the direction of their home and was bound to save them some time.

"Wouldn't it be faster if we cut through the cedars?" Gaven said pointing to the west.

Salathiel looked at the path and seemed to have thought the same.

"Okay but watch your step," Salathiel advised as he diverted them from the main trail, carefully stepping through a screen of thick bushes. As the trail grew steep he tightened his grip on the canvas holding the boar and looked down before taking each step. Gaven and Roselyn followed his footsteps.

Roselyn, for some reason, was mesmerized by the cedar trees around them. She kept her gaze on the tree's ivy leaves and purple petals of all shades. Some petals bloomed and others slept.

Roselyn stopped. She tugged hard on Gaven's sleeve, leaned on his ear and whispered, "What are those?" while nudging her head to the trees on his right.

Gaven took a glance and immediately noticed the herd of leaves and flowers crawling around the trunks. There were a handful, no, dozens of thin vines slithering up the trunks with caution and grace. They were hissing, almost like a den of snakes.

He felt Roselyn's grip on him tighten. Without taking his eyes off his enemy, he reached for the spear behind his back. The other hand kept Roselyn close.

"They look like eater twigs," Gaven said.

"What?" Roselyn didn't like the sound of that.

Some buds began to bloom, and when they did, they turned and pointed at them.

"Ilorinae. Cover your face. Their pollen can knock you out."

Roselyn did as she was told, pulling her shirt up so it covered her nose.

"Sal?" Gaven hollered at him, who was now a couple paces ahead.

Salathiel turned around. His eyes grew wide as the ilorinae started to rise up out of the ground around Gaven. He picked up speed and called out, "Walk fast and ignore them."

Salathiel dashed from the grove of trees, dodging low branches and tiptoeing over thick bushes. Gaven and Roselyn tried to keep up, covering Salathiel's print in the ground with their own.

Salathiel was finally out in a clearing, where the cedar trees were brown and bare, but the two youngsters were still several yards behind. He dropped the carcass and turned to urge them on.

"Faster!" Salathiel yelled, their path growing narrower. He took a step forward, but the vines began to roll at his feet. If he moved, he would surely be dragged along. More violet petals bloomed and they followed Gaven and Roselyn's strides. The ground became a sea of thorns, operated by the flowers that had come alive. The slithering vines advanced, and now there was an angry mob of blossoms separating the path between Salathiel and them.

Roselyn took a misstep back, and Gaven heard a loud crunch as her heel dug into one of the vines. A wail pierced their ears. It was an awful noise that sounded like a cross between engraving metal and a steam whistle. The screaming twig shriveled, as if the escaping sound had drained it. They were easier to kill than Gaven thought. Only now Roselyn had angered every other plant around them, petals fully bloomed with their pistils pointed at the young hunters. Hisses multiplied and echoed from all directions.

Gaven watched the white stamens twitch and hiss. His first instinct was to protect her.

"Get down!" Gaven threw his arms around her, pulling her face into his shirt as he held his breath and tumbled on top of her.

Several puffs of yellow pollen shot into the air, putting on a mesmerizing show of dusty fireworks. The pollen left a mucky coating on every surface it touched, including Gaven's body.

Golden powder fell from his back as he arose to his feet. He held his spear at the ready – but the air around him was still blanketed in particles of amber glow. The particles stung his eyes like water on fire, forcing him to cover his face with his other arm, but not before he took a swipe to his right and sliced off the heads of three sprouts. Even though he couldn't see them, the piercing wails were a pleasing melody.

One of the vines slapped him across his cheek, forcing him to let go of the breath he held in. As pollen funneled up his nostrils and filled his lungs, Gaven choked. With every blink, his eyes lost focus, and the only thing on his mind was sleep.

The powder began to settle on the ground. He felt Roselyn shift, then something pressed against his nose. The gentle scent in the cloth, one that he recognized dearly, brought him back to reality. He forced himself to stay awake. Through his heavy eyelids, he could see the white fabric covering his face and knew it was Roselyn's. He took a deep breath and fought against Roselyn's hand, bringing the handkerchief over her face instead.

"Make a run for it," Gaven wheezed.

There were dozens of buds opening up now. The blooms turned to aim at both of them.

Salathiel was on the tip of his toes, barely able to peer over the wall of aggravated ilorinae. He took a dagger from his belt and slashed at the sterns. They shriveled and died quickly – but none of the flowering buds turned their attention away from Gaven or Roselyn.

"I'll hold them off," Gaven repeated, nudging Roselyn to the direction from where they came. The path was relatively clear. Some trunks were still wrapped in green ivy, but none of them had any aggravated flowers. The bulk of them had already surrounded them. "Keep running until you don't see them anymore."

"I'm not leaving you," said Roselyn. She pulled out a dagger from her shoe and huddled closer to Gaven. Though the feeling of her arm pressed next to his made Gaven feel a little safer, he had no idea what to do – none of them did.

As the petals bloomed and screeched once again, Gaven and Roselyn closed their eyes and held their breath.

It seemed that the worst moment was upon them – and yet he felt overcome by a calm sense of silence and peace. He felt no fear, no pain – only a strange, narcotic warmth that seemed to enfold them.

Gaven forced himself to open his eyes.

To his shock, he was surrounded by fire. It was moving like a hurricane, in a circle around them, enclosing them within the eye. Blankets of pollen burned as they touched the flames, and Gaven felt the dreamy feeling fade away.

The fiery cyclone gradually expanded, reaching the wall of vines that had grown around them, charring the plants and burning off their petals in an instant. The cedar trees that were unfortunately in the fire's path lit up like a candle. The remaining aggressors had backed off, but were waiting for an opportunity to attack again.

The pause in the danger allowed Gaven to glance over at Roselyn. What he saw shocked him. She stood tall, strong and fearless, like a mighty fighter. Only instead of a sword, spear, or bow, the weapon in her hand was a deadly, red flame. The flame swirled around her hand, waiting for the ilorinae to attack. The heat radiating from this flame had no effect on her at all. It was hers to command.

Gaven's stomach lurched with a wave of awe. Yet, what he saw before him didn't make sense. Roselyn was too young to be able to use kore. To even generate a spark of kore would require years of practice, and when Gaven first met her, Roselyn didn't know how to use a single weapon.

Perhaps it was a lie, for what he saw before him told a different story. He saw those marbles of fire dance in her hand with absolute control. The burning pillars of wood towered over her as if everything that glowed red and orange was her kingdom.

Roselyn lifted and pointed her finger at each flower, one by one. A small blast of flame rocketed out each time, hitting each bulb with deadly accuracy. He realized she wasn't merely able to generate a wild, swirling mass of cyclonic flame – she could also strike with pinpoint precision at any target she chose. She pointed – and instantly her target was a charred corpse.

As she continued picking them off one by one, the area was cleared, and Salathiel was in sight of the two children again. He sighed in relief, but then confusion seemed to come over him.

Roselyn was setting the forest on fire. Here was the undeniable evidence – she had the power to summon and control the flames.

Salathiel darted his head across the surrounding area. Small pockets of fire in the ground were being kindled, and in a dense forest, that was not an assuring sight.

Gaven covered his nose, choking on the ashes swirling around them. The smoke was suffocating, and getting thicker as all around them burned – grass, shrubbery, and innocent wildlife, all at the mercy of the flames. Gaven placed his hand on Roselyn's shoulder and gently shook her, urging her to stop.

She reacted like a hound protecting her territory, turning on him in a terrible fury. With seemingly no effort, she elbowed him to the ground.

"What are you—" Gaven snapped, but his voice ran dry as he saw her raise her flaming hand over his head. The flames that had him mesmerized a second earlier now sparked a paralyzing terror through his limbs. Gaven didn't dare move an inch.

His eyes darted to hers, his fright becoming even more paralyzing. Their inviting, attractive purple was no more. Now they danced with a raging magenta glow, which complemented the chaos of the flames. It was intimidating – and mesmerizing to have these inhuman eyes stare right into his soul.

This girl, who he had come to love and trust, now set him trembling with terror.

She was not playing around. From what she did to those plants, he knew that she could easily slay him with a flick of her little finger. And in those fiery pupils there was no remorse, no hesitation, as if she had been waiting years for this opportunity to take his life.

She took her shots. He felt the sharp, hot sensation of the flames rushing past his skin. He quickly checked his body – somehow he wasn't burned. The flames had lightly brushed past his right ear and left shoulder, igniting the grass behind him. Another fireball poked the earth and the grass caught fire inches from his foot. Those misses were deliberate and her message was clear.

Something began to erupt from the earth. Roots and branches poked out of the ground, a trail of bulbs riding on slithering vines. But these plants were not the deadly ilorinae that had attacked them before – they were benign succulents, round like a pumpkin and plump with moisture. They feasted on the smoke around them and drowned the flames. Thick roots rocked the soil, intertwining and weaving through the ground, falling like waves until every last flame was extinguished.

Gaven recognized the slithering movements, the way they slowly encompassed and controlled an area before turning offensive. That was Salathiel's power, and this ability to manipulate the earth was a skill he had recently developed.

Roselyn turned toward the eruption of vines that had engulfed her fire like rolling ocean breakers. She looked disappointed to see that her creation was snuffed out.

Salathiel hurried over to them. All the ilorinae vines were either dead or had retreated. The ground was scorched, but the children were safe. A small bit of smoldering vine was kindling into a tiny flame again. He stomped on the fire, crushing it.

Roselyn shot up, intense rage in her eyes. In her hand were the dancing flames. Salathiel stared back, bewildered but calm. They locked eyes, waiting for the other to make a move.

The flames in Roselyn's hand erupted into larger ones. As soon as his eyes caught her movement, Salathiel flicked his hand in the opposite direction. A thin root burst from the ground next to Roselyn and moved with Salathiel's hand. It slapped Roselyn's small body and sent her flying… until she slammed into a tree with a thud. Salathiel cringed upon hearing the painful impact.

"Shit," he cursed as he ran toward her. He made another gesture, calling the vine to get off Roselyn. But it snapped back hard, and a thorny end cut his cheek. He cursed under his breath again, chiding himself for not being able to master his new ability yet. With another frustrated swipe, he slammed his hands on the ground, and the roots returned to the earth.

Salathiel lifted Roselyn's head onto his lap, combed his fingers through her hair, and carefully tilted her head in both directions, checking for any blood or bumps. Her limp body felt like a rag doll, but she was breathing steadily, and her pulse was strong and regular. Roselyn was knocked out cold, but she would be okay. He looked over to Gaven, who was as pale as a trout's belly.

Gaven sat motionless. His eyes wouldn't leave the patch of smoking grass that was by his foot.

"Are you okay?" Salathiel asked. Gaven looked at Salathiel, blinking out of his trance. Roselyn looked like she was sleeping, and everything around him felt like a dream. But he knew it wasn't when he saw a streak of blood running down Salathiel's cheek.

"I will be," Gaven said. "What about you? You're bleeding."

Absently, Salathiel wiped his face, and his hand came away streaked with red. "Don't worry. It doesn't hurt."

"You almost look like Uncle Rocco with that scar," Gaven said, and snorted. The laugh only lasted a quick second before he started to choke and cough.

A light smile brushed across Salathiel's face, but Gaven knew he wasn't going to be able to hide his emotions from Salathiel. Gaven turned away before Salathiel could see a tear in his eye. He covered it up with another cough.

"Take it easy," Salathiel said. "That pollen is going to mess with your mind."

"Yeah. I need some air."

Gaven picked himself up and wobbled off toward the clearing.

He looked at his dirt-covered hands. Useless. Powerless. In that moment, there was nothing more he wanted than to grow stronger. That way he wouldn't have to depend on anyone to save him. He'd be able to take on anything that met his blade.

And he knew that if he wanted to be stronger, he couldn't show fear. It was time he stopped acting like a child.

CHAPTER FIVE

They continued their journey home, passing by the familiar, white, scrawny trunks that towered around their farm. Salathiel's arms were locked around Roselyn's legs as he carried her over his shoulder. When her eyes fluttered open, she was thinking, perhaps, that she had fallen asleep during their hunt.

Salathiel and Gaven's feet shuffled across the forest floor, crushing piles of crisp leaves that had long fallen from their branches. Fighting the urge to interrogate her, Salathiel held his silence. He figured Roselyn kept her fiery secret from them for a reason, and he was willing to wait until she was ready to explain herself.

Gaven didn't feel the same. His glare on her was as cold as ice, and Salathiel could feel that Gaven was about to burst any minute. Roselyn noticed too. When Gaven didn't say anything, she snapped.

"Who pissed in your soup today?" she asked.

Instantly confrontational, Gaven shouted, "You!"

"Me? What did I do?"

The two children hissed at each other with their ear-piercing voices. Gaven had no filter. He unleashed a string of profanities no child should know. When Gaven called her a liar, Roselyn stretched her arm out as if she was ready to yank his ear off. But Salathiel pulled her back, making sure the two kept their distance.

"He's not lying, Roselyn," Salathiel continued. "We saw you control flames with your hands, and since we live in a forest, you can't use that power around here again. Understand?"

Roselyn tilted her head. "What are you two going on about? I can't use kore. Look."

Roselyn raised her hands to the air, stretched them high and flailed. Nothing happened.

"It's alright if you don't want to talk about it," Salathiel said. "But Roselyn, you really shouldn't be keeping such things from us."

"Seriously?" Roselyn said, pouting, her cheeks puffed and brows furrowed. "If I could use kore I'd be showing it off, not hiding it. And out of all elements, fire? Do you know how hard it is for someone to control fire? And if I can do it, why don't I remember—"

Roselyn froze. Something in her clicked, but whatever she discovered, she kept to herself. She looked down at her clothes, then to Gaven. His face was smeared with soot, mostly on his neck and a little on his cheek. Roselyn leaned forward to look at Salathiel's face and noticed a fresh scratch that was now healed.

"What is that?" Roselyn asked, running her finger over the scar.

"I hurt myself," Salathiel explained. "It's nothing."

"With… what?" Roselyn grew more concerned. "Did… I hurt you?"

"No—"

"Don't sugarcoat it, Sal," Gaven said. "If she wanted to, she could've killed both of us."

Salathiel saw how those words stung her, and he was starting to believe that Roselyn had no idea what had happened. He believed it because he didn't recognize the girl that wielded the flames. She was full of hate and rage, a fierce determination to destroy everything around her. The girl on his back took years before she had the courage to kill her first game.

"I- I'm sorry, Gav," she said. "But really, I don't remember anything."

Gaven turned away. "I don't buy that."

Roselyn sulked. She stayed silent for the rest of the way home, even seemed more upset about the incident than Gaven was. Gaven was trying to give her the guilt trip to cover up his cowardly behavior, and it worked.

But his demeanor completely changed the next day when they discovered that Roselyn ran away.

It took half a day of searching before Salathiel and Gaven found her in a shallow cave formed by large rocks along the shore of a stream they often played at. Roselyn had a stuffed bag tossed to the side, her eyes swollen from hours of crying.

"No, please," Roselyn wailed as she backed away from her friends. "I don't want to hurt anyone."

She wasn't the only one crying; Gaven wiped the tears from his eyes and summoned false bravado.

"Stupid!" He kicked the gravel under his feet. "How does running away solve anything? You don't even know your way around here. You'd get eaten by a boar before you made it to the next town. Was that how you wanted to solve your problem? You didn't even try."

That may have been the moment Gaven realized that even if she could wield fire, Roselyn was still a fragile girl, and he still wanted to protect her no matter what. If Roselyn was afraid of her abilities, then Gaven would help her overcome it, even if he was afraid of her abilities himself.

Salathiel couldn't agree more. Roselyn was young. It was natural for her to feel afraid. Salathiel felt obligated to guide her in the right direction, much like how he helped Gaven come out of his shell. They were family, and he swore they would stick together no matter what.

Months had passed and Roselyn never kindled those flames again. Whether she tried to or not was a mystery to Salathiel, but it didn't seem to bother her. She resumed her studies, chores, and hunts as if it never happened.

It was Gaven who changed. Salathiel didn't sense any hate or disdain. Rather, he talked less because he was always lost in thought, daydreaming and fantasizing.

Now Gaven was in a corner of the room, sharpening the point of his wooden spear with a stone. He had so many weapons in their room that he started a new pile by the side of the house. Salathiel tried to tell him to stop, but Gaven kept going.

"Did you hear, Sal?" Gaven asked. "There's a new Region Leader in Althaea who dueled his way to Region Leader. He's a warrior too!"

"That's great," Salathiel said with far less interest than he had in the bread dough he was kneading. To his side, Roselyn also paid little attention to Gaven, never taking her eyes off the carrot under her fingers.

"They know the value of a great fighter in Althaea," Gaven said. "Not like here. If you're not born to the clan, you don't stand a chance in Minetta."

Salathiel sighed as he watched vegetables sizzle and crackle in the pot. Gaven was working himself up into another sulk. He was always talking about region leaders. For some reason, he'd gotten it stuck in his head that only in Althaea could a master warrior achieve power and respect. In his zeal to become a great warrior, and a region leader, he stuffed himself with unrealistic expectations.

Salathiel wrote it off to a *grass is greener on the other side* attitude. Why did Gaven think his chances were better in Althaea? In Salathiel's opinion, it was a child's crazy obsession.

"One day, I'll be a region leader," Gaven said. "I'll be the best fighter ever."

Salathiel couldn't hold back his smirk and tilted his head to the side. If that were true, poor Salathiel would end up as the master chef of his fortress, destined to never hear the end of Gaven's complaints about string beans. He did what he could to be supportive of Gaven, but his unrealistic optimism was getting repetitive. Besides, he started to wonder if he was doing him any favors by playing along.

"Calm down, squirt," Salathiel said. "Just last week you had trouble catching the chickens in the barnyard."

Roselyn tried to suppress a chuckle, but Gaven seemed to have heard her. He jumped to sit on the counter, and turned to the two chefs. He looked like he wanted to say something, but he just stared.

"Out with it," Salathiel said, before Gaven burst a vein.

The young boy stayed quiet – as long as he could stand it. But Salathiel waited him out.

Finally, Gaven cracked. "I want to go to Althaea."

The kitchen fell silent. Roselyn held the knife, sparing the other half of the carrot, for now. She looked at the eldest, wide-eyed as if confirming she heard him right. Salathiel felt the same. He paused to think about how to respond without hurting the ambitious boy's feelings.

"I understand your impulse. But let's think it through. Because that was just… just…"

"Dumber than a string bean," Roselyn filled in.

"Unrealistic and ignorant."

"Althaea!" Gaven said. "The best warriors are trained there."

"You don't need to go to another empire just to become a fighter," Salathiel argued.

"But I'll never become a region leader in Minetta."

He was right about that, but Salathiel managed not to say so.

It was true that Minetta's region leaders only appointed those in their lineage. It was a tradition for leaders to carry on their heritage this way. If Gaven wanted to become a region leader, he would have to be reborn. Or adopted. Again.

He was right about Althaea in one respect. They praised and fawned over their strongest fighters. Region leaders frequently changed, overthrown by anyone who challenged them and won. It was a system acknowledged long before the alliance of the three empires and had remained that way, but the region leaders of Minetta and the tribes in Valenia respected each other too much to continue such barbaric traditions. Not all thought it was fair, but it was a stable system and kept the peace. As long as one region leader or tribesman didn't misuse their power, other leaders left them alone.

Althaea, on the other hand, never changed. The endless factional wars between Althaean regions were ruinous and deadly. They loved the tradition of duels and battles without end. Once, these wars ravaged entire populations. All-out wars between regions were rare today, but the hostility between factions was still there. It was a volatile environment, the constant competition wasted energy, and the political jockeying kept everyone perpetually on edge. An Althaean region leader today may not be a region leader tomorrow – it was as simple as a single duel.

"Minettans aren't allowed to live in Althaea," Salathiel pointed out, just in case Gaven forgot. The only exceptions were high nobles and merchants traveling on official business. Besides, at that age there was no way he could survive on his own. He would need to spend a few years on the streets with petty jobs – if no one kidnapped him or sold off his limbs first.

"And what if I'm not Minettan? My father is Althaean. Your father said so himself."

"You were born in Saon. Last time I checked, that's in Minetta. Even if you were Althaean, you don't have the paperwork to prove it."

"You don't know!" he said. But even Gaven knew he was going down a rabbit hole. Still, he would not stop clinging to the idea. "It could be true…"

"Argue all day if you want to. But even if you convinced me, it wouldn't matter. To cross the border, you'd have to convince them. They'd laugh at your story, then boot you on your way."

"I don't care what you say. I'll find a way, you'll see."

It was a fantasy, but he was incredibly stubborn.

Gaven had convinced himself that leaving the family that had raised him would be easy. He didn't seem concerned how it would hurt their parents. He acted like none of them meant anything to him. The trouble was, Salathiel knew that in his heart, that wasn't true. But Gaven always had a selfish streak – he was always doing whatever he wanted without limitations.

If he told Marlo and Misa, they would let him go. When Gaven's mother left him, Marlo and Misa promised that they would never stop Gaven from doing what he wanted. As a result, they never treated the two boys the same. Gaven had always been a free child, devoid of obligations and responsibilities. But that didn't mean Gaven should be able to do whatever he wanted. He was careless, hotheaded, and if someone didn't hit him with the hard facts, his recklessness would get him killed.

"I'll be fine," Gaven said. "Right, Roselyn?"

Roselyn bit her lips. She looked at Salathiel briefly, as if she was trying to think of an answer without making either of them angry.

"I don't want you to leave," she said. "Althaea is dangerous. It's full of criminals and evil people. The city, the countryside, they're all dangerous."

"How do you know?"

"Because I've actually been there," she said.

"Ha! Liar."

"It's true. My father had lots of business there."

"Can't prove it."

"Seriously? Why would I make that up?"

"To see me fail!"

"Stop being immature, you two," Salathiel sighed. He was tired of hearing about Gaven's quest to become a warrior, and his petty fights with Roselyn.

They used to get along before the fire. The pranks and jokes were good-natured. Now he was hostile, always challenging her and trying to be better than her.

Maybe that was what this was all about. There was no doubt that seeing Roselyn handle kore before Gaven not only wounded his pride, but challenged his warriorhood. He had liked her just fine as his playmate. But he couldn't live with himself knowing she could kick his ass six ways to Soli. That was what turned a boyish fantasy to an existential demand. Poor kid. Only in his early stages of puberty, and already he was falling into that emotional trap – the pig-headed crap about how being a man could only be proved by physical superiority.

But Salathiel knew that wasn't something you could talk a young boy out of. He would have to learn his lesson the way they all do.

"Look, Gaven," Salathiel told him, "if you want to go so badly, then go. I'm not going to babysit you forever. It might be a good way for you to finally start learning how to take responsibility." He hoped that calling his bluff might make him see some sense.

"Great. I'm leaving tomorrow." Gaven hopped off his seat and stormed out of the room.

Salathiel wanted to kick himself. "Good luck getting there," he yelled down the corridor after him. The only answer was the sound of a door slamming.

He looked at Roselyn, but she just shook her head. "Forget it. He's just blowing hot air."

But Roselyn was just as wrong as he was and, as expected, Marlo and Misa didn't stop the young boy from following his dreams.

Next morning, at the crack of dawn, there was Gaven, ready to creep out of their room. He was holding a small pouch stuffed full of clothes and small weaponry, a defiant look on his face.

Salathiel knew that look. It didn't matter what he said to Gaven now. Even if he physically stopped him, Gaven would find a way to escape. He was going.

Salathiel should've seen this day coming. They were growing up. It was inevitable that they would begin to forge their own destinies.

He still had doubts. It wasn't that he didn't approve of Gaven's quest to become a fighter. Salathiel fully supported his unwavering ambition, but he didn't want him to do it alone.

Salathiel sighed. "Is this what you really want?"

"You know the answer to that." Gaven refused to meet his gaze.

"It's just… does it have to be Althaea? The leaders there are tyrants."

What he said next surprised Salathiel. "Did you ever have the feeling that you were meant to do something? That it was your destiny?"

"That's a very big idea for somebody your size."

"You don't believe me."

"No, Gaven. I know you mean everything you're saying. And I wouldn't bet against anyone as determined as you are. I respect what you want. I just don't think this is the way to do it."

"Something tells me otherwise," Gaven said with true sincerity. "I have to trust my heart. This is what I'm destined to do. I want to hold the greatest sword known to mankind, adorned in battle armor, and really make something out of myself."

"You're going to leave us? Mother and Father? Roselyn and me? For this insane feeling?"

"Just let me prove it. If it doesn't work out, I'll come back. I promise."

Salathiel took a deep breath. "You don't need to prove anything, Gav. I have a map of bruises on my bottom. You will be a great fighter, no matter where you are. I know it. I just want you to be safe, and not make irrational decisions. We should at least find you a guardian or someone to take care of you there."

"I can handle myself."

"Gav."

"Actually," Roselyn interrupted. She stood in the doorway, peeking into the room. "I think I can find you a guardian, or an escort to Althaea at least."

Gaven looked surprised. "Really?"

She walked up to Gaven. In her hands was a folded piece of paper she didn't seem to want to let go. But Gaven accepted it and glanced at the name written at the top.

"What am I supposed to do with this? Who is this... Joe-a-cheem?"

"Joachim," she corrected. "Go to the Hale's estate in Fauna and give him this letter. He's my retainer."

"Your retainer?" Salathiel perked up in disbelief. "Roselyn, if Gaven does that... they'll know you're still alive."

"This is more important. If Gaven is going to take risks then I will too. If he makes it to Althaea then that's all that matters."

Gaven frowned at the letter, as if he was debating whether his quest was worth the sacrifice she was making. "Why would you risk all that? You've tried so hard to escape them and now you're just going to throw it away with a letter?"

"Because you are more of a family to me than they ever were, and I'd do anything for you."

Gaven's cheeks went red. He kept silent like the shy boy he always was. He looked away, still hesitant to accept the letter.

"Just do it, Gav," she said. "Then I won't worry so much. Joachim knows people in Althaea. If I ask him, he'll help you. I trust him."

Roselyn walked over to a shelf next to the door and pulled out the wooden crate that contained her personal belongings. She shuffled and dug deep to the bottom. She knew exactly where to look.

Out came a small, wooden jewelry box with a glimmering, purple gemstone. It was tied to a silver chain that appeared just as expensive as the gem itself. She rubbed her fingers over the stone, admiring the craft and holding back the bittersweet feelings that came with looking at it.

Roselyn handed the necklace to Gaven. He gazed at the gem.

"If he doubts you, show him this necklace. He'll know it's mine."

Salathiel took a few steps to look at the gem up close. He recalled the day they found Roselyn in the woods three years ago; she was wearing that necklace. Not long after, though, she took it off and never wore it again. She told him it was called a kirinvā stone, something every member of the Hale family had, a present given to them on their first birthday. The Hale family were the ones who discovered hāstals after all, and they turned some of them into a fashion statement. The kirinvā stones were forged with divine powers, or so they say, a gift of protection from the Gods.

"Roselyn." Gaven was dumbstruck. "You sure you want to give me this?"

"It's so you don't forget about us when you make it big," Roselyn said in a playful tone. "Give it back to me once you've achieved your dreams."

"Of course." Gaven looped the necklace around his neck, then tucked the gem under his shirt. He took one more look at the letter in his hand before shoving it into his sack. "Thank you."

"What if your retainer comes looking for you?" Salathiel said.

"He won't. I told him not to in the letter."

"And he'll listen, just like that?"

Roselyn opened her mouth, then reconsidered her words. "Joachim has never let me down."

Salathiel frowned knowing that there would be consequences. Would his family be in trouble for not reporting the missing Roselyn Hale? Would Gaven make it to Althaea in one piece and be able to endure the cruel ways of the Althaean army? With the dozens of questions running through his mind, he knew one thing for certain – things were never going to be the same.

Gaven leaned over and gave them a hug. His sudden affection surprised Salathiel but he wrapped his arms around the soon-to-be warrior and pulled him and Roselyn in.

In his left arm was an abandoned foundling.

In his right arm was a runaway from a noble family.

It may be the last time they would get to embrace each other like this. The very thought of it only made Salathiel pull them in closer as tightly as his arms could squeeze.

He valued every second of it.

CHAPTER SIX

The Day of the Grand Ball

As the kōnvoy entered Althaea Main, they passed by street vendors and shopkeepers, their stalls and stores bursting with goods of every kind, scrambling to keep up with prosperous customers, haggling prices and driving bargains. The busy street was alive with buskers – street entertainers, musicians, and story-tellers performing impossible acts of prestidigitation and legerde-main. There were quack medicos peddling snake oil, rainmakers, and frauds of every ilk. Meat pies and sugar cakes filled the streets with their aroma. And of course, plenty of zotweed to pack the pipes of those who sought the illusions of dreams.

The passengers of the kōnvoy admired the city through the windows, but Mirari faced the opposite direction, paces away from the herd. She stood inside a vacant luxury compartment with a compact mirror held up to her eyes, ignoring everything around her.

She heard the compartment door glide, and the banters coming from the other side gradually fade away. She looked up and saw Lucan close the door before sliding his hands into his pockets. Mirari quickly threw the mirror back into her small leather bag.

"No one's going to recognize you," Lucan said with a playful smile.

It wasn't about that, but he had a point.

Mirari Zanette, Knight of the Alliance and partner of the Valiant Tiger, was known as a peasant with no status. The connection people would make to her and the Hale family was slim, but she couldn't hide her features – her sharp chin, much like her father, and her long, lilac hair that curled like ocean waves, just like her mother. And she would be adorned and served to the public in an elegant gown. She would look like a noble. The thought of it tangled a knot in her chest.

Mirari sighed. "But what if— "

"No one is looking for Roselyn," Lucan repeated. "She died in that fire. I'll make sure the story stays that way." Lucan reassured her of that more than once, and she fully trusted Lucan to uphold that promise. Still, it made little sense to her. Her eyebrows pulled up as she turned to him.

"Why would you do this for me, Lucan?" Mirari asked. "Were you never mad that I lied to you?"

"I'm a Hale too," Lucan said. He gave a small shrug. "I know being one isn't easy, but I can't imagine being a peasant was either. I will stand by whatever decision you choose." His smile faded, and in a lower voice he continued, "The offer is still on the table. Everything that belongs to you is still yours to take."

She lowered her head, noticing the white rug between them. She knew it was made of a special type of cotton grown only in the fields of West Valenia, a luxurious item that once laid in her childhood home, and no doubt in Lucan's too. A piece like that could've fed her and Salathiel for a month. But to own one, with no purpose other than to flaunt her status? She couldn't imagine it.

She returned her gaze to Lucan, puffed out her chest and mimicked, *"Business is for men*. But I will be more than honored to sample your finest selection of narcissus tea. For quality, of course."

Lucan returned a broad smile. "You're right," he laughed. "If you were running the Hale business, we'd be missing inventory."

Mirari felt the compartment jolt, and the kōnvoy come to a halt. Lucan turned his head, his gaze fixed on the window looking out to the large fortress towering over Althaea Main.

She followed his line of sight. The last time she saw Gaven's region, a quarter of the buildings had been destroyed, and more than half of the remaining structures, were damaged during the Althaean Siege. As bad as the physical destruction had been, the ravages of war had been so much harder on the population. She recalled people shivering in torn rags, loosely draped over skeletal forms, faces gaunt with starvation.

All of the destruction remained, but there was no doubt that Gaven was hard at work ever since resuming his position as region leader. He wasted no time reviewing and revising building plans, supervising reconstruction, and raising the enormous funds necessary to recover from the Althaean Siege, doing so without taxing his people to starvation.

"You can stay as Mirari, but you need to tell him," Lucan said. The stern look on his face reminded Mirari of her father whenever he caught her eyes wandered during study time. He wouldn't punish her, she knew, but she didn't want to disappoint her father. That same respect extended to Lucan.

"I know," Mirari sighed, but she didn't know how to tell Gaven about her identity. She didn't see a point now that five years had passed since they first met on the battlefield of the Althaean Siege.

"The longer you wait, the more dire the consequences may be." Lucan turned his head toward the sound of footsteps outside the kōnvoy. The main doors slid open, and passengers began to flood onto the station. They had already lost sight of Fangbane and the others. He slid open the compartment door and held out his hand to Mirari. "After you, Miss Hale."

SNOW FLURRIES FELL upon their hair and coats as they exited onto the busy platform of Althaea Main. A faint mist flowed out from their nostrils, that refreshing cold breeze kissing their cheeks. It was hard to miss the two lavish white carriages waiting for them, accompanied by two dozen guards and a gentleman blanketed in a long coat made of wolf fur. He greeted them with a wave.

Mirari nudged her way to the front, kicking up snow along the way, and Gaven intercepted her with a tight hug.

"You're freezing," he said, feeling her shiver. He guided her to the carriage. "Come. It's heated inside."

The guards opened the carriage doors. Fangbane and Mirari boarded one with Gaven, and the rest took the other carriage.

"Have the others arrived yet?" Fangbane asked, brushing the snow off his shoulder as he boarded the carriage.

"Dorain's and Hime's families arrived last night," Gaven said. "I expect Shiba and Neo will be fashionably late, as usual."

"They had matters to attend to in Oban, but I suspect it won't take long."

Mirari felt her cheeks burn as she adjusted to the mild warmth inside the carriage. As their carriage made their way to the fortress, she marveled at the scenery.

"The people," Mirari said as she pointed out the window. "They look so happy. After all they've been through, it's wonderful to see such joy."

"I hope so." Gaven shrugged. "I wouldn't be doing my job otherwise."

Watching her face flicker with reactions relaxed him. The city didn't fascinate Gaven in the same way. After all, this was his region. He had walked these streets countless times. He had seen all there was to see, and it was his hard work that had brought all the remarkable changes.

But to Gaven, much work was still left to be done. Civilians were still dying every day from lack of water, food, and even rowdy roughhousers who knew they could get away with crime. The vision he had for Althaea Main would take time, and frankly, he didn't feel that they were moving fast enough. Gaven would continue to supply and rebuild as many villages as possible throughout the region, as long as he had the funds to do it. He hoped his gifts could help raise the people just a bit higher, and transform Althaea Main into a paradise.

"And you?" Gaven asked Fangbane. "How are things at the estate?"

"Two hundred new volunteers just last month," Fangbane said. "We had to turn some away. The island can only hold so many."

Once just seven fighters, the Knights were now an entire battalion of dedicated egalitarians who believed in Fangbane's cause. Some wanted to be fighters, snatching a taste of justice for themselves, others were happy to clean the stables as long as they could adore the Knights under the same roof. They assisted with petty tasks, mundane asks from townspeople, so the Knights could focus on bigger missions, ones that were often interlaced with politics.

No matter how much support the Knights had, Fangbane

vowed to keep his army small. Support was always welcomed, but the Knights, the faces of equality, would always be the original seven.

The carriage moved through the grand gates, opening into a courtyard of green toppled by fresh snow. They were ceremoniously welcomed by a formation of soldiers, steady at perfect attention. Gaven stepped out of the carriage first, snapping a crisp salute in return to the troops in their dress uniforms.

As Mirari followed, the rows of guards made her oddly anxious. She was used to the Knight's own guards saluting her every time she walked the halls of Fangbane's estate. But they were familiar colleagues; she saw all the volunteers as family. Here, she was unaccustomed to such deference from strangers on this scale of grandeur. She realized it had nothing to do with her being a Knight, and everything about her being the Valiant Tiger's partner.

At the far end of the soldiers' line, they were greeted by a stout lady with a stern attitude. Her brown hair was cropped short, with bangs over her forehead. She wore a cerulean sash with the insignia of Althaea Main, in honor of her position. She was attentive, but gave away no emotion in her serious expression.

"This is Erel, my servant," Gaven joked as they approached her.

"Second in command." Erel was brusque as she corrected him. "Not that this brawling savage could run the show without someone to keep him in line."

"Lovely to see you again, Lady Erel," Fangbane said.

"Erel. Just Erel."

"Yes, yes, of course."

Under his command, Erel assisted Fangbane during the Althaean Siege. She also remembered Mirari, the stranger who offered Gaven mercy when no one else would. She had nothing but respect for them and the Knights they had established. More than anything, she couldn't keep her eyes off Mirari, and Gaven seemed to have noticed.

He said, "Why don't you show them to their quarters while I debrief Mirari."

Erel narrowed her eyes and said, "Fine. The carriages to the ball will be waiting at the west gate." She began walking toward the East Wing, and the Knights followed.

The Grand Ball. Mirari was looking forward to that a little less than gutting and cleaning a dozen giant Valenian swamp bats.

Every five years, the Council held these lavish boondoggles. It was nominally a traditional way to meet and greet, promote peace between empires, and stab a politician, if one desired. All councilors and region leaders were required to attend, and they were often joined by commanders, advisors, and the highest of nobles across the alliance.

This year it was held in Althaea Main, and with the establishment of the Knights, this event inspired high expectations. For Mirari, she would have to double not only as a Knight, but also as Gaven's partner. She would be seeing many of these region leaders for the first time. It was crucial to make a good impression. She despised this kind of attention, but she knew such responsibilities came with being a Knight.

Gaven and Mirari wandered deeper into the fortress' inner courtyard, bustling with training soldiers and servants running errands. One of the officers drilling troops accidentally backed into a servant who wasn't watching her step, distracted at the sight of the nobles passing by. The officer stumbled, knocking a stack of linens out of her hands. As he apologized profoundly, he looked up into a familiar face in front of him. At the sight of Gaven, his face glowed like a newborn pup.

"Haynes," Gaven scowled, "you look like you woke up this

morning and put your legs on backwards." Haynes' clumsy nature was an inherent flaw everyone was used to by now.

Haynes ignored the remark and pulled Gaven in for a rough hug. "Your Honor!" Haynes exclaimed. "Forgive my elation at your esteemed presence."

Gaven pushed Haynes away. "A show of decorum in front of the new recruits, will ya?"

Haynes adjusted his stance and stood straight like the veteran battle commander he was. That only lasted a few seconds — again, he couldn't suppress his joy as he spotted Mirari standing behind Gaven.

"Lady Mirari!" Haynes boomed. He barely recognized her, amazed at how she had blossomed since he last saw her. "Wow. It's been too long. You look... good. With all due respect and such, of course."

The servants were accustomed to Hayne's spontaneous personality and resumed their work. The new trainees lost their disciplined attention, erupting in audible giggles and whispers. For most of the raw recruits, this was their first time seeing their leader. Mirari could hear the trainees murmur in awe.

"That's the Valiant Tiger."

"Wow. He really does look strong."

"Who's that woman next to him? Is that the featherpit?"

"Can't be. She looks too wimpy to be a warrior."

Mirari pretended not to hear these comments. Gaven, on the other hand, exploded in fury.

"Who said that?" Gaven shot his glare at the recruits. Many had taken a step back, now cowering with their new interest of the wet dirt under their feet.

"A-An honest mistake, Your Honor." Haynes chuckled, but Gaven's rage continued to burn.

"We don't use those words here. Say it again, and you'll all be cowering home with a letter of dishonor personally signed by me. Am I clear?"

They nodded without a word.

Mirari placed her hand on his shoulder and with her gentle voice she beckoned him to move. She bowed to Haynes. "It was nice seeing you again."

Haynes gave a crisp salute, with a smile that even Gaven's roar could not penetrate. "We'll catch up later."

"Two laps around the fortress," Gaven said. "If any of them stop, do it again."

"The old Susie's ring," Haynes winked. "You got it, boss." He straightened his stance, and marched back to resume drilling the recruits. No one was willing to talk now, as Haynes battered instructions at them.

Mirari nudged Gaven forward as they continued toward his chambers.

"Don't make it worse," she said.

"I'm trying to be a good example."

"You're trying to destroy my reputation faster than Dorain can aggravate a yeti."

Gaven chuckled. For someone who had just yelled at a group of recruits, he was in surprisingly good spirits. Mirari couldn't feel a speck of tension from her partner. His anger had come and gone like a spark. Perhaps he was never mad to begin with, but rather he was used to putting on a show. It was part of being a good leader.

They arrived in front of a large door guarded by two soldiers. Gaven placed his hand on the aulōg. Veins of blue ran through the pad at his touch, and it clicked open.

Finally, they had a moment to themselves. In his chambers, Mirari took off her coat, but kept it neatly folded and cradled in her arms. Gaven paced over to a tall liquor cabinet opposite the door. Without even asking, he poured each of them a good knock of whiskey, the good stuff from Valenia.

"Aged sixteen years in a cask of finest mast wood." He offered a glass to Mirari.

"No, thank you. A bit early for—"

He cut her off, insisting. "Your butterflies are migrating from your stomach to mine. I insist we drown them."

"I'm not the one who just shattered the dreams of future youths."

He chuckled. "Those who break come back stronger."

"Like your region?"

He gave a hard nudge on her shoulder and swallowed the rest of his whiskey.

Mirari scanned the rest of his room. A large map of the alliance was pinned on one side of the wall, and the rest was largely covered in bookshelves. Gold drapery hung from the windows and over the doors to a balcony that opened out to the distant plains.

Mirari stared at the mountains of paper on his desk. When Gaven stayed at Fangbane's estate his room looked no different. For a man with such power, there was no doubt Gaven was always busy.

Her eyes were drawn to one of the drawers left ajar, and she pulled it open. It was full of trinkets and gadgets, letters bearing seals. Some would've called it hoarder's junk, but Mirari knew there was a meaning behind each item. Sometimes Gaven told her about his adventures, tracking down misbehaving hooligans and repressive guilds throughout his region. But this was the first time she had seen his collection, and it was clear he was targeting a specific type of people.

"Are these—?" She didn't want to say the name.

Gaven bit his lip as he glanced at the array of books and boxes along the opposite wall, he was toying with something in his right hand. He turned and tossed a mask upon the table, cleaved in two and stained with blood. Mirari looked him in the eye.

"Your Honor!" she hissed.

"I didn't *want* to. I was following one of many complaints we received throughout the region. There was commotion in a remote farming community to the north, one of those backwater regions no one really goes to as long as the grain keeps flowing."

"No one watches over the area?"

"It's not that unusual. Honestly, it's far more economical to allow the remote areas such freedom. They rarely cause a disturbance." Gaven reached for a piece of paper buried at the bottom of the drawer and handed it to her. He pointed at the seal of an ox. He leaned upon the table, watching as she examined it. "I was visiting a few farmsteads to get more information about the disturbance, and found a rancher near the foothills. He was a nice fellow at first, very receptive and hospitable, but once my back was turned, he pulled a knife… and he had backup. They didn't like me snooping around their territory, and they weren't willing to let me leave alive." Gaven looked down at his wrist as if something was there. He rubbed it a few times.

Mirari caught the hint. "They had tallas."

"All with that symbol… and that's when I realized that the Blessed may be more active than we think. All this time, we were waiting for the next grand attack on the Council, when the Blessed had already dug their roots in our society, terrorizing people right under our nose. Every member of the Blessed has some agenda that threatens the stability of the empires, and just because they're not all empaths like Laikos, doesn't make them less dangerous. Farmers, housewives, even nobles, any of them could be members of the Blessed."

Mirari stood motionless. Gaven's agenda was clear; he wanted to take out the Blessed before they became a problem.

She didn't disagree with what he was doing, but from the dark edge to his tone, he was likely acting alone.

She knew that rounding up members of the Blessed had a deeper meaning to Gaven — he was still haunted by the events of the Althaean Siege. Over the years, she had seen how the guilt invaded his dreams. Perhaps he felt that taking out the Blessed was the only way he could repent for his wrongdoings, for the comrades he killed and the unrest he created across the empires.

Now, seeing this disorganized drawer dedicated to the cause, she understood how much it meant to him.

"Please don't do this alone," she said. "Tell Erel—"

"Erel still hasn't forgiven me for chasing Laikos."

"Fangbane will—"

"Will have a heart attack. He's not one to poke the lion."

"Then me. I'm your partner."

The corner of his lip perked up. She could tell he was fighting the urge to say something witty, but his humor evaporated into gratitude. "I'll see if Fangbane would be willing to lend you to me for a while."

The thought of it sent butterflies through her stomach. She wouldn't mind a chance to explore the landscape and the culture of the people in Gaven's region, and a chance to spend more time with her partner.

She folded the paper in her hand and placed it back in the drawer. Taking one last look at his collection, she found a black velvet box shoved in the back. She reached for it and held it in front of her eyes, but before she could open it Gaven plucked it from her hand.

Before Mirari could ask about it, he directed her across the room. "Come. Take a look."

On his enormous mattress laid two glistening dresses, one in green and the other in blue, and a white coat adorned in badges on the opposite side.

"Please don't tell me those are for me." Mirari gaped at the sparkling dresses that danced under the sun's rays coming from the adjacent window.

"Erel wants you to choose."

"Do you have anything a bit more… understated? These are for princesses."

"We have crowns too, if you'd like."

Mirari looked them over once more, pointed at the one with fewer ornaments, bows, and less extravagant lace puffing it up. It still wasn't her style, but at least it might draw slightly less attention.

"Blue for Althaea," she said. "And the color shows status."

Gaven looked at the dress and agreed. "You're learning." He took her glass and set it on the bed stand. "Go on. Try it on."

She grabbed the dress tenderly, careful to not wrinkle it. Mirari still had doubts, but she noticed that Gaven didn't put up any resistance to the outfit selected for him. It was a long, white coat that was traditional for region leaders, decorated with cyan and gold trim and the large insignia of Althaea Main sewn on the lapel. It was always simpler for men.

She watched him strip the last of his top, showing off a talla of Althaea Main's dragon emblem on his chest. Every time she saw him, whether it'd be in Minetta or Althaea, Gaven was stronger, his muscles firmer and wider. And though she always enjoyed his company, she couldn't help but to feel smaller every time he grew.

Then, she recalled the way his recruiters looked at her when she arrived. She was a highly-praised Knight in Minetta; here she was but a mere commoner. Respect in Althaea was earned through strength and wealth. She had no political power to support Gaven's region, and there was no way she could match up to his fighting talent. As his partner, what could she offer him besides emotional security and a sound conscience? If people asked what made her special — what made the Valiant Tiger choose her — she wouldn't have an answer. Those questions would inevitably come up tonight. Looking back at the gown, Mirari didn't feel worthy of wearing it, but tonight she had to pretend to be as great as Gaven always made her out to be.

"Do you need help?" Gaven said with a smug look on his face. Mirari blinked back to the moment, unaware that she had chosen the most inappropriate time to daydream — while staring at his bare chest.

She pivoted away and mumbled, "Turn around."

She let her clothes slide down her body, dropping down at her feet. She managed to wriggle herself into the gown after much effort, but the opening in the back was left exposed. She struggled to reach for the back. Then, she let out a gasp as she felt her stomach being pulled back and the fabric pressing her breasts together. Gaven's fingers traced the crosshatches on her back and tied the ends.

Once the ends were secured, Mirari dared to look in the mirror. She was certain she would stick out like a boil on the nose.

But staring back at her in the mirror was a woman who had gone from beautiful, to a genuine goddess. The gown defined her alluring curves, and the lace trim on the cuffs and collar gave a comfortable touch of dignity that almost made up for the arresting effect of the plunging neckline, and the slit that nearly reached the top of her hip. There were subtle patterns in the weave of the blue silk, and tasteful accents decorated with silver gemstones, which emphasized the long flow of her legs from the waist to the ground.

"You look good," Gaven complemented. And she noticed Gaven had already slipped on his full outfit, decorated with badges and a formal tie, though, with little care. He was struggling to fasten his cufflinks.

Mirari smirked and stuck her hand out, snatching the cuff links. "But you're still a mess." They were snugly in place in under ten seconds. While she was at it, she tidied up his shirt and fixed the tie knotted around his muscular neck.

"I hate these damn nooses," Gaven muttered as he raised his chin to give her a little space. "A man should only be hung once." When she finished, he glanced at the mirror. They looked nothing short of spectacular together. It may have even given Mirari a little more confidence about the ball.

"The maids outside will do your hair and makeup." Gaven gestured to the door. "Sorry to rush you. I have some matters to attend to before we leave."

"I've gotten quite used to that." Mirari shrugged, lifting the ends of her gown and giving him a curtsy. "I'll see you later, Your Honor."

CHAPTER SEVEN

As soon as Mirari left, Gaven took out the jewelry box he had hid from her and opened it. The glistening purple gem cradled on a silver chain captivated him now as much as it did the first day he laid eyes on it. The stone had a special kind of kore-infused hāstal that claimed to offer divine protection. Gaven didn't give a damn about the Gods, but the person who gave him the stone, and what it meant to him, was more valuable than anything he ever owned.

Gaven twirled the silver chain around his finger, admiring the kirinvā stone as it twisted and turned in his palm. When he looked at the stone, it reminded him of how it brought him to Fauna. He worked hard every day to become the fighter he said he could become. That child had come a long way, but at the cost of never seeing his family again.

A MERCHANT in Malino was kind enough to let young Gaven ride in their carriage to the glamorous town of Fauna. Gaven looked at the scrap of paper in his hand again – directions to the Hale residence.

As soon as the carriage reached a hilltop, Gaven saw patches of brown rooftops resting in the valleys of green hills and floral fields, connected by the glistening waters of Kestrel Bay stretching over the horizon.

It was the first time he saw any body of water larger than the wide streams near Malino, and Gaven could faintly make out the floating vehicles lined up by the shore. But what captivated him the most was how large the cities were. The people from afar appeared like seeds in a ripe melon.

As the carriage journeyed through the nearest town, Gaven realized just how small he was in this world. He had to lean his head back all the way to see the brick rooftops. Each house had a balcony jutting over the doorway. Street lights lined up into the horizon. Pedestrians paid no attention to the black-painted carriages that passed by, each equipped with leather seats of the highest quality.

There were no beggars on the road. The streets were beautifully paved and kept clean. Despite the heavy ocean breeze knocking golden leaves off plump trees along the sidewalk, the ground was free of debris. It wouldn't surprise him if the roads were swept every day. Twice maybe.

He got a few stares from the townspeople, gossiping behind their silk gloves and feathered wide hats. Of course he stood out. He was in the back of a worn-out wagon and his dirt-covered clothes proved he hadn't bathed in a week. He was an embarrassing contrast to the well-dressed adults in tailored gowns and coats, and it reminded him of when they first found Roselyn in the woods in that laced frock. In comparison to these nobles, he would've considered her under-dressed.

When the merchant arrived in Fauna, Gaven started asking

around for directions to the Hale residence. It was clear that people seemed hesitant to tell him.

"You best keep your nose out. The family's still in mourning," said one man, and many others responded with a similar warning.

But eventually, Gaven found the large estate on the edge of town. Without confirmation from the locals, he would've assumed it was a government building. A tall, iron fence guarded the Hale's vast property. The fence was much too tall for the young boy to climb over. Peering past the fence, he could see a single light beyond the luscious front garden. Gaven bellowed at the gates, praying someone inside would hear him.

Sure enough, a man with wavy brown hair – just starting to go gray at the temples – stepped out and approached the gates. Gaven could see the daggers fastened around his belt. An umbra, if he had to guess. He had an intimidating presence that made Gaven question if he would regret coming here.

"Don't you know how to use the pad, kid?" he said, gesturing to the black slate hung on the outer wall. Gaven hadn't even noticed it.

The guard did a double take on Gaven's lowly appearance and changed his demeanor. It was clear that the boy before him was a peasant, one unfamiliar with the Hale's technology. He let it go and continued, "What do you want, son?"

Gaven hesitated. "A-Are you Joachim?"

"I am."

He gave him the letter in his hand. Joachim read it quietly while Gaven fidgeted, each second longer than the last. The silence was killing Gaven.

"My name is Gaven Zanette," he said. "I want to become a fighter, and she told me you could help me get to Althaea."

"What kind of sick joke is this?" the man said, waving the

letter in the air. He looked like he was ready to take it to the authorities, and send Gaven to prison.

"She wrote it, I swear! Look—"

He pulled out the necklace hidden under his shirt to show him the purple stone. Almost immediately, the man's anger subdued. Joachim shut his mouth and took another look at the letter. At first Gaven was skeptical as to what that tiny hāstal around his neck could do, but he saw just how meaningful it was. One look was all it took to change this man's mind.

"Do you know what you have there, boy?"

"It's… umm… a necklace?" Gaven wasn't sure if that was what he was asking.

"It's a kirinvā stone," he said. "And now that it's in your possession, you must never let it go."

Gaven took another look at it to see if he could figure out why it was so special. To him it was just a rock, but it was the most precious thing he carried only because it was from Roselyn.

Joachim shook his head. Now Gaven could see that he believed him – he just didn't want to accept it. "Well, come on in."

The retainer unlocked the gate and opened it just enough for Gaven to slip through. He locked the gate behind him, and Gaven waited.

Joachim reached for one of the daggers in his belt and tossed it to him. Gaven dropped his pouch and caught the blade. It was crafted in beautiful silver, sharper than any of the hunting tools he had ever used, but Gaven didn't know what he wanted him to do with it. He looked up and saw that Joachim had pulled out a second dagger, ready to swing it at him.

Joachim stepped forward, hacking and slashing with complete disregard to Gaven's preparedness. Gaven barely stepped back in time, and he used the dagger in his hand to block and parry. He was hesitant, confused, unsure if the old man was trying to kill him. And Joachim took advantage of his wavering. Gaven was almost certain that was the intention – to silence the messenger and along with him, Roselyn's secret.

Gaven decided that he had to fight for his life no matter what. He began to push back, transitioning every parry into an offensive attack. His dagger slashed and jabbed forward but Joachim did not sustain a single scratch. He calculated every step, avoiding Gaven's swipes by a hair and not an inch more.

The boy charged at him with a holler. Another swipe, missed. Joachim read every one of his moves. Worst of all, Gaven could tell that the man was holding back.

Joachim lunged forward again, with enough force to knock the dagger out of Gaven's hand. It landed far beyond his reach. He began backing away, now defenseless.

"She's alive but doesn't want to be found," Joachim said, not even slightly winded. "And she gives a peasant her family heirloom just so he can pester me." He stuck the dagger back in his pocket and took out the piece of paper again.

Surprisingly, Gaven's life was not yet over. Joachim took far more interest in Roselyn's letter than in Gaven's life, and Gaven began to understand why. Even though she had been gone for three years, he still saw her as family. Joachim could fulfill his duty and selfish desire to bring Roselyn home, or respect her decision to leave the family. If he chose the latter, he may never see her again. It would be the same as if she were dead.

Gaven retrieved the other dagger and offered it to him, but the loyal servant just stared at the purple stone around his neck. Gaven kept his silence, not wanting to speak out of turn.

"You've got quite the flexibility, enough force in your strikes too; I give you that, kid. But you have no training. If you want to be a fighter, you'll need to learn some tactics. Can you read?"

"And write," Gaven said. "She... Roselyn taught me."

Joachim raised a brow. Surely he was impressed. Gaven perked up. "Does that mean you'll take me to Althaea?"

"Not in your current state. You'd be worth nothing." He paused, then reconsidered. "Let's see if you can move the ores in the keep."

Gaven didn't argue. He was ready to do anything to prove he was worthy.

YOUNG GAVEN COULDN'T CALM his excited heart as he saw cascades of tiny lodges and grand white skyscrapers from a distance. The lower markets were bustling, full of all sorts of produce he had never seen before. Their carriage rolled through stretches of green lawns that overlooked the bazaar and gated homes owned by brawny men with braided beards and fresh clothes on their backs. Gaven watched the mothers laugh and swing their young children in the air, almost with jealousy – it was a luxury he never had.

The delightful scenery came to an abrupt halt at the foot of a massive stone wall that stretched to no end. It was heavily guarded, with soldiers lined up under its cold shadow. But as the gates swung open, a bright light welcomed the travelers into a courtyard of luscious green lawns and pure, white watchtowers as if it was the divine city of Nagama itself.

The fortress was massive, with guards posted in every corner. His eyes traced ornate etchings along the buildings that lead to a series of statues of the mythical winged dragons. In their mouths were glistening gems, the hāstals harvesting the blaring sun. There were soldiers performing drills in the courtyard, and Gaven fantasized about being one of them. After all, this was his new home.

Joachim made sure Gaven proved his worth, testing his abilities not only with the sword but with the pen. After a couple of months, they set off for Althaea Main. Gaven thought he would be taken to the border region of Ophallen, where there was always a need for more recruits, or to Axillaire, in hopes that the new region leader was looking for fresh talent. Never did he imagine he would be ending up in the capital region of Althaea Main.

Joachim hustled Gaven out of the carriage and off to the side, where a scrawny man held a smoldering cigar in his mouth. His hair was disheveled like he had just woken up ten minutes ago, and Gaven could see a small crack along his silver-rimmed glasses. The man's creases lifted as he greeted them with a bright smile.

"Ah, what a fine nicker he is," the man said, leaning down and looking at Gaven closer. He gave the young boy's arm a firm squeeze, almost too hard. "He's got a strong roove... and tates already."

Gaven looked at Joachim. Behind that thick accent, he had no idea what this man was saying.

"This is Stein," Joachim said. "He's one of Region Leader Suzan's commanders, and also my... distant cousin."

Stein patted Gaven's shoulder as if he was an armrest. "Jo-Jo says ya want to be a p-gon?"

Hearing words he could understand, Gaven jumped at the chance to say something. "All I ask is the opportunity to prove myself... Sir."

Stein seemed to be very pleased. He had a big grin as if he had stolen all of Joachim's emotions. "Le best rollos are trained right here in 'Thaea Main. And I can make ya one of them, if ya as dedicated as ya are ambitious."

Gaven questioned whether or not a man like this could really help him. But he didn't have a choice. This was the path he'd chosen, and if he had to smell that wet, earthy stench this

Althaean reeked of every day until he reached his dream then it was a small price to pay.

"If you wish to stay here you have to live under two conditions," Joachim said. "One, you tell folks you are his nephew. You do everything he tells you." He paused for a second before adding, "You won't have to copy his peasant-mouth. Only countryside Althaeans speak like that."

"Yes, sir." Gaven nodded. "I swear it."

Stein threw a metallic tag at him and he caught it with both his hands. It had Gaven's name engraved on one side and the flag of Althaea on the other.

"Two, you're Althaean-born. No one can know you're from Minetta. *Ever*. Is that clear? You're aware that it's against the law for Minettans to settle in Althaea. The instant you're found, it's over."

Of course he knew that. That's why Salathiel and Roselyn were so against him leaving home. The chances of them seeing each other again would be faint. He tried to push the thoughts of home away. He had to lock them in a small, dark room in his mind.

Still, he said a silent thank you to Roselyn for getting him this far – whatever happened from here on would be up to him. He had to prove he could be useful, and evolve into the master of weapons he said he would become. And when he saw her again, if he did, he vowed to be a new man.

GAVEN RELEASED a heavy sigh before returning the velvet box to its drawer. He didn't want to hide things from his partner, but the stone was all he had left of his former self – a past that no one could know about.

He was a region leader in Althaea. His former identity, and

everyone that knew his younger self, had to be locked away if he wanted to stay in command. There wasn't a law that prohibited those born on foreign land to become region leaders; that loophole was always there. But Gaven knew his people weren't ready to accept a Minettan as a region leader. Trust from his people could only be granted to an Althaean-born. That was their society. Althaean was his only identity.

CHAPTER EIGHT

The Grand Ball

A black carriage with golden wheels and curtained windows came to a halt in front of a grand estate on the outskirts of Althaea Main, the grounds alive with a kaleidoscope of bright and elegant evening dress. The atmosphere was vibrant, charged with the kind of energy generated by a critical mass of the rich and powerful. An endless stream of carriages dropped off their precious nobles at the entry. Gaven and Mirari stepped out, walking side by side, up the pearly rose and white marble stairs, and into the grand ballroom.

Impeccably dressed wait staff circulated with trays of delights — crusted lark tongues with spiced torchberry jelly, crispy fried land muffintails and sparkling pine cherry wine. Gaven seized two glasses of Chateau Goethe Merlot, handing one to Mirari. Already, she could feel many eyes on her.

Mirari scanned the crowd for the one couple she was sure she could socialize with, to no luck. She recognized the councilors and a few commanders and region leaders from previous assignments. She found Lucan in the company of two nobles, undoubt-edly talking business, and Kylah captured by a talkative Dorain. The rest were new faces.

"Where are the rest of the Knights when you need them?"

"Well, you know Fangbane." Gaven shrugged, bringing his glass up to his lips. "He's always late."

"Oh, Mirari!" Mirari recognized the princess' sweet voice, but still wasn't used to seeing her with long hair. The young lady wore a long, dazzling white garment with loose pleated sleeves. It was decorated with glistening white pearls from the oyster beds off the coast of Allete. Gems sparkled on her fingers, wrists, and neck, and her dress had subtle, pink floral patterns. Hime gave Mirari a firm hug. "It feels like it's been forever."

Mirari held her glass high to avoid spilling it and gently patted Hime's back. "You were only gone for a month."

"Altha Hills just isn't the same." Hime pouted. "I miss Starlight's cooking… and all of you of course. Politics can be so dry. It's been quite a pain lately." She then turned and bowed to Gaven. "Thank you for your help the other day. I would've never been able to figure out how to deal with those advisors."

"You can come to me anytime, princess," Gaven said. "You'll be a great region leader one day."

Hime smiled. "Only with your guidance."

Mirari could hear rushed taps against the marble floor, coming in their direction. She turned and saw a young man steaming toward them, fueled by enthusiasm, youth, and six goblets of spring meadow ale.

"How's it going, boss?" Dorain gave Gaven a hearty slap on the back. His normally alabaster cheeks held an unusually rosy tint. "Have you tried the boar bacon? Absolutely phenomenal. Apparently they put brandy in it, wrap it with some milark and roast cannonpop, and let it sit for three days. Crazy, right? How is it possible that no one would've eaten it by then?"

Mirari noticed that Kylah was nowhere in sight, and she knew why. Now more than ever, she wished Dorain came with an off switch. Mirari was getting enough attention as is.

Dorain was now taller than Gaven and Mirari. They were still not adjusted to his massive growth spurt since he joined the Knights. Regardless of his height, Dorain hadn't changed much as a person. He was rowdy as ever, full of mischief and the unpredictable.

"I learned a new game yesterday," Dorain continued between a bout of hiccups. "One of the guards taught me. He didn't have the best hairline, though… Anyway, you take a barrel of water… and two strings—"

"That's hazing, Dorain," Gaven narrowed his eyes. "Who told you about that? I want to know."

Dorain leaned in, going for his confidential voice, but missing it by many decibels. "Relax. The new recruits will love it."

As Dorain dissolved in giggles, a young lady approached him from behind and grabbed him by the ear. Her emerald dress bore a crest of the aegises, identical to the one pin on Dorain's vest next to his Knight's badge.

"Your Honor, I apologize for his lack of respect," she said. "Dorain, father is looking for you."

"Later, later." Dorain flailed his arms out, but his sister only tugged on his ear harder. "Goddammit, Cinder!"

"I'll come with you, Dorain," Hime said, trying to convince him. "I haven't seen your father in a while."

"Thank you, Princess," Cinder said, and with the help of both ladies, they nudged him toward another room.

"Good riddance." Gaven let out a sigh, but not long after, a man and woman, linked in arms, approached Gaven and Mirari.

"Your Honor, good evening. I would like you to meet my countess." The noble, adorned in medals and gold links, gestured to the fair lady. She bowed.

"Falina of Millaford, Your Honor," she said. "A lovely region you have. It is certainly prospering."

"Thank you, Falina." Gaven said. "And it's an honor meeting you again, Master Raphen."

The man looked at Mirari, and didn't bother hiding the smug look on his face. He asked, "Is this your partner that I've heard so much about?"

Mirari took a deep breath and dipped into a small curtsy. "Yes, My Lord. Mirari of the Knights."

As if Raphen didn't hear her speak, he continued directing his attention to Gaven. "I hope she will be a good investment to you."

As fast as they had come, they wandered off to greet another pair. Mirari furrowed her brows and turned to Gaven.

"An investment?" Mirari hissed in a low voice.

"Consider that a compliment," Gaven said, patting her on the back. "It gets worse. Try not to punch anyone tonight."

Mirari wasn't sure she could uphold that promise. The night continued in the same chaotic way, one introduction after another without a moment's peace. Mirari knew she wasn't going to remember any of their names after tonight. Secretly, she hoped she would never see them again. In fact, she did her best to avoid eye contact with anyone as they moved through the crowded ballroom.

"Would you like to dance, Lady Mirari?" a drunk nobleman babbled, offering his hand to her. She had met him earlier – the Duke of Pralines, or some other dinky principality. She had wholly forgotten his name.

Mirari wanted to decline, but she couldn't afford to be selfish. If she told this man to go kiss a hammerhog, would it make Gaven look bad?

"Not now," Gaven answered, taking Mirari by the elbow and

leading her away with a curt nod to the duke. When they were alone, he nudged Mirari, reminding her, "Breathe."

Mirari released a heavy sigh. "Sorry."

She felt so overwhelmed. She could only imagine that Gaven had it far worse, since he actually knew almost everyone in the room.

That peace lasted only seconds when another man approached, clearly a nobleman, and a rich one at that by the cut of his clothes. Mirari couldn't spot any kind of insignia or rank on him. She wasn't sure how to address him.

"Well, well, fancy seeing you here," said the man with forced bonhomie. "How have you been, Gaven?"

That calm Gaven had just a second ago was now up in flames. Mirari felt an unsettling prickling feeling in her chest, one she hadn't felt in a long time. A rage that echoed his desire to kill a man.

"I'm busy. Go away." Gaven brushed him off without any attempt to conceal his dislike for the man. He took Mirari's arm and turned away, without once looking the man in the eye.

"Oh c'mon," he called after Gaven. "When was the last time we got to talk like this?" He glanced at Mirari, and took her hand in his.

"Inigo Tepis," he said, kissing her hand, adding, "a pleasure. I'm sorry such a beautiful woman has to put up with that grump."

Gaven spun back to him, and slapped Inigo's hand away from Mirari's.

"Don't touch her."

Inigo smiled. "Sensitive as usual. You'd think he'd treat his investors a little better."

"House Tepis?" Mirari tilted her head. "The winemakers?"

Inigo looked pleased. "Elegant and educated. You should join me for tea sometime, darling. I can tell you all about Gaven's embarrassing stories when we were both still trainees."

Gaven hissed, "What are you doing here? This event is for important people only."

"Good try. But who do you think paid for this venue?"

Gaven clenched his fist, and Mirari took notice. She had to stop him before he lost control.

Mirari leaned into Gaven's ear and echoed his word, "Breathe." That unsettling sensation in her chest lessened. She could tell Gaven was still angry, but at least he was less likely to start a fight. With a quick curtsy, Mirari waved Inigo goodbye. "We'll be taking our leave."

Even as she pulled Gaven away, his eyes didn't leave Inigo. So, she brought him out to the patio. The snowfall had stopped, but the cool evening air was enough to calm an angry tiger. They stepped into a grand garden. Only a few guests lingered out in the cold. There were hardly any lights to guide the way, but the darkness was a welcoming silence after a night of socializing.

Gaven released a deep sigh.

"Am I embarrassing you?" Mirari asked.

"Absolutely not. I… just wish I didn't have to put you through this goat grab."

"Well, I'm still a Knight. I would have to attend the festivities regardless."

"Yeah, but it only now occurred to me that Inigo—" He paused. "Never mind. Just don't get near him."

"What did he do to you?" She could tell Gaven wasn't ready for that conversation. He looked down and bit his lip, as he always did when he was ready to deflect the question.

"I know people have said harsh things to you tonight," he said. "Don't listen to any of them. You are the best partner I've ever had and I never regretted choosing you."

Mirari wanted nothing more than to hug him tight, but in the presence of others it would have to wait. She had her ups and downs, and doubts had the louder voice. She often questioned her value, but whatever she meant to these people, she didn't care. Only Gaven's words mattered to her.

Before she could reply, she felt a tug in her chest. Her partner was alert and locked onto something like a tiger tracking prey. This time, she was sure it wasn't Inigo and she turned to see he was looking out into the deeper parts of the garden. She failed to make out anything but silhouettes of shrubs and gazebos.

"What's wrong?" she asked.

Gaven focused not only on the garden ahead but also on the rustling of leaves and the harmony of the earth. Everything fell silent except for the sound of Mirari's own heartbeat. Then, she was shoved aside by Gaven as a huge, black blade gleamed from the darkness and slammed into the stone where she once stood. Gaven dodged left as the sword cut toward his torso.

To Mirari's horror, the claymore wasn't wielded by any man, but it was levitating. She took note of its lackluster features. It had a basic shape, tied with cheap, tacky leather around the hilt. But she was attracted to the blade, which was crafted with such a dark black material that it seemed to reflect no light. She didn't recognize it as any of the pristine hāstal weaponry the Hales would've forged – it was operated by some sorcery.

The blade spun its point toward Gaven's chest. He called upon the stone power around him, bolstering his stance he slapped and intercepted the flying claymore with his bare hands. The black pommel trembled against him and began to slip from his grip.

Mirari wanted to help, but she was distracted by a dark figure that came out from behind a cover of bushes. A man dressed in formal attire came at her with a bolt of lightning in his palm. Mirari ducked, and the bolt sliced a branch from a tree. She thrust her fist into his stomach. With his body lurched forward, she elbowed his neck to the ground.

Gaven released his grip on the claymore, taking a side step as the sword launched forward. He grabbed its hilt and drove the blade into the chest of their assailant. The man fell dead instantly, the blade protruding from his back.

"Are you okay?" Gaven asked. She nodded.

"I thought weapons aren't allowed at the ball," Mirari said. She took a closer look at the man. He was dressed in a dark suit made of fine fabric but not fancy enough to stand out. His face was covered with a cloth mask.

"They aren't," Gaven said. "He barely put up a fight. Someone like him isn't strong enough to move a weapon with such precision."

"Then was he possessed?"

He pulled the man's mask down. It was a middle-aged man, one he did not recognize. Judging by his unkempt beard and dark circles under his eye, he was but a commoner, a victim of the hard times.

Gaven shook his head. Even if he made immense efforts to help his region rebuild, there were undoubtedly people still at the bottom of the chain, starved and impoverished. There simply weren't enough resources for everyone. Gaven tried to make the poor the minority, but it was a complicated process, one that could take decades to overcome. Not everyone was willing to wait. Many expected him to do better. Some wanted a new region leader. Under such circumstances, Gaven assumed the assassin came for him.

But then they heard a scream coming from inside the venue. A flood of attendees streamed from the mansion into the garden, and one catapulted through the window. Shattered glass rained into the gardens and confused cries could be heard from inside.

"There's more?" Mirari was bewildered.

Gaven didn't hesitate. He sprinted toward the mansion beckoning Mirari. "Come, we must protect the guests."

"In this?" Mirari pointed to her gown that had been dragging on the ground. She groaned, lifted the ends of the gown, and rushed after Gaven.

Gaven and Mirari watched chaos unfold in the ballroom. There were about two dozen assailants, all dressed in black from head to toe, with bandannas concealing all but their eyes to hide their identities. The guards tried to stop them, jabbing at them with their swords without much luck. The fighters, trained commanders and proud region leaders from all three empires, didn't need to think about what was unfolding before them. Even without their weapons, they took on the unwelcome guests head first, driving them into walls, slashing with steak knives and choking them with cloth.

One man turned to Mirari. He spun two daggers in his hand and charged at her.

"Mirari, catch!" She turned and saw Starlight with two round, metal trays in her hand. Mirari didn't have the time to compliment her dazzling pink dress before Starlight spun a tray at her. Mirari caught it and held it above her head just in time as the daggers bounced off the tray. From underneath, Gaven chucked two wine glasses at the assailant. As he shielded his face, Mirari hurled the tray at him. He stumbled back into a displeased man in a suit, a metal mask still shielding his identity. All it took was one pinch at the neck, and the assailant sank to the floor unconscious.

"I thought you might want this," Fangbane said as he tossed Gaven a flimsy spear he had picked off from an unconscious guard. "Guess we arrived just in time."

"Where did they come from?" Gaven asked, clearly upset at the bloodlust all around him.

"Doesn't matter, just protect the nobles. I can't imagine the mess that will come out of this if someone dies here tonight."

Gaven heard a whip snap in the air, then the shriek of a man who had his bottom slapped. He had underestimated the old lady, dropped his weapon and ran for the door. Except Gaven was in the way, and with a single jab through the chest, he fell to his knees, then collapsed in a pool of crimson.

"Permission to kill, Suzan?" Gaven asked. Suzan looked at the dead man at her feet.

"Why do you bother asking?" she said. "Capture as many as you can, but don't let a single one of them escape."

On that order, the team dispersed, tackling as many assailants as they could in their formal attire. It was then Mirari realized that not everyone was fighting, even if they could. The Priest, the Councilors, even the highest of advisors, watched as the guards, Knights, and most passionate region leaders faced their opponents with little to defend themselves. Nothing could break their pride.

Mirari approached the cornered assailants when one of them stood before the rest and raised a hand in the air holding a glowing dark green orb, and cast it upon the ground. A cloud filled the room and Mirari coughed at the first smell of it. It made her a bit dizzy and in the darkness she could hear people scream. Dark shapes began flying about her, great wings and dark bodies flashed about and her head began to pound.

In a panic, she covered her mouth and threw her other hand toward the ground. A gust of wind began to spiral around her, expanding and consuming objects in its path. She heard metal objects clattering as her gust launched trays, silverware, and tablecloths against walls and bodies. It was enough to allow herself to take a breath of fresh air, but did she hurt anyone along the way? When she dropped her hand and opened her eyes, she was surprised to see that the Knights and many of the guards were still fighting despite remnants of the smoke obstructing their view.

Only now many of the assailants had fled through a side passage. She heard Gaven roar, "Move in and seize them!" He and dozens of guards ran after the masked assailants.

Further beyond the escapees, Mirari saw the assailant who had thrown the orb slip through a doorway. He wore a studded, full-faced mask unlike the rest, and Mirari was propelled with curiosity. Gathering her dress she ran between the group of attackers in pursuit.

On the second floor, Mirari saw the assailant sprinting for one of the rooms. Before he could get to the door, Mirari tackled him. He kicked and punched, trying to pull free from her grasp. As Mirari hung on, she could feel the figure underneath was actually a woman. The realization provided enough of a distraction for the woman to escape with a hard kick. The masked woman rolled to her feet and took out a dagger.

It was an odd weapon, dark as void. The dagger was hard to make out in the dim light, but it was no doubt made of the same black steel as the claymore that had attacked her in the garden. Prior to tonight, Mirari had never seen such a material, but now it piqued her curiosity. She had yet to discover effects of this type of metal, and she must be cautious.

The woman moved within arm's length of Mirari. Her fist whipped through the air, as Mirari narrowly dodged her blow. Her opponent wasn't terribly quick. Mirari didn't even need to block her flurry of punches, using her disciplined technique to simply dodge her lumbering assaults.

Then the woman sprung, trying to tackle her.

But Mirari dropped, in a rolling motion, and was lying on her back with her legs drawn in just as she reached her. Mirari's feet struck her in mid-air, and she threw her backwards with the double-legged blow like the kick of a mule to the chest.

"What do you want?" Mirari yelled, but the woman didn't say a word. She was already back on her feet, ready to attack again. An assassin like her was going to fight until one of them was dead.

Mirari slugged her in the jaw, cracking her mask. She caught Mirari's fist before she could pull back. Bracing her feet, Mirari threw her weight against the woman's strong grip. This woman was no amateur in close combat, but Mirari would not allow this woman to best her. As they grappled, she tried to punch Mirari in the face. She managed to land a few punches, but not without Mirari returning a few good kicks. The woman's apoplectic fury didn't slow down. She headbutted Mirari. Dizzy, Mirari staggered back, forced to let her go. The mask cracked further and half fell to the floor. Mirari's eyes widened as she stared at the face under the mask.

"You…?"

Mirari brought her hand up to her pulsing head. She didn't expect it to hurt so much, and the pain was only growing worse. She felt something wasn't right. The pain was expanding to the rest of her head, her body growing heavy.

A dark wave washed over her mind and she looked at the woman, now shrouded in darkness as she overwhelmed Mirari's mind. The woman flashed a wicked grin as the black dagger floated into view. The way her weapon hovered with much precision made Mirari realize that she was likely the one who attacked her in the garden. This woman could control weapons. Maybe minds too. But that was impossible.

Stomach rolling, Mirari lurched to the side when she felt another sharp pulse in her head.

"For the love of Xerxes," she cursed as she placed her hand on her head. Her head pounded again as darkness overcame her vision. The dagger launched at her and Mirari flinched reflexively, the blade grazing her arm. Mirari sneered from the pain.

Mirari reached out to claw at the woman, but missed, and fell to the ground. Did she have a concussion? Was she poisoned? Her strength left her faster than she could process the events unfolding before her, and her senses were drowned out by a hum in her ears growing louder and louder.

Unable to lift her heavy body, Mirari tried to regain visual focus. She blinked several times, expecting to see the dark blade overhead. But the woman was nowhere in sight and the pain never came. What did her assailant look like? Mirari was beginning to forget.

She slowly turned her head, enough to make out another silhouette in the corner of her eye, guarding her body. The shadow was too big to be the woman, and he had a deep voice she didn't recognize. He was shouting at someone, but her ears were too muffled to make out a word. She saw him throw a punch, and his opponent fought back. Mirari wished she could see more, but the more she tried, the more her senses failed.

Mirari swore her eyes were open, but the silhouettes grew until her vision was consumed in black. She tried to move her fingers, toes, anything, but she could only lay there and beg for control.

Then she felt a sense of calm as her world became silent. She had almost forgotten why she was in a panic. Her mind was at peace, her physical state no longer of importance. She allowed her mind to drift... and drift... for what seemed to be an eternity.

AN UNKNOWN AMOUNT of time passed until she heard someone call her name. She felt her body sway back and forth, then a sharp flick to her forehead.

"Ow," Mirari hissed, now finally opening her eyes. Kylah was inches from her face, and her headache was gone.

"She's alright," Kylah said, and stepped away.

"Really?" Mirari said. "You're not even going to ask?"

"You're moving and talking. That's all that matters."

Lucan grabbed Mirari's hands and pulled her up. "We caught most of them. The chaos is finally over."

"Who?" Mirari asked. Lucan tilted his head.

"They must've hit you pretty hard," Lucan joked. But Mirari wasn't joking. She recalled chasing after someone, their faces skewed along with the rest of her memory, but that all felt like a dream to her. Then she noticed the sparkling gown she was wearing.

"The others?" Mirari gasped, remembering where she was. "Is everyone okay?"

"A handful of dead guards and assassins," Kylah said. "Unfortunately, every noble's head seems to still be intact."

They returned to the ballroom, a glaze of red painted on every wall. Dead assailants were piled in one corner of the room, while the rest of the men and women in black were tied up and lined against a wall. They were being interrogated by members of the Council, to not much luck. They kept their heads low, joined in silence.

Gaven was observing the injured guests, all in the hands of capable healers. Their injuries were all treatable, scratches and jabs that missed vital organs. Were they bad fighters or was it intentional?

But the attack didn't add up. For starters, it was foolish for commoners to attack a venue full of the most elite fighters and expect to get much out of it. If their goal was to kill as many nobles as possible, then they failed horribly at it. Much blood was drawn that night but not a single life was lost — on the noble's side, that was. People praised the good work of the guards,

Knights, and healers, but Gaven noticed that every assailant he took down didn't have a fraction of the military training and discipline of a new recruit. The Blessed wouldn't send people like that on such an important mission. He was convinced it was a distraction for something larger, but nothing was stolen and nothing suspicious had been reported since. What was the goal of the attack? The mystery loomed over his mind.

The surviving assailants refused to talk. It was not likely anyone would uncover the answer. He turned and noticed that his partner had woken up.

"Are you alright?" Gaven asked. "What happened?" He placed his hands on Mirari's shoulders, eyeing the nude parts of her body for the slightest bump or cut.

Her cheeks grew hot. She brushed his hands away, saying, "Still in one piece. Any luck with the interrogation?"

"Not much to work off of."

"Someone on the inside must've let them in," Lucan said. "They couldn't have infiltrated this place with so many guards."

Kylah looked over at the injured nobles. "If they were aiming to assassinate someone tonight, they failed horribly at it."

Gaven released a sudden breath. "This is a damn disaster is what it is, for both sides. It's looking like these enemies are able to strike from within any circle around us. How can we hope to find out the truth here, even if we convince some of them to talk? Tonight is proof that we can't even trust our own people."

Mirari scoffed. "That's nothing new."

"Maybe you need to slip your coin in the right hands." Lucan said as he nodded to a group of nobles in heated conversation. They had not a speck of blood or stain on their garments, yet they were bustling with energy.

Gaven narrowed his eyes and gave Lucan that disapproving glare. "You don't mean..."

Mirari recognized one man of the bunch, Inigo, who at the

moment seemed to be calming the other nobles. Inigo seemed to be held in high regard amongst them.

"He paid for this venue right?" Lucan said. "He must have an idea of how they got through. Even a list of staff will help."

Mirari felt her chest tingle again. Gaven was trying to hold back a scowl.

"We're not working with him," he said.

Lucan gave him a stern look. "Inigo knows how to get information. We both know that."

Gaven scoffed, adding, "We're not dealing with him. I have better ways of getting intel."

Curiosity was getting the best of Mirari now. She asked, "What happened between you two?"

Gaven snapped. "Just drop it. I mean it."

Gaven turned to cast a glare in Inigo's direction, then stomped away from them. Mirari stood in shock. She had never seen him so enraged over a single person, especially one that didn't appear to have a fraction of his strength.

But what did she know? Whatever happened to Gaven when he arrived in Althaea was a mystery to her. She was just starting to meet the friends and enemies he made. If she learned anything tonight, it was that she knew little about her partner, and, in light of this attack, truths would be unraveled.

PART II

CHAPTER NINE

It had been four months since Gaven left Minetta. Even though Gaven never talked much, the house was quieter without him. It felt like something was missing. There was one less person to go hunting with, one less person to play games with, and one less person to squeeze into their cramped, shared bedroom.

Roselyn wondered if he even made it to Althaea. No one knew. They never heard another word from Gaven, but Roselyn thought about him every day.

A rich, steamy scent rose from the broth Misa was preparing.

"Dear?" she asked Roselyn. "Could you chop these vegetables for us, please? Nice and fine, the way you do so well."

Roselyn shook the thoughts of Gaven away and focused on chopping the vegetables in front of her. Misa watched Roselyn, and a familiar joy warmed her. The girl had grown so much since the day she walked into their home. Gaunt, timid, almost shrinking into herself. Back then, Roselyn wasn't tall enough to see over the counter top. Now she was capable of cooking a whole meal by herself.

Roselyn felt Misa's gaze, and looked up. "Is this how you want them?"

"Perfect, thank you." Misa let out a sigh, a little smile played on her lips. "Our little Miss Miracle."

Roselyn blushed. It was the cute nickname they had given her after she began living with them. Misa said she was a gift from the Gods. Marlo said it was fate. Salathiel and Gaven used the nickname to tease her whenever she slipped on wet mud or carelessly slingshot a pellet into her forehead.

She didn't dare tell them she hated it. It made her feel like a survivor, reminding her that she made it out of whatever killed her parents. They called her lucky; she called herself guilty.

And now she liked it even less, knowing what *did* kill her parents.

The townspeople in Malino believed it was the kinastōne in the Hale's compartment that exploded. Roselyn didn't believe that theory. Her father told her those generators would be able to fall off a cliff and still function. They would not be so easily damaged by a flame or spark.

Then, there was the other piece of the puzzle that didn't add up. She was with her mother and father next to that noisy generator. Why didn't she perish with them? She never accepted that it was a miracle.

Roselyn had a dozen theories about that day, but the only thing anyone knew for certain was that there was a fire. Where the fire came from was anyone's guess.

But a new theory surfaced after the incident in the woods. What happened in the forest played out like the kōnvoy accident: there was a fire and she couldn't remember it. The source? Gaven said it was her.

Guilt sluiced through her body – then a cold rush of fear and anxiety. She couldn't deny what was looking more and more like reality. If the boys were telling the truth, it would be like the time they found her in the woods – she would have no injuries, which she didn't. The soot on her clothes and smell of ash told her there was indeed a fire, that there was something deadly inside her – likely her kore – she couldn't control.

It was believed that all humans were children of the Gods and inherited their divine ability that would become known as kore. Kore was a skill that could disappear over generations if the wielder did not practice it. As far as she knew, her ancestors had given up that practice long ago.

But if she had fire kore, this ability, she believed, had to stay locked up. The last thing she wanted was to hurt her new family. To this day, she couldn't muster the courage to tell them her theory, in fear that they would hate her, abandon her even. If she told Salathiel, would he call her crazy, or would he believe her? If he called her a monster, she would accept it.

Misa took her diced carrots and stirred it into the broth, bringing Roselyn's attention back to the vegetables in front of her. She thought it would've been better if she could bake bread with her fire kore, but even if she could summon it again, there was a higher chance of her burning the house down.

"Have you ever thought about going home?" Misa said. This was an inevitable question now that Gaven was gone, but Roselyn had long made up her mind.

"This is my home, Mother."

"And you've been a blessing from the day you joined us."

Roselyn knew that. They loved her dearly as the daughter they never had. She could tell; it showed in the patient way they taught her how to do her chores, the amount of freedom they gave her, and how they scolded her as much as they did to Salathiel and Gaven.

Roselyn asked, "Why do you ask that? About me going back to the Hales?"

"No reason, sweetie." Misa said. "But… Well, you know you're free to go back to the Hale family whenever you want. It might be nice to see some of your relatives again."

Roselyn kept her eyes on the chopping. Her silence sparked another statement from Misa.

"Surely you miss them."

"I do, in a way…" Roselyn said. "But…"

"Go ahead, dear. It's all right."

"I think it's better for the Hales that I'm gone. I was always messing up anyway."

Misa stirred the pot a few more times, wishing she knew how to say what she wanted to. "You know why I agreed to let you stay, sweetie?"

"Because you wanted a daughter?"

"It's because that first day you came to us and I gave you a change of clothes, I saw the bruises on your body," Misa admitted.

"Ow!" Roselyn cried out. The cut on her finger was small, leaving only a drop of blood, but Misa fluttered all over her. "Oh, my. Here, here." She took Roselyn's hand and brought her to the sink.

"It's alright. It's nothing."

"I used to have bruises like that," Misa said, as she pressed a clean cloth to the tiny wound. "I know what it's like to live in that kind of household. You looked so desperate to break free, and I… I could see myself in you. It was as if the Gods were giving me a second chance to make things right. How could I have turned that away?"

"Even… if I'm a Hale?" Roselyn's voice broke just a little. It wasn't the cut that made her tears well up – it was the way Misa's love poured over her injury, and patched every other hole in her heart since she began living with them. They embraced her imperfections, and never made her feel ashamed. Roselyn now knew that the world her parents tried to instill in her wasn't the world she wanted to be in.

If living a kind and modest life among the help was bad, then she didn't want to be a noble.

"A name doesn't define what's in your heart," Misa tore a small strip of cloth, and bandaged the finger. "You've brought nothing but miracles into our home, you're our—"

"Oh please, Mother!" Roselyn interrupted her and squirmed, trying to pull her finger away from Misa's pampering.

"Hush, Miss Miracle. And hold still." Misa finished tying off the bandage. "There. You'll be fine," she said. And then, unable to stop herself, Misa pulled Roselyn close to her, hugging her with fierce, protective love. Roselyn embraced her warmth and slightly lifted her head up for the forehead kiss she knew was coming…

"Mother." Salathiel's voice came from behind them. The ladies turned around and saw Salathiel and Marlo enter the kitchen. Roselyn noticed that Marlo looked troubled, and Misa's smile had faded to a stern look.

Misa said, "You know how I feel about all this."

"If you're so worried, then Roselyn can come too."

"What's going on?" Roselyn asked.

Salathiel began. "Near the border, there's a town in Avon called Solarin. It's not much bigger than Malino. But I hear it's growing rapidly. More and more merchants are using the town as a trading center. It's a promising place."

"You're planning to find work there?" Roselyn said.

"I want to move there," he clarified. Roselyn raised her eyebrows. She wasn't prepared for Salathiel to leave as well. In fact, the thought never crossed her mind. But now it made sense why Misa had brought up her family. She was expecting all of them to depart, just like Gaven.

"Merchant towns are so dangerous," Misa said.

Marlo nodded, adding, "We have everything here. Food, open space…"

"We don't have enough income," Salathiel said in a tone that sounded almost stubborn. His sharp words silenced Misa, but that wasn't his intention. Salathiel took a deep breath and considered his next words more carefully.

"Mother, Malino is great. But we could be living so much better. You could have a roof that you don't have to change every winter. You could buy whatever you want at the market and not be worried if we have enough for tax."

"Greed is a sin, Salathiel," Marlo warned with his finger pointing sternly.

"We shouldn't have let Gaven go," Misa shook her head. "This is about him, isn't it? You want to prove you can do something better than him."

"Mother," Salathiel wanted to object, for letting Gaven go without complaints. He hesitated against raising his voice, and Roselyn knew why. Salathiel was older than Gaven and her – the most responsible out of the three – and he deserved the opportunity to discover himself. But he had no real future to look forward to, other than scratching a living from the earth. There were independent people his age, wealthy shopkeepers, even region leaders. He was ready to be like them and live on his own.

"I… think it's a good idea," Roselyn spoke up. She rubbed her fingers together. All eyes turned to her – it left the family speechless. But she pushed ahead. "We can look out for each other. It works out."

She surprised herself – she had never felt more confident. She understood why Salathiel wanted a future of his own. Roselyn felt the same way. It was as if watching Gaven pursue his dream woke her up. She wasn't really living – she was just hiding. She couldn't hide forever in this rustic farmhouse, tucked away at the edge of a secluded forest, for the rest of her life. If Salathiel was going to take a risk, she was determined to follow him.

"Roselyn, are you sure you want to go to Solarin?" Marlo said. "It's a town full of travelers."

"He's right," Misa seconded. "There may be people from the Hale family who recognize you."

"I'll be ok. It's a small town, right?"

She glanced at Salathiel. It pleased her to see he didn't object to the prospect of her going with him.

In fact, he had an idea. "We'll change her name."

"What?"

"Father, do you still talk to Uncle Rocco, the one who can make fake records?"

"Rocco!" Marlo laughed, "What a character! We used to—" and then he cut off, wiping his grin away quickly when Misa gave him *'the look'*. He scratched his scalp, and his eyes and mouth squinted and squirmed as he tried to find the proper tone. "Uh… yes, Rocco. Not the sort of fellow you'd want to trust to hold your purse, of course. But very skilled in his ways. I think I know where to contact him."

"At the alehouse, I'll wager," grumbled Misa.

"We just need to give Roselyn a new name," Salathiel said. "With our family name."

Roselyn tilted her head. "Fake records? You can do that?"

"Uncle Rocco can make tags look like the real thing. Trust me, his cousin works in the records. They just slip in your paper, no problem."

"Then… why didn't we do that for Gaven? Wouldn't that have made his travel easier?"

"Althaean tags are a whole other process," Salathiel said. "Completely different materials that aren't available outside the empire. That's how they make sure they're not fake."

Roselyn nodded. There was still so much she had to learn about the world, things she couldn't learn from books. An adventure was beginning to sound thrilling.

But a new name? She would have to live with it for the rest of her life.

"You want to go by your nickname? Miss Miracle?"

"What am I, a saint?" she said, scowling at Salathiel.

He tried again. "Mira?"

"Hmmm… Too much like Misa, you think?"

"And what's wrong with that?" her mother asked.

"How about Mirari? The Goddess of Miracles." Marlo suggested.

"Mirari?" Roselyn liked how it sounded when she said it out loud. "Wasn't there a Region Leader named Mirari?"

"A couple of centuries ago, I believe."

"Then it won't be strange at all," Salathiel said. "Roselyn, what do you think?"

"Mirari…" she repeated. She touched her finger to her lips as she mouthed the name over and over again. "It'll take some getting used to… but I like how it sounds." The more she uttered those three syllables to herself, the more it flowed naturally. The name was certainly different enough that no one would connect it to the missing girl of the Hale family.

Salathiel smiled. "Mirari. It suits you." His face lit up even more with another idea. "You'll be a Zanette. We'll say you're my sister."

"Sister?" It was only now she realized that Salathiel had always been like a big brother to her, but she never referred to him as one. That was a change she wouldn't mind. The thought of it made her smile.

Misa's hand glided across Roselyn's tender cheeks. Roselyn tilted her head and allowed her face to be caressed. She thought about how she was going to miss Misa's motherly touch. She brought her hand up, squeezing Misa's hand.

"No matter where you go, what path you choose, you'll always be my daughter."

"And you'll always be my mother. My family."

CHAPTER TEN

One Week After the Grand Ball

Gaven and Mirari combed through the streets of the lower plaza. With the attack on the Grand Ball so recent, their steps were shadowed by the guards that followed close behind. Gaven had promised to show her more of the city and now was as good a time as any. The assailants captured at the Grand Ball were being interrogated by the Council and Erel had assured him that another attack so soon after the Grand Ball was unlikely. Still, Gaven kept his gaze alert as he strode next to Mirari.

Her eyes flitted from stall to stall as she gazed in an innocent wonder he wanted to preserve. Gaven felt a light twinge of surprise from Mirari – not unpleasant, just unexpected – and she was drawn to the quirky odds and ends spread out across a ragged stall.

When Gaven followed after her, he saw what had caught her attention. A small, decorative bracelet embellished with two dangling feathers. She bubbled with pleasure and he wondered if she was homesick for Minetta. Althaea must be quite different from what she grew up with.

Suddenly nervous, the peddler began ringing his hands even as his shoulders crept up to his ears. He glanced apprehensively between the two of them and scrambled for a handkerchief. He tossed the cloth over the bauble to hide it and bowed to Mirari. "Please, good lady, do not take offense."

"Offense? How could I?" She tilted her head, glancing over at Gaven. "It was beautiful."

Sighing, Gaven lifted the handkerchief away and said, "Selling Minettan goods isn't illegal anymore, you know." No matter his efforts, he still saw situations like this all across Althaea Main.

"Aye, yes, but…" The merchant swept a surreptitious eye around the marketplace. "Well, old habits, ya know. And uh." He winced and rubbed his shoulders. "Not everyone is so open-minded. A couple of pud-whackers threw a rock at me the other day over it."

Glowering, Gaven picked up the bracelet. "How much?"

"Oh, please." He waved his hands as though to ward off trinket. "Just take it. It's brought nothing but bad luck to me." Ignoring him, Gaven pulled out a gold coin and tossed it onto the counter. Eyes wide like saucers, the shopkeeper spluttered and said, "Oh, I couldn't, Your Honor. I can't make change for—"

"Keep it." He smirked. "Maybe it'll change your luck." He turned to Mirari and asked, "May I?"

Smiling, she held out her hand. "Who knew you were such a gentleman?" she whispered as he fastened it around her wrist.

He ducked his head and didn't answer. Frankly, he had learned it from her. Just watching her every day was a noble lesson. Her compassion and empathy. The way she related to the common people, not just with words either. It was a trait she embodied in everything she did. She mingled with the children, unloaded merchandise, even spent a few coins at struggling shops.

In Althaea, people were expected to mind their own business; kindness was a rarity. Sometimes it was even seen as a weakness, but Gaven didn't see it as a flaw in Mirari. She noticed things that Gaven would've turned away from. When he saw the differences in the people's behavior, her habits rubbed off on him a bit. It made him imagine a kinder future with her help.

Before they could continue on, they were interrupted by Erel approaching them on horseback. She was riding Gaven's favorite mount, a powerful white stallion, and had a scowl on her face with an ominous pinch of her brows.

"Do you think something happened?" Mirari asked, glancing between them.

He grunted. "Yeah. She's got that sour look on her face."

"Really?" Mirari raised an eyebrow. "And that would be different how?"

Erel reined the horse to a stop in front of its owner. Gaven stepped close, ostensibly to run his hand over the beast's snout. "I take it you have some urgent news?" he asked. "Or are you just giving my horse some exercise?"

"Both." Leaning down, she whispered into his ear, "Councilor Suzan is on her way. She wants a word. The council is finished with the rebels caught last week and she wants to discuss it with you."

"Already?" he said, nonplussed. His heart darkened as he thought about the attack. For the dissidents to be so bold as to attack the Grand Ball and the councilors, nobles and Knights, Gaven hadn't thought any information would be garnered from them so quickly. Based on the look on Erel's face, she hadn't thought it either.

"Evidently," she answered neutrally.

"Is everything all right?" Mirari asked, drawing his attention back to her.

"I'll be right there," Gaven told Erel. He returned to Mirari's side. "Sorry to cut our stroll short. I'm needed back at the fortress."

She nodded, looking concerned. "Is there anything I can do to help?"

He thought about it. "Not anything specific, but keep your eye out." Scowling, he looked around the area. "Whatever's going on, we're not done with the Blessed."

<hr>

Suzan had her arms crossed, staring at the seat she once occupied. Gaven kicked his legs on the armrest, fiddling with one of her paperweights in his hand.

"Are you listening?" Suzan said, narrowing her eyes. Her discontent extended beyond Gaven's absent-minded behavior. It was seeing the way he had vandalized her former study with strings laced with citrine, every velvet chair replaced with white leather. Gaven had been region leader for years now, but Suzan was still not used to seeing the fortress with new decor.

Gaven tossed a heavy cube onto the table, sending a loud clang echoing across his room, if not to simply annoy her. He was displeased over Suzan's orders and the Council's actions, and he made no effort to hide it.

"Kill the rebels. Take control," he repeated.

The Council's official report of the attack at the Grand Ball labeled the assailants as surviving rebels of the Althaean Siege, determined to finish what they started. Since the Grand Ball took place in Althaea Main, it made sense. It was a repeat of what happened four years ago at the hearth, but this time it was a direct attack on the high officials.

This information was no secret. Still, Suzan saw to it that she spoke to Gaven regarding this matter in private.

"It's imperative that you do it this time," she said. "Convincing the Council that you had nothing to do with the rebellion was a miracle. Now you must prove it through action."

There would be a public execution of the rebels tomorrow. Gaven knew that killing the assailants would stir an uproar in neighboring regions and empires, just as it did during the Siege. All of Gaven's efforts to improve his region would be gone in an instant, and what purpose did death serve if the Council found no motive for the attack? It would be no different than pinning the blame on every commoner.

Althaea Main had never been so unstable.

Gaven stared at his palm, the hand that had been stained with blood more times than he could count. He didn't enjoy slaughtering civilians, but he had grown numb to it. Suzan had been preparing him for situations like this since the day they met.

WHEN YOUNG GAVEN arrived in Althaea Main, all he did was train, eat, sleep, and grow. Stein was no easy trainer to please. Once he got into a clean shirt and combed his gray hair to the side, Stein became a merciless commander. Gaven learned the hard way that things only got worse when Stein was out of sour herbs.

Gaven was offered no rest. A pulled muscle or a fractured bone did not provide an exception to the rule. Every morning he woke up numb and sore, but he soldiered on. Even if Gaven didn't understand why he spent more time heaving supplies across the fortress than holding a sword, he didn't deny that it made him physically stronger. By the end of the second spring, he had developed the build and strength equal to any warrior on the field. And when he was placed in his first platoon, he bested them all in a duel in less than a minute. All eyes were on the aspiring young warrior.

From a balcony, his grand leader, the most fearsome fighter in the entire Althaean Empire, watched Gaven beat half a dozen teammates in record time. His teammates were much older than Gaven, but withered on the floor like worms in the sun. He slapped the wooden pole on one of the soldier's buttocks to claim his victory.

Suzan took immense satisfaction seeing him stand toe to toe with grown men and knock them to their knees. What delighted her wasn't his fighting prowess; it was seeing the proud, swaggering braggarts, men who never failed to underestimate him, learn a lesson. One that Suzan had crammed down the throats of so many men who scoffed at the very idea that a mere woman could best them. She loved seeing Gaven do the same to those fools who couldn't see past a younger soldier having more potential than them. It kindled her fondest memories.

"What of his kore?" the aged woman asked Stein, as she picked up her cane.

"He resonates with the earth," Stein said. "Not much by far."

A few spectators clapped for Gaven as he wiped the sweat off his face and bare back with a towel.

Stein gave him a thumbs up before trailing behind Suzan.

They were hardly out of sight when someone dumped a half-filled bucket of cold slop on Gaven. Soggy crusts of stale bread and grain rolled down his back. If it had been the first time, he would've thought it was a drunk man's spew. But he knew there was a reason why the servants kept complaining that someone had been stealing the grub meant for the livestock.

"Bartley, you fed the wrong pig!" he heard his teammate holler.

A spectator had Gaven's white shirt in hand. The shirt was

no more than a rag compared to his pressed vest and gold chains. He stood by his two possies and threw Gaven's shirt onto the soiled ground.

"Oops, missed."

"Let that pig eat, Inigo."

Ignoring the snorts, Gaven groaned in disgust as he tried to wipe off the slop. They dropped the bucket and left him in the puddle of yesterday's breakfast.

Suzan and Stein had reached the ground level of the court-yard now, and saw that Gaven had been served another one of his victory meals.

"Your Honor!" Gaven held a crisp salute, ignoring the slop trickling down his body.

"Ah, Young Gaven," Suzan said. "My Valiant Tiger."

The phrase struck him as odd. "Your… who, My Lady?"

"Oh, just a nickname that struck me. It's what watching you fight makes me think of. Your power, your grace, your speed. The mightiest creature of all, seems appropriate to me."

Gaven blushed at the attention. But he remembered his place, mumbling, "You honor me, Great Leader. I haven't earned so much as a single victory in a real battle."

"True. But Stein tells me you've defeated every soldier here in a duel. Even Stein himself."

"That is correct, Your Honor."

"I've observed you, Gaven. More than once. You're a trained paragon, and yet the moves you make, the unexpected revers-es…" She looked at him, and he felt that her eyes could drill right through a diamond. "Those are moves taught in the umbra class. How did you learn to fight like that?"

Gaven wasn't sure if this question was a trap. Almost every trainer would insist his pupils stick firmly to the mastery of one style. But he decided to just admit the truth.

"With all due respect, My Lady… I got the idea from you."

Suzan would have made a great gotchen player – her face betrayed nothing, as she asked, "From me? How do you mean?"

"When you were ten, you switched from being a paragon to an umbra," Gaven began. "You beat all the paragons because you knew how they were trained, how they fought, and eventually, you became the best region leader of all time in Althaea. Because you knew exactly how other classes fought."

Suzan was amazed this child would know about that.

"Did Stein tell you that?"

"Your history is in the fortress archives, Your Honor. It's not hard to find."

"No one bothers to read the archives." Suzan raised a brow. "No one bothers to read at all these days." She knew this boy was an amazing physical rarity, but she wasn't expecting a scholar.

She laughed at Gaven's impertinence. And yet there was something so original, so bold about him. Sure, people used all kinds of persuasion and subterfuge to get their agendas across to her. That she was used to. But this boy? He was so direct. Without a filter, without guile. This was a rare quality – an essential of any good leader.

"You have guts, I'll give you that." Suzan chuckled. "If that ego of yours doesn't get you killed, you might actually have a shot at becoming a region leader someday."

Gaven held his breath, savoring the best compliment he could ever receive from the strongest region leader of Althaea.

He had no shyness regarding his ambition, and no lack of confidence. It was no secret everyone expected a new region leader to replace Suzan in the coming years. But certainly not yet. She still fought just as well as she did in her prime. She was uncontested, and she was a powerful umbra many looked up to. This compliment was so unexpected, it rocked him.

Suzan turned to Stein. "Send him to Desmonda with the rest of the unit departing tonight."

"To…" Stein stammered. "But, Your Honor… ain't he too young?"

"I need to know if he can handle it. Send him."

———

GAVEN COULD HEAR screams filled the air as a new gravesite was being carved in the once peaceful forest outside the town of Desmonda. Looking down, young Gaven saw two stains of blood – black in the early morning – that had run down his tunic.

He turned to the blade in his hand.

It took him only half a second to realize why it looked different. It was coated with the blood of the dead man by his feet. Another body lay five feet away – except for his head, which had rolled off another yard or two. Gaven took it in for a moment – he had killed two men.

He turned away and put his hand over his mouth, feeling his supper rising. The sounds of metal slashing through human flesh — frantic women screaming, knives cutting through children his age — filled the air. There was no avoiding the chaos unfolding around him.

These were families from a neighboring empire that had recently entered into war. The refugees were trickling into Althaea and other nearby empires, well aware of the Separation Law. Still, they took the risk knowing they had nowhere to go. Suzan and the other Althaean region leaders ensured that the law was enforced. There were to be no outsiders. No exceptions.

The soldiers that Gaven tagged along with, men and women some five to eight years older than him, didn't hesitate to use their weapons. They were the lowest of soldiers who failed to ascend, tasked with petty and unfavorable missions like this one. To them this was routine, and they had no need to empty their stomach. Their eyes remained hollow as they slashed and jabbed at anyone who ran.

But for the first time, Gaven had human blood on his hands. This weight sat heavy on his shoulders as he processed feelings he hadn't expected. Would he still be a fighter if he were to cry for the innocent lives he had just taken?

A scrawny man with a gray beard covered in dirt and blood charged in Gaven's direction, with an ax over his head and a hardened battle cry. Still in a daze, Gaven watched as the man got closer, pretending that the ax was not for him. But the man showed no sign of stopping, until the ax was above Gaven's head.

But the man came tumbling to the ground with a dagger through his chest.

"If you're not going to fight, then go back," a soldier hissed, pulling the dagger out of the man's chest. "Stupid kid. Don't get in the way."

His comrade dashed toward the hurricane of butchery, unleashed and slashed his sword through the neck of the first, then ran the next one into a woman's waist. He waded in further, slaughtering with merciless efficiency. Gaven thought there was no way he could do the same.

But he was right. Gaven was sent here to fight, and on the battlefield, there was only victory or death. He had to choose which side to stand on.

There was only one way to stop the refugees from killing him and his comrades. His eyes were drawn to a spear that had lodged between the ribs of a fallen refugee, buried all the way into the man's spine. One look at the man's bloodied face was all it took for Gaven to close his eyes and shrink back.

In the darkness, he could hear himself panting like a hound in a thunderstorm. He hated it so much that he ignored every other sound around him and concentrated on his breathing.

Steady. Controlled. They were just pawns, he reminded himself. Chickens on a farm, fated to be sacrificed tomorrow if not today.

When he opened his eyes, his thoughts and vulnerabilities left him with one exhaled breath. His disgust turned to bloodlust. His mind was clear and focused. As he reached for the spear, he recalled Suzan's words.

"I am a tiger," Gaven said to himself like a chant. With his foot planted on the dead man's chest, he tried to tug the weapon free. Suddenly, he felt his hands tingle, the shaft of the spear illuminating with a faint glow. Gaven stared at it, bewildered, seeing his kore take shape for the first time. The spear slid out like a hot knife through butter, and he felt a rush of power flowing through his veins, a source of strength that fed off his thrill. He held his spear the way he was trained to do.

He turned to the few refugees still standing. They held their blades in front of them, their last sign of hope. Their blades were nothing but dull metal in the presence of Gaven's newfound power. He pointed his spear at his next opponent, and charged with a mighty roar that no witnessing soldier would ever forget.

KILLING DIDN'T BOTHER him now — it was a part of being a fighter. What made Gaven uneasy was being unable to differentiate the good from the bad. If a rebel was anyone who disobeyed the law, did a murder weigh the same as petty theft? If a man rallied for rations to feed his children, would silencing him bring peace to Althaea Main?

The Council's decision to silence the assailants at the Grand Ball didn't sit right with Gaven. A swift decision like that, he knew, meant they were hiding something.

"Gaven," Suzan sighed, rubbing her temples, "this is for your own good. I don't want to risk losing you again. Althaea Main can't lose you either. Can you give me a verbal response? That you *will* take care of these rebels?"

Then, Gaven remembered why he was spared from the death sentence for the Althaean Siege. The Council had swept the existence of the Blessed under the rug, knowing that they had the power to alter Gaven's mind. Was it possible they were doing the same again?

Even after Laikos attacked the Hearth and nearly toppled the entire political system, the Blessed was still a taboo topic, one he knew Suzan would dodge if he uttered their name. How the Council was dealing with the dangerous organization, if at all, was just as much of a mystery to Gaven as it was to Fangbane or any other person outside of the Council.

That was why Gaven had to take matters into his own hands. Even if he agreed with the Council – to weed out every last trace of evil plaguing the empires – they would not approve of him acting as a vigilante. But how could he sit back knowing that the Blessed was behind the chaos plaguing his region? Possibly with an ability powerful enough to control his mind? He couldn't wait for them to make their next move.

Gaven rubbed his hand across his forehead and cursed at himself. They *did* make their next move. The rebels of the Althaean Siege were likely followers of Laikos, other members or possibly leaders of the Blessed. The Council knew this and put an immediate end to them. But why were they resurfacing now? Was the attack at the Grand Ball retaliation? And if so, how would he respond?

"Gaven?" Suzan repeated, her tone now more stern.

The Blessed were long from dead, the threat still looming and growing. Putting an end to the rebellion wasn't fighting his people, but rather fighting the parasites hiding among them.

"Yes, *Your Grace*," he said. There was a spark in Gaven's eyes as he lifted his head. He swore to Suzan, "the rebellion will be silenced."

CHAPTER ELEVEN

Two Weeks After the Grand Ball

"Down with the regions! Long live the fight!"

"Down with the regions! Long live the fight!"

A handful of angered men and women in ragged clothes rallied around the lower plaza's fountain, holding signs calling for Gaven's resignation and the dismantling of the Council. They gathered where dozens of civilians took their last breath one week ago; some of the cobblestones were still stained with splatters of faint red. Some bystanders watched the brave souls trying to rally a crowd. The majority simply looked the other away.

"What are you waiting for?" One man hollered, pointing at a group of men. He was twice the size of his peers, seething behind a full beard. "One life more is one life too many. They will continue to tear us apart until we have nothing left. But we run this society. We paved these roads. And it's time for us to take it back!"

The attack at the Grand Ball undoubtedly stirred up trouble across the empires, gave men like these courage to take a stand.

Some were physically violent, others rallying behind words. The commoners were tired of watching their people murdered without proper trial. Radicals, revolutionaries, even neighborhood vigilantes were starting to raise their voices again. Most were rabble-rousers who lacked the skill and courage to hold a blade. But there were also battle-hardened fighters, who believed that change could only be made through brute force. It was only a matter of time before another insurrection would break out.

The small crowd cheered, as did some nearby shopkeepers. As one bald man applauded from a distance, his wife slapped his hand.

"You better shut your mouth if you want to keep those hands," she said, looking around before heaving her basket of cabbages inside.

"This old hag," he said, shaking his head as he took the coins from his customer. "Afraid to take risks. I reckon you're different. I can see it in your eyes. You'd do something about this senseless manslaughter. Someone ought to."

Mirari bit her lip and nodded. She stored her apples in her satchel and quickly turned away, keeping her head hidden under her hood.

The bustling streets were filled with laborers and merchants, elderly folk and children, rich or poor, pious or profane. An aroma of fresh fawn and pepper skewers roasting over a flaming grill weaved through the market. Despite the liveliness, Mirari knew their lifestyles could be better. Althaea Main was still recovering from the Althaean Siege, and there were many who had yet to see any change in their lives. With protests becoming common, more guards decorated the streets to make sure the wicked stayed out of trouble, but it didn't always make the people feel safe. She wondered if the guards were making it worse, and if her Minettan presence was adding to the fuel.

She scurried to the opposite side of the street toward two

men waiting for her. They had swords strapped to their waists, which was not unusual for commoners in Althaea, but these men were not out for a stroll. While the people around them were distracted by the chants and cheers from the crowd, their gaze never left Mirari.

"We should go before they notice you, Milady," one of the men said.

But Mirari didn't want to leave. Their mission was to find out more about the rebels and what they were plotting next. She had to help Gaven find key contacts to suppress the riots before they grew violent. But all she got were quibbles, complaints about the taste of cabbages, and occasional mouth-breathers, and she didn't want to go back with only a satchel full of fruit.

"We should take them out while we're here," the other guard said. "Beats hunting them down again later. What do you say, Milady?"

That was the popular opinion among the army. They believed that words alone would not stop the rising rebellion, and no one understood how dire it was to contain the resurrection more than Gaven's army. Memories of the Althaean Siege still haunted the region. Every region leader in the alliance was ordered to silence the slightest sign of a rebellion – talks of reform, praise of a new idea, complaints over their region leader – with the blade. Would Gaven make the same decision?

The movement was growing, and time was running out.

"The age of the valiant is no more!" A man shouted near the fountain. "He cowers behind the Council, cowers behind the blade. He's saving his own arse, at the cost of our lives!"

The crowd erupted in another cheer, now doubled in size. But not everyone among the crowd was happy. A young woman, attractive and brimming with confidence, caught Mirari's eye. She was draped in a modest brown cloak, a basket over her shoulder, and two young boys locked in each hand. She tried to walk around the crowd, but a protestor wouldn't let her pass.

Mirari shoved her satchel at one of the guards. "Wait here," she said and paced over to the protestors.

"Milady?" the guards watched her walk toward the crowd. As soon as they realized what she was doing, they sprinted after her, but as the crowd huddled in closer, Mirari was out of reach and out of sight.

"Don't hurt our sister!" a young boy screamed. Mirari followed the sound of his voice and found the young woman at the front. The protestors had separated the woman and the boys, who were now bawling.

"I'm just trying to get her to apologize," the man said with a light chuckle.

"I meant what I said," she barked, pointing her finger at him. "Without the Valiant Tiger, we would've starved to death! Quit whining and put your hands to work like everyone else."

The bark in her voice drew the attention of listeners from afar. But what piqued the curiosity of the onlookers was not the person who countered the speakers, but rather what six brute men were about to do to this woman. They had inched closer to her now, almost completely surrounded. The woman stood her ground, fists raised, but Mirari could see that her legs were trembling. She didn't know how to fight.

Mirari had squeezed her way to the front of the crowd, looking at the largest man, his presence far more intimidating than the others. He had been rallying in the plaza all morning, and he was no doubt the one in charge.

"Let her go," Mirari shouted from among the crowd. She was but a shadow in the mob with her hood concealing her face. The leader almost brushed her away until she lifted her hood and flashed the badge on her chest. She wore it proudly – the gold phoenix of the Knights. Her hair waved through the wind as murmurs flowed, fingers pointed at her direction. The man's eyes widened when he met her intense gaze, then melted into a chuckle.

"Well, well, look who it is," he smiled, turning to the silent crowd. "Don't be scared. Her Lady, the Knight from Minetta, has graced us with her presence." In a lower voice he added, "or cursed us."

"Is this how you plan to seek reform?" Mirari said. "By terrorizing your community?"

The man grinned. "And what do you know about how we run things here? How would you know what's best for us? You have no power here, featherpit. You don't even deserve to walk on our land."

The ruffians released their attention on the young woman. She instantly ran to her siblings and embraced them.

Mirari felt her arms tugged from behind, constrained by the hands of two men, and the people around her backed away. From the way they held her, she could tell they had never been in the army – those were the grasps of men who learned the art of fighting through fellow pub-crawlers. She was ready to twist herself free and give these men a beating they wouldn't forget.

But a thought trickled into her mind, and for a second, her mind slipped from everything around her.

Mirari, the voice scowled. *How many times do I have to tell you to stop getting into fights?*

Before Mirari could respond, she felt a blow to her cheek, followed by a kick to her stomach. She gasped for air as her eyes blinked back to reality, seeing the rough man hunched over her. Mirari seethed, her eyes telling him that she would take her revenge.

"Maybe I don't give you enough credit," he said. "I didn't think you were capable, but now I see it." He turned to the crowd. "Everything went to Inferna the moment she entered our gates. This witch is, without a doubt, manipulating our region leader! Featherpits are a toxin to our land."

The sound of metal rung through the air, and seconds later, one of her arms was freed. The man next to her dropped with blood spurting from his armless body. Not long after, the man on the other side dropped with a hole through his chest.

The crowd began to scatter, screams rolling through the streets and many dropping their belongings along the way. The leader, however, remained unfazed. His followers didn't contain a fraction of his courage as they took off with the rest of the crowd.

"Look at this!" He pointed behind Mirari, at two guards holding bloodied swords. "Where is the lie? They are here to kill us!"

Rubbing her bruised stomach, Mirari turned to them and seethed, "I told you to wait."

"This is unacceptable, Milady," a guard said. "It's against the law to speak ill or harm the region leader. That law extends to his partner."

But violators didn't need to be slaughtered, Mirari believed. And she certainly didn't need to be saved. These Althaeans were quick to draw the sword. It was something that was hard to re-program in their minds.

The leader stood his ground, seething at the guards, regardless of the fact that he now had a blade over his head.

"Kill me like you do to all peasants," he said, his arms spread wide. "Prove to me exactly the kind of monsters you are."

And the guards would've if Mirari didn't stop them.

"Take him alive," she said. The guards looked at her as if she had spoken a foreign language.

"But Milady, the charges he will face will certainly lead to death. There is no reason to—"

"I said take him alive!" They didn't dare challenge the rage in her voice. One of the guards groaned, wiping the blood off his sword and sheathing it before unraveling a pair of aulāce.

The man didn't resist. He willingly placed his hands behind his back, letting the glowing shackles imprison him. He gave one last laugh.

"Mercy will be the death of you," he said as he was escorted away.

That wasn't the first time someone told her that. In fact, the whole incident was déjà vu. More than the pain in her stomach, she was troubled by the voice that thrusted her into a trance. She had never hesitated before. Why now?

Mirari turned to the young woman she saved, the two boys still in her arms. She was surprised to see that they had stayed. Their somber eyes were drawn to the bodies at her feet.

"Are you okay?" Mirari asked.

The woman gazed at her with the same dull look she had given the men. "He's right about one thing," she said. "Everything grew worse after you arrived." She picked up her basket and nudge the children back home.

The weight on Mirari's shoulders felt heavier than ever. She took a deep breath and pretended to wipe dust off her clothes.

"Milady." The guard offered her his handkerchief, pointing to a spot on his neck. Mirari took it and wiped her neck. She took note of the streaks of blood now smeared on the handkerchief before returning it to the guard. "We'll take you to a healer right away."

There was no doubt that Gaven would find out what had happened, and she could already see the scowl on his face.

"No need," she said, keeping her gaze on the floor. "I'll walk back myself."

They hesitated for a beat, but Mirari didn't budge. She waited for the guards to leave with their new prisoner. As soon as they were out of sight, she absorbed the silence in the plaza.

The streets were nearly empty now, but she still felt eyes on her.

Mirari turned to the fountain, her reflection clear against the blue sky. It could've been easy, taking out the rebels like every other street thug she had faced in Solarin. She had done it a handful of times as a Knight throughout the streets of Minetta. What stopped her this time?

She wanted to strangle her reflection. Her vow to serve the three empires was meaningless if they didn't want her help. Fangbane had given her permission to stay with Gaven to handle the riots, but was she only causing more trouble? Gaven had enough on his plate.

If she hadn't interfered with the rally, two men wouldn't be dead. Would it have been better for her to turn away, letting the girl suffer for speaking her mind?

With her head turned, she noticed something glimmering in her reflection. The night Salathiel disappeared, he gave Mirari an early birthday present – a beautiful bundle of white and gold feathers, secured with gold gemstones. It was right after they had a small argument over Mirari's brawl in town.

No matter how much trouble that pin had given her, especially from wearing it in Althaean territory, she never took it off. She stroked the soft feathers as if they granted her a connection with her late brother. Now she realized why she hesitated. Even if she could never see his smile again, his words still haunted her. She could see the scowl he would have if he had witnessed her fight. Her heart dropped like a sandbag. The last thing she wanted was to disappoint him, even in the afterlife.

A SECOND YEAR was approaching since Gaven left, and Salathiel and Mirari had built a humble cottage atop a gentle hill overlooking the growing town of Solarin. Beyond their hill, to the north, they had a sweeping vista of the fertile open plains of Avon, stretching as far as the eye could see. Beyond the plains were vast forests, extending all the way up the foothills of the towering Minettan Alps on the north end of the province.

A wrinkled piece of paper lay on the corner of their dining table. It had some words and a few drawn pictures. It had been sitting there for a while and Mirari kept glancing at it.

"What's that about?" Salathiel asked, enjoying a tender, juicy piece of roast boar.

"Oh, this?" Mirari jumped, not realizing he was watching her. She hesitated before deciding to tell him about it. "There's an innovation fair next week… down south in Falum."

"Innovation fair? You're interested in that stuff?"

"Well," Mirari frowned, "when I was younger, I enjoyed drawing up all sorts of strange inventions. Sometimes my father would take my ideas to the designers and see if it could be done. One of them was a communication glove… and it's here, in this ad."

He looked at her in awe. "You really were Miss—"

"They're just scribbles," Mirari hissed before he could finish.

"Still…" He said and shook his head at how oblivious Mirari was. "If you go, people might recognize you there."

"I know," Mirari said. "But I really want to see it."

Salathiel narrowed his eyes, a look he gave her whenever he disapproved. Roselyn Hale was declared missing, presumed deceased. The chances of anyone suspecting her to be alive were very slim. But they hadn't changed her name for no reason. Though she blended in, Mirari didn't want to take any chances of being recognized.

Salathiel understood how much it meant to her to see what was left of her family's work, so they hitched a ride to the south. The streets of Falum were like Mirari's hometown, where the bright sun caused floral shrubberies to bloom decorating the well-maintained stone pavements. Every carriage that passed was tailored in gold and white, pulled by the largest breeds of horses as groomed and well-mannered as the nobles they transported.

The sea breeze kicked in. Salathiel took a whiff of the salty air coming from Kestrel Bay. Mirari pointed to the clocktower on the other side of the bay. A block away would be the Hale Estate, her home. But she didn't care for that. She turned her focus back to the bustling street in search of her father's inventions.

A whole street was dedicated to the event. Jewelry merchants weaved through the road and food vendors cooked savory aroma in all directions. The fair was open to nobles and peasants alike, and crowds huddled next to wooden decks where demonstrators displayed the less-exciting creations of hāstal technology. In a troupe of laced dresses and feathered hats, Salathiel and Mirari's clean but plain shirts separated them from the beggars, but not enough to pass as nobles. It worked to their advantage as no one cared to look them in the eye. The wealthy were headed elsewhere, to a white mansion with a fence of guards cloaked in red capes, exhibiting glares as sharp as their spears. It was the grand mansion of Councilor Dareh Kampht. Undoubtedly, the most expensive gadgets were reserved for the eyes of the wealthiest.

Salathiel had his eyes on a black slate on display. Pale blue lights crawled through the thin grooves etched into the wedge.

"That's an aulōg." Mirari said. "It can remember auras at the touch. Unless someone is authorized, the pad will not release a door or gate. We had one in our home."

"So… it's a lock."

"Correct."

"Why not… just use a key?"

"Because anyone can turn a key."

"Sounds pointless. No wonder no one is interested in this

one." Salathiel gestured to the few elders nearby who were mesmerized by the slate's glow.

"It's old," Mirari said. "Just like you." She dragged him by the hand to the next stage where more spectators gathered. Their eyes were fixed on an illuminated barrel that hissed like a boiling pot. Had it not been glowing in blue light, Salathiel would've thought it was full of beer.

"What's so interesting about this one?" Salathiel yelled over the screeches of the machine.

"That's a kinastōne. The one used to power kōnvoys." A frown crossed Salathiel's face and he looked back at Mirari. She wasn't bothered by the sight of this machine, but her discomfort may have been obvious. She did her best to not think about the last time she had seen one of those.

Salathiel dragged her away from it, and they continued down the bustling street.

"I still don't understand how these hāstals work," Salathiel said. She knew he was trying to distract her, and it was working. "Care to explain, Miss Brilliant?"

Mirari smirked and began, "Hāstals in their raw form possess a tremendous charge of potential energy. When they're processed, you can control the release of that energy. All these machines, appliances, and weapons with enhanced durability are powered by that energy. And when hāstals are infused with the elemental forces in kore, there's almost no limit to what you can do."

"Like lumastōne, right? Using light kore to replace candle light."

"Precisely." She noticed a large crowd at one of the decks, and tugged him along with excitement. "Look, there it is."

Up on the stage, a man in a grey suit was putting on a black glove. Strands of kore weaved between the threads so faint that one could mistake it as glare from the sun. On the other side of the stage, another man did the same.

"Comstōnes will soon be a thing of the past," the man on the far left said. Those words echoed from the glove on the man on the opposite side. The crowd perked with 'oohs' and 'ahhs'. "We now have the freedom to communicate on the run. Bandits and sea rovers, beware! For the Hales have once again revolutionized our defenses. With the clōve, no enemy will stand a chance."

The crowd erupted in applause. Salathiel did the same.

"Well done, Miss Hale," he whispered in her ear. "Is everything here made by the Hales?"

Mirari scanned the street. She recognized most of the things, and she took little interest in the ones that were not tailored with her family name.

"There are many houses attempting to create new things with hāstals, but in terms of quality, nothing compares to the Hales. That's why nobles and leaders only buy Hale technology. The weaker ones are sold cheaply to peasants in small towns."

The demonstrators were now setting up the next item for show – a metal crate with odd-shaped antlers poking from its side. She couldn't even begin to explain what that was supposed to do.

Behind the demonstrators, she caught sight of someone that most would've dismissed as simply a sturdy guard with a belt full of daggers. Though his age had begun to show, the roots of his hair had turned to white, she recognized the look on his face, and the way he still stood like a kestrel looking for prey.

Mirari's stomach suddenly flooded with ice water. She tugged at Salathiel's arm, almost frantic and pulling him back out into the main road.

"What's wrong?" Salathiel asked.

"We need to go."

They weaved out of the crowd, but Mirari didn't stop. She

took huge strides, as fast as she could without looking suspicious to the others around her. As they made their way past other demonstration stages, Mirari heard rough footsteps from behind, matching their pace. She felt Salathiel putting up a bit of resistance, his hand reaching inside his tunic.

They kept bumping into spectators, and the stranger was getting closer. They weren't going to be able to outrun him for much longer.

Salathiel stopped and pivoted, getting a good look at their stalker. It was an older gentleman, cloaked in an open, juniper cape and dozens of gold-rimmed daggers gleaming underneath. He was a guard at this show, no doubt. He didn't seem hostile but Salathiel was ready to outwit him if things got violent.

"Can I help you, sir?" Salathiel asked. Ignoring Salathiel completely, the guard drew his attention to the girl behind him.

"Miss Hale," he said. It wasn't a question, Salathiel noted. "How nicely you've grown up."

Mirari pulled on Salathiel's sleeve, but he wouldn't budge. He kept one hand on her and the other inside his tunic. "You have mistaken her for someone else. Kindly leave us alone. Good day, sir."

"Miss Hale, is this man bothering you?" he asked. He took a step closer, and Mirari could now smell his whiskey breath.

"We will be leaving now," Salathiel said, but before he could react, the man slid his own hand inside Salathiel's tunic, twisting his wrist in a way that caused instant and breathtaking agony. The dagger clattered to the ground, as Salathiel gave a short, involuntary bark of pain.

"Stop!" Mirari whispered as loud as she could without attracting any attention. She stepped in front of Salathiel. Still, the guard refused to let go of Salathiel's wrist. "You have the wrong person. Please let us leave."

"With all due respect, Miss Hale," he said. "I could identify you in the dark from a block away, and you know it."

Of course, what was she thinking? Mirari cursed at herself. With a sting in her words, she commanded, "Then stand down, Joachim."

"As you wish," said the man, releasing Salathiel's wrist and stepping back. Mirari was shocked to see that he had obeyed her. "At the very least, you owe some sort of explanation."

"And what if I don't want to?"

He furrowed his brow. "Roselyn…"

"Mirari," she huffed, trying to put steel in her voice, yet the tremble of fear escaped. "I… go by Mirari now."

His eyes wrinkled even more. Surprise? Disgust? Mirari couldn't tell.

"Mirari," Salathiel began. He darted his eyes between the two. "Who is this man?"

Mirari kept her lips sealed, waiting for Joachim to say something.

"Perhaps…" Joachim sighed and cleared his throat. "Would you like to discuss it over buzz? Somewhere in private?" With his fine white gloves, he gestured to his left – the grand building on the far side of the fence where nobles had gathered.

Mirari didn't move an inch, trying to decide whether or not to trust him. The silence was unbearable, and people passing by were beginning to take notice of the strange trio that stood in the middle of the road. Salathiel nudged her on with his elbow.

Mirari let out a heavy sigh and began walking to the front gate of the mansion.

"Fine."

With a simple wave to the guards, Joachim led Salathiel and Mirari into the building. Nobles hugged the stairway, gossiping in the long marble halls, and picked at small delicacies presented to them by passing servants.

He guided them into one of the rooms in the hallway. Inside was a marble table with only six chairs and a view of the vendors at the fair. The room quieted as soon as the man shut the door, putting his hand on the aulōg, locking them inside.

"This is Joachim," Mirari told Salathiel. "The retainer I sent Gaven to."

Without the distraction of the crowd, Salathiel got a better look at the man. His lower body was decorated with knives, all sorts of blades and handle designs that he hadn't seen before. His upper body, the broad shoulders and unfaltering creases on his aged face, radiated a terrorizing aura.

"And what do I call you, boy?" Joachim asked, reaching one hand out in a mechanical gesture.

He grabbed Joachim's hand and squeezed it like a lemon. "Salathiel Zanette."

"Zanette." Joachim loosened his shoulders a bit upon hearing his name. He examined Salathiel's physique in detail, noting the familiar facial features. But Joachim frowned seeing that Salathiel – unlike the boy he trained last spring– was just flesh and bone. He turned his attention back to Mirari. "That kid you sent to me, is his brother?"

"More or less," Mirari said.

He lost interest in Salathiel, treating him no different from the furniture.

But there was a mystery Mirari was dying to know, and she jumped at the first opportunity. "Joachim, what happened to Gaven? Did he make it to Althaea?"

Without giving away his emotions, Joachim nodded. "He's

under the guardianship of my cousin in Althaea Main. I heard Region Leader Suzan has taken a liking to him." Mirari lit up. She was happy to have one less mystery in her life, but Joachim continued, "Still, sending a Minettan to Althaea? Giving up your heirloom for a child's foolish dream? How utterly irresponsible of you."

Mirari lowered her head, but Joachim's anger only lasted for a brief moment.

"But now that you've returned," Joachim continued. He walked to the far end of the room, gazing out of the window at the people outside. "I am sure you know that you are presumed dead and most of your inheritance has been divided among your relatives, but you still have the right to reclaim everything that once belonged to your parents. Your cousin Lucan has taken over many of your duties. It was with his delicate use of persuasion that he was able to convince the rest of your family to leave the estate in my hands in case you returned. I advise you, Miss Hale—"

"Joachim, please." Mirari stopped him. She chose her next words carefully. "I... I have chosen my own path. Any fortune I claim will be that which I earn."

Her words brought Joachim to silence and the air grew tense. His glare returned to Salathiel, knowing he was the one to blame for influencing his mistress' decisions. Salathiel kept his hands inside his tunic.

"Well, don't jump to any hasty decisions," Salathiel piped up. "There's a fortune simply waiting for you, right?" But Mirari wasn't listening.

To her, it sounded like a fairy tale life, probably one anyone else would dream of. Mirari knew Salathiel dreamed of it himself. If she could, she would've given it all to him, to her foster parents. It felt selfish not to take full advantage of it. But, to take control of her family wealth would be accepting the heap of responsibilities that drove her to misery. She would be telling the world she accepted her place in the Hale family.

A life of luxury and prestige only conjured visions of her parents throwing crockery at each other and howling like furious gibbons. Mirari's eardrums felt numb. She could practically hear their angry voices.

She felt a gentle embrace on her hand. It forced her attention back on the two men in the room, as the terrible cacophony of her past dissipated like fearful demons in the light of day.

"You don't have to decide right now," Salathiel said. "Just think about it."

But Mirari had made up her mind the day Joachim and Lucan came to find her. Ever since, there was not a day she missed being a Hale. She knew as a Hale, there was no room for laughter or friendship… and she would have to forfeit her relationships with peasants, with Salathiel.

Joachim said, "What have these peasants given you that you would go out of your way to stay with them?"

"They're my family." Resolution flickered in Mirari's eyes. "Joachim, I decided to revoke my birthright as a member of the Hale family. I hope you can accept—"

"If you are no longer a Hale, dear Roselyn…" Joachim's tone grew sharp once again. "Then you will no longer have noble protection."

Mirari lowered her head. She kept her face pointed to the ground, waiting for him to behead her. "That is correct, Joachim. All I ask in return is that you let us go quietly, pretend we were never here. Let the Hales continue to believe that I perished in the fire along with my parents."

Joachim's eyes flickered to Salathiel, then back to Mirari. "And if I refuse, what will you do? Fight your way out?"

Mirari opened her eyes and with a calm grace, she replied, "Yes. I will fight you."

Salathiel appeared to be holding his breath. His free hand was no doubt on the hilt of his dagger again, ready to make a move.

A snort erupted from Joachim. The corner of his lips perked into a grin, an eerie one at that. Perhaps it was for the better that he showed no emotion at all.

"You haven't changed one bit, Miss," Joachim laughed, which was a rare sight to see. "Your bold mouth remains unfiltered."

Mirari's expression relaxed, but she didn't understand.

"You always hated everything your parents made you do. It's no surprise that you've taken a liking to these peasants. Regardless of your status, Miss Hale, it would be my pleasure to serve you until my last breath."

He lowered his head in a slight bow and Mirari returned a small smile.

"Okay," Mirari said. "First, don't call me Miss Hale anymore."

"Miss… Mirari?" Joachim's voice pinched at the unfamiliar words. His face crinkled a bit in disgust. "I suppose you're not willing to come back to Fauna with me, *Miss Mirari*. And if you won't, how will I know you'll be safe?"

"Don't underestimate me, Joachim. I know how to handle weapons now."

Joachim took one of the knives from his belt and tossed it to Mirari. She caught it mid-air, then twirled it in a flourish with one hand.

Joachim smiled, then took her hand and adjusted her finger's position around the knife. He said, "You may be able to fend off a pickpocket, but neither of you will last against a group of bandits. It's a cruel world out there, Milady. If I am not with you, then at least give me the assurance that you would be able to defend yourself."

Mirari wasn't sure she had heard him right. "You'll teach me how to fight? You know my parents would never have let me hold a weapon."

"And when has that ever stopped you?"

Her face lit up like the sun.

Salathiel relaxed, taking his hands out of his tunic.

Joachim turned to him. "You too. If you're going to stay with her, you better be able to protect her."

Salathiel crossed his arms and rolled his eyes. "I don't need training from an old geezer."

Joachim moved in on Salathiel, breathing down his neck. His glare was enough to send a shiver down Salathiel's spine, but Salathiel tried to keep a brave face. Joachim hissed, "Arrogance will be the death of you. If I could choose, I'd rather have your so-called brother look after her. Now, are you going to prove me wrong?"

Salathiel gritted his teeth. Mirari knew how much he hated being compared to Gaven. But from the way Joachim rendered him defenseless moments ago, Salathiel must've thought that there were some useful techniques he could learn from him. She knew he had no desire to become a fighter, but self-defense was essential. Joachim had a point; the world was full of evil, and Salathiel and Mirari weren't prepared for it.

Salathiel took a deep breath and braved, "I can fight too. I can prove it."

Joachim's mouth perked into a smile, and he handed him a dagger. Salathiel clenched the hilt. She could see the scowl in his eyes and knew what it meant – being powerless wasn't an option.

CHAPTER TWELVE

Back at the fortress, Mirari swapped out her blood-stained clothes and swept back her hair. She spent a couple minutes in the dungeon facing the rowdy peasant she had arrested. Every word out of his mouth was profanity, nothing he said would be of use, and she quickly realized he was a waste of her time. He taunted her more, daring her to call for his execution. Mirari simply turned and left.

She opened the door to Gaven's private keep and stepped inside. Her eyes swept the room, ignoring the paper-littered floor and tacky blue curtains that shielded all light from entering. She found Gaven sitting by himself at the far end of the wooden table, arms crossed. Her face flushed.

"What were you thinking?" he said. He rose from his chair and walked toward her, stopping inches from Mirari. His aura could send any hound running with its tail between its legs.

But Mirari took a deep breath and said, "If this is about what happened at the plaza this morning—"

Before she could finish, he lifted her chin and turned her

cheek slightly. She crinkled her forehead. To her surprise, she felt no anger from him. His touch was almost pitiful.

"They hurt you," he said. Mirari thought she did a fine job covering up the bruise on her cheek. Clearly she did not.

"It looks worse than it is," she said.

"Violence upon a region leader's partner is capital punishment. That's a national law. You should know that."

"It's just a bruise."

"Nobody does something like that without the intent of killing." He fumed, releasing his grasp. "Mirari, you can't let people get away with this. There's no place for mercy in Althaea."

Mirari shook her head. "Then maybe there should be. If you want to change Althaea Main you have to challenge the norm."

Gaven crinkled his forehead. She expected to receive another scowl, but instead he let his anger out with a heavy sigh.

"Well? Did you find out anything from the prisoner?"

Her gaze drifted away. She would only be proving his point. "No, unfortunately he's just another loud-mouth. It's not easy, Your Honor. How do you differentiate those with strong desires from those who seek to harm? At this rate it's easier to..." She paused, biting her lip.

"It's easier to kill all of them." Gaven said. That was what the Council had ordered rather than to make space for discussion. "Look at what they did to you, Mirari. You still think they'll listen?"

She could see the limitations of her fantasy. The harsh reality of ruling a broken empire, fueled by centuries of bitterness, left little room for peaceful talks.

Someone cleared their throat. Mirari turned to the door and saw Erel standing with a stack of books in her hands. Towering over her was Erel's *favorite* commander. He gave a gentle wave.

"Hey, I heard what happened at the plaza," Haynes said, grinning.

"Hasn't everyone?" Erel said. Mirari looked away.

"It takes a lot of guts to hold in your anger like that."

Erel coughed. "Or a lot of stupidity."

"Let it go, you two," Gaven said. He gestured to the empty seats at the long table. They had a long evening ahead of them. "Let's start the meeting."

***

GAVEN SAT at one end of the table with Erel and Haynes on either side. Mirari took her seat a bit farther down to watch the three of them strategize. Gaven divided clusters of metal figurines while Erel and Haynes sternly focused on his movements, understanding what each figurine represented as they were moved across a projected map.

The room was awash in the blue light of the oriōn. That metal ball could make any map come to life, from the peak of Mount Kelper to the depths of the Sharcana Ravine. She hadn't seen one since she was a child and was still with the Hales. She recalled how complex it was to operate, fumbling with the mechanics a few times herself, but here was Gaven, using it as easily as breathing. She knew his military expertise was unmatched, but watching him strategize always put her in awe.

Gaven's bark grew sharper as he pointed at the map. A large cluster of figurines were in the south, and Erel had a scowl.

"You're taking up a lot of resources," Erel said, coldly. "Most rebels aren't capable of fighting back."

"The searches must be thorough," Gaven said. Mirari felt a sting in her chest. She drew her attention back to her partner.

"They won't be if you wear out the scouts. Judging by your

temper, you plan on carrying this out for as long as it takes. Even if we do catch them, we don't have enough space for—"

"There's no need for catching. We'll take care of them on the spot, as we have with the violent protestors."

Mirari's heart sank. She turned to Erel and Haynes to make sure she had heard him right. Haynes continued fiddling with a coin on the table, and Erel drew her attention back to the stack of papers in her hand.

"Alright," Erel said, brushing her hand in the air. "That does save us the hassle, but are you prepared for the drawbacks? The people are already petrified. They're starting to question whether we're protecting them or terrorizing them into submission."

Without hesitation, Gaven responded, "If they were truly innocent, then they have nothing to fear. We'll start checking papers. Anyone without them will be executed on the spot."

Mirari was not used to this side of Gaven. As a region leader, he was ruthless, stubborn, and a master of instilling respect out of fear. His orders were absolute, unlike how Fangbane managed the Knights. Or was it only these recent events that had caused him to harden?

Mirari stood up, her hands pressed against the table. "Anyone, Your Honor? Don't you think that's a bit excessive?"

"Oh right," Haynes perked his head up, returning the coin to his pocket. "I heard it's uncommon in Minetta to have welfare checks."

"Soldiers don't show up to our doorsteps with a blade to our neck."

"This is how we keep the danger out," Erel said. "Althaeans know they must have a form of identification on them at all times. In the past we've only arrested them but..."

"We have to assume that anyone trying to hide their identity is doing so with maleficent intentions," Gaven said. "If we don't know who lives on our land, we let risks run wild."

Mirari knew there was a darker reason behind Gaven's sudden, aggressive moves. He was willing to follow the Council's orders because he believed the rebels were members of the Blessed. It was personal.

And now he was willing to run the blade through anyone who stood in his way.

"Besides," Haynes said. With a slight frown he slumped backward against his chair. "Less people means less mouths to feed. We're running out of resources."

"Well, I have some rather good news," Erel said. "House Tepis offered to fund our recovery efforts."

Mirari jolted as if someone had pricked her heart.

"Turn it down," Gaven said.

"Your Honor—"

"I said, turn it down." The room grew silent, but Erel didn't seem afraid.

"You need it."

"He had five years to offer his aid, and he does it now?"

"No one was doing financially well five years ago. I know he's not in your best interest, but with the funds—"

"He wants something and we're not giving it to him."

Mirari leaned over to Haynes, and in a whisper asked, "Is he talking about Inigo?"

"No doubt," Haynes mouthed.

There was something Mirari still didn't understand about Gaven. Why did the mention of Inigo send her partner into a boil? The look on her face must've been obvious when Haynes leaned in again.

"He didn't tell you about him?"

Mirari leaned in closer. "No?"

"Not even about the battle in the Bay of Minetta?"

"Should he have?"

"You two," Gaven snapped.

Haynes returned to his upright position. "Yes, My Lord?"

"Since you're not contributing, go rally a hundred for the south tomorrow. Take Mirari with you."

Mirari wasn't sure if she heard him right. She was used to leading her own team. "You don't want me investigating anymore?" Mirari asked.

Gaven stared her down. "Not after what happened today. Haynes will be watching you from here on."

"Yes, Sir!" Haynes said. Before Mirari could protest, Haynes leapt to his feet and grabbed Mirari by the arm. He pulled her out of the room and around the corner.

"Thank the Gods we got out of there." Haynes stretched his arms to the ceiling. He looked far more energetic than he was a moment ago.

"I don't need to be watched," Mirari hissed.

"Yes, yes of course, Milady." He did a double take in the empty hall to make sure there were no extra ears. "But truth be told, the negotiation stage has passed. Councilor Suzan already got in his head, and after what happened to you today, he's even more certain that this is the path to take."

"Well…" Mirari shuddered at the thought of what might happen. "We can't just slaughter every village until the rebellion stops."

"Region leaders have done it before. It has always worked."

Mirari lowered her head. She wasn't a region leader. She knew nothing about how to control thousands of people. Her inability to control the situation at the plaza spoke volumes – a featherpit in Althaea had no power, not even as the region leader's partner.

Haynes led her down the empty hall. At the end of the hall, he bust open the doors to the courtyard, just in time to see the last streaks of orange sunset fade beyond the walls. A handful of men were bantering under the first batch of twinkling stars starting to appear, face flushed red with an empty tin jug in their hand. Most of the noise was still coming from the dining hall. It brought a big grin on Haynes' face.

"Care for a drink, Milady?" he asked, nudging her. "I reckon you haven't tried larmender wine yet."

Of course not. It was made by House Tepis, available exclusively in the region of Althaea Main, unless one were rich.

Mirari squinted her eyes and said, "I thought soldiers aren't allowed to drink the job."

"Good thing it's an order from you, right Milady?"

Mirari didn't care for it. In fact, retreating to her room after a long day sounded like a haven. Maybe on the way back she could find an icestōne to treat her bruise. But watching the drunk soldiers outside the dining hall, she saw an opportunity. Her investigation was not quite over.

"I'll allow it if you tell me about the battle in the Bay of Minetta." She bit her lip. "Even better, tell me everything you know about Inigo Tepis."

CHAPTER THIRTEEN

Ten Years Ago

In Minetta, a new region leader was expected to ascend. Mallory Zabato, the proud region leader of Avon, was often compared to Althaean Main's region leader, Suzan Naas. Rumored to have come down with an illness, Mallory was inching toward her last years as the head. She had lost most of her strength, but unlike the savages of Althaea, the fighters of Minetta respected her too much to challenge her for the throne. In the coming months, one of her sons would be crowned region leader in her place.

The strongest of the two sons was Commander Shiba Zabato, nicknamed the Shadow Soldier, a name fitting for a man who was as cold as his shadowmancer abilities. He was overseeing the new stream of soldiers being recruited from their region. Few of them were women, and certainly none came from Althaea.

Except one princess from Altha Hills.

Mallory had sent Shiba to the armory with a basket of curated wine and cheese. He didn't know why until he saw a young woman, sitting alone, polishing her breastplate. She stood out in her loose, faded cerulean dress. It was traditional garb in her native land, but in Minetta, it was like waving an enemy's flag.

"Why are you here?" Shiba asked the new recruit.

Mecate paid little attention to the young lord. She was an intense lady, focused on everything she did. Her long, sapphire hair curtained her beautiful profile. When she lifted her head to reveal her face, Shiba stared at her shamrock eyes. She could mesmerize a crowd.

Mallory's decision to shelter the Althaean princess meant that they were drawing Althaea's attention to them, and in the wake of her illness, the timing could not have been worse. They would have to take more preparations to ensure that the celtas of Altha Hills did not try to wage war.

Shiba wanted to know why this princess was chosen to join his army.

"To serve the people, what else?" she answered.

"No, no," he said, frustrated that she was being deliberately obtuse. "Why are you on this side of the border? You're a flatty."

"Oh." She paused and thought for a moment. "I forgot about that." She shrugged it off and continued polishing.

"That's not something you forget."

Shiba already knew the story. She had a passion for fighting, but her father, the Priest, wanted her to be a diplomatic beauty, not a war maiden.

She was unlike the rest of the nobles of Altha Hills. Much of the actual business of governing that region was delegated to subordinates, from the Bishop, to the military commanders, to the local nobles: the Dukes, the Earls, the gentry of the court.

They passed along most of the day-to-day authority to mayors, sheriffs, aldermen, tax collectors. Nobles did nothing but sit on wealth, and she couldn't bring herself to live like that.

What she wanted was to give service to the people, not orders. She believed the function of leadership was to make life better for the people she was supposed to lead. Not to just act in her own self-interest, and of her political allies.

"I've lived in Minetta for a while," she said. "I like it here, and I feel Minettan."

Her words projected more confidence than he expected, but he still looked at her with the same glare he gave all Althaeans. "You're not going to like what they say about you."

"I know what they say. So what? Are you going to deport me?"

"It would be within my rights," he said.

"I dare you to." She didn't back down. "It's disappointing for anyone to believe that they can decide what's best for someone else."

Normally he would've punished any soldier who sassed him as she did, but it only kindled a stronger desire to know her more.

Her eyes shifted to the basket in Shiba's hands. "Is that for me or were you about to throw yourself a picnic in the armory?"

Shiba nearly forgot why he was there in the first place. He set the basket on the workbench next to her. "Milkenkase and larmender." Before she got the wrong idea, he added, "From the region leader."

"Milkenkase. I'm impressed," Mecate said. She set down the armor and examined the basket, reading the fine print on the wine label. "Imports from Eudoxia are a rarity. But larmender? Do Minettans not make their own wine?"

"What do you mean?"

"Larmender is grown by House Tepis. They are arguably the most powerful family in Althaea."

Shiba took the bottle and observed it for himself. He had this wine several times, even preferred it, but he had no idea it was Althaean wine. Knowing now, he would be less likely to drink it again, but he couldn't understand why she had a problem with it.

"Does the Althaean taste not satisfy the Althaean Princess?"

She sighed. "It's not that. Have you ever met a Tepis? You should never believe a word they say. I wouldn't be surprised if they sprinkle zotweed in their products."

A grin crossed Shiba's face. Something about her inflamed him like no one ever had. She held a will of dancing flames, almost like firecrackers ready to set off a chain reaction. He felt her pulling him in closer, tempting him to light the fire.

"I never got your name."

"Mecate."

Mecate was a fierce lady, no doubt. She sat as tall as the dozens of axes and halberds that decorated the walls, projecting a kind of confidence Shiba had yet to see from most of his soldiers. Her aura captured the room and Shiba knew her kore would be more powerful than all those weapons on the wall combined. He was lucky to have her on the team. Still, he wanted to witness her strength.

"Well Mecate, if you're as good as they say, I want you to train the new recruits today."

She raised a brow and smirked. "Having a new recruit train new recruits? That's a new one."

Shiba felt a blow to his stomach. What was he thinking? He wasn't, not in the presence of this lady.

After a faint chuckle she answered, "With Honor, My Lord."

BY THE END OF FALL, Mecate became a lieutenant in Shiba's division. Many said she ascended the ranks too fast. Her qualifications were no contest; it was her birthplace that made the other soldiers uneasy. No one wanted to see an Althaean have power in a Minettan army.

Shiba always kept a close eye on Mecate, if not for personal reasons. She was dedicated to her training, practicing and studying alone in her free time. Nothing she did raised suspicion, and no matter how ridiculous his commands were, she followed them without resistance. Shiba wished he could get the rest of the army to behave more like her.

But right now, he couldn't find her. She wasn't in her usual seat at the library and the armory was vacant. Then, he heard noise coming from the Zabato's private courtyard. It was one that doubled as a greenhouse, and sat on a cliff side that over-looked a glistening lake. From above, a distant Sierra stretched into the sky, and native birds flew their dizzying patterns upon its turbulent winds.

Shiba and Neo often used the courtyard to spar, but Neo never came without Shiba. That was, until now. Shiba followed the sound of the ruckus and found Neo engaging with Mecate. He was using an immense amount of kore to ground himself against Mecate's assaults.

Shiba folded his arm across his chest and watched his partner pound his fist into the ground, cracking the tiles with immense force. That would've sent most people cowering behind the nearest stone, but not Mecate. With a stomp of her foot, the cracks that Neo had created in the earth were filled with shim-mering ice. It was so beautiful it could've been mistaken for a work of art.

A shard of ice formed in Mecate's palm, and she flicked it at Neo. He raised his fist and batted it to the side. She threw another, then another, taking a step forward each time.

"Is this going to leave a dent?" Neo asked over the sound of the ice colliding with his gauntlet. From the way Neo defended himself, Shiba could tell that Neo's objective wasn't to best her — he was letting her use him as a training dummy. Shiba bit his lower lip as he came to a realization. Where Mecate was from, there were no brawlers. She must be thrilled to be able to practice on a target that couldn't break so easily.

With every offensive, Mecate's shards were doing a number on the courtyard. Shiba furrowed his brow after an icicle beheaded a nymph statue, then stomped down the steps to scowl at Neo.

"Shouldn't you be on watch duty?" he said. "And you. This is a private room."

"Your mother was the one who told me to wait for her here," Mecate said. Shiba narrowed his eyes. What was she discussing with Mecate behind his back now? It came with no surprise. Mallory was pampering her, treating Mecate like a daughter. Shiba should've been jealous, but he was already used to not being the favorite child.

Casting Neo aside, Shiba stepped in close to Mecate, his breath tickled her skin as he whispered, "I'm offended you didn't ask me to train with you instead."

Mecate tucked a curtain of hair behind her ear. "I wouldn't dare, My Lord."

The two were locked in a heated gaze. Neo, realizing that he was out of place, began to back away. "I'll... be on watch then, Lord." He bowed to them and scurried out of the room.

From behind Mecate, a shadowy figure emerged, as tall as its owner, its cool presence sending a chill down her spine. She whipped her body in a twirl. A brush of her hand was enough to dissipate the shadow behind her. Now her hand was coming back toward Shiba.

He leaned back, avoiding the swipe of her hand. He

crouched and extended his foot, forcing Mecate to flip over and land on her back. Before she could raise her hand, the shadow emerged from the ground, pulled back her wrist and locked her to the ground.

Mecate raised her knee in an attempt to kick Shiba in the chest, but he caught her leg and forced it back down. He used the weight of his body to keep her down, locking his eyes on her dazzling green ones.

"As I said." Mecate gave him a grin. "I'm no match for you."

But Shiba knew she was teasing him. She was more than capable of putting him in gridlock. He challenged, "It's no fun if you let me win all the time."

He wasn't sure if her reluctance came from her respect for him as her lord, or if she was trying to tell him something more. Mecate had a kind of weakness on him. Even if he enjoyed their scuffles, he could never put a bruise on such flawless beauty. Her creamy skin pulled him in, kindling his desire to touch it. He was only inches away from her lips, and he felt the temptation to move closer.

"Careful, Shadow Soldier," Mecate said. "People might start to think you're falling in love with an Althaean."

Shiba didn't hesitate. "And what if I am?"

"Enemies to lovers is a bit cliché, don't you think?"

He smiled. "You were never an enemy. You're not like them. Mecate, you're—"

Before Shiba could go on, he was distracted by a sound echoing from the corridor. That tapping noise was all too familiar to him. He scrambled, pulling Mecate up from the ground.

A gallant lady in a crimson robe walked into the room. Her long, dark hair and blood-thirsty eyes were almost identical to her son's, but the wrinkles on her hands bore years of experience that Shiba had yet to acquire.

"Ah, Shiba," Mallory greeted. "I see you've become acquainted with Princess Mecate?"

Shiba's cheeks flushed pink as he struggled to come up with an excuse as to why he was in the courtyard.

"Just Mecate will do, Your Honor," Mecate said, lowering her head into a bow. "I am no longer a princess."

"Modest, ain't she? Well, doll, you are what you are by blood, whether you like it or not."

"Did you need something, Mother?" Shiba asked, growing impatient.

"I do, and you saved me the trouble of explaining twice." Mallory took a seat looking out at the lake, slowly leaning back into a bench with the help of her cane. "Keep this between us. I don't want any rumors spreading before I announce it myself."

Shiba and Mecate leaned in closer.

"I invited Mecate here in hopes that she would become a fine commander. You and I know very well that we're not going to find a better spellcaster than her."

"We don't have enough room for another commander, Mother."

"She's taking over for you."

"What? You're replacing me? I've only ever done everything you asked—" Mallory raised her hand to silence him.

"These bones of mine won't let me stand for much longer, Shiba. We need someone strong to defend Avon."

"What do you..." He was not sure what his mother was suggesting. "Shono isn't taking your place?"

"Your older brother would much rather travel with vagabonds seeking *enlightenment*, whatever that means, than become region leader. I have to respect his decision to focus his life on the spiritual," she said, almost dutifully. Then her face hardened. "Don't make the same foolish mistake. You must carry the duty of the Zabato family."

Mallory unfolded a thin letter that was sealed with a blue stamp. The stamp caught Mecate's eyes, the dragon crest had to be from Althaea Main.

"Next spring you will be dueling one of Region Leader Suzan's new commanders. She insists upon it, and I think it would be a good way to show how fit you are to rule Avon."

"She has a new commander?"

"Yes, by the name of Gaven Zanette. They call him the Valiant Tiger."

"The wh—" Shiba gave a loud snort, unable to contain his reaction. "That's… adorable."

"Don't take this duel lightly. This boy has made quite a name for himself throughout Althaea. And it goes without saying, but you absolutely cannot lose."

"I agree," Mecate said, rubbing her chin as she tried to recall a faint memory. "I think I've met him. Her Honor was taking quite an interest in this boy… And if Suzan trained this Violent Panther—"

"Tiger," Shiba corrected, barely able to contain another snort.

"Don't underestimate him, Lord. If Suzan has taught him anything, he will know how to fight like her too."

Shiba puffed out his chest and chuckled. "I'm sure he's nothing I can't handle."

Mallory then turned to Mecate. "If it's no trouble, Lady Mecate, I would like you to teach him a few things."

"Me?" Mecate shifted her eyes between Mallory and Shiba. "Surely His Lord doesn't need my—"

"He doesn't know how sneaky those Althaean nutsacks can be, and you know how they're trained better than anyone else within these walls." She glared at her son. "This one still has the pride of a boy. Teach him how to be a man."

Shiba certainly didn't object to the idea. The challenge? Shiba didn't worry about that. But he was looking forward to the training, being able to spend more time with Mecate. And this time, she wouldn't be holding back.

CHAPTER FOURTEEN

A wind swept through the coliseum, kicking up a dust cloud, twisting and grabbing the tailored coats and frilled dresses of noble spectators. Feathers from hats and coats came loose and took off with the wind before the air began to calm. The dust faded to reveal two men standing in the arena.

Gaven stood confident, unblinking and unaffected, as though one with the wind. He was not fazed by mere dust as his affinity with the earth protected him from the fine particles in the air. He was focused, glaring at the darkly cloaked umbra across from him. He counted over a dozen daggers at his opponent's waist and knew there would be more under that cloak. Gaven admired the fine silver those weapons were made of, and the glare they gave off must've meant they were polished with the finest lorestōnes. A man with such wealth, the next heir to Avon, of course, got the best. Shiba toyed with a pair of daggers and held a sharp grin on his face.

This was the great Shadow Soldier.

Gaven scanned the arena stands filled with noble snobs. A battle like this was worth hundreds of coins just to spectate. He knew he was a mere animal to the spectators, a savage they placed their bets against. It disgusted him more that these were people he once lived amongst – Minettans. But it also gave him pride, knowing he grew up to be better than all of them.

In the stand to his right, he saw Suzan whispering in Mallory's ear. They were close together and flanked by their retinues. They did not display any outright joy but he could see the way Suzan's face lit up when they spoke to each other. They must've had a long history, and a friendly one at that.

Gaven couldn't help but be in awe of Mallory's beauty and the presence she commanded like she was the only one in the stands. He knew she was the Shadow Soldier's mother, but she looked far too young. With Suzan's mouth still pressed closed to her ear, Mallory fluttered her thick-lined eyes toward Gaven. He felt himself blush. Her delicate movements spoke of grace in many ways that Shiba did not possess. A slight smile touched Mallory's lips and he turned away to hide his awe.

He shook his head, forcing himself to focus. He couldn't let all his training go to waste.

He spent nearly half a year preparing for this battle. Suzan taught him how to read a shadowmancer's movements, and warned him of the many tricks Shiba would have up his sleeve.

Gaven assessed the arena, grinding his sole against the loose sand. It was warm and quite dry, but a bit loose, a slipping hazard. He would have more control of his balance and his core would be at an advantage if he was more connected to the ground.

Gaven unbuckled his boots, letting his bare feet sink into the warm sand. Shiba watched as Gaven tested the stability of the sand.

"What's wrong?" Shiba said, almost letting out a snort as he watched the young boy put on a show. "Shoes not to the peasant's liking?"

Gaven didn't respond to his jest. After spending years in Althaea, he was numb to insults like that.

Two bannermen stepped out on the grand stand next to the region leaders, one waving the flag of Althaea, the other of Minetta. The flag's mighty presence immediately silenced all chatter in the arena. The region leaders rose from their seats, and Mallory cleared her throat.

"Honorable leaders and nobles of the alliance," she began. "It is of great tradition, in memory of our long-established peace between region leaders of Althaea and Minetta, that we appoint our greatest fighters to battle in a glorious duel."

She motioned for Suzan to speak.

As Suzan looked at the two young boys, she began, "Today we witness a historic moment, in which this year's two candidates will also hold the future of the two capital regions of the land. May I present – Shiba Zabato of Avon and Gaven Zanette of Althaea Main. Today you two will fight for the honor of your house, region, and empire, in hope that one day, the two of you will succeed the honorable Region Leader Mallory and I."

Mallory stepped forward with a glass swan in her hand, and she extended it out over the edge of the arena. "Ready yourselves. Fight bravely, for Cordelia watches over you. Through battle she helps us see the true hearts of men."

"Shiba of Minetta, are you prepared to begin?" Shiba nodded, squinting as he took a ready stance.

"Gaven of Althaea, are you prepared to begin?" Gaven stepped his right foot back and raised his spear.

At that, Mallory released the crystal swan. For a brief moment the coliseum was silent as the glittering sculpture fell. It let out a clear pop and shattered into powdered glass.

A dagger sailed past Gaven's right ear. Had he not heard it whirl in the wind, he wouldn't have dodged in time.

He didn't even see Shiba move. Gaven circled right and focused on Shiba as he stalked him outside of his spear's range.

The next knife came straight for his chest, but with a quick flick of his spear, ringing with steel, Gaven sent it flying.

Shiba watched Gaven move forward, dragging his heavy spear in the sand. It was a spear bigger than most – with a much thicker shaft and a menacingly long blade. Gaven had the strength, that much he could tell from his physique. But skill? Shiba had his doubts.

He spun a knife in his right hand, taunting his opponent. Both their weapons were blunted with a defensive spell, intended to deliver a stunning shock if contact was made. This whole duel was a show, after all, not a real battle. As much as Shiba was trained to take the heads of Althaeans who crossed his path, he wasn't allowed to kill this one. But he was ready to give them a show *and* put the whelp in his place.

Shiba moved into a dance, spinning and ducking as he sent dagger after dagger at his opponent.

Gaven scrambled and continued to deflect the onslaught.

But he couldn't just stay on the defensive. He moved like a seasoned combatant and his piercing gaze spoke of fierce determination and power. He would have to be careful with this one. Even if he had been educated it meant little – the boy surely had never faced a shadowmancer before today.

Gaven swung his spear like a club, knocking a knife back at Shiba. It gave him enough time to regain his footing before rolling forward, sweeping the spear in a wide arc. Shiba was forced to leap backwards to dodge the blade.

With continued momentum, Gaven planted the spear point into the sand in a feint, cartwheeled over it and slammed the spear down. A shower of sand flew where Shiba had been one second ago. It knocked him off balance, and Shiba slid on the sand, onto his bottom.

Gaven felt satisfaction at the shocked expression on Shiba's face.

Shiba had to re-evaluate his approach. He didn't want to use his shadow so soon but Gaven's attacks had a fury to them. He needed to tame the tiger.

Shiba shuffled back onto his feet and rushed straight for Gaven. Gaven furrowed his brow, taken aback by Shiba's charge and almost didn't have the sense to brace himself against his opponent's stupidity. To Gaven's horror, Shiba plowed right into the tip of his spear. It pierced Shiba's chest.

But he felt no resistance on the spear and Shiba slashed at his face with a dagger. All Gaven felt was a cold, eerie mist as it passed through him. In a blink, Shiba disappeared like the smoke of a dying candle. Coming from below was a fist, buckled in steel and fine leather. The metal knuckles of the gauntlet met Gaven square in the nose. He heard a crack before tumbling into the sand.

"Bastard!" Gaven spat as he staggered back to his feet. His palm came away from his mouth bloody. "Cheap trick."

Shiba grinned and darted left. Gaven reacted with a spin of his spear, nearly catching Shiba's shoulder as the shadow Shiba split once again. Two Shibas stood before him, and he couldn't tell them apart.

They moved to either side of Gaven, trying to force him to face one. He backed away, moving in a semicircle to keep them from flanking him when one of the Shibas darted in to slash him. Once again, Gaven's spear banished the shadow with a slash. Gaven dodged aside as two daggers sailed past him from behind and he turned to face the real Shiba.

Shiba had a dozen polished throwing stars in his hands, all ready to launch at his target. He threw three at first, so fast that Gaven lost his footing and stumbled backward. Shiba tossed two more at his feet.

In a panic, Gaven placed his hands on the ground and called upon the earth. A wall of sand arose before him and shielded him from the throwing stars. His bare feet in the sand sensed movement coming from both corners of his sand wall. He tracked the movement carefully until the Shibas came into view.

As soon as he saw their dark cloaks, Gaven thrust his hand to the right. A geyser of sand launched the real Shiba into the air, and the other dissipated once again.

It was a lucky guess. Gaven sighed in relief, before getting back on his feet.

But while Shiba tumbled in the air, he was able to launch a shower of throwing stars. Gaven swung his spear in an arc, but there were too many for him to deflect. He aborted his defense and rolled aside as the throwing stars pelted the spot where he stood.

He gasped and refocused on his breathing to calm himself. He couldn't believe how much he was shaking. It had been a while since he had faced someone so skilled.

"I'll make it a little easier for you." Shiba grinned as he landed back on his feet, and his shadow rose into form once again. This time it was just a black shape, a dark silhouette with no contour.

Rage was building in Gaven now, along with his frustration from being so easily toyed with. Planting his feet, he began a furious barrage of strikes upon both Shibas. Every cut, stab and parry took both Shiba and his shadow at once. Gaven feinted left and reversed immediately, nearly catching Shiba who bent like a reed as Gaven's spear passed over him. Never could he land a strike on the elusive fighter who was highly skilled at baiting Gaven's petty strikes.

The shadow spun and struck the spear with a powerful kick. Gaven's grip was clumsy and the spear was torn from his hands, landing a few feet away.

Gaven leaned forward and swooped up a handful of sand, throwing a dust cloud in the face of the real Shiba. He heard Shiba sputter and curse, but Gaven turned his focus to his kore and called forth a wall of sand, dividing the two fighters.

Two dark hands rose underneath, clawing at his ankles and climbing up his body. The shadow got one of its hands around Gaven's throat. The distraction forced Gaven to drop his sand wall, but he only grasped the shadow tighter and pushed back, slamming his body into the sand with the shadow as a cushion. The crushing pressure forced it to let go.

"You goat-footed pillock!" Shiba grabbed a handful of sand and drove it into Gaven's face and mouth. "You want to play dirty?" Gaven felt a movement of air just before a sharp pain erupted in his right rib cage and he flinched as though stung by a wasp.

Gaven's abdomen was made of stone. Two heavy blows to his left ribs left him breathless but he didn't succumb. Gaven struggled to get free, but the shadow in the ground held back his arms and legs, and Shiba was free to hit him for as long as he liked.

"You're lucky I'm not allowed to kill you!" Shiba laughed before he silenced Gaven with a headbutt.

<hr>

"IT WAS A GOOD DUEL," Suzan said to her defeated commander. Gaven wasn't as complacent about the loss. He sulked, icing his cheek with an enchanted stone.

"I could've had him if he wasn't using his shadow all the time," Gaven complained. "It's like fighting two people."

"Get used to it," Shiba teased as he approached them. "They call me the Shadow Soldier for a reason." He had two goblets of cold bellberry juice with him. And, in the customary ceremonial gesture of goodwill in Minetta, he offered one to Suzan. "My compliments, Your Honor."

"Thank you, Shiba."

Shiba took another look at the stands. He saw his comrades cheering from the other side, and his mother on the ground level chatting with one of their advisors. She took the time to nod at Shiba, and he knew his mother well enough to know that she was telling him to not underestimate the warrior.

Shiba couldn't just let that go. "What's with the tiger thing, though? Seems a bit of a boast, I'd say."

"I think it suits him perfectly," Suzan said. "In due time you'll see him shine like the predator he is."

"I think he's still a kid."

"Kid? Says the featherpit with the hair of a woman." Gaven couldn't let the jab go.

"Huh, you got a bold mouth you little—"

"Ah, Suzan. What a marvelous commander you've trained," Mallory interrupted their petty fight, joining them. "He certainly lives up to his reputation."

"Thank you, Mallory," Suzan said, smoothing things over. "I hope there will be more opportunities for our successors to duel again. Before they actually kill themselves as region leaders, that is."

Mallory glanced at her son, hoping she was more direct with her warning this time. But to her surprise, Shiba had lost all interest in this competition. He was looking at Neo, the giant known as the Silver Fist.

But no, that smile on Shiba's face... it couldn't be for Neo. His eyes were focused on the lady next to him. Her son was gazing upon her with that besotted look, and she knew he was smitten.

For the past six months, his hair-trigger temper was not just under control – there were times when he actually showed judgment, perhaps he was even on the verge of actual maturity. She gave all the credit to Mecate. She was good for Shiba, and he was on the right path.

Mallory drew Shiba aside, getting back to business. Although in truth, seeing her son take an interest in a beautiful, strong woman gave her hope that perhaps he was now mature enough to become region leader. She hoped that a good woman like Mecate would bring out the best in her son. But she wasn't going to say anything now to ruin it.

"Good work," she praised him. "Let those Althaeans know we still dominate these lands."

Shiba broke out of the spell, realizing he hadn't heard a word she said. "I'm sorry, Mother. What were you saying?"

Mallory rolled her eyes. "You need to watch out for that boy. Rumor has it that soon, Suzan will take a seat on the Council. When she does, this boy will succeed her."

"Then things couldn't look better for me."

"Don't underestimate him, Shiba. This warrior has ambition, something you still lack."

"And I have something he still lacks – a partner," Mallory stepped aside as Neo approached. She sighed, disappointed, but hoped her message was clear enough.

"Well done, boss." Neo nudged him with a fist bump, and Shiba returned the gesture. "Imagine seeing an umbra knock out a warrior with his head."

"I got that one from you, brother. Almost like that tree back in the courtyard."

Neo exploded with laughter, and clapped Shiba on the back – a blow that would cripple the average citizen. Then he remembered the petite princess he escorted from the stands was waiting behind him. He stepped aside and gestured her forward. Neo winked at Shiba before he drifted away. "Don't let me keep you, boss."

Mecate bowed to Neo before he departed and then returned her gaze to Shiba. For a minute, they looked at each other, with a mixture of indecision and urgency.

"What did I tell you about the sand?" she said, arms crossed against her chest.

"I didn't think he would actually do it," Shiba said with a shrug.

She moved closer, and hugged him. "Listen to me more, will you?"

Shiba hesitated for a moment, wanting to believe that this hug meant what it felt like. A moment later, he let his arms encircle Mecate.

"I... Yes, Lady Mecate."

Shiba pulled back and held both of her hands in his, staring deeply into her emerald eyes.

"Mecate," he nearly stuttered. "When I become region leader, I want you to be there with me."

"You know you can count on my loyalty."

Shiba took a deep breath. "No… I mean…"

The glint in her eyes made him even more nervous. He could never tell when she was playful or serious, but he found the mystery alluring.

"You really don't know when to shut up, do you?" she said. She leaned closer until her lips were on his, and the spark that passed between them set their world on fire. "I said yes."

CHAPTER FIFTEEN

On their journey back to Althaea Main, Suzan resumed quizzing Gaven on a thousand topics, none of which had anything to do with battle. There was nothing there she had to worry about. What concerned her were the rumors that Gaven's fellow soldiers didn't show him proper respect. It wasn't easy for the region's toughest, fiercest fighters to be beaten by a soldier who had yet to master the use of a razor. If they wouldn't follow, he couldn't lead them. She had hoped the battle with Shiba would solve that issue, but his defeat made her turn to her second option.

"Have you thought about what I said?" Suzan asked to see if he was still paying attention. Gaven kept his eyes on the view from the other side of the carriage, a sight that wasn't so common in Althaea – the forests that stretched over valleys and mountains tingled a faraway memory.

He wondered if his old family were watching, but as far as his eyes could scan, everyone in the coliseum were nobles. It was hardly likely that they would be there, but the proximity to

Malino made him wonder. A part of him wanted to jump out of the carriage and run off into the woods. But his conscience told him to stay put and remember his place. His thoughts spiraled to his humiliating defeat at the hands of Shiba, and suddenly Gaven had the urge to set the whole forest on fire.

"Gaven?"

"I told you. I don't need a partner."

"Did you see how big Shiba's partner was?" Suzan pointed out. "Half of his strength is being channeled into his partner. Shiba is a skilled umbra, no doubt, but I think he was only able to win today because he has a partner."

"What are you implying?" Gaven spat. "You already know there isn't an Althaean fighter out there better than me."

"You're correct about that," Suzan agreed. "But there are other benefits to a paragon's partnership."

"Such as?"

"There is more to leadership than physical conflict."

"I know that, but—"

"But you are no politician."

"Thank you for the compliment."

"You can understand why some men would resist following you. At least for a little while. On the other hand, a partner with the right social skills and connections can open doors you can't chop your way through, even with the very best of swords."

"Cut to the chase, Suzan. You already have someone in mind, don't you?"

Suzan pierced him with a knowing gaze. "Inigo Tepis is a great match."

Inigo was in Gaven's squad during their early training days. His cowardly face flashed in his mind. He whined whenever dirt got on his pressed shirt or if his sword wasn't the sharpest of the stack.

"That noble prick can't fight for sour owl shit. The guy holds a sword like he has his hands on backwards."

"That "prick" happens to be funding a third of Althaea's businesses. His family has all the social connections you'll need. They might as well be the only family that has as much influence as the Hales."

This got Gaven's attention. He almost jerked up in excitement, but managed to keep his body planted on his seat.

"But most of the Hales are too posh to be dabbling with swords. So the best you can do, politically, are the Tepis. Plus, you and Inigo have been advancing through the ranks together. You'll get along perfectly."

FOR HIS EVENING MEAL, Gaven joined the rest of the army in the Dining Hall. Inigo eased into Gaven's space as he was served his ration.

Gaven ignored Inigo, who had once again changed his shirt for the evening meal. His silver hair was tied back and his eyes matched the golden chains on his uniform. Despite all the food on his plate, Inigo's limbs were still sticks. He never attended training sessions, after all, and he got away with it.

"Could you spare a moment with me, Commander?" Inigo asked.

Gaven wanted to say no, but knew he would have to answer to Suzan. If he sucked it up now, he wouldn't have to deal with him later. Gaven gave a hefty sigh and gestured for Inigo to take the lead. They headed for a table off in the corner and out of anyone's earshot. Even as they passed other warriors, Gaven couldn't miss the taunts of his fellow trainees.

"Are you babysitting tonight, Inigo?"

"Don't forget to cut up his meat for him!"

Inigo wasted no time in getting to his pitch. "Look, Gaven-may I call you Gaven?"

Gaven sighed but didn't respond, so Inigo went ahead.

"I've spoken to Her Honor. I understand that you don't want me as your partner."

Gaven shoved a hunk of lamb stew into his mouth, not caring for whatever sales pitch he was about to throw at him.

Inigo didn't let his rudeness faze him. "Do you always hold a fork like that?"

"Like what?"

"Like you need to kill your meat before you put it in your mouth."

Gaven almost took offense – then realized Inigo was trying to make a point. "I'm sure you can teach me all about fancy table manners."

"I can teach you how to eat a meal with the right people and not sell yourself short by looking like a bumpkin."

"And why would I give an Eudoxian water rat's ass?"

"Again, Gaven. You don't need to play brute with me. But what you may need to play before long is the role of region leader. And I know you take that seriously. Don't you?"

"Go on…"

And so he did. He explained how important it would be for Gaven to feel at ease in social situations with nobility. Because like it or not, as region leader, he would spend half his time either with politicians, or haughty barons of industry. Or, just barons, period. Nobles – snooty, clannish, condescending, but they were essential to a leader, if he wanted to make his region run smoothly.

"Because if you're not uncomfortable with them yet, they will do their best to make you uncomfortable. They'll push you around, because they won't respect you. They'll smile, but behind your back they'll write you off as a muscle-bound cretin."

"And you can do… what?"

"I can do more than teach you which fork to use. I know these people. I've dined with them, gone hunting with them, attended concerts, stage plays, and weddings with them. Courted their daughters, taught their sons fencing. They treat me as one of them because, my young friend, I *am* one of them. When my fellow nobles see me treating you as my equal, my leader, even as my superior, they will get the picture."

"Because you're so rich and popular," Gaven said.

"More than that. Because if someone from a family as powerful and influential as mine kisses your ring, these high and mighty grandees will ask themselves – *why?* What power does this upstart have that he can cow someone like the Tepis' into such obedience? In their eyes, if you can dominate me, you must be more powerful than I am. And I'm more powerful than most of them. So they will take their cue from me."

Gaven considered this. He nodded in the direction of the other warriors in the room. "What about these loud mouths?"

"Good. You ask the right questions."

"I can't lead men who think I'm a joke."

"They don't think you're a joke. They think you're a threat." Gaven looked surprised. "That's right. There are some mighty big egos here. Every one of them thinks he's nearly invincible. But you? You put a kernel of doubt in them. Make them question themselves, think about who they are. You give them a touch of fear, which they aren't used to. That's why they put you down all the time. They're scared."

"And how would you change things?"

"You've seen me fight, haven't you?"

Gaven burst out laughing, and had to fight to keep the food in his mouth. "Sorry. I didn't mean…"

"No, you're right. I can't fight for… what was it? Sour owl shit?"

"She told you that?"

"No, she didn't." Inigo let a sly smile curl his lip. "But I know how to slip a coin into the right purse. My information is usually quite solid."

"You have spies."

"I call them… *eyes*. But yes, they would be quite useful in your service."

"I don't think much of dirty business."

"Which is why you need someone who does." Inigo steered back on track. "The soldiers don't have any respect for my martial skills, obviously. But they take me very seriously. I have earned their trust, and I'm owed a lot of favors. The fact is, they know how special you are. They just need the right push to make them admit it. No one wants to jump off the cliff first. But when they see me dive in…"

"You sound pretty sure of yourself."

"I am. And that is something people respect."

Inigo took another glance at the steak Gaven was skewering.

"Come with me." Inigo took his plate and headed out of the tent. Gaven really didn't want to follow him, but he was curious to see what Inigo would sell him next.

They walked across the courtyard to the private quarters. They were empty, as expected at supper time. Inigo walked to the row of rooms on the first floor, the corridor lit only by dim lumastōnes hanging on the cobblestone walls. He stopped at the center and took another bite from his plate.

"Now, which one of them do you hate the most?" he asked, his voice echoing in the hallway.

"I don't hate anyone." Despite the unmarked wooden doors, Gaven knew which belonged to which warrior. Most of them were in his own team.

"Don't give me that load of toad's spew. How about Devin, the one that spat in your soup last week… or Koma. Did you know he was the one who left that pig's head on your bed?"

Gaven shook it off, ignoring Inigo and taking another bite of his steak.

"Oh, I know." Inigo perked as if he had come up with a plan he couldn't resist. He headed for one of the doors. It was the aegis on Haynes' team who had skewered his pants and hung them like a flag on the outer wall. Inigo knocked on the door to make sure no one was inside. The knock elicited high-pitched barks, not aggressive, only a response to the banging.

Gaven raised his brow. "Is that a hound?"

"It is."

"Pets aren't allowed here."

"Exactly. And as our commander, you should do something about that, shouldn't you?" Inigo took a thin piece of metal from his pocket and wiggled it into the lock. It clicked open within a few seconds. He had experience with this.

With the tips of his two fingers, Inigo took his piece of steak and set the rest of his plate on the floor. He slowly opened the door, wavering the fillet through the crack. The barking stopped. They could hear the snuffs of the canine, its nose glued to the savory red meat. Inigo opened the door wider, leading the pup into the hall. The brown and white mongrel stared at the meat with beady eyes, ears alert and perked as high as its fanning tail. It was small enough to fit into a satchel. Gaven figured that's how it got into the fortress in the first place.

The pup never once took its eyes off its treat, putting a spring in each paw as Inigo threw it down by Gaven's feet. Ignoring the strangers in front of him, it began to feast.

"You got your dagger?"

"Of course I got my dagger." Gaven rolled his eyes. He was

armed at all times. But what did that have to do with… "Oh no, Inigo, don't you dare."

"The mutt doesn't belong here. What if he kills someone? Spreads a disease? If you knew about it and did nothing, it's on your head. Her Honor would not be pleased to know you made an exception to the rules."

Gaven knew he was right, but the animal had done nothing wrong. He would rather set it free or give Lorrek a warning before taking action.

Inigo crouched and took the steak knife from his plate, offering it to Gaven. Gaven gave him a look that showed he questioned Inigo's sanity.

"In your skilled hands, may it have a painless death." Gaven examined the edge of the steak knife. It would be enough to kill the dog, but only if he stabbed it a dozen times. The very thought of hearing the hound whelp in pain and watching it bleed to death made him uneasy. He didn't want to do it.

"Do you see what I'm trying to teach you here, Gaven?" Inigo said. "Ignoring the problem doesn't make you a better man, it makes you an easier target. And people will keep at it until you put your foot down. Show them that you control them. Show them that you grant no mercy."

Gaven clenched his teeth knowing that there was some truth behind his words. Killing is what a fighter did. He was trained for this, but to kill for fun? As far as he knew, the animal had done nothing wrong. Must it suffer for the wrongs of its master? Just to send a message?

Gaven admitted that he knew nothing about how to please others. He had trained hard to earn his role and always did what was asked. But all his comrades saw a young commander who prematurely ascended the ranks and dishonored their veterans. What could he do to prove he was in charge?

An opportunity was before his eyes. He decided to take a chance.

He tossed the knife aside. It spun down the hall and out of sight into the dim hallway. Inigo was ready to scowl at him, until he noticed Gaven reaching into his belt for his silver dagger. In one motion, faster than a blink, Gaven sliced the hound's neck. Without a single cry, as if it had simply fallen asleep, the hound rested on its side. Silent.

The shiny silver of the steel was dripping with blood and there was a dead animal at his feet. Gaven took it in for a moment. It wasn't like him to kill for power. Yet he didn't regret it.

He finally understood what was holding him back. His past and the weaknesses he dragged along with him since his parents tossed him away. The memories he hung onto of the people he treasured the most. His Minettan morals were no good here. And by killing this hound he became a beast himself, one full of power, determination, and resilience. It was what he wanted.

Inigo was surprised at how fast it all happened, but his amazement soon turned into giddiness.

"Absolutely marvelous," Inigo said, applauding. "No one can work a blade as well as you do."

"Let's go," Gaven grumbled, turning back to the courtyard. He had no intention of returning to the Dining Hall. He had lost his appetite and was ready to retire. Inigo opened his mouth, wanting to say more, but he let the man walk away. The job was done, and his plan was in place.

By the first assembly, every soldier had heard of the rumor surrounding the pup's death. When Gaven lined up his soldiers that morning, he was mildly shocked to see that they didn't banter amongst each other. It was quiet enough to hear the chambermaids gossiping. The platoon kept their heads lowered, away from his gaze.

"Heads up unless you want to get yours chopped off!" Gaven said. At the sound of his roar, their chins snapped up in fear.

"Yes, sir!"

It was only then that Gaven realized he couldn't have chosen worse words. They would think he'd cut their necks like he did to that hound.

He almost wanted to apologize, but he couldn't deny that he enjoyed this newfound power. Inigo's scheme had worked. It only took a fraction of his effort to get his men to listen to him now. For the first time in months, no one took his ration of bread by the door, his belongings stayed where they were, and he was certain no one would dare pour slop over him. It was the respect he long wished for, and deserved.

Gaven spent the rest of the afternoon consulting with Suzan. She avoided the topic of the hound for much of the discussion, focusing only on the array of letters sent by civilians asking for the army's assistance.

"Did you really kill that pup?" Suzan finally asked.

"Are you shocked?" Gaven raised his brow.

"Yes. I've never seen you kill anything but your supper."

"Dogs aren't allowed on fortress grounds. I had to take care of it."

"Well, I don't disagree, but… killing it on the spot? That's not like you, Gaven."

"Weren't you the one who told me not to show vulnerability, Your Honor?" Suzan raised a brow, and waited for his justification. "What good is a fighter who doesn't raise his blade? How would our enemies know fear if you do not show them the rivers of red?"

Suzan didn't disagree. In fact, she had been trying to teach him this very thing since she began training him. But this sudden change in his mentality? She figured Inigo had something to do with it.

Almost as if he had been listening to the whole conversation, Inigo knocked at that very moment and invited himself into Suzan's study.

"Did you enjoy your day?" Inigo smiled at Gaven. "Refreshing, isn't it? Like a brawler off your chest."

Gaven ignored Inigo. But Inigo already had his next pitch prepared.

"Gaven, you need me," he insisted. "Not to watch your back, but to guide you forward."

Suzan agreed, pitching in, "A paragon's partner doesn't have to be physically strong. They just need to counter your weaknesses."

Gaven knew that, but he didn't want to admit it. He grew up believing only the strongest ascended to the top, and he worked hard to get there. In came this slackard whose only talent was being able to toss a coin at any time. For Gaven to share his hard-earned position with such a coward was insulting.

But Inigo could command a thousand swords with mere prose. If he could make an entire army kiss his feet, imagine what he could do to other empires. Gaven was certain this combination could take over the empire, perhaps even the whole alliance. His quest to become the strongest fighter was within reach. He would obtain everything he desired; the respect, the control, and the pride of a man. The answer seemed so simple.

"I call the shots," Gaven reminded him. "If we're doing this, you serve *me*."

"I wouldn't dare ask for it any other way, *Commander*."

Inigo pulled the sword from his belt, a studded beauty that had never clashed with more than a training sword. In an elegant swaying motion, he took it in both hands and raised it to Gaven.

"*Gaven Zanette. By my blade, I hereby request your alliance to become your eyes and ears in the time of uncertainty.*"

And Gaven held back his ego like a stubborn child ready to swallow bitter medicine. But he was ready to seize that express ticket to becoming region leader.

"*Inigo Tepis, by my blood, I swear to be your sword and shield in the battles to come.*"

CHAPTER SIXTEEN

Nine Years Ago

Since Salathiel and Mirari arrived in Solarin six years ago, the booming town had nearly doubled in size. The clang of hammers and groan of saws cutting planks of wood never seemed to stop, and it quickly became a bustling town known across Minetta as one of the empire's centers of trade.

New shops and warehouses were built every day, and there was never a shortage of work. Mirari found her place in Solarin helping shopkeepers with inventory and retail trading. It wasn't customary for modest merchants like her to be carrying a sword. Salathiel forbade it himself, fearing that it would draw attention and cause unnecessary trouble. That was no problem for Mirari — she was better with her fists. Still, she practiced the sword techniques Joachim taught her every morning before her first trade. She had no doubt those skills would be useful one day.

But Salathiel had it different. He made his living as a retinue, a hired guard who protected anything from cargo to shady travelers. He was a scrawny, young umbra who looked like he could be dragged off by the wind, but his hands could handle knives better than the finest dart players or the most skilled seaside chefs. Mirari was trained by Joachim in the same manner, only her throwing skills were more dangerous than a cart with one wheel. Javelins and knives were out of the question, so Joachim gave her a sword, something that would never leave her hands.

"I may be out late tonight," Salathiel said as he grabbed his coat by the door. The last streak of light was parting the sky – he timed it perfectly. He didn't particularly like evening jobs, but they paid the best. Besides, this one was different.

Closing her book, Mirari sat up on the couch and watched as Salathiel swiped his hair with his fingers in front of a small mirror by the door.

"What is it this time?" Mirari asked. "Smugglers from Morenta?"

"Even better," Salathiel smirked as he glanced back at her. "A request from Region Leader Nivenda herself."

Mirari furrowed her brows. "From Oban? What business do they have with Avon? And why you?"

Salathiel shrugged. Ignorance was a bliss – it was to protect himself and Mirari from the dangers of this cruel world. As long as he didn't ask questions, he had nothing to fear. His job tonight undoubtedly came with secrets, but it was no surprise why he was chosen – he was the best retinue in Solarin.

Salathiel waved goodbye as he headed for a small park at the edge of Solarin. It was desolate as it should be after dusk. He waited for his clients under the faint glow of a lumastōne-lit lamp with a throwing star spinning on his finger.

Though Oban was just a couple mountains over, Salathiel never expected to be hired by the renowned region leader, defender of the border to Althaea and Valenia. What could she possibly require from him that she didn't already have?

He heard their armor clanging with each step, but the first

thing he saw creep out from the shadows were a pair of yellow cat eyes, fixed and staring back at him. Salathiel grew stiff, but took a deep breath to calm his nerves.

Aegises. He had to remind himself. The penniless clients he normally served didn't own animals. Still, every so often he would deal with some kestrel or ape, and most commonly, saber-lions like this one.

Once his guests came within distance of the lumastōne, he saw their snake-like crest embedded in their shoulder pads. They were Nivenda's commanders − a young woman with dimples that could replace the warmth of the sun, and a dark-skinned giant, curly redhead with limbs firmer than the sierras of Oban. Accompanying them was the yellow-eyed saberlion with fur darker than twilight.

"You're smaller than I expected," the larger one said. She held out her meat cleaver of a hand. Her skin-tight under-armor showed off her hard-earned six pack. "Commander Hilda, and this is Fig."

"Salathiel," he greeted as he shook her hand. The saberlion sniffed his hand; Salathiel waited patiently before it pulled away. Tall as Salathiel was, Hilda still towered over him. On her toes, she would be able to touch the tip of the streetlight over his head. But it wasn't her height that perked his curiosity − her body was exceptionally toned for an aegis. Considering archers didn't need a lot of strength, it was strange.

The other lady reached out her hand. "Commander Iphige-nia, a pleasure," she beamed as she shook Salathiel's hand. "You can just call me Iffy." Her innocent and sweet composure reminded him much of Mirari. Her long, periwinkle hair, much lighter than Mirari's darker shade of violet, wavered over her cute smile. Without the Oban insignia on her armor and a sword strapped around her waist, no one would have assumed that the petite sparkling young woman was a fighter.

"The pleasure is mine," Salathiel said. "Her Honor said you are after a fugitive from Valenia?"

"Are you aware of the poisoning that happened in the Tribe of Paragons a couple of months ago?" Hilda asked. Salathiel nodded. It was an infamous story among the townspeople and travelers alike — a witch, they called her, for her bold action in poisoning a mistress of the Tribe of Paragons. It awoke centuries of unrest between the Tribes of Celtas and Paragons, and now a war was brewing.

Hilda continued, "An informant told us that the person who poisoned the mistress is hiding around Solarin. The Tribe of Paragons were ready to march an army into Minetta, but Nivenda forbade it. Instead, we are tasked to capture her and bring her back to Valenia."

Salathiel now understood why Region Leader Nivenda requested his assistance. It wasn't to protect them, but to escort them around the area he was familiar with. Salathiel swallowed his nerves and guided the ladies to the nearest forest.

It was untamed wilderness, where any traveler could easily get lost, but Salathiel had guided plenty of merchant caravans through these woods. Locals knew to stay away, but many of Salathiel's clients conducted shady business in these parts. A smart man would not ask for details; his job was to know how to get his clients where they needed to go, and make sure they got there in one piece.

"Hold on," Hilda cautioned as she raised a fist. She observed Fig, who was taking big whiffs of the air around them. Hilda nodded. "I smell it too. Someone's lighting a fire."

"Would that be wise to do in these woods?" Iphigenia questioned. "It's tinder-dry."

"It's not a wood fire. It's fire kore."

Fig glued his nose to the ground and carefully tracked the source of the smell, creeping through the thick undergrowth.

Following the scent, they approached a small clearing where the remnants of a small campfire smoldered. All that remained was smoke and a few hot embers. They could see green, glowing crystals scattered in the glowing coals. They scanned the surrounding area. No one seemed to be there.

Hilda let out a frustrated grunt. "She caught onto us."

Fig snarled.

"What is it, boy?"

Salathiel could feel the ground underneath him begin to shift. His instinct told him to jump, and so he did, leaping for the branch above. As soon as he did, he heard Iphigenia yelp.

Something grasped her ankles. She looked down; they had been immobilized by roots wrapping around her legs like snakes.

"She has trapped us!" Iphigenia cried out. She unsheathed her sword and with one swipe, split them apart like they were a stick of warm butter.

The roots under Hilda's feet also began to creep upward, but Fig pounced on them, pressing the roots down with his enormous paws and severing them like jerky. Hilda readied her bow and took a shot at the ground. The arrow penetrated the soil, and an electric pulse lit up the roots in cracks of light. The roots withered, then fell lifeless on the ground.

Iphigenia saw a flash of light from the corner of her eye, and shifted her gaze to what she realized were balls of fire coming at her.

Before the fire could make contact, a wall of mud, gravel and twigs sprung out in front of her. The fireballs landed against the makeshift wall, disintegrating into puffs of smoke.

The wall tumbled forward like an ocean wave, crumbling back into dozens of boulders and loose dirt. But they didn't stay there; Salathiel planted his feet back onto the ground, then swiped his hand through the air. Stones and pebbles followed his movement – some to the side but most had flung forward – flying into the depths of the forest.

Salathiel listened closely until he heard one of them land a soft hit.

"There!" he said pointing to Hilda's right. "Someone's over there."

Hilda's arrow aligned with Salathiel's finger, and she took her shot less than a second later. Fig followed the arrow, jumping over tall bushes and blending with the dark forest. They heard a metallic clang, possibly the arrow being deflected, followed by the screams of a woman.

The trio rushed forward in the direction of the noise. They could hear Fig's growls and snarls, but could not see him. They saw a blonde woman on the ground, wrestling what appeared to be a shadow. The only thing holding Fig back was the metal staff in the woman's hands, forced forward as she tried to keep the cat's teeth away.

Salathiel was surprised that the woman was young, around his age. He'd expected the poisoner to be a seasoned assassin. But this woman didn't look the least bit threatening, just unfortunate to have been trapped under the jaws of a beast. The only terrifying thing about her was her ruby eyes – radiating a fiery defiance that looked like she could kill anything with a single glare. He noticed that the glare was on him.

Iphigenia caught sight of the colorful stones on the spellcaster's bracelet. That was all they needed to confirm her identity. She said, "They call her the Witch of Aten."

"You graceless featherpits. I am not a witch!" the young woman screamed. She was aggressive and put up a great struggle, but the beast on top of her was at least four times her weight. Hilda caught a spark of fire growing from her hands.

"Stubborn," Hilda mumbled as she reached for one of the arrows in her pouch, and stabbed the witch's neck. She yelped. It was an enchanted arrow, designed to disable with minimal pain. It should have knocked out a rhinoceros — yet the woman kept screaming and squirming. But at least, nothing else was coming out of her hands. The arrow had disabled her kore.

Realizing she was defeated, the woman finally stopped struggling and gave in. Hilda stuck two fingers in her mouth and whistled. Fig hopped off his prey and returned to his master's side.

As the woman sat up from the ground, Iphigenia knelt down and locked the spellcaster's hands behind her with a glowing pair of aulāce.

"You have the wrong person," the witch said, scornful but not putting up any resistance. "I did nothing!"

"I'd be more inclined to believe that if you hadn't attacked us," Hilda said. "Clearly, you know why we're here."

"Was I supposed to just let your cat eat me for supper? *You* invaded my home."

Hilda turned to Salathiel. "Does anyone live in these parts?"

"They'd be stupid to. There are bigger things to worry about in these woods at night than saberlions."

Hilda looked back at the witch. "Anything else?"

"Alright. I made the potion, but that's all I did!" She seemed desperate for them to believe her. She went on, saying, "The Tribe of Celtas told me they wanted better euthanasia for the injured they couldn't save. So I made up something that would kill quickly and without pain. But they lied to me. I swear. No one was supposed to use it as a poison."

"It's your word against theirs."

But Iphigenia sensed the woman's sincerity. She furrowed her brows, adding, "Hilda… what if she's telling the truth?"

"It's not our decision to make."

"But the celtas? You know how they are. Lying to an outsider is considered a virtue. If we give her to the paragons, they'll just kill her. This won't end the war – the real people behind the assassination are still out there."

"I just did what I was told," the witch said. "After I found out what the celtas were doing with it, I destroyed all traces of the spell. Believe me, no one can make it again. No one else will be poisoned."

Salathiel started to have doubts of his own. Her story was plausible. Despite the ghastly rumors, he couldn't sense any hostility in her. He had journeyed with a handful of wicked, crude people, the banes of society. He knew what a tainted aura felt like, and this woman didn't have one.

Hilda was focused on the witch, still weary and suspicious, but Iphigenia yanked the arrow from the woman's neck.

"Hey!" Hilda looked like she was ready to unleash a series of profanities, but Iphigenia crossed her arms and pouted. The way her cheeks puffed only subdued Hilda's rage.

"See, she's cooperating," Iphigenia said.

"We were sent here to retrieve her. I don't care if she's innocent or not." Hilda gritted her teeth, but seeing how the witch didn't move an inch, her shoulders unstiffened. "Don't feel like throwing more fireballs at us?"

"Why would I waste any more of my precious crystals on you?" she said. "I'm an alchemist, not a fighter."

"We ask Nivenda." Iphigenia said. "The paragons are waiting by the border. We need to make the decision here and now."

Hilda groaned. "Fine, fine." She turned to Salathiel. "Does your town have a comstōne?"

"Of course," Salathiel said.

"Could I burden you to watch over the *alchemist* until Nivenda makes a decision? I don't want to have to go looking for this witch again."

Before he could answer, Iphigenia placed a key in Salathiel's hands. A smile crossed her face. "We'll be in touch."

Salathiel arrived at his cottage when the sun rose. The witch trailed by his side, not saying a word. She was calm, a simple person, and the only thing she cared about was keeping her dark cloak over her head.

Salathiel was ready to restrain her if she tried to run away, but she didn't seem to have taken this whole incident as a capture, rather a rescue. And it made sense; only the insane would live in the outer woods.

Mirari was already awake and practicing her sword technique outside with a wooden stick. She beamed upon seeing Salathiel... and with a woman.

"Welcome back," Mirari said. "You two dating, or just friends?"

"Very funny," Salathiel said, nudging to the woman's aulāce.

"I'm his prisoner," she said, in a tone that said she could take off at will. Which, in fact, she could.

"This is Mirari, my sister. This is... um..."

And it crossed his mind that he didn't know her name at all. All this time, they had been referring to her as a witch.

"Kylah. You can call me Kylah."

"Kylah. Turns out she's the one who allegedly poisoned the mistress of the Tribe of Paragons. But without proof, they may let her go. She'll be staying with us until Region Leader Nivenda makes a final decision."

Mirari furrowed her brow in how crazy that all sounded. He brought his capture home and was introducing her like a friend.

He gestured Kylah to the door and handed Mirari the key to

Kylah's aulāce. "I need to report to my employer, but I'll be back soon."

Mirari looked at the stranger, then back to Salathiel who was already leaving. "That's okay. Just leave me with the murderer you were hired to capture. No big deal."

Salathiel gave a carefree wave without looking back, leaving Mirari in an awkward situation.

Kylah stared hard at Mirari. She wouldn't speak but her eyes were judging her in some way. Dirt on her face? A jealous girlfriend? Mirari couldn't tell what was on her mind.

She rolled her eyes, opened the front door and waved the guest inside. "Water? Buzz? Or do you prefer herbal?"

"Did you just assume I like herbal teas because I'm Valenian? I don't know whether to be impressed or offended." Kylah raised a brow as she scanned the small cottage. Last night's dishes were still in the sink and the corners of the room were stacked with crates. But Kylah didn't care. She was drawn to the cozy, velvet couch in front of her, and was glad it was free of any stains or personal belongings. She invited herself to it, leaning her head back and resting her eyes.

"Herbal it is." Mirari opened one of the cabinets and scoured through the back for the box of tea leaves. The kettle on the stove had already been heated earlier that morning. She sprinkled a few yellow petals and tangerine skins into a clean, ceramic cup.

"*Mirari*, huh?" Kylah prompted. "So this is where you ended up." She admired Mirari's composure, but wondered how long she would be able to keep it. She watched the girl move the kettle in a circular motion with two delicate fingers taped to the lid. "You still pour tea like a noble."

Mirari's hand wavered slightly, flooding the cup.

"Badger bollocks." She cursed while reaching for a towel.

"So. You are."

"Am what?" Mirari kept her gaze on the floor, wiping the spot of water over and over, anything to avoid the stranger's gaze.

"The missing Hale girl… was it Roselyn?"

"And what gave you such a preposterous idea?"

"I did a few jobs for the Hales, in Valenia, that is. Your family's portraits are still up on their wall, including a younger portrait of your mother. You look more like them than your so-called brother."

"You can't—" Mirari started. "I mean, you have no proof."

"She looked so young and happy. Must've joined the Hale family at your age. Then every portrait after that… Well, I guess she made some bad decisions." Kylah leaned against the couch, her back pressed against the satisfying cotton despite her hands still being restrained. She looked up to the ceiling, beams stretching from one end to another, and it reminded her of home in Valenia, a place she knew she could never return to. "Lucan told me what happened to young Roselyn – or at least what people think—" She let out a small yawn and closed her eyes once again. Last night's adrenaline was starting to fade. "You're not kidnapped. You're not even lost. You ran away, didn't you? Look how cozy you are in this cottage."

Mirari's hand tightened around the handle of the kettle. She wondered if it was necessary to silence the stranger. Kylah was restrained, and it was a perfect opportunity.

"Don't worry, I'm not after that reward money," Kylah said. "Even if I owe Lucan for sneaking me out of Valenia. If you don't want to be found, I can certainly relate. It's none of my business. Everyone thinks you're dead anyway." A small smile perked on her lips. "Wish I thought of that."

"Thought of what?"

"Playing dead. They quit looking if they think you're dead."

"They do?"

"Mostly. Lucan won't, but I persuaded him to let it go. Hanging onto someone's death for nearly a decade… it isn't healthy." She looked Mirari over again, nodding. "But I guess I was wrong about that. May I ask why you're in hiding?"

Mirari released her grip on the pot and relaxed her shoulders. She could see why Salathiel invited this stranger into their home. Kylah didn't seem dangerous, just a modest woman trying to get by.

"I just… I don't know, but I really like this new life," Mirari said.

"I hear you," Kylah said, as she recalled stepping into Lucan's mansion. The recently polished marble floors had nearly blinded her, and the Hales owned more classical décor than the number of guests that would probably see it. "The Hales… I couldn't believe there are people living like that. Not with so many barely having enough to eat."

Kylah looked around the shabby cottage, from the unwashed pans to the blackening fruits on the countertop. It was a fairly empty house, she thought, a striking contrast compared to Lucan's estate.

"Mansions, servants, mountains of gold. Who needs all those things?"

Without hesitance, Mirari answered, "I don't."

"Salathiel seems like a nice person. You prefer him over being a noble?"

"A thousand times over."

In those elegant eyes, the one part of her that would forever be a Hale, Kylah knew her answer was genuine. And that made two Hales she knew that defied their birthright – born into privilege and luxury, but chose a different, much more complicated path out of goodwill. Perhaps not everyone was as selfish and materialistic as she believed. There was still some good in the world.

Mirari set the cup of tea on the table in front of Kylah.

"Well, I'll tell you what," the witch said. "We can both play dead. You don't tell people I exist, and I won't expose your little secret either."

Mirari stared at her faint reflection in her cup, then to the key clenched in her other hand. "Deal."

CHAPTER SEVENTEEN

A ball of light formed in Mirari's hands, bright and delicate like a sunflower. She caressed it in her cupped palms. Kylah gently guided her.

"That's amazing!" Mirari was awed. The rumors said the Witch of Aten was an expert spellcaster, and Mirari believed them now. From firecracker fingers to object levitation, even making water taste like wine, Kylah showed off her skills to Mirari, using her kore to create the impossible.

Mirari was never able to do much with kore. After Joachim trained her, the most she could do was swipe wind and cast barriers. It was simply not in her blood. The Hales were aristocrats; few practiced the ways of a fighter, and their ability to link their aura with nature gradually diminished generation after generation. Even if Mirari practiced her kore for the rest of her life, there was a limit to how much she could improve.

"There are some skills that don't require a lot of kore," Kylah explained. "Even with low kore affinity, you can win a battle if you play smart."

Kylah raised one hand above Mirari's ball of light. It

followed her hand and stretched upward like taffy, then pulled apart into a dozen smaller strands of light, all straight and pointing at Kylah's hand. If they weren't glowing, Mirari would've thought they were raw spaghetti.

"Sit up straight," Kylah instructed, and Mirari quickly adjusted her position. "Now close your eyes and imagine you are one of these strands."

"Close my eyes?" She was excited to see the dancing light in front of her.

"Do it."

Kylah's sharp tone reminded her of Joachim when he tried to teach her how to use kore. He told her that kores were like personalities. Gaven and Salathiel were headstrong, determined and full of pride. It came to no surprise that their auras resonated with the earth.

But Mirari was shocked when wind spiraled from her hand. She was confident − based on her fiery incident on the kōnvoy and in the forest − that her kore was something more destructive. Being able to use more than one type was unheard of, unless one was naturally talented like Kylah.

Then, why was she able to unleash fire?

With complete trust in her retainer and desperation for the truth, Mirari told Joachim her secret − how she believed she was the one who caused the fire on the kōnvoy that took her parents' life. Joachim didn't believe her, but he neither laughed nor questioned it. He didn't know what started the fire, but he took one look at her aura, and knew it was impossible for her to have been responsible for it.

"Though it is shallow, you are gentle and nimble like the wind," he said. "Fire is as impulsive as it is destructive... It's not your style."

But Mirari knew Salathiel wouldn't lie, especially not about what happened that day she set the forest on fire. So, where was this ability? And why couldn't she control it?

"Back straight," Kylah repeated. Her words dragged Mirari back to reality, and Mirari gathered hope once again. "Eyes closed. Focus on the energy in your hands."

Mirari wanted to ask Kylah about it. She saw Kylah work up flames to light the candles by their door earlier, and was thrilled to finally meet someone who knew how to wield fire. But no matter how close they'd gotten, Kylah was still a stranger that Mirari had met only a few days ago.

With her eyes closed, Mirari felt Kylah's hands lightly touch the back of her palm. Kylah guided Mirari's hands apart, drifting them to the side until her chest was open and her arms relaxed in a welcoming, meditative position.

"Okay, now open your eyes."

Mirari's eyes shot open, expecting to see the bands of light still in her palms. Instead, her mouth dropped when she saw that they were spread apart, hovering in the path that her hand had moved in. They were like prison bars between Mirari and Kylah, but Mirari felt anything but separated from her. It was beauty that stemmed from her own hands, and a feeling of control she never had.

"This is an aegis skill that mimics a cluster of arrows," Kylah said. "Many don't know this, but as long as you have the endurance, you don't need to use a lot of kore for this skill. And if you choose to continue using a sword as your main weapon, performing an aegis skill will shock people. It can be your trump card."

"How do I throw it?"

"Nuh uh," Kylah hushed, pulling Mirari's hands back together in a flash. At the sound of her clap, all the light arrows dissipated, and the room became dark, lit only by the faint moonlight shining through the window on the roof. "I can't imagine the look on Sal's face if he comes back to holes through his walls."

Kylah's sharply tuned hearing detected footsteps tapping against the pavement on the stone path to the cottage. Her eyes focused on the shut door, and Mirari noticed Kylah's hand slip inside her tunic. Last time she heard noise in the backyard, Kylah threw a handful of paralytic powder out the window, and two raccoons had seizures. Mirari didn't want to guess what she had in her hand this time.

The door cracked open, and a familiar pair of dark boots stepped into their view.

"Why are you both sitting in the dark?" Salathiel glanced at the two ladies on the couch, before igniting a match from his pocket and lighting a row of half-melted candles by the door.

"Umm… surprise?" Mirari joked. Salathiel rolled his eyes.

"I saw some light glaring from the window," he said. "Are you showing off again, Kylah?"

"Actually, the little one's got some talent."

Salathiel blinked in disbelief. "Mirari? Really?"

Mirari laughed nervously. As eager as she was to show him, she wanted to perfect her new skill first. Then she remembered that Salathiel was supposed to deliver more important news.

Days had passed but the paragons from Valenia refused to leave the Minettan-Valenian border until the terrorist was in their possession. Nivenda's commanders hustled back to the border to negotiate with the angered paragons. Salathiel would have heard the final verdict over a call from the town's comstōne.

"So? What did Region Leader Nivenda say?" Mirari asked.

Salathiel pulled up a seat from the dining table and Kylah leaned in anxiously. With his fingers interlaced in his lap, he began, "Kylah, Witch of Aten, the most brilliant spellcaster in all of Valenia…" He took a dramatic, deep breath. "You are offi-cially sanctioned to live in Minetta."

Kylah and Mirari hollered and high-fived each other.

"You're free!" Mirari cheered.

"Not necessarily," Kylah said. "I'm assuming Valenia wasn't okay with it. It won't stop bounty hunters from trying to bring me back."

Salathiel said, "Then you'll just have to not get kidnapped, Kylah Kein."

Sparkles of kore wavered in her hand, which quickly formed into a pellet-shaped crystal. She flicked it at Salathiel and it ricocheted off his forehead.

"Ow," he said, pressing his finger where it had hit him. "Easy. I'm just the messenger."

"How about you go get us some beers to celebrate, *messenger*."

<hr>

IT WAS PAST MIDNIGHT, and Kylah was still up on the couch working on a spell she had started earlier. She tinkered with the tiny sparks of light circling her fingers. Her concentration was interrupted by the sound of footsteps coming from outside. But Salathiel and Mirari were both home. This could be anyone.

Kylah quickly put out the sparks, leaving her in the darkness. She listened closely. The lock on the door jiggled quietly, then the door creaked open. Moonlight shone on the stranger's face. He wore livery with the insignia of Oban.

He peered around in the dark room, trying to see if anyone was there. "Hello...?" He turned in Kylah's general direction, not quite spotting her.

Kylah's senses were on high alert – something didn't seem right, and she remained in the shadows, silent.

"Sorry about the hour. I didn't mean to disturb you," he said. His eyes could only see pitch darkness. "I'm Officer Keff, in the service of My Lady, Region Leader Nivenda. I have a message...

for Kylah Kein." He took another step into the room, still peering around to find her. "Please, come with me, I have a coach waiting…"

Kylah kept still, not moving an inch from the couch. The door to Salathiel's bedroom opened. Keff turned his head at the sound, but he could only make out a tall figure. Salathiel looked at the intruder in his living room with a glare.

"Get out of my house," he said. "I will speak to Her Honor herself on this matter."

Mirari's door slowly creaked open, just wide enough for Salathiel to see her eye through a small crack. He shook his head, gently shooing her back inside.

"Look, if I go back empty-handed, she'll have my head," he answered. "She said she wants to speak to Kylah in private. It's urgent."

"Really? If you're going to impersonate a soldier of Oban, then you should've at least done your research. Men aren't allowed in their army."

Keff tried to plaster an innocent look on his face, and said in his smoothest tone. "Fetch her now. You don't want trouble."

"I have trouble. Standing in my doorway."

A dagger flew across the room, but Salathiel was expecting the stranger to make a move, and he jerked his head just as the blade buried itself in the door frame, barely missing him. Salathiel took a lunge at Keff, who then shouted, "Rever!"

A second man crashed through the front window, tackling Salathiel. As they grappled on the floor, Rever pulled a dagger of his own. Salathiel was quick to get back on his feet, ready to fend off both intruders.

From the corner of his eye, he saw a streak of light illuminating the room. It was Mirari – she held a growing globe in her cupped palms. Wide-eyed, Salathiel took a quick dive to the ground, right before she pushed it forward. The light knocked

Rever back out the window through which he came, like a swinging hammer. But the light didn't dissipate – it bounced off River, ricocheted against an empty kettle, then drilled a hole in the floorboard in front of Kylah.

"By the shredded wedding gown of the Goddess Felicia!" Salathiel shouted, ready to scold Mirari for the damage, but there was still one intruder left in the house, and his lecture would have to wait.

The light revealed Kylah's location, and Keff saw the blonde woman sitting on the couch. He staggered for her, dagger in hand. Kylah had been muttering a spell for quite some time, and now she was ready. She drew her hand out and the red stone on her bracelet sparkled with a faint glow.

With the snap of her finger, the dagger in Keff's hand began to glow red hot as if a blacksmith had just pulled it from the fire. Keff screamed in pain, dropping the knife.

Kylah couldn't contain her devious grin. "Aren't you a hothead?"

Proving her right, he roared and came after her.

She tried to chant another spell, but only got one word out when he slapped her hard across the mouth. He was about to take a swing again, but he felt two stings against his back. He had no time to check what it was before Kylah raised her hand for a punch. Keff caught her wrist, and tore her bracelet off with one firm yank.

"Hey!" Kylah fumed, ready to fight to death for her bracelet. "Give that back!"

Upon hearing Kylah scream, Mirari scanned the dark room for the nearest weapon. She grabbed the dirty pan from the sink, dodged the dining table chairs on her way to Kylah and readied a strike…

Wham!

Rever drove his knee into Mirari's stomach, knocking the

wind out of her. There was a discomforting *crack!* when another kick hammered her to the floor. He pushed his knee into her fractured ribs, twisting and grinding the air out of her.

The stabbing pain in her ribs flared up, and blackness was creeping over her. Mirari was on the edge of passing out when she heard a strange whooshing sound, followed by a meaty thud. Rever's full weight pressed on her, and something hot splattered on her face.

Keff was ready to escape with the jewelry in his hand, but as he made to turn around, he was met with Salathiel and his wooden umbrella. Keff dropped to the ground.

Kylah snap her fingers. Instantly, a small flame appeared, floating in the air, and it zipped to the mantel, where the conjured flame lit the candles along the window. The room filled with soft, yellow light, illuminating the bloodied umbrella snapped in half, and a lifeless body lying by Salathiel's feet with two knives lodged in the back. Mirari was squashed under Rever's body, her screams muffled by her tears, which rolled down her face, dragging splatters of blood down her cheek.

Rever's body had a scythe protruding from his back, the other end barely missing Mirari's shoulder. A towering woman stared at the weapon from the doorstep. She had light wrinkles over her truffle skin, body decorated with a kind of matte blue armor that Salathiel knew didn't originate from Minetta. Her waving blue cape showed off her high rank.

She heaved Rever's body off Mirari, then tried to dislodge her scythe from Keff's upper torso, where it was jammed between his ribs. Planting her boot on Keff's corpse, she used both hands to yank and tug, trying to work her bloody blade loose.

"Gods be damned!" she cursed.

Salathiel rushed to Mirari. He couldn't care less about the scythe, the mysterious woman, or the dead bodies in his home.

He tried to pull Mirari up by the arms, and when that didn't work, he grabbed her waist. With every touch Mirari yelped and begged him to stop. He didn't know what else to do.

"Don't move her," the woman said. The blade finally popped out with a sound like uncorking a bottle of sparkling muddleberry wine. Her weapon glistened next to her sapphire eyes. "If you're not a healer, don't touch her unless you want her to break another bone."

"Who are you?" Salathiel shouted at the last stranger in his home.

"Hopefully someone you'll never see again." She pulled aside her cape and flashed her circular badge, engraved with curved lines that drew a figure with a cloak, representing the divine.

Salathiel knew that symbol. He had seen it in papers hanging on the town bulletin board, but never thought he would see the badge in person. He almost didn't believe it, but after everything that had happened since he took this dangerous job, he had begun to accept the impossible.

"Councilor."

"Correct. I am Councilor Julie of Valenia, and you are commanded never to speak of this incident to anyone."

"Really?" A voice shouted from the far end of the room. Kylah showed no restraint, pointing a nasty finger at the lady. Salathiel wouldn't be surprised if she picked a fight with the councilor. As Kylah spoke, she loomed over Keff's body, and dug her bracelet out of his bloody pocket. She gave his corpse three hard kicks for good measure. "You sent these mercenary bastards after my scalp. Don't think you can sweep this under the rug, *Your Grace*. I'll make sure Councilor Tarek hears of this."

"You are mistaken. I'm not here on behalf of the paragons. I was sent here by Region Leader Nivenda to officially put an end to the madness you caused between our empires."

Kylah blinked a few times. Though the woman before her

was supposed to be a representative of her empire, it was no secret that her origins were from the Tribe of Paragons, the very people after Kylah. Kylah never would've imagined her assistance. It almost seemed like a trap.

"*I* did nothing," Kylah hissed, now only a few steps away from the councilor, but Julie kept her ever unwavering cold glare. "What the Tribe of Celtas did with the poison was out of my control."

Julie didn't seem to care about her explanation. She gave her scythe a fancy twirl, and Kylah held her breath. She went on, "Here's how we play it, Witch of Aten. You died here tonight at the hands of these assassins. I paid the assassins their rewards, and they vanished without a trace, as they always do. The paragons acknowledge your death, they send their men away from the border, and you won't have assassins looking for you anymore."

Julie snatched the jewelry in Kylah's hand.

"Now, hang on a minute—"

"You either play dead or I will be forced to put you on trial at the Hearth. If that happens, I guarantee I won't take your side."

Kylah realized what was happening. This councilor was acting out on her own. Was it bribery that drove her to turn away from her duty?

"You owe this favor to Region Leader Nivenda," Julie said. "Had she called anyone else, you wouldn't have been spared."

"And I should believe a councilor who makes deals under the table?"

"This saves us all a lot of trouble, and legal proceedings would've been a waste of time. It's easier when someone's dead, isn't it?" Julie dangled the bracelet in front of Kylah before storing it in her pocket. "I'll need this as proof of your death. As soon as all parties acknowledge your death, I'll send it back. Anyway, you must learn to live without it. It'll help a spellcaster like yourself blend in with the rest of the crowd. A good thing, wouldn't you agree?"

Julie said something that Kylah hadn't considered. Kylah was an acclaimed spellcaster across Valenia, and her parents, brothers and sisters lived most of their lives in the spotlight as renowned spellcasters with the powers of Aten, the God of Elements. But her clients, the Tribe of Celtas, had turned her product against her. After years of crafting her name was ruined in a matter of days because she didn't question the integrity of her clients.

With Kylah's bracelet in her possession, the mysterious woman walked out the door. Salathiel wanted to call after her. He still had an injured sister and two dead bodies to deal with, but realized it was better that the councilor left as soon as possible. He let her go and turned his focus to Mirari.

Kylah ran over to the kitchen, shuffling through faintly labeled bottles of herbs in the cabinets. She took a few from each jar, measuring only with the touch of her hands. She soaked them in water before wrapping them in a kitchen cloth and a long string she found near the sink. Kylah took her remedy to Mirari, lifted a corner of her shirt and wrapped the medicine around her bare skin with the string.

"It stops inflammation," Kylah said, patting the cloth. "Will also help with the pain, but I can't put your bones back together. Healing is not within my knowledge."

But it was enough to calm Mirari, who kept one hand on the cloth and the other tightly squeezing Salathiel's hand.

"That's okay... this... doesn't hurt," Mirari lied, teeth clenching and grinding with every breath.

Kylah looked at the girl with pity. She took another glance at the bodies, the blood splattered over the floor, the overturned furniture, and finally rested her gaze on Salathiel. "I've stayed here long enough. I'll get the town healer, then be on my way."

"You don't have to go," Salathiel said, knowing that Kylah

didn't have anyone else to turn to, and he didn't want her living out in the woods again where anyone could be a boar's supper.

But she was sick and tired of this useless bloodshed over her life.

"It's not worth the risk. For all we know, there could be more assassins trailing me. You will both get hurt."

"Kylah, don't."

"We'll protect you," Mirari croaked, hoping she would stay.

But there was nothing either of them could say to make Kylah change her mind. Her thoughts drifted back to her own family. Her brothers and sisters were right — she was a living curse, and misfortune was her best friend. Being a prodigy, being the one chosen to carry Aten's power came at a cost. She was fated to never stay with anyone for too long.

She reached for her cloak. The hood fell perfectly over her head, hiding her face from the moonlight. She pulled out a pouch containing a glistening red and yellow powder and handed it to Salathiel.

"Wear gloves and a mask when you are handling it," she said. "Take the bodies outside. Sprinkle this on the corpses and they'll decompose by dawn." She edged closer to Salathiel and whispered in his ear, "Until we meet again."

She pressed a light peck on his cheek before stepping down the porch stairs, and marched straight ahead into the night.

"Kylah!" Salathiel called to her one last time, but she ignored him.

Fireflies fluttered up from the ground, almost as if they were guiding her home. Every step was filled with determination, but in truth, Kylah didn't know where she was going. Forward was the only direction.

CHAPTER EIGHTEEN

The morning after Shiba's coronation, Neo rode into the Agna fortress with the force of a dozen kinastōnes. Each step he took shook the floor, and he continued down the hall until he made it to Shiba's room, busting it open without knocking. He was assaulted with a shriek and the bare back of a celta princess on Shiba's bed. She glanced over her shoulder.

"Neo!" Mecate shouted as she buried herself under their silk sheets. Shiba sat up.

"Really, Neo?" Shiba grumbled, scratching his disheveled hair. After his long coronation ceremony, he thought he would have plenty of time to rest.

"Sorry, Lord." Neo closed the door, quietly this time, and shouted through the closed door. "I'm afraid you'll have to sober up. We got word that Althaea Main is sending fleets to the Bay Islands."

"They're… what?" Shiba wasn't sure if he heard right, but he was ready to explode. Those remote islands were Minetta's territory and Althaea had no business there.

Mecate pulled on his arm and stroked his hair like he was a

lapdog. His anger dissipated with a sigh. Now that Shiba was region leader of Avon, Mecate had stepped up as his first commander. But she did more than just command – she was possibly a far better tactician than Shiba, and she was the perfect companion to rule alongside a hot-headed Minettan.

Their relationship was no secret. She had as many ill-wishers across the land as supporters for being betrothed to a Minettan region leader. There was a rumor that the marriage was arranged to ensure that the impulsive Shadow Soldier wouldn't wage war on Althaea. But Mecate was more worried about how her people in Altha Hills would retaliate. Though she had left home behind and her father's dangerous and traditional ways of thinking, a part of her was still afraid of what he could do.

"Shall I send our water fleet, My Lord?" Neo called out.

With a couple of grumbles, Shiba hurried to get dressed – it wasn't an option for him. They had to get to work.

Suzan strode to the battle room to look for Gaven and Inigo.

"Sea rovers raided Desdemona. We need to—"

Inigo was already looking over a map of the area. Gaven leaned back on his velvet chair, one almost as grand as Suzan's throne.

"My sources sent word an hour ago," Inigo piped up. "The rovers hit before dawn. Two villages burned to the ground. Hundreds slaughtered."

Suzan gave a startled cry. "But... I just got word about the attack," Suzan said. "How do you have intelligence on the casualties already?"

Inigo feigned modesty with a shrug, and said, "I'd heard rumors yesterday about some suspicious activity from boats treading through the Althaean Sea. I expected an attack on shipping, but…" Inigo shook his head. "By the beard of Saint Tox himself, nobody expected them to take land."

"What else did you hear?"

"They took everything they could carry, and were back at sea before word ever reached us of an attack. By then, the raiders were sailing hard with the wind due west."

There was a knock at the door, and a tall lad peeked inside.

"Excuse me." As he stood up, Inigo bowed to Suzan and shooed his messenger back into the hallway, then closed the door behind him. Suzan walked to Gaven's side at the table map.

"What's your move?"

"I say we chase them." Gaven's chin rested on the balls of his fist. He nudged one of the two metal figurines of a warship placed on the map. "We already have two fleets scouting for those savages, but it's likely they'll try to take land on the Bay Islands. The dense forests are a perfect hideout. They're not easily accessible and nobody lives on those islands. They could take shelter there for a few days, wait for the threat to pass, then sail back to wherever they came from."

"Why not land in Oban or Ophallen?"

"That would be daft. They would be trapped between the Minettan *and* Althaean forces. The only way out of the Bay of Minetta is sailing north." Gaven pointed to the islands. "This area is too narrow and the waters are much too shallow for large ships to weave between these islands. They think we won't go near the islands, but if we trap them there they won't have anywhere to escape."

Suzan nodded. "So you plan on charging straight into Minettan territory to catch the sea rovers?"

"What choice do we have? Can you get word to Mallory?"

"Not to Mallory. As of yesterday—"

"Shiba," he groaned. "I forgot that weasel was taking over."

"He might not be happy about you sending Althaean forces into his waters."

Before Gaven could answer, Inigo stepped back into the room, leaving his courier at the door.

"Shiba? I expect he may be grateful for the help," Inigo announced.

"What makes you so sure?" Gaven asked. Inigo walked over to the comstōne in the far corner of the room. He glanced over the thick directory for the fortress of Agna, then lit the comstōne with a wave of his hand.

"Tepis," a feminine voice answered with no enthusiasm. "I see you got my message."

"Princess Mecate," Inigo sassed back, "or is it Lady Zabato?"

They could hear a bit of shuffling, and a few angry curses in the background. As he got closer to the stone, they could identify the husky voice.

"You got some rat's balls pushing those sea rovers into our territory," Shiba spat.

Mecate hushed him and said, "Would you like to explain the situation?"

"We are trying to catch the thieves that invaded our town," Inigo said. "Hand them over to us, and we won't have a problem."

"Problem?" Shiba's faint voice yelled from afar. "You're treading in *my* waters, flat rat."

Mecate rephrased his words. "Since your ships are already out there, we might as well make them useful. Here's the plan. We'll squeeze them like pincers. We'll drive them from the front, and you'll hold them from the back and cut them off from retreating to their ships."

It was exactly what Gaven had suggested. He smirked at Suzan, waiting for her to stroke his ego.

"With all due respect, Princess Mecate, why should we trust someone who turned against her people?" Inigo said.

"Because your ships aren't going to make it far in the Bay Islands. They'll get stuck in shallow waters, and then you'll have to send more men after your thieves *and* a rescue crew. Do you have that many soldiers to spare, Tepis? And would you be willing to leave Althaean Main so defenseless?"

Inigo narrowed his eyes and looked at his partner.

"She checkmated you there, pal," Gaven said. He pulled himself out of the comfort of his seat and walked over to the comstōne. Along the way, he took his coat and pair of black clōves. Buttoning up his coat, Gaven leaned into the stone. "Shiba has my aura registered in his clōve. Send me the coordinates once they take land, will you Mecate? We'll meet you there."

"Of course, Commander."

Gaven nodded to the door, urging his partner who seemed less enthusiastic to leave.

———

Neo fastened his massive silver gauntlets, while Mecate buckled her armor, and strapped on her shoulder and wrist pads.

"Where do you think you're going?" Shiba asked her.

"To fight. Where else?"

"Not without me you're not."

"You already know why I need to go," she said.

"I do?"

"The sea rovers may be a diversion for Althaea Main to invade Avon. Since it's your first day as region leader, it all sounds too much of a coincidence. You think they're taking advantage of you, and you're right. It's absolutely something

207

those back-stabbing flatties would do. So, you must stay and protect the mainland."

Shiba agreed with her theory. As a former Althaean, Mecate was the logical choice to command this mission in his place. Still, he tried to find an excuse for her not to go.

"I didn't say—"

"Say it fast enough?" she cut in. She tightened the last of her wrist straps, then soothed his burning cheek with a stroke of her loving hand. "You guard the mainland, and Neo and I will take care of the sea rovers. You can handle that, can't you?"

"O-of course."

But an uneasy feeling washed through him as he watched Neo and Mecate rally an army of fighters, and rushed them out of the fortress. Shiba paced around his desk, dreading the silence of the room. How could he sit idle knowing she was about to face danger without him by her side?

CHAPTER NINETEEN

It was the largest fleet of sea rovers anyone had heard of – five vessels that could hold two dozen men each, accompanied by a squadron of fishing boats, smaller and faster. Inigo's sources estimated their numbers to be around two hundred. Once the thieves reached an inner island in the Bay of Minetta, they docked their boats in a hidden cove, nearly out of sight. But the army of Avon had been watching the vessels from afar, waiting for them to choose their island before positioning their men.

Mecate and Neo had brought along a force of a hundred fighters on foot – umbras, aegises, paragons and celtas – trained for years, all bearing the same black shadow crest on their shoulder pads and breastplates. Each of them was instilled with iron-willed discipline.

Mecate examined the island the thieves had chosen. It was covered in dense trees. She understood why they favored this particular piece of land. The center of the island was abundant with fresh water and fields of wild berries. They could survive on the island's natural resources alone for weeks. But the island also offered an advantage to Mecate and her troops. The open land had a field of concave hills, perfect for observing long distances, and perfect for trapping. The battlefield would be a broad valley, bordered by steep hills to the east and west, which would make it nearly impossible to escape, other than by retreating to the beaches. She rallied her ships to dock on the opposite end and set up at the top of the hills.

Gaven and Inigo boarded a smaller, faster boat that was able to catch up with the two ships they had sent earlier. The large ships were stuck at bay, unable to move forward into the island's shallow waters. They began lowering and boarding smaller wooden boats equipped on the ship, and the army of eighty followed their commander to the island of corsairs.

Gaven waved his hand left and right, observing the green light on his clōve, the signal sent from Mecate. It pulsed faster when he pointed it toward one of the islands in the inner bay, vast and decorated with natural forests seemingly untouched by humans.

They found the cove where the sea rovers had docked their boats and landed their own boats along the sandy coast. Their men began rushing in, sand flying from their huge strides. But one person didn't dare step beyond the shore – his partner.

Gaven wasn't surprised. "What's your problem?" He scowled. "You're going to sit this one out too?"

"Commander, if I may? An item of strategy I'd like to point out."

Gaven knew his strategy – anything to avoid a fight.

"Quickly," Gaven demanded. He was anxious to be with his men, cutting through the enemy, instead of cutting through bull-shit with Inigo.

"You're sure to turn the tide in this battle—"

"Not back here I'm not."

"But when the sea rovers find their position hopeless, they

will have to retreat. If not to their boats, then to ours. They have a dozen fine boats to choose from. Someone has to make sure they don't escape. And the last thing you'd want is to be stranded on Minettan land, correct?"

As obvious as it was that Inigo had played another one of his excuses, the idea was rock solid. He hated how persuasive Inigo could be.

"If you leave me with a small force at the beach, we can ensure that not a single one of them will escape. They'll be panicked, disorganized, and I can make them pay with just ten men."

It was hard to argue with such reasoning. Gaven knew he would be doing most of the work, as he had since they became partners.

With Shiba's forces also fighting, he could spare a few. Gaven gestured to the handful of men still getting out of their boats.

"Ten of you stay back with Inigo." As he said that, Gaven rushed into the forest to join the rest of his soldiers.

THE ARMY of Avon created a wall of men across the peak of the hills. They covered shore to shore, making sure not a single one crossed their line. But Mecate and Neo noticed that Inigo's information didn't add up — there were more men on the island than they had expected. Three, no, maybe four hundred sea rovers were laying in the open valley around small campfires and rolled out blankets.

"There's no way those boats carried all these men," Mecate said.

"They must've already been on the island," Neo said, realizing something even more dire. "That means they'll know where to hide."

"Not if they're dead."

Neo chuckled. "You really do think like a flatty."

As soon as they got word that Gaven's army had landed on shore, Mecate led the first charge of men down the hill.

The sea rovers heard their unexpected guests roaring with battle cries. They saw the army advancing with red flags from the hills. They hurried to regroup and formed an offensive line. Others made a swift retreat, taking only the soiled and torn rags on their unwashed hairy bodies.

Mecate began to mold a collection of crystals in her hands, as menacing as a lady's stiletto heels. With a single sweep, the shards rained down on dozens of thieves. The first three men fell before they could take their next breath, crystals nailed to their skulls. The archer's arrows impaled their comrades, and the remaining crooks were left to clash swords with the foot soldiers.

The retreating rovers didn't get far before they met the blades of another force coming from the shore. In blue uniforms, they hurdled over bushes and charged like scattered bees. Their job was to simply hack at anything they encountered, and if one of them slipped by, they knew the criminals wouldn't be able to get far without encountering another Althaean soldier.

Gaven's men had caught them completely off guard, tearing into their rear like a cloud of wasps. Now forced to defend both their front and back lines, the rovers had no choice but to put up a fight. Weapons clashed as a choir of metal sang through the island. From the more skilled fighters on Gaven's team, waves of kore elements – earth, lightning, and all – danced through the air.

The barbaric hooligans were no match for the trained armies of Minetta and Althaea. The sea rovers were used to boarding fat merchant ships manned by terrified crews, or looting defenseless villages that couldn't fight back. Facing a real army? This wasn't what they had signed up for.

Gaven felt his pride swell, watching the way his men advanced into the enemy lines. Four rovers broke loose, now running toward him.

Without much thought, the men raised and swung their cutlass. Gaven slashed his spear through the neck of the first, then ran the next one through.

He stared at the bodies at his feet.

He was still not used to it – not to the sight of decapitated men and definitely not to the sour stench of blood – but it was a feeling he had kept suppressed for the sake of the soldiers he led. It had to be done. Without hesitation. Without mercy.

Caught between the buzzsaw of Gaven's ferocity and the mechanical effectiveness of Mecate's assault, the sea rovers were being decimated. They were a disorganized force at the best of times, relying only on the shock and speed of a sudden attack. Their only plan was to roll over the armies like a wave – hacking, slashing, cutting them down with nothing but a dull blade and a man's pride.

The wall of soldiers at the top of the hill charged behind Mecate, sweeping down the last of the thieves. With his heavy armor, Neo was nothing less than an overgrown armadillo, almost impervious to swords or spears. He snapped spines and crushed skulls like a child kicking down his little brother's sand castle.

The sea rovers had disintegrated, and their entire force melted like a mountain of sugar in heavy rain. As panic spread, it became a rout. They paid a terrible price trying to fight past Gaven's forces, falling like wheat before the scythe.

As the bloody clash raged in the valley behind her, Mecate caught sight of advancing men in blue uniforms. She was drawn to the glow of a spear, a magnificent display of power that she knew could only be from the one they called the Valiant Tiger.

He was mercilessly hacking at the rovers, one soul leaving after another.

Even though Mecate had taken life herself, there was something about watching Gaven fight that made her queasy. He was ruthless, like a predator playing with his food, disregarding the pain his enemies endured. That was the way they trained soldiers in Althaea, something Mecate had always disapproved of.

"Flatties." Mecate grunted, mumbling a rainbow of disparaging slurs under her breath. "Pure savages."

Almost as if he had heard her, Gaven pounced over the dead bodies and greeted the exiled princess.

"I thought we had more men than the thieves," Gaven said. "This is almost double."

"There were some already hiding out on the island. We'll have to be a little more diligent to make sure we get every last one of them."

Gaven nodded and trotted off to swing at the next rover who was coming at Mecate from behind. She sensed his presence but didn't bother moving away, knowing that Gaven would take care of him.

Gaven's spear slashed the man's chest, and he died instantly. Mecate could feel drops of blood splatter on her, and felt mildly agitated that he soiled her garments.

"Easy there, Tiger." She gave him a warning glare, but despite the firm expression on her face, Gaven knew she was joking. The few times he had seen her before she was exiled, Mecate had seemed a modest woman, the kind who couldn't care less about wealth. And though her confidence had skyrocketed, Gaven could sense that her tenderhearted aura had not changed in the slightest.

"Don't tell me you've lost the thrill of fighting, Princess."

"I certainly don't enjoy it as much as you do."

A hum rung in his right ear, and the discomforting sound of

arrows whirling through the air caught his attention. Gaven hesitated, not wanting to admit that countering against a herd of arrows was one thing he still couldn't master in a real battle. He could easily parry fighters at close range. He could deflect throwing stars. But there was little he could do against flimsy points on a stick.

Mecate waved her hand in a circular motion, and a thin disk of ice formed in front of them. The ice stretched as tall as their bodies and she threw one toward Gaven. He reached forward to catch it, but the disk hovered in the air in front of him, deflecting the incoming arrows. Then, the disks launched toward the archers, weaving through roots and bushes until they knocked the archers off their feet.

Mecate caught sight of a dozen more archers running from the corner of her eye. They scattered, running for the shore. She tried to chase after them, but more thieves blocked her way. Gaven skewered one with his spear and flung him away from her. He did the same with the next, and headbutted another before hacking each limb off. Mecate turned away. His savage tactics were proving her point. A fatal blow would've been enough, but Gaven was making a show out of the dead.

"Can you cut them off?" he asked.

"Can I what?" She seemed offended by such a request.

Gaven gestured to a rocky stream not far from where they were.

"Most of us are on this side of the island. Inigo has the shore, but I doubt he'll be able to hold off that many on his own. You go after them and I'll stay on this side with the Silver Fist to take down the rest of them."

Mecate now understood what he was getting at, but it also meant that she had to trust the Valiant Tiger not to double-cross her army. She hadn't known him long enough to be comfortable with either decision, and the fact that Gaven was her fiancée's sworn enemy made the situation even more difficult.

It was time to rely on her firm belief that not everything could be answered by logic and reasoning. The celtas in Altha Hills called her crazy, but the pull in her chest was far stronger than their baseless words.

"When our mind fails to reason we must follow the heart," Mecate had told her father before she left the temple, and now those words were coming back to her. Her mind told her to never trust Althaeans, but her soul had a speck of faith in this rising warrior. She could tell he was here to fight, not to conquer. Perhaps he didn't even see blue and red, just one side fighting against a common enemy. Mecate could sense that beyond all that bloodlust was a greater spirit of loyalty, a quintessence of faith and resilience that could even make Oris question his judgment. She would trust anyone with characteristics like that, Althaean or not.

Her eyes darted back to the stream. Focused and steady, she raised her arms up high. Water began to climb and mold like a solid element, dancing in the air. It towered higher than the trees, stretching as far as the stream ran on the island, from shore to shore. It took the unfortunate men in its path along before it froze into solid ice. Mecate gave a firm nod to Gaven before dashing toward the shore.

The battle had lasted for only thirty minutes when some Althaean soldiers came racing back, chased by a flood of savage men with scimitars. Inigo let out a small yelp, seeing rugged barbarians advancing toward him. The men that were left with him charged back at the rovers, defending their fleeing comrades.

Inigo had his sword drawn, waving it in front of him with a quaking hand, hoping to scare off the barbarians. But they didn't scare that easily. One charged at him and swung down his ax. Inigo jumped away in time, the insides of his shirt and shoes now coated in white sand. The ax lodged into the stump behind him, and the barbarian tugged hard, trying to pull it out. Inigo raised his unsteady blade and cut down the distracted man.

The bearded man's head tumbled onto the sand and hit Inigo's feet. He cringed, almost ready to puke, but before he could, another man came at him with a mace and a sneering set of yellow crooked teeth. Three more advanced from his right. Inigo threw his sword at them, hoping it would either scare them away or lodge into their limbs. But the dull side of the sword hit one of the men in the chest, and he ignored it like it was a bug on a log.

Inigo fled like a brown hare caught in the middle of hunting season, dashing to the side of the forest where no men had emerged. Mecate caught sight of the coward with four men on his tail, wondering why he didn't just take a boat.

Then it came to her in a beat; he probably didn't know how to row one.

She raced after him.

They reached a thick part of the forest covered in shrubbery. She could see no one in front of her. She scanned the area left and right, searching for Inigo and the rovers.

One misstep and Mecate's foot slid against the soft mud. She felt her body free-fall for what seemed to be an eternity, until she crashed against a cold surface. Rubbing her dirt-covered bottom, she shook off the pain and looked up.

"By Oris' soggy balls, this trench must be fifty feet high!" She saw no easy way out, but the trench was wide enough to run two carriages through, giving her some options.

Mecate heard the battle cries of men rushing in front of her. She held her hand up, creating a shield disk moments before a blade reached her head. Then came more, from left and right. She pushed her ice shield forward, launching away the man in front. She needed both her hands to create the ice shards that circled her body. With a swipe the ice chards launched forward, piercing the limbs of the first line of men. But there were more.

She noticed about two dozen men had also fallen into this trench, or maybe had taken refuge in it. Two dozen untrained crooks were nothing to her, but Mecate stood up and felt her leg tear like it was being pulled apart. She slumped back to the ground.

She gasped, realizing she would be unable to walk or stand. With an ice shield in one hand and a herd of needles in the other, she tried to hold off the thieves. She glanced around for Inigo, who was nowhere to be found. Then she caught sight of the fox peeking from behind a tree at the top of the pit.

"A little help here?" Mecate called out, barely able to keep up her shield. But he only stared. She even saw the edge of his mouth perk into a smile for a split second before he dashed out of her sight.

"Tepis!" she screamed, but she knew the chances of him coming back were close to none. Distracted, Mecate's chest suddenly exploded with pain, then she heard the crack of a rib or two. She coughed forward, choking out red. In a fury she yanked the dagger from her chest and headbutted the man who had stabbed her. Now she had no shield and the surrounding men raised the blades over her head.

She rolled out of the way just in time to avoid the daggers and swords, but she had a broken leg that left her immobile, and now a hole in her chest. Another blade slashed across her back, opening a streak of red under her torn robes.

A sense of hopelessness overwhelmed her. She clenched her teeth, wanting to scream and cry. Her nails dug up loose dirt as she tried to endure the pain. She knew she was better than that, and her mission was far from over.

"I will not die here!" She screamed at herself, thinking of the people in Avon she had yet to help, the men here that relied on her leadership, even her little sister who would be waiting anxiously to hear another one of her stories.

Then her thoughts drifted to Shiba. He was waiting for her to return home – to rule by his side – and she was not going to fail him.

With a loud battle cry, Mecate focused her remaining energy on her kore. Her hands erupted in a blinding blue light that shone beyond the ditch and above the treeline. In a gallant roar, she stretched her hands wide, and the ground erupted into a cavity, a geode of sharp geometric shapes as azure as her silky curtain of hair that covered the gashes on her back. The crystals pierced and crushed all in the ditch, swallowing enemies faster than a thorn-tailed whale, and continued to rise.

As suddenly as it had begun, all was calm. Mecate had won the fight, and her crystals were tall enough for her to climb out.

But with no strength left in her, she curled in the smooth center of her frozen masterpiece, protected by the spikes around her, caressed like a sleepy fairy in a flower. The ice numbed her pain and the last of her strength flowed to her eyes, trying to keep her eyelids up. With her thoughts slowing and her consciousness being pulled down, she saw herself home, in Avon, wrapped in Shiba's arms as he kissed down her neck. When he called her name, she couldn't find the strength to respond. Instead she smiled and closed her eyes, sinking into the warmth of his body and giving into the relaxing temptation.

And with one last, shallow breath, Mecate drifted into a peaceful slumber.

CHAPTER TWENTY

Shiba didn't have it in his heart to be angry. He was consumed by grief so crippling he could neither sleep nor eat. While they had successfully killed most of the sea rovers and captured the others, Althaean–Minettan relations only got worse. Shiba felt a blood-boiling thirst for vengeance on Gaven and Inigo, the people who were responsible for Mecate's safety.

The Council knew if this feud escalated, it would plunge the two empires into open warfare. They had managed to force Shiba to keep the peace for the moment.

The princess was welcomed home with a grand ceremony, covered in the beauty of white and violet flowers that bloomed only in the coves of Allete. It may have been the largest gathering of foreigners on Althaean soil since the birth of the alliance. As beautiful as the day was, no one entered the city with a smile. Every noble house in Minetta came to pay their respects to the Althaean princess that fought on their behalf. Six councilors and representatives of the main tribes arrived from Valenia. And though many still looked at Mecate as a traitor, she was hailed from peasants across the land, from the wealthy merchants of

Axillaire to the sea-faring fishermen of Nanaka. They brought flowers, gifts, even cattle for the royal family of Altha City.

This was not the way the High Priest had imagined her homecoming. His thick, white beard absorbed single trails of tears before anyone could notice. He could see the brutal cuts on her cheek and hands that the maids had tried so hard to cover with powder.

One of his mistresses and her daughter held on tightly to each other as they looked at Mecate's body, eyes pooling with tears. Still well short of her teens, Mecate's sister was devastated, swaying between wailing hysterics and fainting spells.

Shiba's silence had Neo more concerned. Neo could feel Shiba's stirring emotions in his own heart. Shiba was anything but calm, and Neo wondered how much longer the numbness would last.

"Come, Princess Hime," her mother said, pulling the distraught child to her side. The Priest had prepared a eulogy and had asked the Bishop to read it in his place. The Bishop praised the ambitious nature of their late princess, and also reminded the crowd of why Mecate should've never left her duty at Altha Hills. Oris had disapproved of her actions, and his judgment was clear.

"Oris can go judge rat sacks for all I care," Gaven muttered. But his partner had a different opinion.

"He's got a point," Inigo said. "If she didn't leave, she would've still been alive."

Gaven clenched his teeth. There was nothing that irritated him more than a coward's words. But out of respect for Mecate's funeral and Althaea Main's reputation, Gaven held back his trembling fist.

Inigo's official statement claimed that he hadn't been with Mecate at the time of the attack, and by the time he reached her she was already gone. Gaven didn't believe a word of it. The snake had dropped one of his signature-gold daggers not far from the pit where Mecate was found. It wasn't hard to piece the story together, but Gaven, for the sake of Althaea, had to discard the evidence before Neo's men arrived.

What was worse – the emotions he felt in their bond told a different story. Inigo didn't weep or panic; he was as calm as ever, filled with pride over the fact he survived and she didn't. During the battle, Gaven felt a spike of adrenaline that wasn't his own, one that was accompanied by a speck of joy. It was a disgusting, nauseous feeling, one he often had to suppress since they had become partners. But for how much longer could he put up with the curse of the partner bind? Inigo provided political benefits – that he didn't deny – but things were much easier on the battle-field when Gaven was on his own.

At the end of the service, he caught Shiba's soulless eyes, now swollen into a furious lightning storm. But he could tell it wasn't meant for him. The merciless umbra was heading toward Inigo.

Neo saw the advance and went after his partner. He grabbed his arm but Shiba pulled free, ready to take a swing at the stuck-up noble.

"This is your fault!" Shiba shouted. He pulled his hand back ready for a hard punch.

Gaven stepped in just before Shiba unleashed his rage. Gaven felt a slight impact, but the punch wasn't strong enough to knock him down. If Shiba wanted to, Gaven would've let him take another swing. He closed his eyes, lowered his head and waited for the Shadow Soldier's punishment.

"Stop, Shiba!" Neo said. "That won't help," The giant was capable of carrying his partner away, but he didn't want to belittle his region leader in the public's eye.

Shiba's anger, on the other hand, flared like a rabid hound's and he showed no signs of calming down.

"Why do you protect him?" Shiba scowled. "He's a disgraceful coward!"

Gaven said, "It was an accident and there was nothing we could—"

"Damn you to Inferna, Gaven! I'm not going to let him off so you can put him on latrine duty. I'll have him flayed to the bone. I don't care if he's a Tepis. He killed Mecate!"

The accusation drew all eyes on the warriors and their partners. Gaven knew he had to deny the allegations; it was his duty as a partner and as an Althaean. As much as he wanted to hold Inigo accountable for his negligence, his coin-soaked royal lineage wasn't going to allow it. Arguing about it was pointless.

"You are not in your right mind," Gaven said, now gesturing over to Neo. "Please excuse us—"

Shiba struck Gaven in the jaw with his head, and Gaven stumbled backward.

"STOP!" Neo pulled them apart like they were nothing more than two schoolchildren in a flailing temper tantrum.

Shiba was apoplectic with fury. "You better think twice about becoming region leader because once you do, I'll be the one coming into your waters. You're going to beg—"

Neo clapped his huge, open hand across the back of Shiba's skull. It looked like barely a love tap. But from Neo, it was a lot of love. His partner was immediately silenced, now slumped over his arm. Neo apologized profusely to Gaven and Inigo as he carried Shiba's body away.

"Quite a temper that one's got, hasn't he?" Inigo said, fixing the wrinkles on his button-up shirt.

"I should've let him hit you," Gaven spat. He dared Inigo to feed him the same lies he had to the public. "Everything he said is true. She would've been alive if you had done something."

"What could I do? There were too many of them, I—"

Gaven slapped him – his open-handed blow had enough

power behind it to flatten Inigo to the floor. As blood seeped from his mouth, Inigo knew enough to stay down.

"You share my strength! Even that wasn't enough to shroud the cowardice in your blood."

With a hand over his cheek, Inigo hissed, "Things happen in battle, events that no one can control. Perhaps if you had more command experience, you'd know that."

Gaven raised his hand to strike again. Of all the times he had to endure his partner's bullshit… this was twisting his last strand of patience. One slap was barely enough to satisfy the emotions raging through him. The only reason he couldn't act on them was because he had promised Suzan to not make a scene at the funeral.

"I'll let you sell your story to Shiba, Suzan, and all the Council, but don't think I don't know when you're lying." Gaven lowered his hand and spat at Inigo's feet. "I felt what you saw. You used Mecate as bait, and you don't feel even a hint of regret or mercy."

Inigo picked himself off the ground.

"And do you not feel the rush of joy when you have outwitted your enemy?" He said, inching closer to Gaven until he was breathing down his neck. "If you're going to talk about guilt, you should look at yourself in the mirror, *partner*. Think carefully, Gaven. Whose side are you on here? After all I've done for you? You would stand with the Minettans against your own partner? That won't sit well with the public."

Inigo had a point. Why did Gaven care about this one when every other life taken before him meant nothing? Though it wasn't within his rights to have an opinion about Mecate's heritage, he saw her neither as Althaean nor Minettan. She was an ambitious fighter, and a remarkable spellcaster who knew no fear. She had Gaven's respect. If he was given the chance, he would fight by her side on the battlefield a thousand times over.

"I'm done covering your lies, Inigo," Gaven said. "I'm sick of looking the other way when you cheat, and steal, and blackmail anyone you can."

"And yet you still don't understand. This is how the game is played. You have the upper hand because of my family ties. I'm the reason you are who you are today."

Gaven knew he was right. Gaven was willing to do anything to become the next region leader. The prize was so close, but to live another day with Inigo as his partner? No, he couldn't. No position was worth the cost of treachery and betrayal. He would rather die as a forgotten man than to live with dishonor.

"I don't need your connections," Gaven said. "And I don't need you either."

He waved his hand and drew a symbol with his finger. A path of light followed, and a seal illuminated in front of him. Inigo's eyes widened when he realized that his partner was not bluffing.

"I hereby vanquish this bond…"

"Gaven, you can't…" Inigo pleaded, his voice had lost all of its calmness. "Without me your whole battalion will be talking shit behind your back. Suzan isn't going to make you region leader without a partner."

"I'll take that risk."

He swiped his hand downward, shattering the seal in two. In an instant, Gaven felt as if a boulder was lifted off his shoulders, his limbs light and nimble. His body welcomed a new, refreshing breath of air as the light faded, and their partnership was no more.

Gaven gave Inigo another rough shove that made him stumble back. When he turned, he caught Suzan's glare. A crowd had just witnessed him debase one of the most prominent families in Althaea.

Good or bad, Gaven was used to this attention; all these expectations to be fulfilled, judgments over every breath he took.

He may have been a child prodigy, but like delicate ruthia petals his reputation fell apart as fast as it had bloomed. Was it downhill from now on? Were his glory days over?

Gaven seemed to have made every mistake he possibly could have. His careless actions took the life of an Althaean princess. Now, he anticipated a war with Avon's region leader, and he didn't have Althaea's wealthiest nobles to back him up.

Yet, he didn't regret it. For once, he had acted on his conscience.

He turned to Inigo and the rest of the bewildered attendees. In a dramatic swipe, he yanked Inigo's badge from his vest. "The army gladly accepts your resignation. Now get out of my sight."

GAVEN RETURNED TO ALTHAEA MAIN, shaken and ready to collapse. He was tired of the straight face he had to put on as he passed by the soldiers and servants. A commander could not show weakness, but after all the mistakes he had made, what harm would it do to surrender for just one night?

The road to region leader required more than he could have ever imagined. And now he wasn't sure if it was worth it.

The soldiers passed by him without a word. They had no doubt, by the fire in his eyes, that Gaven would tear them to shreds, or send them to the guillotine if they angered him.

Gaven could hear the soldiers whispering. Mecate? Inigo? Whatever rumor was stirring about him now, he couldn't care less.

Gaven took a seat in front of the lily pond in the courtyard. It was the perfect place to meditate, but he found it hard to convince himself to close his eyes. He liked the still night, the trickling of the water and the dance of the rainbow trout. The water reminded him of Mecate, the master of water and ice kore. Their victory would not have been possible without her. To die young was such a waste of talent.

But that was the nature of war, the cost of being a fighter. And if he were to continue going down this path as a commander of Althaean Main, he surely had more losses to come.

He heard footsteps shuffling across the garden. From the sound itself, if not from the distinctively jolly aura, Gaven could tell who it was. The bulky soldier approached Gaven, and invited himself to the seat next to him. Gaven was ready to berate his comrade for disturbing his peace, but found he had no energy left. He knew this particular fellow liked to talk a lot, was dumb as a trout, ran his mouth at the worst of times, but he sure could fight. His smile was always as bright as his hair, complementing his perfect set of teeth. He was handsome enough to make the ladies swoon, and rowdy enough to rally a team. But Gaven didn't want rainbows and sunshine right now. He sighed and continued to stare at the moon's reflection in the water.

"What do you want, Haynes?" Gaven grumbled.

"Nothing. You just look like you need some company," he said, stretching his arms and yawning. "Too bad with Inigo, huh? You think Her Honor will be mad?"

"Geez, word sure does travel fast," Gaven said, but he was prepared to justify his actions to Suzan and every soldier on fortress grounds. "I don't care if she doesn't make me region leader. I'd rather stay as a commander than spend another day with that lying bastard."

Haynes nodded dramatically after every word, as if he wanted to make sure the gods above saw that he agreed with his commander's decision.

"You know what makes you great, sir? You live by the Paragon's Conduct. You are as perfect as a warrior could get. Inigo? Well, he doesn't have courage, justice, or loyalty. Scums like that couldn't possibly match your level of integrity. I'm sure if you tell Her Honor that, she will understand."

"Without a partner, I won't be the leader she wants."

"Don't be so hard on yourself. You keep blaming yourself, carrying everyone's burden, but you don't need to. You don't need a partner, you have us, your team. We're here for you."

Gaven snorted at the thought, but Haynes was happy to finally get a chuckle out of him.

"There's no one carrying my weight," Gaven said. "Half of the people here despise me."

"No! I mean—" Haynes paused. "Yes, you're intimidating, but sir, I think anyone who has followed your command agrees that you act with a big heart, and that's something not a lot of commanders do. If the tiger fights with all his might to protect the people around him, then there's no reason to fear its roar or fangs."

"What a bucket of feces." Gaven knew Haynes was trying to help, but it wasn't working.

"I'm serious, sir! You act all tough but… deep down I can see that you always have good intentions." He smiled big, nudging Gaven to get some emotion out of him. Gaven was sure he was asking to get punched. "C'mon Tiger, lighten up. I miss that old side of you."

The old side of him? The old farm boy who spent his days hunting boar, or the new recruit who cleaned up his comrade's slop?

Both of them were long gone. Where he was going, there was no need for trivial friendships and emotional attachments. He closed his eyes and thought of the only words that mattered.

Keep moving forward.

CHAPTER TWENTY-ONE

Four Weeks After the Grand Ball

A longside Haynes, Mirari rode behind the dozen guards sent to the surrounding villages. She kept focused on the imperfect dwellings they passed. She would've thought the villages were deserted if not for the half-dozen commoners, tending to their potted plants and haggling over prices.

She heard a woman beg for her life… followed by a scream.

Mirari didn't dare look. All silent once more, the soldiers trudged onto the next house. One of the homes had a large hole in the roof. Only a cannon could have caused such massive damage. She gazed at the rooftops as soldiers checked identification tags and residential papers. If the villagers didn't have them – if they were simply misplaced – it was enough to mark them as a traitor. There had already been two in this village.

"Please, good sir. I haven't done a thing." Mirari heard the homeowner beg just like the last. She knew what came next. "Oris, have mercy—"

His words were cut off with a strangled cry.

Mirari tightened her grip on the reins. The numbers would only grow as time passed. As word spread, most complied without a struggle, weary and resigned. Occasionally there were those who resisted the army. They greeted merciless death at the door, hoping their last would make an impact. So far, it hadn't.

"This area was hit hardest by the Althaean Siege," Haynes told her, coming up to her horse and offering an apple. Her steed seized it in one bite.

Mirari could see the truth in his words. Many of the buildings were left torn and damaged, some on the verge of collapse with dangling wood exposed like a badly broken bone. But Mirari had no true interest in the buildings. There was a somber feeling draped over these villages. The people should've felt safe knowing the army was there. Instead, they cowered behind their doors, barely showing their dirt-covered faces.

"If you told his Honor you don't want to go on these raids, I'm sure he'd understand."

That wasn't an option. Mirari swore to help Gaven contain the rising rebellion. Even if she returned to Minetta, her duty would be more of the same. As a Knight, she had to ensure there was peace between the three empires. The rebels must be stopped. She knew this. She understood this. However, there was a persistent thought that dogged her steps as she had spent the last week scouting with Haynes.

"Do you truly believe this is working?" Mirari asked, her gaze drifting to the ground. She had faith in Gaven's decisions, but no ability to execute them.

Haynes sighed loudly with a similar frown on his face. "Loyalty is important in Althaea," he said. "The price to pay for betrayal is non-negotiable, but the reward for loyalty is bountiful. Once we weed out these rebels, we can focus on supplying these villages again."

"But—" Haynes looked at her and she bit back her words. He was right. She knew Gaven had the interest of the people in mind. Even if she didn't understand, she knew that much. It didn't matter if she didn't agree with Althaea's policies. It was her duty to support Gaven. "I understand," she said firmly. "Thank you."

"Of course, Milady," Haynes said with a big smile. A soldier waved to him. Mirari could see that most of them had turned around as the last of the soldiers finished checking the last house. Haynes clapped his hands. "Excellent. I think now's a good time for some ale. What do you say?"

"Go on ahead," she said. "I want to look around some more."

Haynes scanned the area, but said, "Okay. Don't stray too far." She watched Haynes pat a few soldiers on the back, nudging them toward the alehouse and disappearing inside.

Leaving her horse tied to the fencepost, she made a slow circuit around the town. It wasn't big, just a collection of misshapen houses bunched together like a cluster of mushrooms. The shriek of children's laughter caught her attention, but she barely caught sight of the young ones before they were hustled inside under the weary eyes of their parents.

Sighing to herself, she turned around to rejoin Haynes. She stopped in sight of the tavern. There was a nobleman by her horse, running his hand over its mane. She recognized him, unfortunately.

She approached slowly, glancing toward the alehouse. As though sensing her presence, Inigo calmly looked at her with a friendly smile. Narrowing her eyes, Mirari coldly asked, "Did you follow me here?"

He laughed. "Me? No, of course not." He waved his hand toward a wagon stacked with crates. Two men delicately unloaded the crates into the tavern while more soldiers entered the tavern. "Just business as usual. Care to sample our finest batch? On the house for a friend."

"I have work to do," she said, stepping around him.

"No, no, I insist, darling." He stretched his arm out before she could walk past. "I really think we should be friends."

Mirari considered forcing the issue. It wouldn't take much effort to twist his arm and shove him over the fence. Gaven wouldn't mind. He'd probably even be happy about it. Unfortunately, attacking someone from the House Tepis wouldn't help Gaven either.

"Don't you think we have a lot in common? His Honor's former partner and his *current* partner."

She pushed his arm aside. "I know about you. We're nothing alike."

"Would Gaven agree?" Smiling, Inigo reached into his inner pocket and pulled out a folded piece of paper. Unfolding it, he glanced at the words written within. "Miss Mirari Zanette or so it says." He handed it to her.

Mirari stared at the crinkled paper. It had her name, her birth town, family. There wasn't much else on it. "What do you want, Tepis?" she demanded. Doubt started to creep over her as a self-satisfied smile grew across his face.

He snatched the paper back. "It looks pretty official, doesn't it? Could've fooled just about anyone." He held the paper up to the light and pointed at the stamp. "Except it's missing the reflective mark." He leaned against the fence, tucking the paper away.

Mirari felt a knot in her throat. Holding her breath, she tucked her trembling hand behind her back.

"You see, I wanted Gaven to take a look at this to make sure I was seeing this correctly. I mean, it's hardly fair that you're checking everyone's papers and no one's checking yours. But I thought I'd give you a chance to explain yourself, friend." He waved his hand toward her. "Well? Go on. Explain. Why are your records fake?"

"This is ridiculous. I don't know where you found this, but no one is going to believe this lie."

He chuckled. "I found this in the House of Records." Narrowing her eyes, she glared at him. He patted his pocket. "And don't think about just taking it. It'll be worse for you if someone were to go looking for your records and found this missing."

Mirari swallowed hard, heart nearly jumping out of her chest. He smirked at the discomfort she couldn't hide.

"Yes, I think we're starting to understand each other, aren't we, Milady?" She didn't say anything, voice caught in her throat. "Because we're such good friends now, I'm willing to overlook this for a small favor," he continued. "Forget the search. Just sit back and enjoy some quality wine." He narrowed his eyes. "Leave the towns alone and tell Gaven you didn't find anything."

She hissed. "Is that it? You're hiding something out here? Is that also why you're funding the relief efforts? So Gaven won't find you out?"

He laughed. "Nothing so nefarious. I just think Gaven is acting a little rash. Storming through towns, beheading villagers. It's bad for business. You're a merchant. You understand." She scowled at him.

He shook his head, placing his hand on his forehead before brushing back his pale hair. "I was his partner. I know how he thinks. He has a tendency to make things personal; surely you agree. And frankly, I think you're the only one who can make him see reason."

She scoffed and took a glance at the alehouse. Why did she bother? No one could help her escape this fate. She anticipated the day when someone would unravel her past... but didn't expect it to be held against her like this.

"And if you can't, well…" He patted his pocket. "This might fall into the wrong hands. What do you say, darling?"

Mirari's gaze drifted to the ground. What if he found out more about her? What consequences would be brought upon her or the Knights? Or even Gaven? She couldn't bring herself to make a deal with Inigo. Then again, what choice did she have?

PART III

CHAPTER TWENTY-TWO

Eight Years Ago

Loud men bantered and hollered with beers in a crowded tavern. A sturdy old man cloaked in a dark hood sat at the bar. He nursed a lukewarm ale with a bored look on his face. He looked like a gentle giant, stopping for a drink before heading home, and no one dared to approach him; not with the dragon talla inked across his arm. He had fought on behalf of the Althaean army for two generations. There was nothing he loved more than his region, and he wore his mark with pride. But in the dragon's mouth was a special symbol – a swirl of fire, an ancient symbol of prosperity. That was the part that made all heads turn away.

"To hell with region leaders," a drunken man spat. "They don't care about us small fries. We got nothing to offer them."

"Sure we do," mumbled his drunk buddy. "The fruit of our labor. The sweat off our brow."

"The sweat off your balls, more like!" He earned the gruff laughter of several fellow pickled drinkers.

The man had his eyes on his drink but his ears perked in the direction of the conversation. Sundown was the best time to pick up the latest information around town, but mostly all he heard was braggarts touting their sexual conquests, and angry commoners on the verge of revolt. The latter was getting worse. He tilted his head back to soak in his ale.

The rise of their new region leader brought as much good as harm depending on whose side they were on. No one challenged how strong their region leader was. He was undoubtedly the best in the empire, perhaps the best in the alliance. But he was different from Region Leader Suzan, who had moved on to take a seat on the Council. Suzan focused on military strength, keeping Althaea Main and its borders secured for decades. This tiger was more progressive. He shifted the region's priorities to more infrastructure, more agriculture, and the strangest of all, more foreigners.

There was nothing wrong with demanding new infrastructure. He would've liked to see fewer buildings in shambles, windows that weren't broken, and alleys that didn't reek of feces. Plus, as the capital of Althaea, it was about time Althaea Main kept up-to-date with the growing hāstal technology.

He saw agriculture as the main problem. Most of Althaea's lands were dry, useless. And as much as Althaeans didn't want to admit it, most of their produce was imported from Minetta. The only lands that were sustainable for growth were patches in Althaea Main and Evaleen. Region Leader Gaven's solution to this issue was clear – lessen Althaea Main's dependence on other territories and increase jobs for the locals. It would take time, but with the help of hāstal technology and diligent landscaping, the poor would thrive off the production of local goods.

If people could bear the struggle for a few years, they would see that it will benefit them in the long run. He knew that Althaeans were impatient. They liked immediate results. Being

Althaean was a game to see who could milk resources the fastest. They didn't believe that hard work paid off, because it simply wasn't true in Althaea. Here, you had to be born lucky. The nobles only got wealthier, and the peasants only got starvation. That was how life was, and if one did get lucky, they devoted their lives to Oris if they wanted to keep such luck. The atheists? Well, they were in the alehouse.

As for bringing in foreigners…

He heard that Region Leader Gaven was planning to abolish Althaea Main's Separation Law. It would be the first Althaean region to do so, and it may be the last straw for some Althaeans. Yes, Althaeans were used to foreign merchants and nobles traveling in their empire, but those people came only on official business. A Minettan, Valenian, or any other person of a different origin was forbidden to plant their roots on Althaean soil. That was the way the law was set since the formation of the Council hundreds of years ago.

The Separation Law never applied to Valenia, and over the last century every Minettan region leader had abolished the Separation Law. Co-existence was the norm in those territories, but Althaea stayed frozen in time.

Revoking the Separation Law would be the right move, but too sudden. The problem was that he was instilling change and Althaeans weren't used to that.

His decisions sparked debate across the lands. Some conspiracy theorists believed that Region Leader Gaven had bigger, more nefarious plans, ones that disregarded the interest of his people. Perhaps he even had an agenda to strike Minetta and break centuries of peace. But those who saw the benefits of open borders said he did what should've been done decades ago.

The man watched the empire began to split. He scoffed, knowing this was what happened when the young and ambitious ruled before they had matured.

The last drop of ale fell down his throat, just as the men behind him became louder. He watched the short, brown-cloaked woman next to him hop from her seat and make for the door. No doubt, she got her pay for the week.

"Brothers!" one shouted, pounding on the bar. "The only way to stand up like a man is to throw off the yoke of our noble oppressors!"

The man nodded. This drunk would have no problem gaining supporters for his cause, but the rising cacophony reminded him that it was time to leave before a fight broke out. He shoved his way through the foul stench of sweating men.

The man exited the tavern, keeping the cloak over his head. He had taken only a few steps before he was drawn to a commotion a few steps away.

Two soldiers from the army of Althaea Main had detained the small woman he had seen earlier. Ignoring her false protests of innocence, the soldiers secured her hands behind her back. One of them patted her down more thoroughly than appropriate. But he seemed to feel justified as his search paid off with two daggers, a throwing star, and a stash of small pouches, each with a handful of coins. She struggled to break free, trying to reach for the coins the soldier had just confiscated.

"I reckon these don't belong to you," the soldier said. With her hands cuffed behind her back, she was tugged along, heading for Althaea Main's fortress.

The man sighed in relief. Perhaps it was a sign that luck was on his side. The time was now to carry out his plan.

CHAPTER TWENTY-THREE

A long line of unhappy prisoners were hustled toward the dungeons. The string of miscreants reached the fortress, and the lead soldier saluted.

"Your Honor," he greeted the young region leader. Gaven looked at the captives, noting their worn-out clothes and dirty skin.

"Keeping the streets safe for the common man, I see," he commented.

"Just as you like, Sir."

"How many today?" Gaven asked, sounding glum about the whole affair as he turned to Commander Haynes.

"Twenty-six," reported the bubbly stump of muscle, glued to his lord like a newborn pup.

Gaven shook his head. "I only wish there were enough jobs to keep men from stealing just to feed their families."

"May Oris hear your plea, Lord," Haynes said. "But if it's so damn hard for Althaeans to make a decent living, why have you opened our borders to admit foreigners? Sounds like even more idlers without jobs, if you ask me."

"Are you actually asking?"

Haynes grinned big hoping his master would forgive him for the hundreds of questions he raised on a daily basis. Gaven only wished Haynes had as much brain as he had muscle.

"Foreigners aren't here to grow carrots and herd cattle. No, they could do that in their native empire. The people who want to settle in Althaea are the people who want to expand their businesses, look for more qualified men and share with us their new inventions. If we want Althaean Main to prosper then we must—"

"You there!" shouted Haynes, pointing at a prisoner. "If you want to keep that hand, put down that rock, or else!" Haynes turned back to Gaven. "Beg pardon, Your Honor, you were saying?"

"Never mind," he sighed, and nodded at the chained captives. "Carry on, Commander. Put them on mining duty."

As the soldiers guided the prisoners, Gaven analyzed each of them, memorizing every face and aura. One in particular stood out to him – her golden eyes stared back at him with the ferocity of a predator.

"You're too soft, Tiger," Commander Haynes chuckled. "More prisoners means more mouths to feed."

Gaven gave Haynes an exasperated sigh. "What else would you do? Execute them?"

Haynes shrugged. "People say if you instill fear, there will be less crime. But give thieves a job and a roof over their head – well, who wouldn't want to steal?" The twinkle in his eyes showed he didn't really believe that – Haynes simply loved giving the boss a hard time.

Gaven clapped Haynes on the back. "If I thought you

believed that, Haynes, I'd send you down to the mines with the rest of them."

A GENTLE WIND played with the foliage on the cold ground. With every step she took, her bare feet smashed the long-dead leaves. It felt insulting – disturbing things that had already died. But how could she avoid it? As far as her eyes could see through a curtain of smoke, there wasn't an inch of ground that wasn't covered in orange, red and brown.

Then she stepped in something even colder, wet and slightly sticky. Droplets from the mist? Moss on rocks? She looked down; it was as if the leaves had melted. She watched the helpless leaves drift away and get caught, down the stream, in a pile of dirt, twigs... and limbs.

Men, women, children. Face down and naked. In a mechanical gesture they rotated their heads, and with a desperate wail, they gazed at her... with no faces.

The woman gasped as her eyes shot wide open.

It was dark again and she stared at a concrete ceiling. She heard incoherent mumbling from a ways down, strange noises that could only be made by the insane and looked around to see the cell bars.

Right, she was back on mining duty. But she wasn't planning to work another day. She stretched, trying to iron out all the creaks and aches from sleeping on a cold stone floor. Her eyes wandered to the young guard on duty, whose head was swaying like a falling tower.

She smiled.

She rolled out a thin, stiff metal wire that she had hidden in the heel of her shoe. She eased the makeshift pick into the cell's lock and worked at it until she heard a small click. Without a single creak from her cell door, she slipped out.

She stood tall and inhaled deeply, chest out as her skin shifted and her muscles molded into a new form – a tall man, uniformed in chain mail, with an armored breastplate just like all the other guards in the fortress. She rubbed at the grizzled reddish stubble, considered for a moment, then sprouted a thick dark beard and locks of curly black hair instead.

She moved confidently toward the semi-dozing guard on duty.

He heard her footsteps, snapped up, startled, red-faced at his failure to remain alert. "When did you get in here?"

"His Honor asked me to check on a prisoner," she responded in a deep baritone.

"But I never saw you come in." The drowsy guard locked over the hairy man in the uniform and checked for the empire's insignia on his shoulder plate to confirm that he was a guard.

"Got to stay awake, friend." she winked. "Don't worry, I'll keep mum."

The guard blinked, confused, but didn't stop her from exiting the dungeon.

In the skin of the guard, she weaved through hallways and greeted some passersby to avoid suspicion. It would not be her first exploration on fortress grounds, but it was becoming harder to escape. Her last strategy no longer worked – the hole in the wall in the back of the laundry room was now guarded by two men – and she continued walking down the hall in search of a new exit but came across her biggest challenge.

Rounding a corner, she saw a young man dressed in a gold-rimmed white coat with a long, sapphire cape hanging from his shoulder pad. He approached from the opposite side of a long hall. She remained tall and confident, projecting the rugged personality of the man she was impersonating. They exchanged a quick nod as they passed.

But after a few steps, Gaven stopped in his tracks.

"You there," he called out. "Officer Urrea, isn't it?"

She yielded obediently, but she hesitated to turn around. Whatever her adopted name was, she didn't know. But what choice did she have? She wouldn't be able to silence him if it was truly a trap.

Officer Urrea now turned around and lowered into a bow. "Yes, Your Honor?"

"Aren't you supposed to be stationed in the West Wing today?"

"I'm terribly sorry, My Lord. I must have been misinformed. I will proceed immediately." Officer Urrea saluted and strode off before Gaven could get in another word.

Gaven narrowed his eyes, waited until Urrea was out of sight, and then began to follow him. With the quietest of steps, he shadowed Urrea, until they were in a desolate hallway and the guard was within his reach.

Gaven grabbed Urrea by the shoulder. His tight grip made the soldier grasp his wrist out of reflex. Gaven expected this much. He threw Urrea into a reverse arm bar, forcing him to the floor. Gaven rested his knee on top of the soldier.

"Not bad, shapeshifter," Gaven complimented as he secured Urrea's hands behind his back and wrapped them with a pair of aulāce. A click of the lock and Urrea knew he was defeated.

"How did you know?" the soldier groaned, struggling to break free. But the huge man, even though he was twice Gaven's size, was no match for his lord's strength.

"Your appearance is perfect," Gaven replied. "But physical appearances can't hide your natural aura."

Gaven pulled the soldier up off the floor. She resumed her regular form – a relatively young woman, two heads shorter than

Gaven. Her brown cowl covered most of her face – but not those golden eyes. He nudged her forward and escorted her back to her cell.

After a few choice words for the guard Gaven had to wake up to get the keys, he locked her back into her cell. He waited for her to say something, but she avoided his gaze. He dismissed the guard and pulled a chair in front of her.

"They say shapeshifters were extinct thirty years ago," Gaven said. "Yet I have one here in my prison. Records say your name is Eir?"

She held her silence.

"Not much for words, I see. But I have an offer for you." He waited patiently for a response. He knew she was in no position to bargain. "You're here for two murders, and—"

"Self-defense!" she blurted.

He smiled. "Ah, so you can talk after all." She looked away, and clammed up again. "I know who you killed. They were hired assassins."

"Not working anymore," she said, unable to resist.

"You're also charged with, I believe... it was thirteen robberies?"

"Fifteen."

"So far this month, anyway. Have we missed a few?"

"Why would I tell you?"

"I wouldn't if I were you. You're already looking at hard labor for the next twenty years."

"Twenty years… or as long as you can keep me."

"I don't want to lock you up at all. A waste of talent."

"Ah, here we go." She turned those amber eyes on him now. "So, what do you want?"

"Duel me."

His answer surprised her and she laughed. "That's what excites you? Beating up women?"

"You win, you're free," he said. "Best deal you can get."

"You take me for stupid?"

"I take you for extraordinary."

"I am not some rare creature to be used for your amusement."

"I want to study your mechanisms. I read that you can replicate a person's physique. Their strength too. If so, then it'll be a fair fight."

"If you know that much, then you also know that skill and training cannot be replicated."

"Still, I want to see what you can do."

She walked to the far end of her cell, keeping her back facing her unwelcome guest. Dueling the empire's strongest fighter was a joke, and she knew it.

THE NEXT DAY, Gaven visited her again. He sat, relaxed, with his arms crossed, glancing at the curled-up girl behind bars. They sat in silence for nearly twenty minutes. She knew precisely what he wanted, but she refused to acknowledge his presence. He was willing to wait her out – even though the chair he perched on was a literal pain in his ass.

Haynes came looking for him, with some convoluted story about an arms merchant trying to work a fast one down at the armory. Gaven was relieved that he had to leave, rubbing at the pins and needles where his butt fell asleep.

The next day he returned with a seat cushion in hand. Gaven pulled up the chair, arranged the pillow, and sat with a satisfied 'aaaaah'. They stared at each other in silence. After an hour, Gaven woke up to Haynes shaking his shoulder, mumbling something about meditation.

Sounding more curt than he intended, he prodded Haynes. "What now?"

"Rust."

"Rust?"

"That new shipment of helmets. They're starting to—"

"Never mind, show me," grumbled Gaven as he got up. He followed Haynes for a couple steps, then remembered. He went back and snatched his seat cushion.

This continued for over a week. She had finally had it. "Don't you have something better to do, Your Honor? Temples to bless? Banquets to stuff down? Peasants to oppress?"

"Oh? Not happy with the rations?"

"Me? I love bread and water… Make that stale bread and water."

"You obviously want to get out of here. I don't see why you won't duel."

"Yeah, yeah, if I win, I go free. What's the deal if I lose?"

"Then you show me your real form," Gaven answered.

"What?"

"What you really look like."

"You're looking at it, stupid."

"I know that's not your real skin." The Belligmn Tribe was declared extinct before Gaven was born, yet this girl didn't look a day older than him.

"Believe what you want."

"If this is your real skin, then you have nothing to lose."

Gaven beckoned one of the guards, who trotted over with a generous tray of savory meats, fresh vegetables, and ripe fruit. As Gaven slid it through the slot in the bars, she had to control the urge to drool. She hadn't seen so much food on one platter in a very long time.

"What's wrong? Not to your taste?" Gaven asked.

"No, this is fine. Thank you," she muttered. Or it sort of

sounded something like that, it was hard to understand her as she shoveled in one mouthful after the next.

"It wouldn't be a fair duel if you're not at full strength."

"Fighting fair?" she garbled, her cheeks stuffed with food. "You're a strange one."

Gaven marveled at her gusto. She belched loudly without the slightest modesty, and flopped down on her thin blanket of a bed, letting out a groan that was half pleasure, and half discomfort from being overstuffed.

"There you go," Gaven chuckled. He started to leave, saying, "I'll come back in a couple of hours for the duel. Wouldn't want you to cramp up."

LATER THAT AFTERNOON, she was escorted to a private storage room, spacious but empty, where Gaven was waiting, stretching and warming up. He had ordered all the guards to remain outside, respecting the privacy of their duel, and most importantly, Eir's secret.

"Oh, rat socks," she muttered, rolling her eyes at the flaunting warrior. "Let's just get this over with." She took a deep breath and her brown hair turned black, her chin firmed, muscles bulged and she shot up to reach her opponent's height.

She snatched a spear, and noticed the blood-drained look of her challenger. It was the same uncanny feeling everyone had once they saw a walking image of themselves. A huge grin crossed her low cheekbones. In his deep voice she echoed, "Something wrong?"

"Uh... nothing..." He tried to focus, twirling his own spear around in a fancy drill like a baton-twirling maiden. She responded with her own show with the spear. It was like watching himself in a mirror. In a nightmare.

He muttered, "I thought you said you can't replicate skill."

"I never said that," she teased in a manner that fed her amusement. "You must be thinking of someone else, like Eir?"

She broke out in a charge, spear pointed up and landing a slight nick on Gaven's arm.

Gaven looked sideways. It wasn't the wound he was worried about, but his torn shirt. "Why, you dirty sneak. I wouldn't do that."

"If I kill you, would it be suicide?" She made another lunge at him, but this time he was ready to parry.

He felt power in the impact from her spear striking against his. Gaven took it easy at first, probing defenses, examining her footwork and counting the rhythm of her breathing. He only attacked with caution, using simple counter techniques and evaluating how she followed up.

She, on the other hand, did not hold back. She attacked fiercely with all her might, one strike after another. Gaven couldn't believe that this was what it was like to feel his own blows.

But he knew his blows would've been worse. She wasn't using any kore.

Then he realized that she hadn't been lying – she was truly limited to his physique, forced to rely on strength and her own knowledge to win the battle.

But she was no mere peasant who knew how to hold a spear. The way her body jerked and her feet danced across the stone floor told him she was trained in the umbra style. It was no wonder she got away with picking so many pockets, and how she was able to stay alive in the slums.

Once he had seen enough, Gaven snuck in a quick fling that knocked her spear out of her hand. The spear clattered down, far beyond her reach, and though she could've retrieved it, she didn't bother.

He was holding back all this time. Continuing would've been a waste of energy.

"Well fought," he said.

"Yeah? Well, we all knew who the winner would be." She crossed her arms. "But I suppose even you would get tired of looking at yourself eventually."

"You know what I want to see."

"I didn't know you were into older women, Your Honor."

Gaven rolled his eyes. "Your real form, Eir."

She shrugged, and the air around her seemed to shimmer like a heat mirage as the transformation took place before Gaven's eyes. He knew he wouldn't be looking at that short fireplug of a woman this time, but he didn't expect the vision of the lady who appeared before him. Her lime-colored hair swayed like a willow tree, tumbling past her flat chest, down to her hips. She was at least a full foot and a half taller, stick limbs only a fraction of Gaven's size. The only thing that stayed the same was her pair of amber eyes.

Gaven hadn't expected any of the nobles to be alive. He dipped his knees slightly, nodding in a respectful way.

She kept her arms across her chest and her chin high as she looked down on the warrior. "Why the long face? Not what you expected?"

"What's your name?"

She had nearly forgotten. When was the last time she uttered those words? It took her seconds to remember, and for the first time since she was a child, she said, "Erel."

"Your other form," he said. "The one you normally hide behind is Eir? Was she a shapeshifter too?"

"No, she couldn't shapeshift," Erel said. She had always admired her companion's cedarwood tone more than her own. To her, the bark of the tree was more interesting than its leaves.

Their rings told a story, and their thick stumps protected and nourished the others. Eir was nothing short of that.

Erel's best friend had been a normal, average servant girl that looked just like any other human. The chances of anyone recognizing her were close to none, not that anyone would give two donkeys about a servant with no ability. But if any bounty hunter knew there was a rare specimen like Erel wandering around, the whole empire would be drooling over the price of her body. Would she be sold to the circus, the whorehouse, or as a concubine for a noble? She wasn't going to let anyone treat her like a prize.

And so, she took on Eir's name and identity. Though the creases under Erel's eyes were starting to show, she kept Eir's appearance relatively young, her perception of what her friend would've looked like had she made it to adulthood.

"You're honoring her memory," Gaven realized.

"And her sacrifice."

Young Erel was a coward. She didn't have a fraction of the courage her best friend had. Even now, she didn't have the courage to live in her own skin. She could only pretend to be brave like Eir.

"Are you really the last shapeshifter?"

Erel turned away. Her silence neither confirmed nor denied his statement, but still she answered, "Even if I wasn't the only one who made it out of the forest that night, I'm the only one still breathing."

"Then you may go on doing so. Your secret is safe with me."

Erel tilted her head, unsure if she heard right. "I lost. You're still letting me go?"

"Along with all your charges," Gaven said with a sweep of his hand. "It would be a waste of talent keeping you behind bars."

"You'd rather have a criminal up and about on your streets?"

"You steal because you don't have a choice, like far too many in our empire. I know you do only what you must to survive. The assassins you killed were after you because you're a shapeshifter, correct? What did you call it? Self-defense?" This got a small smirk on her face. "I expect a princess of the Belligmn Tribe to know what's right from wrong without having to keep her locked up. All I ask, Erel, is for you to live by your real name. There is no shame to who you are. Wear it proudly."

"'Killing is easier than tolerating'. That's the mindset of Althaeans." Erel shook her head. "It's easy to imitate Althaeans, but you, you put up a challenge. You're not like them."

Gaven kept a stern look on his face. He appeared more serious than he did a second ago. "Althaea likes to take shortcuts instead of facing the issues. It's the reason why we don't progress."

"Hah. No wonder your region is in shambles."

"What was that?" Gaven raised his brow.

"Don't get me wrong. I agree with everything you've done in the last fifteen months. But the time right after an exchange of power is most vulnerable. Yet, you dove balls first into politics. That's a quick suicide. Did Her Grace not tell you better before she left the region in your hands?"

Gaven scratched his chin and chuckled. Anything Suzan had told him was now a distant memory. "She may have said something along those lines."

"But you ignored it. You're incapable of leading on your own. You're no politician."

Gaven had heard those words more times than he was willing to admit, and he was getting tired of it. "Your point being?"

"To be made region leader at such a young age… You're still prone to mistakes."

She made herself comfortable on the ground, crossing her legs as she began her pitch. "You need an assistant. Someone who can help you secure territorial deals as well as get in and out of a bad situation."

The idea tickled his mind, but it brought back unwanted memories of his former partner. Gaven shook his head as unwelcome memories raced into his mind. "It sounds like you have something unsavory in mind. You know I'm not taking any partners."

"Ew, no." Erel felt her hefty meal rising from her stomach. "I don't want to be involved in that cheesy chest-thumping paragon crap."

"Then you must be after the cheese itself."

Erel's smile perked up and she felt her mouth begin to water, recalling the taste of roquefort and manchego she had not long ago. "You said it yourself. You have a shapeshifter in your prison. Why not put her to use? And you know I'm not just some professional actress. Unlike your fish-brained former partner, I can take care of myself. I know how to command men, and as you saw I can put up a fight. Region leaders, nobles, even innocent children, I've played them all."

Though it was Gaven who had kept her locked up, the one who forced her into this duel, Erel had claimed the position with her words. An alliance with someone from a supposedly extinct tribe, well-versed in politics and a master of disguise – it was an offer too good to refuse.

She took note of the look on his face. With her head held high, Erel stuck out her hand. "Do we have a deal?"

CHAPTER TWENTY-FOUR

Five Weeks After the Grand Ball

"Aias?" Mirari said, looking at the map and the hand-drawn notation of the northern village. She didn't remember Aias specifically, but from what Erel had just described, it was the sort of place she'd been steering the patrols away from for the last month. She skimmed past a handful of such villages. "Sorry, it wasn't a memorable place."

All was quiet in Gaven's study. He typically opened his window in the early morning, inviting a calm breeze and letting the sound of his drilling soldiers motivate him. But today, Erel called an emergency meeting before he had a chance to begin his routine. She was typically busy rallying guards and assigning duties, but here she was, wasting time staring at a nonexistent town on a map. She darted her eyes around its surrounding area without making a sound. Gaven and Mirari waited for what seemed like minutes.

Finally, Gaven sighed, crossing his arms. "I take it from that sour look on your face that the news is bad." Mirari peered at Erel, but she looked as bitter and withdrawn as usual.

"Our soldiers broke up a bar fight yesterday. Nothing noteworthy, except…" She tapped that drawn spot. "They were from Aias and they all had markings on their wrists."

Erel reached in her pocket and unraveled a drawing of a spiral flame. Mirari had never seen it before, but had an idea of what Erel was about to say next. Her body grew tense.

Gaven narrowed his eyes. In a low voice, he asked, "Are you suggesting…"

"We know what type of degenerates bear markings like these," Erel said. By inking their group's insignia on their wrists, those men made no effort to hide who they were. They were proud of it and whatever destruction they caused.

Mirari flinched from the blackened anger she felt from Gaven. They were members of the Blessed, and Mirari failed to catch them. She wasn't sure what she feared more: the fact that she failed to detain members of the Blessed, or Gaven and Erel finding out that she had been neglecting her duty out of a deal with Inigo.

"I'll go look," Mirari blurted out.

The anger faded and Gaven looked at her in surprise. "You?"

She nodded. If the men were from Aias, there was no chance Gaven would let the village go without further scrutiny. "It's my fault that I let them slip in the first place. I'll see if there are any more members hiding there. I can do it."

Gaven was already shaking his head. "It's too dangerous. As a Minettan, you have a target on your back." He looked at the map, then turned to Erel. "We'll send the fifth unit. Erel, will you—"

Mirari's hands tightened into fists underneath the table. "Your Honor!" He looked surprised at her outburst. "Let me do this. The people," she hesitated. "These people have nothing.

There's no reason to send an entire squad after a bunch of farmers barely scraping by."

Gaven stared at her intensely. "I do what I have to to protect my people. To find the root of this evil."

"If there were truly any members left, it's best that we first assess the situation, discreetly, before sending a battalion. Wouldn't you agree?"

He sighed, crossing his arms. His eyes had softened into that pout he gave whenever he didn't want to admit he was wrong. He turned to Erel and asked, "What do you think?"

She shrugged. "Three from such a small village might've been all of them. As she said, there's not much a bunch of poor farmers can do. They'd be daft to pick a fight with her. Mirari can handle her own."

He nodded, a decisive look overtaking his face, and got to his feet. "Then let's do that." He frowned at Mirari. "In the meantime, you may investigate the village on your own. However," he held his finger up to her face, "if you come back with so much as a scratch, Haynes will take over all of your assignments."

She nodded. "I understand."

<hr>

MIRARI RECALLED THE VILLAGE NOW, and it was smaller than she remembered. The tiny village rested in a small clearing surrounded by densely packed trees. She had only found it again by following the sound of metal clanging in the distance.

Uncharted on the maps, it was a town unknown to most. The handful of abandoned dwellings — decorated with fallen beams and swaying trimmers — were remnants from centuries ago. It was practically deserted, with a few children playing in the streets and farmers tending to a small row of crops behind their homes.

Around the corner, she found the source of the sound

propped up between two broken buildings: a broad-shouldered artist hammering away at his anvil. Even with bandages on, she could see the inside of his scarred arm and Althaea Main's crest inked there. Fitting for a man who, despite his age, looked like he could wrestle a gritbear.

She continued on, roaming the streets of Aias, making sure to keep her sword tucked under her coat and out of sight. With her association with the army, she knew she didn't have the villager's trust, even less as a Minettan. However, she only received a few stares as she walked by. Most didn't pay her any mind as they went about their tasks. Even then, if there were any rebels, or members of the Blessed, hiding here, it was unlikely the villagers were going to give them up.

She reached the edge of town within minutes, baffled at how little there was. Who in their right mind would stay in such a depressingly confined area? She pivoted and began walking back. This time, she followed the sound of the hammer and approached the smithy, admiring the blacksmith's work.

He paused. "Looking for something, miss?" he asked in a gentle yet persistent tone.

"Is that a rapier or estoc?" she asked.

He briefly shifted his eyes to look at her but continued his rhythmic hammering. "A rapier. You have a good eye."

The discordant sound of wood scraping across the ground drew Mirari's attention to a young man with ragged clothes, dragging a few piles of wood to a corner of the smithy. He placed the plywood down and stared at Mirari with open disgust. "We have nothing for you here. Now get." He placed his hands on his hips, scowling over his unmanaged stubble.

From where he was standing, she could see a mark on his inner wrist: a circular one.

She felt the world around her come to a halt.

Though she couldn't get a full glance of the symbol, she

knew it was the same one Erel had presented. Why did she hesitate? She knew encountering members of the Blessed would be a possibility, and she was ready for it. But now, standing face to face with the enemy, that bravery was swept away with a flood of panic.

She shuddered, remembering the uncanny feeling of Laikos invading her mind. Was this man also an empath? Was he something more dangerous?

Mirari swallowed hard, reminding herself that she was different now – wiser, stronger. She could take him on, no doubt. Her hand wanted to reach for her sword.

But then, Inigo appeared in her mind. She wasn't allowed to harm or arrest anyone. Did that include the Blessed? For a moment, she was torn between Inigo's impossible demand and her duty as a Knight. Before, she'd convinced herself that steering the patrols away from these villages wouldn't hurt Gaven's goals, but these were the exact people he was looking for. Could she really justify not reporting this?

She was drawn from her thoughts by the scruffy man. "Hey, featherpit, you deaf?"

The blacksmith raised his hand without taking his eyes off the sword under his hand. Scowling back at the blacksmith, the man pointed at Mirari's bracelet.

Mirari hesitated to look away. She slowly raised her arm, then glanced at the soft downy plumes hanging from her wrist. She had nearly forgotten she was wearing it, and she was glad she did. Her fingers glided over the soft feathers. Peace. Clarity.

Breathe.

They didn't know who she was, only that she was Minettan.

"That's the region leader's partner," the man said. "Must be. 'Fair skin, haughty eyes, a golden pin tucked in a hair of lavender.' What other Minettan'd be fool enough to step foot around here?" Mirari let out a sigh. What was the point of hiding it now? His glare deepened and he sneered at her. "What're you here for? Looking to break up more families? Maybe strip away the last of our coin?" He waved his hands. "Look around you. There ain't nothing left to take."

He was angry and maybe he had every right to be. She trespassed into their home. The town had barely enough to eat and Gaven's men had seized three of his friends. Even with her agreement with Inigo, she wouldn't want to do more to trouble these people. As she'd told Gaven, they didn't have much left. Even if these people were members of the Blessed, she was beginning to think there wasn't anything dangerous about them. They were villagers, tired and famished, just like everyone else. She needed more information before she could decide their fate.

"Why haven't you asked for help from the army?" she asked. "They must've offered some aid."

He snorted. "Yeah, right. We don't exactly take a liking to the army," the man said. "They caused this mess in the first place." She kept her face clear. Arguably, the Blessed played a role in the destruction as well. "'Sides, we can fix things ourselves."

Mirari's eyes wandered to the house on the right where a wooden plank swayed from the top, threatening to fall on anyone who walked under it. It was clear they weren't managing, not if this was how the village still looked five years after the siege. And with a winter storm approaching, Mirari couldn't imagine anyone living in such conditions. They couldn't all be members of the Blessed. Some who lived here were children and they were all people with basic human needs.

Then, she had an idea.

"We can help," she said. "What do you need? Wood? Clean water," she muttered to herself, looking around and making a list.

"Don't bother." The speaker was a woman, approaching from the smithy. She was a fair-skinned brawler with a tint of pink on her lips and angry hazel eyes. She regarded Mirari with the same distaste as the young man. "All we want is for you to leave." With her hair in a tight bun, she looked ready for a duel. She pounded her gauntlets together and stood aggressively by the young man. "I'll be honest, *Milady*, it's not safe for the likes of you out here. We don't need assistance. Not from the army and not from the featherpits."

Mirari lowered her gaze. Even if she had no right to tell them how to think or live, weren't they being a little too stubborn?

Regardless, all eyes were on her, waiting for her to leave. Frowning, Mirari turned on her heels and walked away. Talking wouldn't get her anywhere. As she stalked off, she heard the young man spit.

"Good riddance."

A BAG of grain tipped over onto its side when Mirari tossed it down at the blacksmith's feet. Thumbing over her shoulder, she motioned toward the cart hitched to her horse. "There's also some barrels of water and wood. I grabbed what I could on such short notice."

The blacksmith looked at her under heavy brows. "Thought you'd left."

"And now I'm back. It would be a waste to not take these." Under her bravado, Mirari worried they would once again reject her help.

Sighing, the blacksmith set down his hammer and stood to his towering height. Lifting her chin, Mirari waited. "Kinneth, Myrana. Get out here," he called out.

The man and woman from before returned, adopting near identical looks of disbelief when they caught sight of her. Mirari saw Kinneth reach for a dagger on his belt.

Mirari's gaze darted between the two fighters and the blacksmith. At this point, she was confident that they were not empaths. They hadn't anticipated her return and surely they would've used their abilities by now. It was possible that they didn't know how to use kore at all. They were nothing but simple villagers.

"Back again," Kinneth said, but the blacksmith raised his hand.

"She brought supplies," he said dryly.

"Oh, yeah?" A smirk crossed Kinneth's face and he laughed. Minettans really are naïve."

Mirari's eyes narrowed. "I'm trying to give you a chance here. How is it naïve to want to help people? You should be thanking me."

"Thank you?" Myrana hissed. "I don't think so. We already told you we don't need your help. We don't want to be indebted to you."

"Enough," the blacksmith said. He rolled his shoulders, approaching Mirari. "You just want to help us? Is that right? Out of all the villages the army's run roughshod over, you want to help us?" He glanced down at his arm. "You're awfully persistent about helping us, aren't you? And bold for coming alone." He scanned the area. "Out with it. What are you here for?"

Biting her lip, Mirari chose her words carefully. "I…I do want to help." The blacksmith snorted and she knew that she had to say more. Even as she looked at him and his companions, part of her only saw a group of humble villagers, no different from anyone in the other dozen towns she'd scouted. Could people like this truly be members of the Blessed?

"I also want to know what you want. The Blessed." Myrana sucked in her breath. Mirari felt the tense air around her, but continued. "I want to know why you attacked the Grand Ball, what you hope to gain from all these riots."

Myrana stepped forward, raising her arm and Kinneth tightened his grip on his dagger. "I knew it," Kinneth hissed. "She's here to kill—"

"No!" Mirari said, raising her hands. "I'm not."

Myrana pointed her finger at Mirari. "No? You'll just run back to report this, won't you?" Kinneth and Myrana circled her like howlers around a piece of meat. Mirari looked at the blacksmith, who remained unfazed. Myrana scowled. "Eoin, she knows who we are. She'll capture us like His Honor did to Bernice and then—"

"Quit it, you two," Eoin said. He went back to his seat, sitting down with a heavy sigh. "Don't pick fights you can't win. Even if you did, the region leader will have your heads."

"So we just let her go?" Kinneth argued. "She's with the army *and* the Knights. Even if she helps, the rest of her allies want us dead."

Eoin raised a brow at Mirari, daring her to prove Kinneth wrong. She lifted her chin. "I want to do this peacefully," she said firmly. "We can all get what we want without sacrificing another life, but only if we can talk to each other."

"Talk. Right." Myrana pounded her fist together. "I think the time for talk is over."

Growling, Mirari laid her hand on her hidden sword. "Don't be stupid. I killed Laikos and I'm not afraid of you either!"

There was a beat of silence and then, "Don't compare us to that psycho!" Myrana was livid, shaking. "That's the problem with you nobles. If someone is beneath you, then they're all the same. Vermin! When you're the blight on our lands."

"Myrana!" Eoin said. Myrana hissed something, but retreated back to his side. "She has no idea," he continued, looking at Mirari. "More than that, I think this one's gone rogue."

"I haven't!"

"Is that right?" He didn't sound like he believed her. She

wanted to argue more – she would never betray Gaven – but then he sighed and began unraveling the bandage on his arm. The dragon's tail peeking out from under the wraps was slowly uncovered.

"Eoin!" Myrana said, horrified but the blacksmith continued until the detailed masterpiece was fully revealed.

"You know what this is?" he asked, holding his arm out for her to see. Swallowing hard, Mirari nodded and forced herself to look. This was what she wanted, after all.

She could see the symbol of Althaea Main in full. It was a beautiful work of art that captured grace and power in the talla that ran the length of his arm. There was a flame caressed in the mouth of the dragon and guarded like precious treasure. Kinneth and Myrana's talla only had the flame. She concluded: Eoin was their leader.

Eoin fastened his bandage and stretched his fingers. "What if I told you Laikos wasn't behind the Althaean Siege?" he said.

Mirari snorted. "I came here for the truth." She crossed her arms and glared at him. "Don't lie. Gaven didn't join the rebellion. He was possessed."

"Not by Laikos."

She opened her mouth, but couldn't think of anything to say. She couldn't trust these strangers and yet they spoke of what she feared, that there was another empath out there capable of forcing people to act against their own will.

"What are you saying?" she asked. "Is there an empath stronger than him?"

Eoin looked away, but she caught a hint of sorrow in his eyes as he seemed to recall some past memory.

"There's something out there far worse than empaths." He turned back to Mirari. "You want the truth about the Althaean Siege? Sit down and I'll tell you."

CHAPTER TWENTY-FIVE

The Althaean Siege

Months after Althaea Main abolished the Separation Law and welcomed foreigners into its region, riots began sweeping across Althaea. Most blamed it on the actions of the new region leader, pointing their patriotic fingers at Region Leader Gaven.

But he knew it was much more than that. Gaven had seen the unrest and dissatisfaction festering for months, years in fact, even when Suzan was in power.

It wasn't about the Althaean reluctance to live among Minettans and Valenians; it was about the unreasonable taxes levied by the Council, the heavy hand of law enforcement, and decades of frustration for the common man who had no say in anything the ruling class did. The priests had their endless demands, the wealthy controlled all the sources of capital, and all of the oligarchy leaned on the region leaders to be their enforcers. Factory owners and land barons controlled vast farms and estates and all abused their workers.

Hate toward Gaven's revoking of the Separation Law was an excuse for the real radicals to start trouble. He admitted that his actions tipped the scales and were perhaps the final straw for many Althaeans, but he had no regrets.

"Every great idea sounds delusional at first," Gaven said. He was confident he was making the right decision.

But despite all he could do to uphold justice, to reform the bureaucracy and give citizens more of a voice, Gaven found all his efforts to improve the lives of his people to be futile. The Council wanted the Althaean region leaders to crack down on the insurgents. Gaven, on the other hand, insisted on opening negotiations with the rebels.

"Forget it," Suzan said, now the high representative of Althaea. "The Council wants to make an example of these radicals. All the folks with money are out for blood. They want this stopped."

Gaven was left with no options. Against his beliefs, he had his army crack down several riots throughout Althaea Main. Even his new advisor and second in command, the young woman named Erel, disapproved of the Council's ruling.

"Unless you want career suicide, you have to listen to them," Erel said. Gaven always found her opinions invaluable. Her leadership was needed during this chaotic time. Much like Gaven when he was a trainee, Erel earned her respect through his army's ranks the way all Althaeans did – through duels. Her flexibility was nothing short of a wild chimpanzee's and though some soldiers were still a ways from accepting this new, mysterious lady, she could humiliate all of them in combat even without using her shapeshifting abilities.

The city of Rhea was next. The rioters there had burned the local garrison, taken over the city granaries, looted a temple, and occupied city hall. The Earl of Rhea fled for his life, and his estate was sacked and burned.

"Haynes will surround the city with troops," Gaven said as he looked at the map of Rhea in the back room of the keep with his two most trusted allies. The table was hardly visible underneath the papers, crumbs from this morning's bread, and the map with several metal figurines placed on it.

"We'll go with the same ring strategy we used in Desdemona," Erel said, and Haynes responded with a firm nod.

It was an efficient plan if all one wanted to accomplish was a slaughter. Gaven knew it was an unfortunate case where he would need to show brute force to calm the people. He hoped that this would be the last time he would have to commit another massacre.

"Are we done yet?" Haynes whined as he stretched his stiff legs. The three had been working since dawn, feet sore and mouths parched from hours of discussion.

Erel slapped Haynes's bottom with her long wooden pointer. "We still haven't talked about the supply allocation. You only get two shield tanks this time."

"Two?" Haynes slammed his hands on the table and wailed like a child. "Last time it was four."

"That was before you broke one."

"That was an accident. Tell her it was an accident, My Lord."

Gaven was distracted by a knock on their door. Haynes and Erel had ignored it, much like they had ignored every disturbance that day. But the knocks were frantic and Gaven thought they could be urgent. His team was supposed to be left undisturbed for the rest of the evening as they planned for tomorrow's massacre. Gaven left Haynes and Erel to their bickering, and went to answer the door.

Gaven stepped out into the next room, a waiting area that he had remodeled into a reading nook. It contained walls of bookshelves, a few velvet couches, exotic rugs from Axillaire, and the door to the hallway. Gaven was ready to yell at the soldiers for disturbing him, but when he opened the door… it was no soldier.

A thin man with a faint scar over his left eye, and slightly taller than him, stood before him. He was dressed in a simple white shirt and dark pants, and Gaven assumed that he was either a lost peasant or an assassin in a bad disguise. He was probably not much older than him.

"How did you get in here?" Gaven demanded. The man didn't yield to his roar, showing a lack of interest and no respect for Gaven's position.

The man darted his eyes left and right before leaning in and whispered, "Gav, we need to talk."

His silvery voice sent a tingle through Gaven's chest, kindling a fire that he thought had been put out years ago. It took a second for Gaven to remember the last person who called him by such a nickname. He was desperate to get a look at this stranger's face. That was the only reason why he hadn't shut the door on him yet.

This man was Minettan. That was Gaven's first thought upon seeing the stranger's sharp chin and a clean shave. No man who valued their pride would shave off every bit of stubble, at least in Althaea.

The stranger's chiseled eyes and nose were similar to his own. Even his dark hair and coral eyes made Gaven feel like he was looking at an alternative version of himself. And now he remembered who that voice belonged to.

The man pressed on, stopping not one second. "May I come in?"

Normally, the answer would be no. They were crafting a top-secret mission in the back room. But that mission was nothing compared to the arrival of his guest.

Gaven gestured for him to enter, and closed the door behind him. A curtain separated the back room and the small library they now stood in. Gaven took a glance at the curtain, making sure Erel or Haynes didn't come out. He could hear Erel raising her voice every so often, trying to hammer sense into the commander. Then Gaven focused back on the man he hadn't seen for years.

"What are you doing here?" Gaven asked.

The man shook his head and spoke with a strange urgency. "That battle you're planning in Rhea, you need to stop."

Gaven raised a brow. "How do you know about Rhea?"

"You need to let it go," he repeated. "It's a trap. They know you're coming."

"Gods, slow down." Gaven almost laughed at his insistence. "It's been nearly ten years, and the first thing you say to me is about politics? Are you going to explain how you know about the mission? Or why you're in my region? Talk to me. I'm afraid I'm going to need more details."

"There's only so much I can say. You just have to believe me."

"You know you sound like a spy, right? I sure hope you're not, because I can't make any exceptions for you." The man let that sink in, and it silenced him. Gaven wondered if he was even listening. He tried again, returning to a playful demeanor in case he had offended him. "You okay?"

The man shook his head and repeated. "What you are doing, it isn't right. People are dying on both sides. Is this truly the way you want to rule Althaea Main?"

"With all due respect, you have no idea what's going on. And I suggest you stay out of it."

"Gaven, look me in the eye and tell me you're going to end the raids."

Gaven ground his teeth. He had just about lost his patience. "Okay, I'm afraid you have to leave. I—"

He was lifted by the shirt, feet barely touching the carpet.

The man no longer held his voice at a whisper. He tugged on Gaven's shirt and demanded, "You have to call this mission off."

"Let go of—"

"You have to!"

He yanked Gaven's shirt again, and by instinct Gaven grabbed the man's wrist and rotated his body. With his feet back on the ground, Gaven pulled him with his upper body, flipped him over, and he crashed onto the wooden floor with a loud thud.

"What is wrong with you? Have you lost your mind?"

The man raised his hand and managed to grasp Gaven by his wrist. Gaven tried to pull free, but only managed to drag him around like a broom.

Gaven was ready to take extreme measures, but he hesitated upon seeing a wave of dark mist surround the man's hands. Elegant and alluring, it unraveled like a coil of ribbons and crawled up Gaven's arm. His face drained to white as he was confronted with an eerie presence, something that challenged every bit of logical reasoning and physical training he had ever come across.

Gaven let go in a panic. He watched as this unknown matter moved up his arm, then consumed his body in a matter of seconds. He felt his heartbeat growing louder, faster, and soon he found it hard to breathe. He felt the weight of a dozen hammers upon him, and no matter how hard he tried to keep his eyes open they wanted to drift into slumber.

Sleep… he heard the voice of a young girl say. *Don't resist.*

He knew it was coming from his mind, but it calmed him and he wanted to hear more. His eyes couldn't make out anything but blurs of grey and white, and he focused all his attention on the voice.

As Gaven's resistance disappeared, he felt a kick to his knees and they caved in like jelly. He fell with a loud thud to the ground.

The warrior felt his strength disappearing along with his consciousness. He felt an overwhelming sense of loss, as if the mist wasn't entering him, but rather he was entering the vague cloudiness of the mist. Every muscle in him surrendered, as he felt his soul become absorbed by the vapor.

The man saw the light in Gaven's eyes go dull as death, and his confusion evolved into panic.

"W-what…" he stuttered, watching Gaven clawing for help. He grabbed his hands and pleaded, "Gaven, what's happening?"

Gaven grunted as his body jerked in sharp movements, trying to regain feeling. Then, he got what he wished for, only now he was rolling on a bed of thorns, each movement stabbing into his skin. His body was burning, seared both sides on a hot pan.

"Aaaagh!" Gaven yelled, wishing he could rip his skin apart.

The fighters in the next room would've surely heard Gaven's cries. The man gritted his teeth, and made the difficult decision of ignoring Gaven's deteriorating state. He brushed himself off the ground and headed for the door. He skidded to a stop when he noticed a figure blocking his way. What he saw before him was impossible – The Valiant Tiger a mere breath away with a glare that could kill.

"Gaven… How did you…"

"Who are you?" demanded the warrior before him.

This puzzled the man – who turned back to check if he was delusional. Sure enough, the region leader was still on the floor, now in his numb slumber. As he turned back, the man reached for the daggers in his belt, but before he could pull one out, the apparition was gone.

He felt something tackle his abdomen, and noticed a petite lady had replaced the second Gaven. She shoved him into a bookshelf, grappling as they went down. As novels and textbooks whammed their heads, Erel snatched the daggers from his belt and lodged the weapons into their owner.

He snarled, feeling those blades dig deep into his shoulder and chest. With her hands still grasping the daggers, Erel pushed herself up, sinking the weapons deeper in the intruder's chest.

Her eyes were drawn to the strange wounds. A black liquid oozed out, like oil in place of blood. Her brows furrowed in confusion and disgust.

She stared at it for far too long. With his free hand, the man grabbed Erel's left wrist and squeezed it tightly. She tugged and punched, but he felt no pain and he didn't let go. The mist returned like a plague, and Erel's face went pale.

She leaned forward and sunk her teeth deep into his hand. What was it? Would it be poisonous? She didn't care. The man grunted and yanked his hand back, readied it into a fist, then launched forward again.

She tumbled to the side, cheek in pain, but her focus was on the strange mist that was still on her hand. She shook her hand, hoping the mist would dissipate, but it was imprinted on her body. She could do nothing but watch as it wrapped around her, and she felt her body grow heavy.

She struggled to catch a breath. Through her blurred vision, she thought she saw young Eir. No face, but she knew that physique better than anyone. She placed her hand over her mouth, beckoning herself to stay calm.

It was Erel who heard suspicious shuffling outside their hut. She carved a hole, big enough for them to escape, in the back of the hut with the dagger she always kept on her boot strap. As they broke for the woods, they heard a scream, then another.

The screams shook Erel's attention, but her servant kept her hand chained to hers and she refused to stop running. Cries of agony echoed through the foggy forest. In the gloomy dark, only dancing fireflies and phosphorescent cryphedeon flowers lit their way.

Erel felt a warm gust of air from behind, followed by odors that she instantly identified as the smell yerna hay gave off when used in bonfires. But it was summer, and burning yerna hay during summer was forbidden.

Erel turned around and saw an orange glow coming from the village, the fog blurred the source but her ears could still pick up the sounds of screams and clashing daggers. Her heart tore open when she realized that the screams were of her family being slaughtered.

Tears ran down her cheeks, as she resisted her servant's pull. She stopped, feet planted into the ground. "Eir, release me. That is an order."

"I refuse your command, My Lady. We must get away. We must."

But Erel shook her head. "I can't just leave my people to—"

"Your duty is to survive!" Despite being a servant, she had twice the bravery of Erel. Her eyes projected nothing but fierce determination.

More howls startled the two young girls, and Eir pulled them into motion again. This time, Erel was more willing to run, afraid of how close the screams were getting.

Neither of them questioned why this was happening. This attack was Erel's worst fear coming true.

One night she had overheard her father speaking to a few other tribe leaders. From outside their tent, Erel could only make out a few muffled words. She heard the name of their Goddess' messenger, Laikos, followed by a series of words including 'crazy' and 'kill'. While none of it made sense to her, the words 'the Blessed' added to the existing confusion.

When Erel asked her father, he denied ever having uttered the words. Yet Erel found it hard to ignore what she had heard. Her father and the rest of the leaders hadn't been the same since the meeting. Their fighters had stopped going on missions, their hunters were forced to return by nightfall, and their group prayers were more… subdued.

The two young girls stopped at the next fork in the road to catch their breath. Erel shrieked. "I told you they were coming! Now what? What do we do?"

Eir looked back and saw nothing but the faint orange glow. In front of them was a clear path to safety. She pointed to the dark path on the right. "Keep walking right and you'll reach the port. There'll be plenty of fishermen there. You can impersonate one of them and cross over to Althaea."

Erel now realized that her friend had no intention of going with her. But the princess had never traveled this far out on her own before, not a step outside the forest, and she was scared.

"Why aren't you coming with me?" she asked.

"You want me to help your brothers and sisters, right? Keep running. I'll catch up."

Yes, Erel wanted to make sure her family was safe, but she also didn't want to be left alone. "I'll come with you!"

"Absolutely not! If anyone needs to make it out alive, it's you." Eir placed her hands on her shoulder. "The shapeshifters cannot go extinct. I have a duty as well. To lay down my life for yours."

Before Erel could convince her otherwise, she smiled and ran back in the direction they had come.

Erel stood there for a few minutes with the haunting howls of the wind… and possibly other creatures. The screams had stopped, leaving only the occasional chime of metal on metal.

Eir was so far gone that Erel couldn't see her anymore. She stared at the gray, making out nothing but the silhouettes of dense trees. She listened for footsteps, the sound of her friend sprinting back. But soon it grew quiet enough for her to hear her own breath… and that was all she heard.

This was when she typically woke up from the nightmare, but this time Erel saw a figure emerge from the fog. Her heart leaped, blessed to know that her friend was safe. But it wasn't just her. A dozen more figures began to emerge from all directions. When they got close enough, she saw her parents, and her siblings. Their faces remained obscured, but she recognized their honeydew hair and golden eyes.

Her vision began to mold. The figures transformed into dark silhouettes with blood-shot eyes. Gashes covered their bodies, and opened a waterfall of blood down their arms. The harrowing cries of her young siblings filled her ears.

Why did you leave, Erel?

Why didn't you come back for us?

How could you have run off?

Erel screamed, begging for it to stop. She reached out with her heavy hand, trying to claw at the tiny shadows. She wanted to strangle them, kill them.

You… do not get to judge me. You… do not control me!

She grasped onto those shadows, yanking them apart. She clawed and pulled at every last one of them. When she got to Eir's shadow, she had to step back. The shadow grinned at her condescendingly. That was how Erel knew it couldn't be her friend.

You let me die, you coward! The shadow hissed at Erel, reaching for her throat.

But before Eir could grasp her, Erel reached out. She grabbed the shadow by the neck, strangling her best friend.

"If I could go back and save everyone, I would," Erel said, with a tear ready to fall down her cheek. "But I can't change the past. You will never come back. All I can do now… is what you told me to do… to live!"

Erel stretched the shadow harder until the body split open and white light emerged from the center, growing brighter and brighter. The light took along the shadows and red tainted the room…

Everything disappeared.

HER VISION WAS STARTING to come back into focus. She could now make out the blond commander standing where her family was just a second ago. Color had returned to the room, the rainbow of leather-bound books, mahogany tables, and sapphire curtains. The blood was gone… and so was the perpetrator.

Above her Haynes examined the dark mist that made her look like a steak fresh off the grill. He reached his hand out to touch it and Erel hissed at him intimidating as a six-fanged snake. He retracted quickly.

"Get… him…" Erel said.

"But…"

Erel nudged him. "I said go…"

Haynes stumbled for the door, tripping over himself only once, in pursuit of the intruder.

Erel took a deep breath and relaxed into her true form, letting her body conserve the remaining energy she had left. The mist started to fade, shedding like her transformation. Her head still throbbed and her limbs writhed as if she hadn't moved for weeks. She turned to her lord, who didn't seem to have the same luck.

"Your Honor?" Erel called out. "This is no time for a nap."

The mist surrounding him had also disappeared, but his eyes

stayed shut. She shook him again with her frail hand. His body wobbled like a drunk bum but he remained still.

"By the Gods," Erel cursed, as she pulled together the last of her strength to carry her leader over her back into his private chambers.

CHAPTER TWENTY-SIX

The Althaean Siege

It was dark. Blackened shadows stretched across his vision. People were talking to him, near him, about him. They called him 'Your Honor' and touched his shoulders with concern. He responded. Or rather his mouth moved and his throat vibrated but he couldn't hear the words he spoke. Somewhere in the darkness, voices cried out, taunting him, chastising him. The voices were faded whispers, but he knew the meaning.

Failure.

The Valiant Tiger who steps on the backs of his friends, his family, his people.

The leader whose region was buckling under the weight of corruption and evil.

He blinked and looked around. He wasn't sure where he was or how he got there. His hands were clenched around leather reins and beneath him, his white stallion was breathing out steaming breaths. By the depths of the night, it was late. So late, it was already ticking toward morning.

Dismounting, he approached the ridge he'd ridden to in the night. Down below, there was an unassuming, little town sandwiched between the ridge and a moonlit river. Village would be a more apt description.

Rhea. The name came to his mind.

With painted wooden rooftops and worn limestone walls, it was fairly unremarkable except for the burst of activity happening in what should be a sleepy village. People were hauling sandbags from the docks that stretched out into the river. The bags were transported to the main road in and out of the village where they were piled up into a makeshift barricade.

The memories were thin, but solid enough for Gaven to understand. The troops under his command would storm through that barricade and those weary peasants would meet them at the gates, not knowing there would be a second force on this very ridge to finish them off. They would all be dead by nightfall tomorrow.

A waste.

The thought struck him like a bolt of lightning. It didn't have to be that way. It didn't matter how he got here. He was here for a reason. Invigorated, he climbed atop his mount and took off down the ridge.

From his white stallion, he was not only noticed immediately but also recognized. Someone released a scream and a door slammed. Soon enough, the clopping of hooves against the road was his only companion. He loped through the quiet streets of Rhea, toward the half-finished defenses, when a door creaked as someone emerged from the house behind him.

"Eoin, wait!"

"Stay there," the man said. He spoke with authority that expected to be followed. Gaven directed his horse to turn slightly, blocking the road and waiting for the rebel leader to approach. The person on the other side of the door pleaded with Eoin to stay, but he shook his head, implacable. He was a large man, built like a steel wall. He wore simple leather armor over a dark tunic.

After closing the door firmly on his subordinate, Eoin came out to meet Gaven, facing him with a large battleaxe resting across his broad shoulders.

"Your Honor," he said, insincerely. Though he presented a tough front, when he looked around it had a frantic edge. "All alone? Why? Where's your army?"

Gaven swung his leg from over the side of his horse and turned to fully face Eoin. He felt weighed down by a strange confusion. Eoin's sleeves were rolled up, revealing a talla of Althaea Main in the form of a sleek dragon inked across his arm that flexed when he readied his weapon. The talla sharpened Gaven's focus as he remembered what he was here for.

Gaven tilted his head to the side, eyeing the ax. "Do you intend to fight *me*?"

"I'm not sure I'll have any other choice," Eoin responded warily. He shifted his weight toward his right foot. "Did you come to finish us off? I suppose mere peasants don't stand much of a chance against the council's dog." He kept his gaze moving as though he didn't truly believe Gaven had arrived alone.

The shadows that edged Gaven's vision retreated slightly as he pushed toward his objective. He glanced at the talla again and took a step forward. "You're the one leading these people."

"I am." Eoin's lip curled. "Why do you ask? Want to talk?" He barked out a disbelieving laugh. "Yeah, right. We already tried that. Didn't work. So, Valiant Tiger, what exactly are you here for?"

Gaven glanced toward the ridge that would bring their death soon. "In a few short hours, you and all of these people here will be dead."

Eoin tightened his grip on his weapon and anger darkened

his features. Despite this, Gaven didn't sense any killing intent in his glare. He must've known Gaven spoke the truth.

"I know we haven't got much of a chance against you or your army," he said. "But don't expect us to just lay down our arms and our lives while our people are dying. While you trample over our people like we don't matter."

Gaven's head cleared as his own thought managed to break free from the shadow and voices. "The people… matter." He started pacing, ignoring Eoin's furrowed brow. "Our actions… irredeemable. I want to help the people. My people." He stopped to stare at a modest house. "Althaea Main are my people. I've sacrificed… so much."

Roselyn.

He squeezed his eyes closed and shook his head. "As you said, the time for words is over. The Council has gone too far, and they won't listen."

Shock crossed Eoin's face, but it was quickly replaced with disbelief. "You tried? Why?"

Gaven thought about it, but there was really only one answer. "For the people."

Eoin snorted. "So you're done talking. What do your actions look like? Why are you here?" he asked again. "What do you expect to get out of coming here in the middle of the night. If the army is planning on slaughtering us all, then how do you imagine we'll have peace?"

"Peace? Is that what your people want?"

Eoin met his gaze, not saying anything for a moment. "There's a lot of things our people want. Sure, at the end of the day, after all the fighting's over, I'd like peace." His harsh glare softened and he glanced at the ground. "But do you really think that's possible? Do you see a path out for us?"

Gaven nodded, straightening his back. "The only way out is through."

"Through what? The army? My brothers and sisters in arms who've gone against the army haven't had much luck." He motioned toward the barricade. "You said it yourself. We don't stand a chance."

Gaven motioned behind him. "A squad will come through your barricade. It won't last long as is. It wouldn't matter if it did. Your death will arrive the same way I did." He motioned up toward the ridge and Eoin turned to follow the direction of his gaze.

His jaw slackened and Gaven could tell the moment he made the connection. "There's a way down from the ridge," he muttered to himself. "If they can get a squad up there, we won't stand a chance. We'll be butchered between the two forces."

"You said 'we.'"

"You won't last without my help."

"And why should we trust what you say?"

Gaven shrugged. The voices in the back of his mind lifted to a wail and he wondered if he'd really be able to walk away from this. He didn't want to. "Whether or not you trust me, doesn't change the facts. You don't have the strength to stop what's coming. Make your choice."

Gaven watched the struggle cross Eoin's face as he stared at the ridge. Finally, Eoin swiped his hand over his face, cursed and turned back to the house he'd come from.

"Levi, Lena!" he called. A man and a woman burst forth as though they'd been waiting by the door. They rushed to Eoin's side, taking up battle positions on either side of him. "None of that," he said, waving his hand. "We need to evacuate the village."

"Why?" Lena asked, clenching her hands into tight fists. "We can take him. Not even the Valiant Tiger can take all of us."

Eoin looked slightly annoyed. "That aside, we don't have

time." He explains what Gaven had told him. About the ambush that would come from the ridge.

Leviathan glanced between Eoin and Gaven with a deep frown. "It has to be a trap, doesn't it? Why would the region leader warn us about an ambush? Especially if that's their ace in the hole."

Eoin nodded, but said, "By that reasoning what kind of trap starts with sending the region leader into a village alone?" Eoin's words were getting to Leviathan and Lena. They lowered their guard and turned toward the large man. "Regardless, evacuating the village is a good idea. They put us up, but there's no need to bring them into this mess if there's a chance to save them."

Convinced, Lena nodded and said, "I'll go find the mayor to start the evacuation." She turned on her heels and set off at a steady jog.

"What about him?" Leviathan questioned, thumbing derisively at Gaven. "Are we just going to let him go?"

Gaven snorted to the other two's consternation. It wasn't like they could keep him anywhere he didn't want to be.

"There's still much to be done," he said as he pulled himself back up onto his horse. "There's not a lot of time to do it in."

"Oh, yeah?" Leviathan said, taking a step forward. He stopped when Eoin placed his hand on his shoulder.

"Enough. Go help Lena. I'll stick close to the region leader for now." Leviathan huffed in dissatisfaction, but moved when Eoin pushed him gently. Once the other was out of sight, Eoin stared at Gaven through distrusting eyes. "What do you mean? Just what else do you have planned?"

Gaven started toward the ridge at a slow enough pace that Eoin could keep up with. The horizon was lightening, bringing change with the sun. "The second squad will be in place soon." His voice lowered to a growl. "We'll destroy them."

"Your Honor?" He laughed incredulously. "Destroy them? Are you mad? We don't have the equipment or military leadership to even compare."

Gaven jerked the reins to face Eoin from atop his mount. "You have me." He looked off into the deep shadows that surrounded him. "I swear to lead our people to victory today."

It was quiet in the thick forest by the ridge where Gaven waited with Eoin. Behind them, the rebels Eoin had gathered shifted with unease. Gaven could feel the worried glances toward him from the assembled peasants. Eoin was perched on the balls of his feet, nimble for a man of his size, with his arms resting on his knees. Gaven glanced over at the ink on his arm.

"Problem?" Eoin asked in a soft voice. The muscles under the dragon moved as he clenched his hand.

Gaven lifted his hand, pressing his palm against the talla on his chest. "No," he said. There was no time to say more. Hand in a fist, Gaven lifted his hand though it didn't mean much to the untrained peasants behind him. Eoin tensed, bringing his finger to his lips.

"Quiet," he hissed.

They watched the small, but well-armed squad ascend the ridge on horseback. Just as Gaven had warned. Gaven could feel the anticipation growing in the rebels, but they had to wait. Soon the trap would ensnare all those who would seek to bring ruin to Althaea Main and his people.

In the distance, a bugle sounded and there was a battlecry as the two squadrons down below joined each other to sweep through the town. They'd take a moment to check that the town was truly abandoned. And in the meantime…

"Now," he said to Eoin and motioned for them to move in on the reserve force. Untrained as they were, they moved stealthily enough – not through any skill but because the peasants were dressed primarily in cloth and leather. Not much steel between them to give away their location.

Gaven shrugged his bow off his shoulder and crept toward the soldiers waiting for the call they would never hear. He was the force that would prevent these sinners from laying a hand on another soul.

"ARROWS!" he shouted, and a couple dozen arrows shot into the sky and rained on many men. The soldiers scrambled to find the source of the attack. That was their chance. Gaven wouldn't give them the opportunity to regain their bearings.

"Forward!" He led the charge to the symphony of the peasant's war cries. He surged forward into the fray, wielding his spear like death.

Blood splattered his face as he hacked a man's hand off. Spinning around, he blocked a blow from a bold soldier. He kicked and the man went down. He jabbed his spear and twisted. The soldier stayed down.

"Please, Your Hon—" Gaven was deaf to the cries of mercy that his former soldiers pleaded for when they recognized who was the harbinger of their death. They made short work of these enemies, but the battle wasn't over yet.

Gaven struck down the final soldier and looked up. There was a man just coming over the incline, accompanied by five other men. His eyes were opened wide as he looked upon Gaven's ambush.

At one time, Gaven was sure he knew the name of the commander selected to lead the reserve force. He was a tall, muscular man, and no doubt, with that twinkle in his eyes, his soldiers trusted him. But he seemed average in every other aspect. Men like him would be easy to predict.

The commander rallied himself faster than the others. He held his arm out to the reckless men by his side. Tugging on the reins, the man jerked his horse around and ordered the others, "Turn back!"

"After them," Gaven called and dug his heels into the side of his stallion. The beast leapt forward. An arrow whizzed by him, striking one of the men in the neck. Gaven returned fire, striking an arrow into a soldier's arm. With two slashes to the horse, the mount tossed its rider to the ground.

A soldier looked at his fallen comrade, then turned to his leader. His voice was hoarse when he asked, "Commander Haynes, what do we do?"

Haynes. That was his name, but a name was all it was to him.

"Go, now!" Haynes shouted as he pushed his horse to sprint.

Trampling the fallen man under the powerful hooves of his horse, Gaven lifted his spear upward, pointing to the sky, and bellowed a war cry. The call was taken up by his peasant soldiers and they lined up on the ridge and looked down on the fleeing man.

"Archers, keep firing. Warriors," Gaven called, riding behind them. "Too long has your will been trampled by those who know not how you suffer. Today, you will take the fight to your oppressors. Take back your home. Take back Althaea!"

"For Althaea!" Eoin roared, taking up the proclamation. The call traveled through the line. Any hesitation the men had felt about working with Gaven was long gone. Emboldened by the early victory, the rebels charged forward toward Rhea where the soldiers were hastily trying to reorganize.

With a wave of his hands, the archers among the rebels released a hailstorm of arrows that cut through the mist, but clanged a metal shield wall. The rebels that had descended came to a halt as they faced over a dozen mounted spearmen. Half stood with their shields up over their head, providing cover to the commander that had fled while the other formed a border with their shields pointed toward the rebels.

Haynes was joined by a woman and Gaven managed to salvage her name from his memory. Erel. A shapeshifter. Not an insignificant opponent, but also not one he would struggle to defeat. She brought a surge of men and Haynes got to his feet, clearly reenergized. He stood at Erel's side and shouted some blasphemy to keep the morale high of the soldiers.

From the ridge, Gaven took aim. Haynes was moving too much for a good shot, but the barrel chest of the lancer next to him made a good target. Gaven released his arrow and it thudded into the chest as intended. Smirking in satisfaction, Gaven watched the man topple off his horse into the mud where he belonged.

Gaven stepped forward and watched the confusion and horror dawn across their faces.

"Raise the flag," Eoin ordered and the blue flag of Althaea was raised… with an image of a bloody tiger painted over the dark dragon. No one would doubt who was standing with the rebels.

"ONWARD," Gaven shouted. He lifted his spear and urged his white steed forward. Behind him, he heard the thunder of hundreds of men following him through the mist and toward the spear wall. The spearmen stood firm and the rebels who were already down the ridge threw themselves foolishly into the fray against the heavily armed soldiers.

"Wait, you fools," Eoin cursed as they rushed to join them.

Gaven lifted his unencumbered hand and felt for the ground beneath the soldiers' feet. He gripped the earth and tugged. There was an eruption of dirt and cobblestone. Soldiers and horses were scattered, disrupting the shield wall and saving the men below.

Eoin looked at Gaven with genuine respect since they first started this endeavor. Gaven nodded to him and continued to disrupt the earth underneath his enemies' feet. Erel was thrown from her horse. Haynes fell to the ground allowing a rebel to come at him with an ax.

In the beginning, Gaven hadn't thought much of the forces at his disposal. Eoin was an ex-soldier turned blacksmith, but the others were nothing more than peasants equipped with garden tools and secondhand arrows and axes. Gaven had resigned himself to taking the brunt of the attack and using the sheer numbers of the rebels to instill fear into the soldiers.

Now, Gaven watched the rebels surge forward like an unending tide. While they didn't have much in the way of fighting experience, there was a zeal in their attacks and thirst for blood in their eyes that bridged the gap between the experienced soldiers and the untrained rebels. Gaven was swamped with a heady feeling. The smell of blood was so thick he could taste it in his mouth.

Screaming along with his destrier, Gaven cut through men and horses with single strikes. Nothing could stand in his way. He charged through, revitalized in a way he hadn't felt in years. The shadows nipped at his heels urging him. He was a harbinger of death. Destruction and blood followed in his wake. His brothers in arms responded in kind, matching his energy as they fought the soldiers.

Gaven felt a sharp killing intent at his back. He twisted in his saddle to confront his attacker. He batted the javelin aside with his forearm, using the motion to bring his spear around with his other hand. Swinging around, steering with his knees, he thrust the spear forward. Haynes was behind him, but the coward managed to get his shield up in time to prevent a killing blow.

Gaven put enough force into the attack that Haynes tumbled

from the saddle and fell to the ground, head over heels. He fell into a crowd of rebels that pressed in on him with death in their eyes. Gaven swept aside the soldiers who tried to attack him from behind, but didn't get a chance to press his advantage and take out the commander.

Erel was suddenly at his side, bringing more men to engage the rebels and help Haynes recover from his fall. She was on horseback and directed the mount to stand between Haynes and Gaven, looking at the region leader with disgust in her eyes.

"You're insane!" she snarled. She spurred her horse forward, charging him with her sword out and blade up. Sparks flew as steel clashed. The impact diverted the weapons up and they rode past each other. Gaven spun his horse around and she was waiting for another go. "Do you have anything to say for yourself?" she screamed.

He looked at her dispassionately. Once she was dead, he would move on to the next battle and the next. He knew Erel was his second in command, but he didn't know her well enough to be riled by her words. She was nothing more than his enemy.

"Answer me!" she continued. "Or answer to your men!" She waved her hands to indicate the carnage around them. Around him, soldiers and rebels alike were dead and dying, bleeding out and praying for mercy. There would be no mercy until Gaven's enemies fell at his feet.

He lifted his spear and looked at the woman who searched his eyes for something she didn't find. "I fight..." He struggled for the words, unsure how to speak of the darkness around him. "For the will of the gods," he finally said. "It is fate that you all will be silenced here by my blade."

He shook his head to try to clear his thoughts. Though his heart was beating wildly like the battle around him, he kept his breathing controlled and steady. He was the Valiant Tiger. He wouldn't be shaken by mere words or this woman. He watched her slow her own breathing. He thought she was gearing up for something, another attack probably, but then her eyes widened and shock crossed her face. She must've come to some realization.

Tilting his head to the side, he watched her like an insignificant insect. He wanted her to charge him again. To waste her energy so he could strike her down and move on.

She roared and charged at him with her sword at the ready. Their blades met once more, but only for a heartbeat before she abandoned her sword and surged into his space. Her steed gave her leverage, and she yanked Gaven off his horse and into the mud. Her strength was always her cleverness. Erel kept charging forward… past him… and by the time Gaven was on his feet, she had Haynes on the saddle behind her.

"Cover us," she ordered as she galloped away as fast as she could in the terrain. "Archers, ready for retreat." The soldiers parted, making room for them to escape while the lancers prevented any rebels from following after them. The archers stayed behind, waiting for the rest of the soldiers to clear the area so they could lay down cover fire.

Lifting his hand, Gaven parted the earth beneath the archers. Screams of terror mingled with the voices in his head in an ever-increasing cacophony. Cries of victory joined the noise like a roar.

A hand clapped his shoulder and the noise ceased, if temporarily. He turned to find Eoin standing by his side.

"We did it! Your Honor! We drove them back." Inclining his head, Gaven looked around. Indeed, the only soldiers that remained were drowning in their own blood. "Your Honor." Eoin spoke in a more somber tone and Gaven turned to face him. He held out his hand, extending the arm with the dragon ink. "It was an honor to fight by your side."

Gaven glanced from his extended hand to Eoin's face. He

gripped his arm in camaraderie and cheers rose up around them.

But Gaven wasn't celebrating. He gazed at his bloodied spear and said, "There's more to be done."

CHAPTER TWENTY-SEVEN

The Althaean Siege

After Eoin grabbed his dinner rations – hard bread and cheese – he picked his way through the camp, making sure there weren't any issues that needed to be addressed. Fortunately, there were none. They found peace camping in forests and valleys as they made their way southeast toward the Gulf of Oris. It heartened him seeing people coming together for a common cause and taking care of each other. Many of these people were strangers, but that didn't stop them from acts of kindness that were so rare nowadays.

He didn't think such camaraderie and brotherhood would be possible without the Valiant Tiger. What had started with barely a hundred had grown to nearly two thousand compatriots. More and more people were taking a stand against the Council and their actions.

Eoin scanned the area once more and found Gaven sitting near a campfire with his own rations, accompanied by a few of the other commanders. They were those, like Eoin, selected to lead a group of rebels.

As Eoin took his seat across from Gaven, the other two commanders were finishing up with their dinner.

"All quiet?" Haveron asked.

Eoin nodded. "Yeah. It's a good night." Nodding to Eoin, they saluted the region leader and left to go on patrol. It was just Eoin, Gaven and the crackling campfire.

Gaven sat quietly. He didn't care to engage with others. He found solitude staring into the flames as though they had the answer to some unfathomable question. He did this sometimes. Eoin didn't know if that was just a part of his personality or if turning on his former comrades, even for a good cause, was troubling him.

Regardless of Gaven's occasional oddities, he was a charismatic leader that had even Eoin full of a vigor he'd thought long since lost. For the others, just having the mighty warrior walk through their camps was enough to raise their spirits.

Sighing, Gaven set aside his rations and pressed his hand to his head.

"Your Honor?"

Gaven lifted his head with a frown. "What?" he asked gruffly.

Put on the spot, Eoin didn't know what to say. While he admired the region leader, they weren't exactly friends for him to inquire about his wellbeing. Eoin settled on saying, "This is good, what we're doing. We're going to change a lot of lives."

Gaven exhaled a solemn, weary sigh. "I have to fight," he said. "I have to keep fighting. I left my home... my family. The only way to make it up to them is to keep fighting." Gaven shook his head as though to clear it of his dark thoughts. "I'm going to patrol," he muttered, turning away.

Eoin wanted to call to him, but decided to let him be. Whatever was on his mind, Eoin hoped he'd find a resolution for it soon.

"Was that the region leader I just saw?" He looked up at the new voice. He was joined in the circle of the campfire by a dark-haired woman with her lower face concealed with a mask. Though he rarely saw them, she had stars in her eyes – dark with a rare glimmer of amber. She was one of the younger commanders selected by Gaven, and though he didn't think she had any military experience, she more than made up for it in enthusiasm and zeal.

"Soteria, right?" She nodded, ducking her head a little with a plate of bread and chopped carrots in her hands. He motioned toward the recently vacated seat. "Join me." She was a waif of a thing – though maybe everyone looked tiny next to Eoin – but she was confident with her daggers, and fast.

"Thanks," she murmured and began tearing at her bread like a starved child. Eoin looked at her closely, but she kept quiet. That's right. He didn't know much about her because she usually kept to herself. He wouldn't call her shy though. Too many times he'd overheard her grandiose speeches of a new world order that always managed to rouse at least a dozen peasants to join the rebellion on the spot.

As though she could sense his attention, she looked up with a small smile. "And you're Eoin, right? Did you serve with His Honor?" she asked, glancing at his arm.

He shook his head. "I never had the pleasure." By the time Gaven had joined the army, Eoin had already long become disillusioned by the Council and their unequal brand of justice.

"But you were the first who joined him in this movement, weren't you?"

He laughed lightly. More like the region leader joined Eoin, but to the same effect. "Yeah, I was the first."

She hesitated, then set aside her rations. She leaned forward, eyes bright. "How did it happen? I've always wondered how the hand of the gods was chosen."

She wanted a story? He could give her that. "He came out of the fog riding a white steed," he started. It sounded mystical, but it was also the truth. Region Leader Gaven really was a bit like the god's own herald.

The problem was, Gaven was not a herald. He was just a man leading a war that was ugly.

"WE'LL REST HERE for the night," Gaven said. *Here* was a small valley next to Fox River, sheltered by thick forests. It was a day's march from Ganmali, where Gaven had informed Eoin and the other commanders of a shipment of hāstal weaponry. Once they rode into Ganmali and liberated those weapons, they would almost be guaranteed to have the advantage in any fight. They would be a powerful threat to the royal army, and the Council would have to take them seriously. No longer would they just be rowdy peasants who needed to be put in their place, but a proper army to be reckoned with.

At the moment, discretion was vital. If they were found at this junction, all their plans would be scuppered and they'd have to scatter to the winds and wait for another opportunity that wasn't likely to happen. As such, patrols along the edge of camp were vital enough that not just the commanders were taking a turn, but also the region leader as well. That was why Eoin didn't think anything of it when Gaven's patrol took him by where Eoin's on watch.

"All quiet, Your Honor," Eoin reported as Gaven patrolled another circuit around Eoin's watch. Gaven seemed restless and uneasy, checking and rechecking the sentries for anything unusual. At Eoin's words, Gaven stopped and stared silently out into the night. "Is something wrong, Your Honor?"

Gaven jerked as though startled by Eoin's presence. His jaw flexed, teeth gritted, as he mulled over his answer. "So much..." he said. "More than any of us knows..."

Eoin shook his head. Sometimes the region leader's thoughts were hard to fathom. Eoin still endeavored to try. "If this is a success, if we get the weapons at Ganmali, cross to Valenia, fight off anyone who stands in our way for, I don't know, years to come... what then?" When Gaven didn't react to his question, Eoin pressed on.

"What's in it for you, I mean? We fail, you'll lose your head. We succeed, you'll eventually be overthrown. Doesn't matter if you're on our side. Your Honor. In our future, there will be no more region leaders." That was the point. That was the end goal for them. That would be the sign that they had made it and their futures were their own again.

"For me..." Gaven hummed, his gaze still fixed on the dark. "I will protect my people... and everyone... who cannot protect themselves." Neck prickling with unease, Eoin looked into the forest. Nothing.

"Your Honor?" Gaven kept walking, stepping beyond the sentry line and disappearing into the pitch black of the night. Shrugging, the puzzled blacksmith resumed his posted position, tucking away any doubts he had. Now was not the time. Gaven would return soon enough and if there was anyone who would be safe on his own, it was the Valiant Tiger.

Without the region leader's uneasy steps constantly loping past, Eoin was able to relax. It was a quiet night, peaceful even. They were making good time and they would arrive in Ganmali soon enough. With the mana neutralizers, they'd be one step closer to equality, safety, and freedom. Peace.

Althaea favored the bloodthirsty and violent. Region leaders were determined by might, not by who had the people's interest at heart. Even if Gaven hadn't answered his question, he'd said enough. To protect those who couldn't protect themself... That was a worthy goal.

Somebody bellowed from the southern edge of the camp. Eoin took a hesitant step forward. There were a few more shouts and he shook his head. It was too late to be making all that noise. While they were a fairly large force, avoiding detection from the army was paramount. They should be resting in anticipation so they could set off first thing in the morning.

Swinging his head around, Eoin kept an eye out for the other commanders closer to the area. He saw one heading in the direction of the commotion. Off to Eoin's right, he saw Soteria standing on stacked crates, looking toward the noise with her head tilted like an inquisitive bird. She held her hand up again, ready to attack at a moment's notice.

Instead of quieting down, there were more quick bursts of noise that died down as quickly as they started. And then the occasional glow of the campfire began to burn brighter as though someone were lighting a bonfire to attract the attention of anyone who looked in their direction.

That uneasy feeling was back and Eoin took another step. What if it were a distraction so that once he abandoned his post, a full attack would come from this side? He hesitated until he could no longer stand to hear the crescendo of voices raised in alarm. They were under attack.

Soteria jumped down from her crates and took off into the fray. Small and quick, she soon disappeared out of sight.

Taking off, he headed toward the south side. Panic was setting in and he had to fight his way through as people tried to flee in the other direction, heading toward the river and the safety beyond.

It was chaos when he emerged on the other side. Charging

forward, Eoin struck down a woman just as she pulled her blade from the flesh of one of his comrades. Too late for him, Eoin moved forward to cover the backs of others retreating. Their attackers were finely armored soldiers, but they had cloth wrapped around any loose metal to muffle the sound of their approach while they slaughtered Eoin's people in their sleep.

"Cowards," he snarled, ramming his shoulder into a man's chest and bearing him to the ground. His shout was true because though he managed to slay a handful of them, the enemy was already melting back into the shadows from where they came. Eoin received a few scrapes, but the worst injuries were to his heart, seeing the hacked bodies of his friends and comrades left behind in the burning wreckage of the camp.

There were more screams from afar until finally, there was the sound of the bugle calling for their retreat from their own camp. He looked out toward the river and saw the massive form of the Valiant Tiger driving away the enemies by the water.

Eoin moved automatically, helping the injured into wagons and strapping them onto horses if they could ride. Even if those who had attacked them had been forced to retreat, the camp had been compromised and they needed to find a new place to rest and treat the wounded.

"This way, this way," he called, directing his people with a wave of his hand. As more people left, it grew quieter and he could hear the sounds of those who remained.

The sound of those breathing their last breath.

He kneeled next to a young man and held his hand as he choked on his own blood and expired. Eoin lowered his head and said a prayer. "I'm sorry, brother. I will return to lay you to rest."

Though it pained him, Eoin found his own mount and caught up with the others. There was some hesitation as no one knew where to go next now that they'd been found by the army.

Eoin soothed them as best he could, but he was relieved when Gaven emerged to take charge once more.

He looked bruised and battered, covered in cuts and gashes, but he rode tall and strong in his saddle. At the front of the company, he lifted his hand in a fist to direct them forward. "Keep it moving," he shouted. As Eoin came to ride next to the region leader, he noticed Gaven had blood smeared across his bottom lip that he didn't seem to notice. His eyes looked vacant as though he were rallying them without any conscious thought. "Press on! Don't stop until we're on the other side of that mountain."

IT WAS late and nearly pitch black, but they kept moving. They stumbled forward while their minds were stuck in the Inferna they had just escaped. Eoin snorted and shook his head. They hadn't escaped that Inferna. They were living in it. He glanced over to Gaven, but no longer felt that same rush of morale. People were dead and dying. The weapons at Ganmali seemed farther away than ever.

The sun was just beginning to lighten the sky when Gaven finally let up from their forced march. He scanned the area with a disinterested gaze and said, "We'll rest here. Be ready to move again in a couple of hours."

Eoin's shoulders hunched and lifted his bone-weary body from his horse in a controlled slide. A woman approached him. Her hair was escaping her tight bun and there was a fatigued arc in her steps.

"Lena," he said, relieved she was still alive but apprehensive to see her alone. "How's Bernice? Is she...?"

"Resting," she said with a nod. She helped him dress his

minor cuts but he could tell she wanted to say something from the way she awkwardly held herself.

"What is it?" he asked.

She glanced over to where the Valiant Tiger was restlessly pacing to the consternation of the medics attempting to treat his wounds. "Do you know what happens next? Where will we go?" she asked as they watched the region leader.

"I'm not sure. His Honor might know of another shipment we can hit. They'll be watching Ganmali if they knew where we were."

She leaned forward and lowered her voice. "I heard it wasn't just Althaean. It's a whole alliance. Featherpits and swines all working together. Against us. Could they really?" Her lip curled. "Would the Council truly let outsiders into our affairs?"

Times were changing. That's all there was to say. He patted her hand. "It doesn't matter who they send against us, we have to stand strong."

She nodded slowly. "I want to but…" Gaven shrugged off the medics and stalked away. "Things have been odd in the camp. Have you noticed?"

"Odd as in?"

She scraped back the strands of hair drooping in her face and shook her head. "Nothing exactly. It just seems like some people here are starting to have doubts. They're worried about their families. Will we get to see them again? Will we even survive this war?"

"It's normal to have doubts under these extreme circumstances. All we can do is keep moving forward toward that future. Some of our brothers and sisters have already fallen. We…" He struggled for the words. "If we give up now, what does that mean for their sacrifice? Was it in vain?" He shook his head, feeling like he was talking to himself now more than Lena.

"Why don't you go back to Bernice," he said, patting her

back. "Rest while you can. Whatever happens next, you'll want to be ready for it." She nodded and let him steer her back in the direction she'd come from.

Troubled, Eoin looked around the camp and found the region leader standing near the edge, waiting as though he were counting the minutes until he would rally them to march once again.

Clearing his throat, Eoin approached the man. "A word with you, Your Honor," he said. Gaven swung around to look at him intensely. "We lost a quarter of our men last night. Since we would be unable to take them home to their families, it seems that the least we cand do is give the fallen a proper burial."

His heart sank as he watched the disinterest on the region leader's face as he rubbed his hand across the bristles on his face. "In war," he finally said, "the dead are dead, and the living must keep living. We need to move."

"Move where?" He looked around at their hastily constructed camp to keep his composure. "They know where we are now. There's a high chance they know we'll be after the weapons in Ganmali. If we march there now, we'll be asking to be trapped." It didn't make sense why Gaven was so adamant that they stay the course. Eoin wanted to question him again about Gaven's purpose for doing all of this. It couldn't be for the common man. There was something else going on. But Gaven just patted him on the shoulder and started to move away.

"Move it, people. We're wasting daylight. GO!" Gaven stormed off, no longer interested in what Eoin had to say.

Shaking his head, Eoin turned away. He caught sight of the medics who hastily looked away when they saw they had his attention. They were bent over, packing up blankets and cookware in anticipation of the upcoming march.

Since they'd already overheard, Eoin approached them and asked, "Could you? A short prayer and a hole in the earth." Eoin stroked his hand over his face, feeling older than ever before. "I'll join you." The medics nodded, looking pleased to stay behind. Eoin couldn't blame them. After last night, he wasn't sure if the battle was worth fighting anymore.

Could even the most idealized version of their end justify the cost? He focused on what he'd said to Lena. At this point, they could only keep moving forward. The Council wouldn't stop until they were all dead.

Before he left, he collected a small group to help him and the medics with his self-appointed task. Gaven's disregard for the dead was unnerving, but Eoin kept it to himself. He didn't want to undermine the morale that had already taken a beating thanks to the night's casualties. Perhaps Eoin and the others had built Gaven up in their heads, but for now, that was how it had to stay. Gaven *needed* to be the Valiant Tiger, strong, charismatic and one of them.

"Eoin." Eoin turned around and greeted Commander Haveron with a clasped hand. "Good to see you survived. Have you seen the Valiant Tiger?" He spoke confidently, but his gaze hopped around, nervous. "How is he?"

"Undeterred," Eoin assured.

As expected, the commander sighed in relief. "Good, good."

With Haveron's obvious agitation, Eoin didn't think he'd be a good fit for the burial. His arrival did remind him of someone else though. "Have you seen Soteria? I wanted to ask her for a favor." His voice trailed off at the somber look in the other commander's eyes. "What happened?"

"I only saw her for a moment, during the battle," the man said. "But it looked like she took a bad blow." He motioned across his chest. "Fatal. Or close to it. If she survived, she won't be joining us any further." Closing his eyes, Eoin lowered his head and offered his prayers up to another fallen soul. To have such zeal snuffed out too quickly. He wanted to give her a proper burial if he had the opportunity.

"Thanks," he said, clapping the man on his shoulder. "We'll make those cowards regret this night."

The commander nodded. "Indeed, my friend. I'll let you continue. Take care of yourself."

"And you."

CHAPTER TWENTY-EIGHT

One Week Before the Grand Ball

The steady, rhythmic pounding of the hammer on heated metal was soothing to Eoin. Five years after the failed Siege and somehow, he was still alive. Not okay. Not happy. Just alive, burning away his last years in the town of Aias.

Needless to say, the rebellion didn't make it to Ganmali. Their forces were decimated by the thousands of unexpected fighters across the three empires. Gaven was defeated and arrested for treason. The fortunate escaped, including Eoin and some of his comrades.

There was still more work to be done, but he felt stuck, unsure how to continue. Things needed to change, within Althaea and within the Blessed. How they would go about doing things must justify the sacrifices made along the way. Many wanted another rebellion, but Eoin knew that wanton destruction was not the way to go.

Kinneth stuck his head around the corner. "Jep is back," he announced.

Eoin got to his feet. "How'd he do?"

Grimacing, Kinneth shrugged. "Not nothing."

Nowadays 'not nothing' was the best they could do. Villages on the outskirts of Althaea were struggling to rebuild while also becoming a dumping ground for the elite and wealthy. Aias, their new home, faced the same struggle, but they had vowed that they would rebuild on their own without becoming beholden to the corrupt Council.

Eoin helped unload the grain that would be just enough if they stretched it. It was enough that he didn't think anyone would argue over whether or not they should accept the region leader's charity for now at least.

Sometimes Eoin didn't know how he felt about Gaven. Glad that he had survived the Council's trial? Probably. If only because he imagined whomever they got to replace him would be a thousand times worse. It was a shame that the cost of his life was the region leader becoming a lackey to the Council. There'd been a lot of potential before, his reforms and ideas, but the Council would be keeping him on a short leash now.

"Eoin?" He looked up from unloading the last bag. Jep, a middle-aged man with a scruffy beard, stood waiting with Kinneth. He looked jittery and glanced back toward Eoin's shop. "Can we talk?" He tapped his wrist, right where a marking would be under his work gloves.

"Sure thing." He motioned and Jep and Kinneth followed behind. Myrana was already inside, leaning against the wall with her arms crossed.

Jep had a field along one of the roads that led to Aias. He went into the city to sell his wares and brought back supplies to Aias. That often included information. Whatever he'd learned, he looked equal parts nervous and excited.

"What'd you hear?" Kinneth asked, leg bouncing with nervous energy. Myrana had a bit more poise.

"There's going to be a revival," Jep started. From there, he detailed a plan to hit the Council. Not just where it hurt, but to hit them directly. Someone planned to attack the Council while they were all assembled for the Grand Ball.

"Yeah, yeah." Kinneth pumped his hand. "That's perfect."

Myrana punched her fists together, excitement lighting up her face. "We don't even have to kill them. Just one will send them into a frenzy. It's time they learn that they aren't safe anywhere."

Raising his hand, Eoin got to his feet before they could continue. "And then what?" He glanced from Myrana to Kinneth to Jep. "What do you think will happen after we do that? After we show them that they aren't safe?"

"What do you mean?" Myrana asked.

He scraped his hand across his face, feeling tired. "Let me explain. When we marched through Althaea five years ago, the Council established an alliance with Minettans, Valenians, anyone and everyone. Why?" He didn't wait for them to answer. "They don't care about the villages. It was a show of power. They were putting us in our place, which is on the ground under their boots."

"All the more reason we should take the fight to them," Jep said. His words were confident, but he spoke as though he thought that was what he was meant to say.

"I disagree. They didn't care if a few villages got damaged during the Siege, but they would care if their homes were threatened or their lives in danger. Do you understand?" At the confused look on their faces, he continued. "Underneath the Council's glamour and wealth, they are just animals, and animals bite when they're afraid. Imagine who is going to feel the brunt of that retaliation." He dug in his point. "It's not just a poorly thought out idea, it's a dangerous one."

Jep nodded, subdued and troubled. "That makes sense. I

once had a mare that I had to put down when she broke her leg. She loved me, but in that moment…" He shook his head. His frown helped him hold back a tear. "She bit me when I got too close."

"The Council will do more than just bite. Understood?" Eoin scanned across the room, but Kinneth and Myrana lowered their heads. He didn't expect them to agree, but he knew they would listen.

Jep pushed away from the wall. "Thanks for talking this through. I'll go let the others know. If no one joins her, I'll doubt she'll carry on with her plan."

Eoin sighed quietly in relief. "Good man."

ONE WEEK LATER, the sound of hooves on the road roused Eoin from slumber. There was a frantic edge to the gallop and he hastily shrugged his tunic on. He was downstairs and waiting by the time Leviathan came to a stop in front of Eoin's shop. His mount was breathing heavily, sides lathered with sweat.

Dismounting, Leviathan approached him. He was scowling and agitated. "I thought… you said… we weren't." Catching himself, he lowered his voice. "I thought we weren't attacking the Grand Ball. That's what Jep said your orders were. Did that change? Did you hear something else?"

"Slow down," Eoin said, holding his hand up. Leviathan looked as wild eyed as his horse and Eoin directed him to take a seat. "What are you talking about?"

Leviathan pressed his hand to his mouth and took a few deep breaths to calm himself. "Last week, Jep came back from delivering supplies here." Eoin nodded, resisting the urge to hurry him along. "He told us what you said about – about the fallout of attacking the Grand Ball."

"That's right. It won't turn out well."

That didn't seem to assure Leviathan as much as Eoin thought it would. "I knew it." He lowered his gaze. "I lost a lot of friends during the Siege. Jep is all I got left." Eoin placed his hand on his shoulder. "If attacking the Grand Ball will only make it worse, I... Anyway, I, we all, agreed with what you said. It's too risky."

"But? Did something happen? Why are you here instead of Jep?"

"Jep had another meeting with her last night to let her know our decision."

"Her? Who's that?"

Leviathan shrugged. "I never met her and Jep never gave her name. All I know is that they call themselves the Defiants. Rumor has it that they're the last of Laikos' followers." Humming, Eoin motioned for Leviathan to continue. "He met her last night and this morning..." He ran his hands through his dark hair. "He was a completely different person, dead set on joining the attack."

What could that woman have said to convince him otherwise? Jep hadn't seemed doubtful about Eoin's words. And yet? "He changed his mind?"

"That's the thing," Leviathan said, shaking his head. "He always listens to you. I thought, I hoped, maybe you had said something to convince him or..."

"No. I haven't seen Jep since he dropped off his supplies. Are you sure he wasn't possessed? You know those empaths..."

Leviathan pressed his lips together. "Eoin, when I say he was like a completely different person, I mean it. Everything he said felt... genuine." He glanced at Eoin and then away. "He drew his sword on us. We let him go even though I knew we shouldn't."

Leviathan sounded almost ashamed, but Eoin assured him, "You didn't have a choice."

"No, of course not." Leviathan snorted and mimicked, "'Can't stand in the way of the hands of the gods.'"

"The what?"

"Sorry. That's the line Jep was saying. This group… they think they're doing the work of the gods." He clasped his hand to his chest. "He spewed out that nonsense and then drew his sword. I really thought he was going to attack us."

Eoin furrowed his brow. Where did he hear that one before? He shook off his thought and brought his attention back to Leviathan.

"You were right to let him go," Eoin assured. "Sometimes you have to pick your battles."

"Right, right." Leviathan nodded, looking more confident. "But then, what do we do now?"

Eoin thought about it. If these so-called Defiants had a proper force to attack the Grand Ball and leave a mark, there was going to be retaliation. He looked at Leviathan and suspected he wanted a chance to go after his friend.

"They have to be stopped," Eoin said. "Do you know of anyone else who would be willing to try?"

"I would," Leviathan said immediately. "And I know of a few others as well."

"It'll be dangerous," he warned. "We'll have to break into the Grand Ball ourselves to intercept them." Leviathan nodded along. "We'll have to protect the Council. And to do that, we might have to fight our friends and comrades," Eoin said slowly.

A realization dawned on him like the sun beginning to peek over the horizon. Eoin had accepted Gaven's assistance and leadership during the Althaean Siege and chalked up his strange behavior, but why had Gaven had such a sudden change of heart, enough to turn his back on his army? Gaven claimed to have no memory, and the Council believed it was the work of Laikos, but no leader of the Blessed claimed responsibility for the attack. Eion himself had doubts that it was Laikos – he must be in range of his victims at all times, and Eoin would've detected him if he was with their group during the Althaean Siege. And now, Laikos was gone, stabbed by his obsession over overthrowing the Council. Whoever forced Gaven to turn against his compatriots may be the same person affecting Jep... and that meant for certain it wasn't Laikos.

There was someone else controlling people, someone with an ability stronger than Laikos. Could it be this woman?

"It doesn't matter," Leviathan said, bringing Eoin's attention back to the present. "I'm willing to die to save our land, and our friends." He lifted a fist. "If we must protect the Council for now, then I'll do that. It's not the first distasteful thing I've done for our people and I doubt it'll be the last. And I know I'm not the only one."

There wasn't time to come up with a good plan. They would just have to do the best they could. They only had one day to prepare.

PART IV

CHAPTER TWENTY-NINE

The Grand Ball

Eoin observed from a distance as dozens of carriages pulled up in front of a grand estate. He could name most of the nobles that stepped out — Seneschal Hermington, Lord Davier from House Frilla, even the grand region leader himself, Gaven Zanette. He had never seen the woman who was accompanying him, but it was no secret. The arrival of his bonded partner was the talk of the town: the Minettan named Mirari.

Behind him were a few armed men and women, all dressed in black rags. The last of them secured their bandannas around their mouth.

"Y-You are t-t-traitors," a young man said from the far back, the snow numbing his naked skin. He was hogtied, stripped to nothing but his underwear as his mustache collected frost. In such weather, it was a rather cruel act, but it was nothing compared to what he and his accomplices were planning to do that night. Six of his comrades were in the same condition —

knocked out and stripped to barely nothing. This man had only just woken up, and his rambling was blowing their cover.

"You can't g-go against f-f-fate. S-she won't let you—" A whack to his head was all it took to silence him again. But the young woman who had knocked him out heeded his words.

"He's got a point," Myrana said. "We are all the same to those nobles. What's the point in saving their skin?"

These revolutionaries called themselves the Defiants. They were identical to the rebels — justice seekers who sought better lives, freedom from the few that stood at the top. But their leader, whoever she was, was willing to start another war. Even if both Eoin and her were leaders of the Blessed, he couldn't support what she was doing. Her actions would only make region leaders and nobles despise the Blessed even more, to the point where negotiation would no longer be an option. To the rest of the world, they were all revolutionaries, all the same. The Blessed were responsible for each other's actions, no matter how much their opinions varied.

"I won't let the Defiants give the rest of us a bad name," Eoin said. Eoin was lucky to have five comrades follow his lead: Myrana, Kinneth, Lena, Leviathan, and Raiden. They had been loyal to him for years, unwavering to his ambitious ideas.

It was someone like Myrana's brother, Kinneth, who was waiting for the day Eoin would pick up a sword again. Kinneth had grown restless with his thirst for battle. He and many others believed that Eoin had retired after the Althaean Siege. But those closest to him knew that Eoin never abandoned the journey for equality. He simply began believing in their new region leader.

Eoin had a change of heart after fighting alongside Gaven during the Althaean Siege. He looked up to the warrior, striving to accomplish the impossible, burning with a passion to help the common people in ways that no region leader had ever bothered to before. He believed that Gaven was leading Althaea Main on the right path.

And now, Eoin had the crazy idea of protecting the region leader against some members of their own, who Eoin believed had fallen to the wrong side.

Eoin waved his team forward, and in the Defiant's disguise, his team dodged the incoming carriages and scurried toward the side of the mansion. The magnificent building was decorated with a cascade of vines trickling up to the third floor. They were sturdy and secure, and Eoin saw an open window on the second floor. Leviathan and Raiden tugged on the vines, got a good grip, and started to ascend the wall. They were insurance, in case any assailants were hiding out in the mansion before the attack, but Eoin hoped that they would be able to stop the Defiants before a fight broke out.

The rest followed Eoin into the garden. Except for a few lights, the backside was completely dark, and they avoided the guards with ease. Eoin's team was scattered across the garden, hidden behind luscious bushes, hoping to pick off the assailants before they entered the mansion. They waited for a while, anxious but alert, until they saw a few shadows lurking through the garden.

Lena was the first to come within range of an assailant. The man was dashing between bushes, believing he had the grace of a fox. He was so focused on his task that he didn't notice Lena stalking him from behind. Once she caught up to him, she grabbed his head and tilted it back. In one quick motion, the blade slashed his throat. She grabbed his body and let him down slowly before tiptoeing to another man. She held a cloth to his face, and the man drifted into peaceful slumber in a matter of seconds.

Myrana and Kinneth followed two men crouching toward the mansion. The dark garden gave Kinneth the advantage of charging at them for some distance before the assailants noticed. By the time they saw him, Kinneth lunged forward with the spring of a Valenian toad and tackled him to the ground with a dagger in his hand, and jabbed the man half a dozen times. Myrana stabbed the other assailant from behind, thrusting the dagger through his heart.

The assailant gasped, blood flowing up his throat as he struggled to pull the dagger out of his back. He turned, now ready to pounce on the woman. But in one lunge she locked his head between her arm. The assailant flailed in her grasp and she pressed harder, until he passed out.

Lena watched an assailant sprinting to the front, far beyond her reach, and the others were out of her sight. With her attention diverted, she barely noticed a man wielding a pike charging straight at her. She spun, her blade deflecting the point of the pike only at the last instant. But the man barreled into a smile for a split second before he rotated his weapon and jammed the pike through her heart.

Kinneth went berserk trying to reach her, his dagger like a buzzsaw cutting his path. By the time he was within arm's reach of her, he was knocked back by a punch to his face.

Two masked assailants stood on each side of Eoin. Eoin ran his sword through one assailant, but wasn't fast enough to block a punch to his face from his partner. Two heavy blows to his left ribs left him breathless, but he had survived far worse. He waited for a third punch and twisted away from it before grabbing his neck and pulling him down into a backdrop. Only the assailant kept him in a tight embrace and pulled him down with him. Eoin kept his lock around the man's neck… until he passed out. That should've been the last of the assailants, but Eoin saw that one assailant had escaped Kinneth's reach and was making a break for the mansion.

Now there were people in the garden. The region leader

himself stepped out onto the patio, his partner dragging him by the hand. Kinneth cursed, quickly launching a dagger toward the assailant with little aim. It was just his luck that it landed a fatal hit in the back of the assailant.

The assailant's sword launched forward, slipping from his hands, blade pointed at Mirari. But she was abruptly shoved to the side, guarded by her partner. They watched the blade tremble, and quickly yanked itself out from the stone. It made an abrupt pivot toward Gaven. He caught it with his bare hands before it jabbed into his chest.

"By the Gods," Myrana let out a gasp. "Is that sword… floating?"

Eoin was equally bewildered. The sword had no wielder, but carried every intent to kill the people before them.

Eoin wouldn't know how to counter such a formidable ability, especially not without knowing the master's location. Against such a powerful kore, he and his team would be a dandelion in the wind. He looked at Myrana, then to Kinneth approaching with Lena in his arms. They were focused on the wave of nobles rushing into the garden, their screams filling the lively night. Eoin knew their mission had failed when he saw silhouettes dash past ballroom windows faster than the Liborian Waltz.

"Fall back," he commanded. "I'll go get the others."

"You're crazy," Kinneth said, but Eoin was gone, dashing toward the mansion from the way they entered. He stopped by the wall decorated with vines, no one in sight. He gave the vines a hard tug before pressing his heels against the wall and ascending to the second floor.

He entered a room through an open window. It was a modest living quarter with plain baby blue furniture and drapery. He could hear the muffled screams and battle cries of the fight downstairs.

Thud!

He was startled by something large that had fallen on other side of the wall. He waited for a moment – took note of faint fumbles and grunts – before peeking out into the hall. He saw two ladies, one in a black suit and the other in a long, blue gown, wrestling each other to the ground. Mirari had pulled off the assailant's bandanna. Eoin got a good look at her... and his eyes grew wide.

Soteria.

She was no doubt the one in charge, judging from the rage in her eyes. Eoin's confusion quickly turned to anger when he saw a black dagger hovering by her side. Had she been hiding her ability this entire time? Soteria's fist met Mirari's head, and she stood her ground, but something else brought her pain. Mirari lurched forward with her hand to her head.

Eoin shook off his anger, taking a deep breath to clear his mind. He noticed the air around him was different; tense, yet unfamiliar. There was something new and eerie about Soteria's aura. No, she didn't hide her ability before... she somehow acquired it within the last five years.

Eoin looked back into the room, searching for a durable weapon. He picked up a metal stool and returned to the hallway. While Soteria was focused on Mirari, Eoin roared and charged forward.

"Soteria!" He yelled, slamming the stool against her head. Before the stool crushed her against the wall, Soteria grabbed the chair by the legs and shoved it back at him. "I thought you were dead! You played us."

Soteria picked up her dagger and attempted to slash at Eoin. He used the stool to block her swings. Another swing knocked the dagger out of her hand as it tumbled down the hall.

"You are a coward," she said, her husky voice spoke words full of contempt. "You lost your war. Don't interfere with mine."

She kicked the stool out of Eoin's hands, then landed another blow to his stomach.

He stumbled backwards. He knew he couldn't win, not with his strength gradually departing with his youth, and certainly not against whatever ability she gained. He could tell from the strength in her kick that her physique had improved, but Eoin was only a fraction of the warrior he was during the Althaean Siege.

He peered over the spiral stairway next to the bedroom and watched chaos unfold in the ballroom. Leviathan and Raiden were struggling. In disguise, they looked like the assailants and took them on by surprise, even saving one noble from having his head hacked off.

But their treachery didn't go unnoticed. Distracted, Leviathan met fate with a dagger in his chest, then there was the crack of a rib or two. He coughed forward, choking out red. In a fury, he yanked the dagger from his chest and headbutted the man in front who had stabbed him. Now he had no shield and the surrounding assailants raised blades over his head.

Raiden put up an incredible fight, but after taking an arrow to his arm, the blood loss had weakened him. An assailant swung a glass bowl at his head, knocking him to the ground. He struggled to get up, but two assailants held him down with a fury of kicks. A spear ran through his leg, taking his last chance of escape. An ax hovered over his head. He stood frozen, knowing it was the end.

Eoin was too late. He knew he had failed. There was little he could do now, except to stop this madwoman.

"This is wrong," he said, turning back to Soteria. "You're making the situation worse."

"You're just jealous that the Defiants are doing more than your group ever did. Look at yourself, rotting away quietly. How could you even call yourself a member of the Blessed?"

Eoin threw a punch at her, which she dodged, and grappled his body, pulling him forward into a backdrop. Eoin cursed as his chest exploded with pain. A fractured bone or two wouldn't stop him from fighting, but he wasn't sure if he could take any more. Soteria's dagger gravitated back within her range, blade pointed at his throat. But then, she was intercepted by a flying kick to her back that sent her tumbling down the hall. Eoin felt his body being forced up.

"We have to go!" Myrana urged. She threw his arm over her shoulder, carrying his weight.

Eoin pressed his hand against his chest, his eyes weighing heavily. The last thing he wanted was for Soteria to escape, knowing that the chances of him finding her again were slim. But as much as he didn't want to admit it, he needed someone to lean on.

Eoin glanced back at the ballroom. Before, the fighters were begging for their lives. Many took shelter under tables and behind guards before they knew what had happened. Now, they had begun attacking in groups of two or three, coordinated offenses with them guarding each other's backs. What had been a dribble of terrified nobles had turned to roaring rapids, hacking and slashing in the manner that they were trained to do. The fight was almost over, but Eoin already lost his men.

Myrana must've read the look on his face when she said, "We did all we could. You don't need to die here today."

Eoin nodded, and he followed Myrana's lead out the window they had come in. He knew when to take a loss.

By the time Soteria regained her balance, Eoin and Myrana were gone. A clatter of footsteps came from the bottom of the stairway, and she shuffled back on her feet, moving to an adjacent room and out a window.

Her plan being foiled was an unexpected nuisance – rival members of the Blessed, seeking to tear her down as much as region leaders, the Knights, and the Council. They couldn't see her vision, and the time for talk had long passed. Her master was once the same, sold on the idea that he could create a better world through a level of honor and code. Perhaps that was his mistake. Change had to be executed by force, and her newfound power enabled her to do just that.

Under the moonlight she sprinted away from the scene, disappearing in the shadow of the woods. She glanced at her black dagger, the only piece she had left of the one who cared for her throughout the decades. There was no doubt in her mind that she was brought back into this world to fulfill his mission.

CHAPTER THIRTY

Six Weeks After the Grand Ball

Mirari focused on the kids running down the street, laughing and playing some obscure game. Farther down, Kinneth was balanced on a rooftop, repairing it with the wood she had bought. Eoin finished speaking, but she needed a moment to process the story she'd been told.

Shaking her head, she got to her feet and walked a few steps away. "Why should I believe you?" she asked.

He snorted, crossing his arms over his large chest. "You're the one who keeps coming back. Why would you indulge in stories you don't believe?"

It was true. It had taken a few days for her to get the whole story without arousing Gaven's suspicion if she were gone too long. Every time she returned to Aias, she made sure she brought supplies and materials to help them rebuild. She stayed for an hour or two, providing help and listening to Eoin's tale.

"It went just as I predicted." Eoin concluded grimly. "Our

people are being hauled in by droves or murdered in their homes by order of the Council. Soteria is on the loose, and I have no idea how to find her."

"Are you sure Soteria is the one who possessed Gaven?"

"No, I never said that." Mirari raised a brow and Eoin continued. "I know for certain she is the one leading this uprising. On behalf of Laikos? On behalf of some other sage she met within the last five years? I have no idea." He shook his head. "But this is not like her. Soteria fought with words, not her fists. Our only way to find out what is really going on is to find her."

Eoin wasn't going to wait for Mirari to feel convinced. He picked up his hammer, ready to get back to work.

"How do I know you're not like her?" Mirari asked.

"My goals haven't changed. I'm an old man, but I want to leave this world better. For them." He nodded toward the children. "But I know, unlike your Knights, unlike the region leader, unlike the *council*, about priorities. My people bled and died to protect the council. If you don't believe anything, believe that. There's a war brewing and you better prepare."

Grabbing the reins of her horse, Mirari pulled herself into the saddle. She turned the horse in the direction out of town, but didn't leave. She glanced back at Eoin. "Why did you tell me? Why would you trust me?"

Grunting, he shook his head. "Don't be naïve. It's not about trust." He was silent a moment, jaw flexing like he was chewing over his next words. "It's like I said earlier. Priorities, is all. I don't aim for the easiest target to make myself feel better. I look for the most dangerous one." His eyes narrowed as he looked up at Mirari. "You tell me, Milady. Do you honestly think we," he thumbed his hand at his chest, "are the most dangerous thing out there?"

Mirari looked away and her gaze landed on Kinneth. She

thought about the disgusting feeling of Laikos invading her mind and how much destruction and death there had been from controlling just Gaven. Could she say these poor peasants railing against the system were the most dangerous thing? No, of course not. But she also couldn't bring herself to agree with him either.

Pressing her lips together, she snapped the reins and took off at a trot.

"Bye bye, Miss!" Mirari looked over her shoulder to see the three kids waving at her. Their cheeks were red from exertion, if not from eating. Mirari waved goodbye and silently cursed herself. Just what was she going to tell Gaven?

MIRARI KNOCKED on the door to Gaven's office. When he bade her enter, she had to straighten her spine to keep from skulking in like a criminal. He was bent over his desk, looking over some papers when she slipped through the door and closed it behind her.

He did a double take when he saw her standing in front of the door. He scrutinized her through narrowed eyes. "Mirari." Rising to his feet, he motioned for her to take the chair across from him. "I haven't seen you in a while. You must have been busy. Is everything all right? No damage, I assume?"

"Oh! No, I'm fine."

Exhaling softly, he nodded to himself and sat back down. "Good. Haynes hadn't said anything, but…" He swiped his hand over his stubble. "Seeing you there just reminded me of what happened in the plaza." He looked tired and drawn, but he shook his head and focused on her. "So, did you find anything else out about Aias?"

"Ah?" Getting right to it? She'd wanted a little time to bring him around to the idea. She didn't know how he would react knowing the person who had controlled him and made him do all those awful things was still out there.

He raised his eyebrow when she dithered on answering.

"No, no. There, ah, wasn't anything to see there. Just another poor village."

Swearing, his hand tightened into a fist. She could feel the burning rage in him like a punch to her gut. "We'll find them. Every last one of those scums no matter where they're hiding."

"Do you think," she started and found herself caught by Gaven's intense stare.

"Think what?"

"Do you think the Blessed are *all* like Laikos?"

"What do you mean?" He turned his fierce gaze out the window. "Do I think they're all empaths? Impossible. Do I think they're all evil? Without a doubt. Don't let yourself be fooled by their circumstances, Mirari."

"I know," she assured him. She didn't know how to talk to him without triggering his anger. If only there was some way to prove it to him. If only she could show him people were still being possessed, he would shift his focus away from rounding up the poor and the weak even if they were associated with the Blessed.

In Eoin's tale, he talked about the people they'd subdued during the attack on the Grand Ball. There was something there and she followed the thought. Like Jep, he'd been wildly antagonistic and violent. That was it. Those actions were familiar and not just what she'd encountered when she confronted Gaven. There was someone else like that too.

She brightened in realization – she still had a prisoner from the plaza. When she'd gone down to question him, he'd been obsessed with antagonizing her. Someone in his position surely wouldn't act like that if he were in his right mind. Like Eoin said, there was someone powerful at work trying to restart the rebellion and using people to do it.

She jumped to her feet, feeling reinvigorated. Now that she knew more about it, she could maybe find just the right question to get him talking about the Defiants. If there was proof that they existed, she'd be able to give the evidence to Gaven. No longer would there be any need to indiscriminately attack the villages.

"Mirari?" Gaven said, looking up at her. "I trust you understand where I'm coming from." He searched her gaze like he was looking for trust and understanding. She hoped he found it there.

"I do," she said with a nod. She glanced at the door, eager to find someone else to corroborate Eoin's story without having to mention him to Gaven.

"Going somewhere?" Gaven asked, amused.

"I just remembered something I wanted to ask that man from the plaza," she said, heading toward the door. "I'm going to question him again. I think he might know something."

"Mirari." Something in his voice called her back. Staring at her in confusion, he motioned for her to take her seat. "You want to *question* the man who attacked you?" She nodded. "I'm afraid that that's impossible."

"Why? I—" She leaned back in her seat, taking a calming breath. "I know he's dangerous, I'll take precautions." She had an idea. "I'll take Haynes with me. I'll be completely safe." Even as she was speaking, Gaven was shaking his head.

"He's already been executed."

"What? Executed?" She leaned forward. Had the taunts escalated? What could justify executing someone who'd already been caught and detained? Someone who hadn't even killed anyone? "Why?"

He looked at her like she'd grown a second head. "Why? You can't have forgotten that he attacked you."

"B-barely," she said through a suddenly dry throat.

He slammed his hand on the desk and she jumped. "Barely is enough. He attacked you. He bruised you. And now he's dead. Problem solved."

"He wasn't a problem, he was a person," she argued. "A loudmouthed jerk. Nothing more than that."

"Why are you acting so surprised? I told you, violence against a region leader's partner leads to capital punishment."

"Yes, you told me that." And that there was no room for mercy in Althaea – she couldn't forget that. "But your people are acting out of fear. Don't you want to change that?"

His jaw flexed as he gritted his teeth. "Change is important, of course, but that doesn't mean I should let dangerous criminals roam free. I have to protect the people of Althaea Main and that means cutting rebels like a rot."

"Did you execute him because he was a criminal or because he attacked me?"

"He almost took your head off. It was justice."

Mirari almost scoffed. It was retribution, not justice, and she didn't want any part of that. "If there's no chance for mercy, how can there be a place for justice?"

Mirari felt Gaven's anger fading. For a moment, she thought she'd gotten through to him.

He waved his hand at himself. "I'm not saying there's no reason for mercy – I'm only here because of mercy, but not everyone deserves it. Someone who attacks you, doesn't deserve mercy. People who disrupt Althaea Main don't deserve mercy." Then his face hardened and his words tightened. "The Blessed don't deserve mercy."

Mirari's lips parted, but she closed her mouth before she could speak. There really wasn't anything more to say. Gaven had taken a hardline and she knew her words alone would not be enough to convince him.

Worse still, as things stood, she didn't have another way to convince him. Her one idea to talk to someone who might be under the control of Soteria was gone. Dead, because of Gaven.

CHAPTER THIRTY-ONE

The people of Aias never left Mirari's mind. For weeks, Mirari kept the newfound information to herself, trying to find and stop the Defiants without bringing harm to Eoin's people. Her mind went blank. It was impossible without getting the people of Aias involved, and she knew Gaven would oppose the idea of working with the Blessed.

She couldn't afford to stall any longer. Every day she waited to gain more information on the Defiants was another day that innocent people were being slaughtered under the Council's order – not just in Althaea Main but across the Alliance.

Mirari leaned into the comstōne in Gaven's fortress and dragged her finger along the metal edges of her badge. After listening to Eoin's story she understood the matter wasn't as simple as she'd thought. The Defiants needed to be stopped by any means. It wasn't just about her new knowledge of the Defiants, but spending time with Eoin and Myrana, even Kinneth in his own fashion, made her realize that the Blessed weren't all cut from the same cloth.

Kylah voice rung out from the stone, and Mirari filled her in with Eoin's tale. Kylah was sharp-witted and knowledgeable. If there was a way to get through to Gaven, she thought Kylah would be able to figure it. She hadn't managed to tell Kylah everything, but Mirari still wanted her advice on how to proceed.

"I can't say I agree," Kylah said and Mirari's heart sank. "I don't fully trust these people. Even if the Defiants truly exist, those villagers were still once rebels, and living poor doesn't dismiss war crimes. I hope you understand."

Mirari's eyes drifted to the ground. It was the response she expected, but she had hoped for better.

"Mirari? Are you still there?" Kylah's voice, ringing from the stone, was sharp, but kind and Mirari hummed in response.

"Yes, but." Clenching her hand into a fist, she pressed it to her forehead. "I just think our focus is in the wrong place. They aren't the ones inciting the riots."

Mirari strengthened her voice. "The Defiants don't represent the majority. I think we can find members that don't want this rebellion *and* will even work with us to put a stop to it. It makes sense to try."

"Or it could be a trap." Kylah's sigh was small, but rang loud in Mirari's ears. "I can only imagine where you got this information from, but this could easily be a part of a greater scheme. A ploy to get to you or Gaven or the Knights. To me, it doesn't seem worth the risk to try."

Mirari stared hard out the window, watching soldiers march by in the courtyard below. She knew Eoin and the others were telling the truth, but Kylah hadn't even left an opening for her to talk about actual members of the Blessed that Mirari had met. If she couldn't convince the pragmatic Kylah, there was no way to speak to Gaven.

Kylah blew out a harsh breath. "Tell me. Why are you trying to convince me instead of talking to your partner? After all, that's what he's for."

"Talking to Gaven," Mirari said. "It's been… hard. He can't forgive what happened to him during the Siege."

"And he has every right to feel that way."

"But not every member was responsible for that. The person who possessed him may still be out there, and more powerful than Laikos." There was silence on Kylah's end. "You don't believe me, do you?"

"Sorry, Mirari. I can't validate the source of your information. I can pretend this conversation never happened, but you should be discussing this with His Honor, or Lord Fangbane." Something creaked behind Mirari but when she turned around, there was nothing there. "Please don't act out on your own. Sorry, I've got to go."

"Wait, Kylah—"

"Goodbye, Mirari."

With a small frown, Mirari took a step outside the room. Staring at the long, empty hallway, she realized she hadn't progressed at all. Perhaps it was better if she did talk to Gaven. But would he listen?

As soon as Mirari took her first step back to her chambers, Gaven came around the corner. She smiled at him, and then tempered her smile when she remembered their last conversation.

"Your Honor," she greeted.

"Mirari." He walked past her with his head held high, barely meeting her eyes. Then he stopped and looked back at her. "I meant to ask you about your patrol in Aias."

"Aias?" Her heart pounded in her chest, but she managed a casual shrug. "I submitted that report a month ago."

Gaven nodded. "Right. And you said there was nothing out of the ordinary."

"That's right."

"So there's no reason for you to return."

The way he asked… Did he know? He must. If he knew she'd been back, he'd know she was lying if she denied it. "I, yeah, but I did take them some supplies."

There was a moment while Gaven looked at her. Then he nodded. "Good." He started walking toward his office.

"Good?" She called after him. Gaven waved his hand without stopping.

<hr>

GAVEN STRETCHED his shoulders out as he slumped back into his chair. Maybe he needed to take a break before getting back to the paperwork. With Erel gone to investigate the Council, the annoying minutia of the region fell to him. He scrubbed his hand over his scruffy face. Maybe that's why he was so short with Mirari. It's just… He thought she understood, but then she was pressing him about the nuances of the Blessed. What nuances?

He was getting himself worked up all over again, so he was grateful when there was a knock on the door. However, before he could bade them to enter, they walked in on their own. He scowled at his own figure as 'he' slipped inside and shut the door.

"I'm glad you're back," he said. "But why do you look like that?"

"Oh, this?" As Erel stepped forward, she molded into her true form. Despite her flippant tone, her features were pinched and he felt a sense of foreboding at the look in her eyes. Whatever she had to say, it wasn't going to calm him down. "I ran into something interesting on the way back."

"And? What did you find?"

She sat down in the seat across from him, crossing her legs on his desk. "Nothing much. Oh." She snapped her fingers. "Except our cute, little Mirari is capable of deception. Who knew?"

"Mirari?" He shook his head. He could tell when Mirari was lying. It wasn't possible for her to deceive him. "Wait, wait. You spent two days in Adder's skin. What's Mirari have to do with what you learned from the Council?"

"As we expected, the Council has been looking for possible accomplices for the attack at the Grand Ball," Erel said. Gaven nodded. Since the entire Council was assembled in one area, security should have been tight and yet rebels had been able to march right inside. "Mirari was one of the names that came up," Erel finished.

His heart skipped a beat hearing those words. Gaven got to his feet and began pacing. His mind was racing, replaying the events that happened that night. She was with him almost the entire time, if not greeting the noble snobs then fighting the rebels. She was injured during the attack. How was it possible? Why her?

"Who would even consider…" He stopped, seething anger rushing through him. "Inigo."

"That would be my guess."

Bracing his hands on the desk, he shook his head again. "He's lying. He's only doing this to get back at me."

Dropping her feet, Erel frowned at him, serious now. "I don't doubt that's the reason, but don't just dismiss it out of hand. You know how he operates. Three truths and a lie. If Mirari had nothing to hide, not even Inigo's word would have brought her to the Council's attention."

Gaven cursed to himself. She was right. Inigo's money bought him a vast information network. But perhaps it was something innocent that Inigo was warping to his own agenda.

Sinking down into his seat, he motioned to Erel. "All right. What is it? What's Mirari hiding?"

"Aias."

"Aias?" The name sounded familiar. "Isn't that the town where we found three members of the Blessed?"

Erel nodded. "It's also the town we sent Mirari to do a second patrol. At her own insistence, remember." Erel's eyes narrowed as she glanced toward the door. "Mirari said she found nothing. When I questioned her just now, she said the same."

"You think she's lying about that?"

"Well according to the information the Council received from *someone*—"

"Inigo," he cursed.

"Mirari has been seen visiting Aias multiple times since that second patrol. Ostensibly to provide aid, but…"

He filled in the blanks. Aias has denied assistance for years. How could Mirari, a Minettan, convince them otherwise. And why wouldn't she tell him?

"Should I question her again?" Erel asked. She leaned forward, dragging her hand across the edge of the table. Lowering her voice, she continued, "I can think of a couple of ways to get her to talk. She's easily flustered. If I keep pushing, she'll crack."

His mind raced. Erel was good at what she did, but…

Gaven shook his head. "No. That's not necessary."

Frowning, Erel dropped the seductive act. "Why not? We know she's lying about something. You don't mean to just let it go, do you?"

He waved his hand dismissively. "I need you to quash these rumors. Get the Council to let this go. Can it be done?"

She stared at him for a moment. "Your Honor, I don't understand. These aren't just rumors. It's the truth. She visits Aias frequently and she let one of the assailants slip away during the Grand Ball. It'll only be a matter of time before—"

"Erel," he said sharply, thunder in his voice. "Can it be done?"

Sighing, Erel closed her eyes and nodded. "There is a lack of true evidence. As long as they find nothing else and she stops going to Aias, I can make them overlook it."

"Good." He exhaled slowly. A little bit of tension in his shoulders eased with that assurance. "Good. You handle that. I'll talk to Mirari."

Erel leaned forward with a sense of urgency. "Why do you protect her? After Inigo, I thought you would be—"

"Erel," he snapped. She pressed her lips closed. "She's not like him." He clenched his jaw against the onslaught of undesirable memories. Taking a deep breath, he forced the thoughts away and repeated to himself. Mirari was nothing like Inigo. And he had warned her to stay away from him. This wasn't the same situation at all. "Take care of the Council," he said wearily.

After a beat of silence, Erel flashed him a grin. Rising, she stretched her arms over her head. "Whatever you say."

As soon as she left, Gaven gripped his chest and stared out the window in silence.

CHAPTER THIRTY-TWO

Mirari and Gaven weaved through the crowds of the lower plaza on their horses. Gaven had said it was just a small patrol to make sure everything was well with the people, but Mirari could sense there was something more going on. She glanced around, noticing there were fewer people roaming the streets than before. In contrast, there was a higher number of military soldiers snooping around. She struggled with the knowledge that even those with nothing to hide now sought life outside of major cities. Where there were many people, there was danger.

For now, she could only do what she was able. She looked over to Gaven and couldn't take the silence any longer. "You're not going to say anything?"

He glanced at her out of the corner of his eye. "About what?"

Things had been different ever since that odd conversation they'd had a few days ago. She couldn't put her finger on the reason why though. She hadn't really seen him since then. That's when she realized. "You've been avoiding me."

He didn't try to deny it. Instead, he turned away and muttered, "It's because I don't know what your relationship is with the people of Aias."

Mirari looked down at the reins in her hand. "Relationship? I already told you. They're people who need help and I'm helping them. Their living conditions are poor and I deliver supplies to them. It's my duty as a Knight."

He exhaled sharply through his nose. "Mirari." He pounded his chest. "I can tell when you're lying."

She could feel his frustration and felt her own rising. "It's… not a lie. It's a truth you don't want to hear." That was the crux of it. What she'd learned from Eoin was a truth he didn't want to hear so she had to bite her tongue and skirt around the issue.

"Tell me what's going on. They've declined our assistance for years. Those poor conditions are what they chose. Why do they suddenly want our help. Why you? They've never cared for Minettans before."

"I… convinced them." She glanced at Gaven, praying he would believe her.

For the first time, Gaven turned his gaze on Mirari. She met his glare. It came with a wave of hostility he had never harbored for her. She took a deep breath, attempting to calm herself, but it was too late. There was something broken between them and she didn't know how to fix it. At this point, even if she wanted to, telling him about Inigo, the Blessed, the Defiants, all of it wouldn't change anything.

She turned away, unsure of what to say. They were about to pass a stall where two unkempt men were loitering, staring a little too intently at the wares. One of the shaggy ruffians engaged the vendor in a loud, distracting conversation. As he did, his partner snatched a dented, old bronze pitcher.

Mirari was almost relieved at the cry of, "Stop! Thief!"

Mirari was off her horse without a second thought, sprinting after the pair of thieves as they fled down the street with the bronze pitcher. She heard Gaven follow at first, but when she glanced back at the sound of him cursing, she had lost sight of him.

It didn't matter. She'd be able to handle a couple of crooks on her own.

Mirari chased the shoplifters, closing the distance. They dodged pedestrians, knocked over a cart of fruit, then cut down a side street. As she got closer, she could hear their labored huffing. She knew she'd catch up to them soon.

She was only thirty feet from grabbing the one with the bronze pitcher, when they swerved off into an alley. She chased after them, following deeper into the warren of slum dwellings. It was a narrow path, crowded between residential hovels, and littered with all manner of filth. As the ruffians disappeared around the corner, she lost sight of them for a second. She sped up, not wanting to lose them in the twisty alley of this reeking slum.

As she raced around the corner, she held up. Ahead of her, she could see the two thieves had stopped short. The alley came to a dead end. Mirari grinned, savoring the thought. But instead of attacking, she gave them a calm stare, and held out her open hand.

"Why don't we skip ahead past the part where I kick your asses, and cut right to the part where you give me back that pitcher?"

The bigger man wheezed out. "Why would we want to miss all the fun, little missy?"

"Hand it over," Mirari demanded. The two men gave each other a grave look. Then they burst out in mocking laughter. The thief threw the pitcher behind him, hitting the wall with a loud clang.

They didn't exactly look terrified. But before she completed the thought, Mirari's ears perked up.

The squeak of a door hinge behind her to the left…

The scrape of a boot on the cobbles to her right…

Her hand instinctively went to the hilt of her sword as she turned. Behind her were four more hard looking men. Slowly they edged closer, cutting off any chance to escape the way she had come. Now there were six men surrounding her, and none of them looked friendly.

Gaven squeezed into the alley, rounding the corners. He stopped at a crossroad, unsure of which direction Mirari had taken. But then he heard a loud clang coming from the left. He was ready to turn in that direction, until he felt a malicious aura looming behind him.

There was a wooden club over Gaven's head, and although he couldn't see it coming, Gaven whirled on the man with the club. His flashing steel took off the man's club hand with a clean slice. There were more. Before the ruffian next to him could raise his dagger, Gaven bashed his skull against the wall. As he fell, Gaven grabbed the knife from his hand, and hurled it at another thug blocking his way. It nailed him dead in the chest. He dropped to his knees, his hands pressed over the wound as his blood pulsed out in spurts.

In that moment, Gaven realized that this was no regular burglary. No one would be foolish enough to try to mug him, but they had separated him from Mirari. For what reason, he was afraid to find out. Leaving the injured ruffians in pain, Gaven rushed down the alley in the direction of the noise.

Mirari cursed at herself. Slowly, she began to draw her sword. The sound of steel sliding out its sheath spoke of certain mayhem, portending a mist of fresh blood would soon fill the air. But her sword was only half drawn, when she heard a voice from behind.

"Let's not scare the young lady," he said, waving the men back. His voice sounded like a friendly purr. Except the tone lacked any hint of warmth. Mirari knew that voice, and the heartless man it belonged to.

"Tepis," she said.

"You remember me," he smiled, brushing his long, white hair away from his face. "But you seem to have forgotten about our agreement."

"I did as you asked," Mirari hissed. "I left those towns alone. Some of your clients are members of the Blessed and I didn't even question it. What kind of game are you playing?"

"Just a little wake up call," he said. "I think you could do better. People are still being taken away from their families, some even murdered on the spot. And that is your fault, Mirari. Perhaps I expected too much for a peasant, a Minettan one at that." He let out a disappointing sigh, then took a good look at the brown paper in his hand. "Fake identifications are a chargeable offense, and with you on the watchlist, I reckon the Council would want to see this."

Mirari was holding her breath, unable to hide her growing sense of doom.

"What more do you want?" she said. "What His Honor does or doesn't do is beyond my control."

He placed his hand on his lip. "You're right. As his Minettan partner, what power do you have? With all due respect, you lack the breeding for such an exalted position. A poor, feather-draped merchant, from a sleepy backwater, a bump in the road. You're way out of your league."

He smiled at her, and Mirari instantly understood. The anger she felt a second ago had evaporated. She stuttered, "You want me to break the partnership."

Inigo nodded. "It's for your own good, and the least you can do for tarnishing our heritage. If you do sever your relationship with him, I'll ask no more of you, darling. I couldn't care less what fun and games you get up to with the Knights. But see to it you keep your affairs out of Althaea." He clapped his hands together. "This is the best for everyone."

Mirari was in a daze, stunned at the decision before her. If this fool was able to uncover her fake records, how far was he willing to go until he got what he wanted? It would only be a matter of time before he unraveled her connection to Gaven, to their Minettan origins. It was what she had feared all this time. The decision shouldn't have been hard to make, but still she hesitated. She couldn't imagine how it would devastate Gaven to lose his partner.

She looked around. "I suppose you're not going to give me time to think about it."

"Here and now, darling." Inigo said. His thugs took a step closer in case she decided to resist "Say the words right here."

Mirari bit her lip. Was keeping her identity a secret worth more than her relationship with Gaven? But it was much more than that. It was a matter of keeping Gaven's secret and preserving everything he had worked hard for. She didn't care if she had to surrender her title, got banned from Althaea, or hanged for treason. The most honorable thing was to not let anyone go down with her.

But before she could answer, the thug to her right dropped to his knees with an unbearable anguish in his ribs. From behind her stood her partner, an undeniable anger in his eyes. He grabbed another man and shoved his head into the wall, his unconscious body dropped face down into the damp ground.

The remaining four thugs exchanged a look. Then they sprinted away, stumbling over each other to get out of that alley while they still had their heads attached.

"Cowards!" Inigo shrieked after them. "I'll have you all flayed!"

"You're the one to talk!" Gaven said as he shoved Inigo against the wall. "To set up this elaborate scheme just to get under my skin. You're predictable, Inigo."

"I've only ever tried to guide you in the right direction. Bonding with a featherpit was a grave mistake."

Gaven punched the wall next to Inigo's head, leaving a hard dent in the stone. "You keep her out of your childish revenge." He snapped with a frustrated rage, seasoned with a dose of revulsion. "Give it to me, now!"

But Inigo didn't tremble or flinch. He simply handed Gaven the paper in his hand. He let go of Inigo and snatched the paper, but didn't look at it in the slightest.

"No matter," Inigo said, fixing his collar. "I'll leave you two alone now. I trust you have a lot to discuss."

Inigo stalked away, and as soon as he was out of sight, Gaven examined the paper, rotating the seal of authenticity in dim light. For some reason, it didn't surprise him that Inigo was right.

Mirari shrunk in herself. Rubbing her hands, she asked, "You heard everything?"

"I warned you to stay away from him," Gaven sneered. "You went behind my back and made a deal? You really were letting the Blessed go free?"

"You think I had a choice?" she said. "Inigo, he—" She took a deep breath; she still didn't have the courage to tell him.

He held up the paper. "Mind telling me what this is about?" Mirari lowered her head. He could tell she didn't want to say it. But that wasn't going to fly with him. Inigo had something on her, and he was completely unaware of it.

Gaven wasn't worried about the evidence. In fact, fixing her records would be no problem. He could have Erel slip in the officer's drawer, stamp the real thing, and replace it with an authentic sheet. But what kind of lie would he be protecting? He had to know.

"Mirari is not my real name," she admitted. "I abandoned my birth name after I was adopted."

He wasn't surprised at that. He was aware that Mirari had been hiding things since the day they met. Gaven didn't care. Everyone had their secrets, some less willing to discuss their dark past more than others.

"Name changes are completely legal, but fake records and tags are not. Why didn't you just change your name?"

"It would still carry my real name in the records and… I can't have people knowing my real name."

"Why? Are you a spy?"

"No." She raised an eyebrow.

"Did you kill someone?"

"I—" Mirari hesitated on that question. "No, I didn't."

"Then why would you need a fake name?"

"Does it even matter?" Mirari asked. Gaven was growing upset. Even though she was telling the truth, it was hurting him. Little did he know, the full truth would hurt even more.

"It does. The Council is already on edge with you. And now this? Do you know how much trouble you're in? And worst of all…" He paused. "I don't even know who you are. You swore to me by oath under a fake name."

"I-I'm sorry."

"Then who are you?"

She paused. With a plea in her eyes, she answered, "I can't tell you. Believe me, it's to protect you."

"Protect me from what?" When Mirari didn't answer, he

beckoned her again. "And the Blessed? Did you let them go to protect me too?"

"You're not in your right mind, Your Honor," she said. "You're hurting people. The Blessed are the people you swore to protect, loyal Althaeans, honest workers—"

"The Blessed are violent people no matter how you sugarcoat it. If they want to survive, they need to work for it, just like everyone else. Not by terrorizing neighbors or assassinating nobles."

"You don't understand—"

"I've captured dozens of these ruffians. I think I do. Evil is evil, and if we don't stop it now, it will only rise tenfold in the future. Once the foundations of justice crumbles, then we do not just fail the people, but also the future generation."

"But is it really the future generation you're thinking about? Or is this about taking revenge on the Blessed for tainting you during the Siege?"

Seething, Gaven bared his teeth. "What difference does it make? A threat left unmanaged is still a threat." He took a breath and she hated the way he looked at her. "Out of everyone, I thought you'd understand."

Mirari took a step forward. This was her last chance. She had to convince him. "They're not the ones," she started. "Laikos, these people, they're not the ones who possessed you."

Gaven thrust his hand through his hair. "More lies? Really?"

"I'm not lying. There's—" He barked a dark laugh, shaking his head. "Gaven, listen!" She held her hand out and spoke quickly. "There's something else out there. Something worse. We can work together and—"

"Enough!" he roared and her mouth snapped closed. He took a breath and then another. "That's enough, Mirari." He paused and snorted. "Mirari, or whatever your name is," he repeated bitterly and shook his head. "You're done."

"What do you mean?"

He tossed the paper at her feet, letting it fall onto the damp, soiled floor. "Exactly what I said." He turned and started walking away from her. "A carriage will be waiting for you at dawn. You've done enough."

Alone in the alley, Mirari dropped to her knees. Pain shot through her and she realized she had lost his trust. No longer would they share each other's burdens. Not since Salathiel had died had she felt such a crushing loneliness.

Her arms hung loose by her side and when she stretched her fingers out, she brushed against the paper Gaven had dropped. She stared at it, cursing it, cursing Inigo, cursing herself.

Was Inigo right? She knew that he was only looking out for himself and his business, but could there have been some truth in what he said? Had it been a mistake to stay in Althaea Main? She was making the situation with the military and the peasants worse.

She pressed the back of her hand to her mouth, thinking about the carnage that would follow. Gaven wanted to do good and to protect his people, but this wasn't the way. He was going about taking down their enemies the wrong way. And he was making enemies that didn't need to be made.

And she knew Gaven better than anyone else – that seething anger wasn't going to go away. And now, the only people who would bear the brunt of the anger were the people he swore to protect.

Shaking her head, she slowly climbed to her feet. Even though she thought this, there wasn't anything she could do. She was powerless, and it was time to go home.

CHAPTER THIRTY-THREE

Mirari's room felt cold as she packed her bag. Hugging her arms around herself, she sat down on her bed. There were still several hours before she had to be on the carriage. Then, it was back to home alone. Collapsing back onto the bed, she braced her hand across her eyes. Something cold touched her skin and she opened her eyes.

The metal of the bracelet rested against her forehead and when she moved her arm, she was greeted with a feathery touch. She bit her lip and sat up.

"What are you going to cry?" she said harshly to herself. "Get a grip." The words brought her neither comfort nor hope. She got up to start packing again, but couldn't concentrate.

She dropped her clothes, left her room and strode down the hall. The comms room was empty, and she locked herself in it. Mirari took a deep breath, then touched the comstōne. It illuminated in a heartbeat.

"Mirari?" She squeezed her eyes closed at the sound of Lucan's voice. "Sorry, I can't talk long, I'm... well, it doesn't matter."

"I understand. Thank you for all the work you do, Lucan. I can't imagine how difficult it is for you to handle the Hales *and* the Knights."

"It's not so bad once you know how to keep the Knights distracted every now and then." He let out a chuckle. "I know we're all busy trying to handle this rebellion, and it doesn't look like it'll be ending soon, but you should come back when you have the chance. We've missed you."

She took a sharp breath and he fell silent. She couldn't explain, exactly, what was going on or rather, she didn't want to tell him that Gaven had rejected her as his partner. She just wanted to speak to someone who didn't think she was terrible. There was no one left in the fort who thought well of her. She hadn't seen Haynes and Erel had given her a deep frown, more frigid than her usual dark looks.

"Mirari, are you okay?" Lucan asked in a soft voice.

"Yeah." She sniffed. "Yes, yeah."

"You don't sound okay."

"I just got a little cold today." she explained.

"Hmm, okay. Drink warm fluids. Remember to rest."

"I will."

Silence settled in for a moment. "Mirari? Is there something you wanted to talk about?"

Mirari. Mirari. He kept calling her Mirari, but did he ever wonder?

"Do you ever wish I would reclaim my name?" she asked. She ran her finger along the creases of the wall while the silence stretched out for even longer.

"No."

Her head jerked up, surprised. "Really?"

"Ah, Mirari." He sighed. "I'm not insulting you. Of course, I'd love it if you came back." He laughed. "I'd appreciate letting someone else go to these engagements." That prompted a light chuckle from Mirari. "At the same time, I'm proud of you."

"Me?"

"Of course. You know, all I ever wanted was for you to be safe and alive. You've done so much more than that, how could I be anything but proud. You have a way that's... good. You're really good, Mirari. No matter what name you go by. Know that, no matter what, I'll support you as best I can."

She didn't know what to say. If she told him the truth now, would he be disappointed? Fortunately, there was murmuring on the other side of the comstōne. "I'll let you go now."

"Are you sure?"

"Yeah, of course. Thanks for talking to me, Lucan."

After the call ended, Mirari finished packing her things. Had that been worth it? Did she feel better? She didn't know. Lucan thought she was good, but she couldn't say the same. Would being good feel this bad?

Inigo? Gaven? Eoin?

She felt like she was being drawn into a million different directions with no chance to make a choice of her own. If she could choose, she'd choose... Her eyes widened as she realized. Why couldn't she choose? Inigo no longer had her false papers and for a while now, she hadn't felt like she was diverting the patrols just for him. Inigo had just been the excuse to do what she'd felt was right. The soldiers killing people for the crime of not having their identification papers, not even people connected to the Blessed, was wrong.

Gaven was wrong. The words felt discourteous to even think, but people were dying and Gaven didn't or couldn't care. There was something dark brewing and if Gaven couldn't see reason then... then she would have to see to it on her own. Gaven had chosen to dissolve their partnership, but she was still a Knight.

Everything she had feared had happened. Inigo had revealed

her secret and Gaven had reacted. There was nothing more to fear. The worst had happened and she survived. Now, anything else that she did would only be on her head. She couldn't say she was following the region leader's orders or capitulating to a blackmailer. She was on her own, yes, but maybe that wasn't so bad right now.

It was all her choice now. She thought about Lucan's words and felt the courage to do what she felt called to do. The Defiants were out there. They were dangerous and capable of something Mirari could only imagine. The only one who had an inkling of the danger on the horizon was Eoin, and she doubted Gaven would waste any time marching on Aias on his vendetta.

If Mirari had a choice, and she did, she would choose to stand against the Defiants and to stand with Eoin and the other Blessed. It made the most sense if she wanted to stop this impending threat, but she'd also grown fond of them. She liked them and didn't think they deserved whatever retribution Gaven was going to rain down on them. She couldn't watch more people die while she stood aside helplessly.

Mirari galloped her horse through the empty streets of Aias and dismounted in front of the smithy. The oven was emitting an orange glow, but the blacksmith was nowhere in sight. But she noticed a soldier tied and slumped over a post next to the stable.

"A scout," Eoin said. "A gift from the region leader."

She followed the sound of his voice and found the blacksmith washing his face in a basin in the back.

Mirari didn't even know where to begin. She failed to convince Kylah and Gaven to reconsider their alliance with the Blessed. Now, she was certain Gaven was out for their heads. How could she tell them that they would all be slaughtered? And if not, where could they run? She was powerless, nothing more than a messenger.

Eoin raised his head, splattering excess water over the ground and wiping his beard dry with a cloth. He turned to Mirari and didn't seem surprised to see her in the late evening.

"Not safe to be riding out at this time," he said. Then he asked, "Why the long face?"

She knew most of the townspeople by name now, even considered some of them her family. But she knew she could never be friends with the Blessed, not after what they did to Salathiel, not after what Laikos did to her and the Knights, or to Gaven during the Althaean Siege. The Blessed were a threat to society — troublemakers, killers, and ruthless tyrants. But the people of Aias were civilians, shopkeepers and merchants, mothers and children, and Mirari saw nothing wrong. No, they were peacemakers, passionate but not aggressive. If the Council wanted to silence every voice that disagreed with them, they wouldn't be any better than the Blessed.

Then there was Gaven, a troubled man fueled by rage and his desire for closure. His quest to take down every member of the Blessed had become unstoppable. It wasn't something he did for the people anymore. It was personal, and Mirari was Aias' last hope.

"Everyone needs to leave," Mirari said. "His Honor wants to raid the village."

Eoin nudged the unconscious scout tied up. "I got the message."

"Then why aren't you running?"

Eoin let out a laugh. He nudged to the spears, pitchforks, and shields lined up against the wall. Mirari had just noticed it. These people were ready to fight, but she knew they couldn't win. They would be marching to their deaths.

"Where would we go?" he said.

Mirari looked around, realizing it was nothing but forests as far as the eye could see. That wasn't the problem. Wherever they would go, Gaven would be able to track them down. Eoin seemed to have made his decision, and the other fighters would no doubt follow his lead.

"This is our home. We defend it with our lives." Eoin put his hand on Mirari's shoulder. "And you? Treason is a death sentence."

Mirari held her Knights badge in her hand. She wasn't sure if it was a good decision. She would be throwing everything she had worked hard for and saying goodbye to her friends in the worst way possible: on the other side of the battlefield.

But her heart knew better. She wouldn't be able to live with herself if she had walked away as Gaven had asked her to.

"This is wrong," she said. "I'm going to make sure I stop him."

She turned her attention to the row of crafted steel, works of art that would soon be stained. Her eyes locked onto her reflection gleaming on a sword's surface, and she instantly noticed something off. Her eyes... were a different color. She jolted back in surprise, terrified, but it had gone in a blink. Mirari grew breathless. This time she knew for sure it wasn't a hallucination.

CHAPTER THIRTY-FOUR

The village was quiet in the early morning. A dozen horses neighed over a ridge, the sound of soldiers accompanying their leader on his white stallion. His piercing gaze spoke of fierce determination and power as he scanned the terrain, then looked down at the village.

A woman was watering the flowers on her porch, and took notice of the cavalry over the ridge. She scrambled inside, waking her family, then knocking on the house next to hers. One by one the villagers emerged onto the main road, woken by the sound of frantic cries. Men hustled to the smithy, grabbing what spears and shields they could, tossing a weapon to every person willing to fight.

Their low-class weapons weren't going to last more than two strikes. Gaven counted the number of traitors he would soon have in his possession, and stopped when he saw Mirari shoving her way to the front. When Erel told him Mirari did not return last night, Gaven assumed she went back to Minetta on her own. But to fight on behalf of the Blessed? He never could've predicted this.

Mirari was always impulsive, always striving for her sense of justice and righting every wrong. But Gaven never would've imagined he would have her standing in the way of claiming his own justice. He thought they had an understanding of how dangerous the Blessed could be. They fought them together, worked together to unravel their mysteries. And now, she was siding with them. Her act was an embarrassment in the face of his soldiers, and with so many witnesses, her treachery could not be denied.

"That man was with you during the Althaean Siege," Erel said, pointing at a tall and heavy man standing next to Mirari. "He may be your best bet to finding out what happened that day." He looked like he could block half of Gaven's small force by himself. Gaven wouldn't underestimate him. But he spotted the ink on his arm — a familiar crest residing in the work of art — and it sent Gaven's blood boiling.

Gaven shouted at the village. "You're all being held for treason against the empire. We know you are sheltering rebels. Your crimes will not go unpunished." Gaven turned to the rest of his squad. "Take all of them, but no one touch those two." He pointed at Mirari and Eoin.

"If they resist, sir?" a soldier asked, taking note of their swords and pitchforks raised high.

"Kill them."

"Onward!" Erel yelled as she pointed at the village. The soldiers kicked their horses into full charge and began to descend into the valley. The commoners readied their swords and shields, and the rest without weapons scattered back into their homes or hid in the surrounding forest. Those who stayed and fought met the soldier's blades, some striking a few jabs and counterattacks. With their iron will, they would fight to the death to protect their homes.

Mirari and Eoin now stood two paces away from Gaven and Erel.

"You." Gaven narrowed his eyes at Eoin and scoffed. He got off his horse and pointed his spear at him. "Were you the one who did it? Did you make me fight on behalf of the rebels during the Siege?"

Eoin wasn't fazed. He had an ax over his shoulder, ready to swing it at any time. But the calm aura he presented told Gaven he wasn't going to fight unless he made him.

"So it's true," Eoin said. "You really don't remember anything."

"Answer me!"

Eoin shrugged. "You're asking the wrong person, Valiant Tiger. You came to me in that state. We were comrades. I'm sad to see that is no longer the case."

"You deceived me," Gaven sneered, taking a strike at Eoin's head. It was quickly blocked with his ax overhead. "We will never be comrades!"

Gaven took another swing. This time, it was blocked by Mirari's sword. She shoved their swords upward, rotating their posture returning them both to a readied stance.

She had her sword drawn with a mirrored stance, and a defiant glare in her eyes. He recognized that look — the eyes of a warrior, one who had sworn to protect and would die for the cause. Such pride and loyalty, he wished he could reward, if only she wasn't standing with the Blessed.

"What are you trying to accomplish here?" Gaven said. "This is the endgame. You just destroyed every chance of clearing your name."

"This is my decision," she said. "I fight for the people, not for a murderer."

"This is going nowhere," Erel said, pulling two daggers from her belt and twirling them in her hand. "I suggest we end this."

Eoin readied his ax, and in a split second Erel jumped off her horse and struck at the blacksmith. She had enough force in her blow to make him stumble a few steps back. Eoin raised the ax again and struck at her.

Gaven couldn't agree more. He raised his spear and struck down. Mirari blocked Gaven's swing overhead, but Gaven swiped his foot under hers, and she fell on her bottom. He had trained Mirari, fought alongside her for years. He knew the tricks she could play, and her weak spots just as well. This duel was all for show. If he wanted to end her, he could do it in a heartbeat. But no matter how much her treachery left a scar in his heart, he found himself struggling to land a killing blow.

Gaven pushed her, propelling her against a tree. As her shoulder slammed painfully into the stump, her anger triggered. She shoved him back. Mirari had no intention of letting this raging warrior chop her into ground steak. She brought her blade over her head as he struck again. She tilted her blade slightly to the side, letting him fall off balance for a half a second, just as he taught her. But she didn't follow up. She stood there, waiting for Gaven to hack at her again.

It was then Gaven realized that she had no intention of winning the fight either. He groaned, striking his spear into the ground between them.

"Do you always have to right every wrong?" he said.

"Look at yourself," she said, lowering her sword. "This whole thing, your obsession over finding the Blessed. This isn't who you are."

"You have no idea who I am." He scoffed, then smiled. "I guess we never knew each other at all, Mirari, or whatever your name is."

He didn't deny that she made him hesitate in ways he never did before. But her lie carved open a wound that Gaven thought had healed a long time ago. The thought of Inigo's manipulation tore at him. The soldiers he harassed, peasants he killed, the lies he told knowing they would suffer at the cost of his gain. How long would it be before Mirari would do the same? What did this cunning woman have planned for him? What was so bad about her past that she would need to hide it? He began to question whether anything she told him was the truth.

Gaven felt like a fool. He had opened himself to an unknown threat. He should've stopped at Inigo; someone as strong as him didn't need a partner. It annoyed him that she was in his heart, violating every emotion he felt. He should've known, and he should've kept it the same — it was better to work alone.

But if that was the case, why did he become partners with her in the first place? Inigo was a snake, a dangerous manipulator without a sprinkle of humanity. Mirari was never any of that, but the part of her he knew wasn't real. To Gaven, it was all the same, and there was only one way to deal with those kinds of people.

"You can't be my partner anymore," he said. "I put up with your lies, but I can't put up with this betrayal."

He began chanting quietly as he raised two fingers, drawing symbols in the air. A small glowing light appeared at his finger-tips and began to trace his movements, leaving a shining text of glowing characters, the words floating between them.

Mirari's mouth dropped. "You wouldn't…"

His fingers swiped down quickly across the emblem of light he had generated.

"I hereby vanquish this bond."

The letters shattered, glowing shards filled the air, then vanished.

He felt his body grow heavy, what was once a source of warmth had now gone cold. Half-stumbled, Gaven was weakened. A familiar energy was missing. The empty space inside him gave off a dull, aching sensation, multiplied by physical pain. His heart felt hollow and dark.

Mirari was hunched over, no doubt feeling the same. Her hand clutched her chest as she felt her strength being pulled away.

"Go home," he said. "There's nothing left for you here."

Gaven looked over at the town now painted with blood. Erel had Eoin in shackles, her foot over his body as she wiped the blood off her face. They had won the battle. He turned back to his defeated partner.

In a blink she rose in fury, screeching and lunging forward with her other hand drawn back for a powerful punch. Gaven was ready to intercept it, but he lost his concentration when he saw her hand erupt into fire. Instead, Gaven crossed his hands over his head, and her punch ricocheted off his barrier. It was strong enough to knock him back a few steps. He stumbled. His mind was now alert, adrenaline fueling his movement. He blinked twice, almost refusing to acknowledge what he saw before him. Mirari was engulfed in anger, so much that it had taken the form of fire. Swirling waves of fire caressed her body, waiting for Mirari's next command.

"Don't underestimate me," Mirari said, with a low hiss in her voice he had never heard from her before. She threw a fireball at Gaven. He ducked as it set the barrel behind him into flames.

"Stop this!" Gaven commanded. He took one step forward, but that was as far as he could go before Mirari threw another fireball at his feet. The speed caught him off guard, and he nearly fell backward. The flames had a familiar red glow, and it entranced him. He was never afraid of fire, but now his body refused to move, frozen as the flames tingled a distant memory.

He saw a scared child, curled into himself as he was

surrounded by fire. Gaven couldn't blame him. That young boy was helpless, too feeble to have been able to do anything. If he could go back he would've told that boy to stand up, look fear in the eye as every worthy warrior would. Seeing the boy reminded him that he couldn't repeat the same mistake.

His heart sank – he blamed the recoil of the partner's bind, but he knew that wasn't true. With reluctance, he turned his focus back on Mirari. Now he was older, more aware of the little things around him. And whoever he saw in front of him, it wasn't Mirari. She had been in his heart for so long he knew her like the back of his hand. The rage this fire-wielder carried – that bitter and disdainful look in her eyes – was not the woman he knew.

But if he didn't put an end to her, the chance would be gone, and chaos would undoubtedly follow.

"Who are you?" Gaven yelled, but her glare told him she didn't want to chat. She had another fireball ready in her hand, and she took her swing.

Gaven crouched, and in one swift motion, he unsheathed the dagger from his boot and whirled it at Mirari. It nailed her right above her chest, blood streaming out as she wailed and sank to her knees. The flames surrounding her began to fade.

Gaven rushed to her side and placed his hand on the hilt of the dagger. He grew with discomfort seeing her bleed red. But before he could pull it out, he heard someone approaching from his right.

Emerging from the alley of the building was a soldier trembling behind his spear. He was relieved to see his leader, but shrieked at the sight of his hand on the hilt of a bloody dagger. He held his spear out, ready to protect his leader.

"Sir? Are you alright?" he asked.

Gaven had to act fast. He darted his eyes between the soldier and the dagger in Mirari's chest, then gave her a hard shove, the dagger sliding out from her chest. Her scream didn't go unnoticed. She wobbled back, barely able to stand up, but she wasn't going to surrender so easily. Mirari tried to generate another flame in her hand, but it disappeared like a feeble candlelight.

She snarled at him with her hand over her wound, and began to back away. She gave Gaven one last look, then dashed into the forest with her hand over her wound. He watched until she was out of his sight.

The soldier asked with a tremble in his voice, "Do you want us to pursue her?"

"No, she won't live from her injuries," Gaven said, handing the dagger to the soldier. The soldier looked disgusted at the sight of it, his face wrinkled as if he was holding back his breakfast. "What's the status?"

The soldier regained his composure and gave a crisp salute. "We got most of them, sir. Just executing the last of the ones resisting."

Gaven strode onto the main street, seeing the road paved with lifeless bodies, dolls and heirlooms abandoned in front of homes.

A young girl was hiding behind a barrel, clutching onto a doll. He could hear her whimpering, her courage gone with the souls of her caretakers. When she looked at the Valiant Tiger, Gaven saw a familiar face. Her eyes were pleading, yet accepting of the fate that awaited before her.

They were just like hers, the girl from his childhood. She was the one who encouraged him to become a great fighter, and gave him a reason to protect the ones closest to him. Even if it was fifteen years ago, he owed it to her for helping him get to Althaea, enabling him to become the great warrior he was today.

The soldier with him noticed the girl, and drew his spear.

"No," Gaven said, "that's enough. Leave the rest alive." The soldier saluted, then grabbed the little girl. She didn't put up any resistance as he pulled her up and led her to the rest of the army.

Gaven placed his hand on his chest. Even though Mirari was not in his heart anymore, it was like he could still hear her voice, dousing his impulse to solve everything through violence. It would take some time for him to get used to this hollow feeling again.

CHAPTER THIRTY-FIVE

A set of keys jangled outside the cell door. When Eoin looked up the shackles that bound him to the wall clanked against the rough stone. There had been some cursory questioning, but ultimately he'd been left alone to await his trial and inevitable death. He was old enough that he had plenty of regrets, but standing his ground in Aias wasn't one of them. Plenty of his people had died for this cause, he was just the latest who fell. Straightening his back as best he could, Eoin waited. He'd march to his death with dignity and take one last chance in front of the Council to warn them of the Defiants.

The door creaked open. The person was backlit by the lumastōne outside the cell, but Eoin recognized the figure anyway. Eoin tried to roll his shoulder and bit back a wince when the shackles prevented it. He hadn't expected the region leader to be the one to escort him.

When the Valiant Tiger stepped inside and swung the door closed behind them, Eoin suspected that Gaven wasn't here just to take him to the trial. As Gaven approached, Eoin could read the somber look on his face, the look of a defeated man. Just who was the real prisoner here? It reminded Eoin of that strange conversation they had had once.

The exact words didn't come to mind, but he remembered some. "You know what you told me?" he asked, but Gaven pretended not to hear him. He fiddled with the ring of keys in his hand and Eoin continued. "We broke bread together and you said you wished you'd never left home. That you had regrets for abandoning them." He lowered his voice, but in the silence of the room, it rang loud. "You said you were fighting for their forgiveness." Gaven's nostrils flared. "Are you still fighting?"

Shoulders tightening, Gaven sneered at him. "I'll be glad to see your body swinging in about an hour. You won't be getting out of this." Though he spoke sharply, he avoided looking Eoin in the eye.

"Even if I don't survive the day, your problems won't be over and I think you know that, at least a little."

"Silence," Gaven hissed, taking another aggressive step forward.

Eoin wouldn't be silenced though. Couldn't be. He'd lost his leverage among the Blessed. His staunchest allies were dead and soon he would be too. His window of opportunity was closing. If the real puppeteer behind the Blessed was to be stopped, she would enact her final plan and it all would be lost. To stop her, Eoin needed help from good-hearted people like Mirari. And Gaven, if the man couldn't get out of his own way. "Bennet, the Bishop, Valara, Nora, Laikos. Me. You caught us all, but we are *nothing* compared to the real leaders you are looking for. You'll never find peace at this rate. Not until you find—"

Gaven snatched Eoin up by his collar. Eoin's arms strained behind him as he jerked far forward. "Is that the cow-slaver you filled Mirari's head with? Lead her down a path that—"

"Whatever path she went down didn't have to be her last." He breathed sharply as pain twinged down his arms as Gaven gripped him tighter. "You killed her. Ladies and gentlemen, our Valiant Tiger." Gaven shoved him hard enough that Eoin hit the wall. "Now what?"

Chest heaving, Gaven stared at him with a wild look in his eyes. Gaven cracked his knuckles. "Guess."

<hr>

GAVEN DRAGGED Eoin before the council, still seething. The blacksmith stumbled in his grip. One eye was swollen closed and the burn scars on his arms were eclipsed by the bruises. Gaven forced him down to his knees before the circle of the six councilors. The councilors looked down on Eoin with almost identical frowns on their faces. The look was reflected in the others invited to the trial: region leaders, commanders and even some members of the Knights.

Fangbane rose to his feet. "What is this? What happened to him?" Gaven shrugged and moved to take his seat in the stands. Fangbane opened his mouth to speak more and Gaven sent him a glare.

Suzan sighed wearily. "He can't speak if his jaw is broken."

Glancing back, Gaven looked Eoin over. He was swaying lightly where he was kneeling, trying to compensate for the bruised, maybe broken, ribs. Gaven shrugged again. "He can talk."

"Let's just get started," Councilor Julie said. "What's done is done. There's no need to delay any further."

As promised, when the councilors brought their questions before Eoin, he managed to choke out some answers. It didn't matter though. The trial was largely performative. Eoin's execution was inevitable. He denied nothing they accused him of, and by the end of the trial the majority of the Council was pleased with catching what they thought to be, possibly, the final leader of the Blessed. Problem solved.

Gaven didn't pay much attention to the actual trial. With his elbows braced on the desk he sat behind, he had his mouth covered by his interlocked hands and he kept his dark glare on Fangbane. He had known. There was no way he hadn't known and yet hadn't seen fit to share Mirari's true identity. Because of that, there had been no way for him to save her. During the trial, Gaven's dramatic final moments with Mirari played in his mind over and over. If Fangbane looked uncomfortable, it was only what he deserved.

As though Julie was the one who could read minds, Gaven heard her say Mirari's name and tuned back in. What were they talking about?

"You want to speak to Mirari?" Fangbane said, glancing at Gaven.

Julie tapped her desk. "Yes, of course. We need to corroborate the information we've received. According to all accounts, Mirari Zanette was present for this final encounter with the leader who attacked the Grand Ball." She raised an eyebrow. "In fact, didn't we hear something about her returning to Aias on multiple occasions." She glanced toward Gaven and then the other Knights. "Where is she, Region Leader Gaven? She needs to answer a few questions."

Gaven's hands clenched tight enough to turn the knuckles white. "That's impossible. She can't answer anything now."

"What happened?" Fangbane asked in a low voice.

Gaven resisted the urge to snarl at him. *You already know,* he thought darkly. "During the battle... Mirari was injured." He closed his eyes to hide his fury, knee bouncing underneath the desk. "She didn't make it." He ignored the shocked cries coming from the other Knights. He kept his thoughts focused on his anger. "Whatever happened, it's all in the past now. There's not much to corroborate anyway."

"So you say," Julie said, but she looked down at Eoin with rage glittering in her eyes. She sighed. "Very well, I suppose I'll have to be satisfied with that. Anyone else?" Down the line, each of the other councilors voiced their agreement and the trial was over.

The decision: Eoin was to be executed immediately. Before Gaven could descend the steps to take Eoin to the gallows, already set up and waiting, he was intercepted by Fangbane and another guard took his place, forcing the blacksmith to his feet.

The council chambers quickly emptied of everyone except the Knights who attended the trial. The others were eager to witness Eoin's public execution and put an end to the investigation of the Grand Ball attack.

Snorting, Gaven walked around him and headed toward the hallway that led to the gallows. "Gaven. Gaven, wait."

"You've got a lot of nerve talking to me about her," Gaven said, keeping his pace.

He didn't slow down when Fangbane rushed to stand in front of him, but the other man grabbed Gaven's arm before he could walk past him.

"What do you mean she's gone? What happened?" Fangbane whispered.

Gaven turned the full force of his glare onto him. He snapped, jerking his hand from Fangbane's grip. "Doesn't matter." Shoving his hand into his pocket, he dug out the golden phoenix badge that once belonged to his partner. "She's gone, Fang. Let her go."

When Gaven turned around to keep walking toward the execution, he was blocked once again. This time by Shiba. Neo stood by his side as though he hoped to stop Shiba from acting on the impulse they could both see in his eyes. "Don't you have anything to say?" Shiba demanded through gritted teeth.

Keeping his face like stone, Gaven shook his head. "There's nothing to say."

Neo grabbed Shiba's arm, but was shaken off. Shiba pulled back and Gaven braced himself. The punch was hard enough that Gaven rocked back on his heels but maintained his footing.

Spitting out a mouthful of blood, Gaven asked, "Satisfied?"

Shiba tried to rush him again, but this time Neo hooked his arms underneath Shiba's shoulders and held him in place. Fangbane stepped between the two, holding his hands up to them both. "Now's not the time for this." He glanced around. "Nor is it the place."

Gaven swiped his hand across the back of his mouth, licking the taste of blood from his lips. "I should be there for the execution."

He started walking again. Shiba shouted behind him. "Go on. Leave. You leave a trail of blood and death everywhere you go."

"Shiba…" Neo said softly.

"Give him time," Fangbane said. "He's been through a lot."

Before Gaven could gather enough steam to reveal Fangbane's duplicity, their conversation was interrupted by a scream. Exchanging a look with Fangbane, Gaven chose to put his anger aside and run toward the commotion.

Gaven ran out into the arena where the gallows had been erected. Guards were standing around with their weapons drawn, but there didn't appear to be any fighting going on. Shouldering forward, Gaven grabbed one of the men. "What's going on?" He looked around wildly, catching sight of councilors and region leaders. No blacksmiths though. "Where's Eoin? Where's the criminal?" he demanded, shaking the man.

Appearing beside Gaven, Shiba swore harshly. "This was his plan all along. Going along meekly with his execution."

"That's why he was so quick to confess to everything," Gaven said. He clenched his hands around his weapon even if there was no point in drawing it. Holding it made him feel in control, and he enjoyed the thrill that coarse through his veins. "The coward might have fled, but I swear I'll find him."

EPILOGUE

Her body shivered, feeling the chilly air brush against her naked arms. It was too cold to open her eyes. She wanted to stay curled up, comfortable in this warm, almost fetal position.

The first sensation she noticed was blades of grass tickling her nose; sharp green edges, brushing against her face. They had a refreshing smell, like the dancing waters of the fountain in the courtyard of the Hale's estate, mixed with the soggy dirt that would accumulate on the pastel-colored shoes she always wore at home.

But that was nineteen years ago.

Mirari's eyes shot open.

It was pitch black. She blinked a couple of times to make sure they were open. It took a few moments, but as her eyes adjusted, she saw stretches of dark green oaks, shrubs, and dandelions. The longer she stared at them the more she realized the dozens of trees in front of her saw no end.

Where she was now wasn't that different from when she woke up in the forest where Salathiel and Gaven lived. Except this time, she didn't want to be found.

And this time, no one was going to save her.

She raised her hand to touch the scar on her shoulder. How she got it, she couldn't remember. It was now sealed, thanks to the spare renastōnes she carried, but she could still feel the numbness of the impact.

And she lost a lot of blood. She could feel her fingers and toes growing numb, her body refusing to move. She could only sit and wait to freeze to death.

She recalled what happened that morning like a dream, only she knew it wasn't. There was an empty feeling in her chest — only a fraction of her energy remained. How far had she wandered from Aias? Was the battle over?

Mirari banged her head between her legs, screaming as tears rolled down her face.

Where would she go from here? She could survive out in the woods for as long as she desired. Was that truly her fate?

Part of her was relieved. At least she was finally free from her duties and the expectations that society had heaped on her. There would be no more Althaeans telling her how to behave, scorning her for nothing other than the place of her birth. She could never please them.

The other part of her wondered if this could really be her destiny – stranded forever in a forest, having accomplished nothing, never to be remembered as anything but a disappointment, a traitor, and a disgrace.

Yet, a sense of calm was blooming in her.

She couldn't remember the last time she was able to sit outdoors like this. Despite the cold weather, the gentle breeze was cradling her to sleep. In the still night, the forest sounded at peace. It had nothing to worry about, no interfering humans. Perhaps a human had never set foot in this side of the forest. It was just her and nature.

Perhaps humanity was a lost cause. She was a fool to believe she could change it. In the end, people were no better than animals.

She thought back on her old life with Salathiel. How they had enjoyed their quiet life in a small town, away from all the drama and dream-seekers. If she hadn't joined the Knights, if she had just stayed in Solarin and lived the quiet life she vowed she would, she wouldn't be in this mess.

Be a merchant — just her and Salathiel. In that moment, she wanted nothing more than that.

As she closed her eyes, she rested her back against a stump, slipping into the velvety darkness. She wouldn't mind enjoying this moment a little longer.

She felt a warm cloak fall over her body, sheathing her from the cold. Who was there? She didn't care. She had nothing left to live for. This person was wasting their time.

"Mirari? Hey. Can you hear me?" It was a man's voice. It was gentle, comforting, enough to caress her to sleep.

Her eyelids were too heavy to budge, but the scent from the cloak triggered a sense of delight. Hueburry? Lactetara? She took a whiff of it again.

Bossle figs. They were a delicacy in Minetta, and it wasn't something that the average person carried. It reminded her of someone, someone she knew, someone who always carried a handful of those figs in his pocket.

She felt for the pocket of the cloak and reached inside. She judged its rough texture, and she was right. She opened her eyes to check, holding up the bossle fig to her eyes.

"No no no, don't eat that. You're dehydrated." The man plucked the fig from her hand and gave her his flask instead. He practically had to force it down her, tilting her head back as the water dripped down her throat.

She wanted to scold this man for forcing her to live. She

didn't ask to be taken care of, and she certainly didn't ask for his help.

But when she shifted her eyes to see her savior, she flinched and choked. She snatched his wrist, keeping him within her grasp until she could regain her breath. Then she got another good look at him. Surely she must've been hallucinating. Her body was on the verge of collapse and her senses couldn't be trusted. She reached out to touch his face, and when she felt the warmth radiate from his cheeks, her mouth dropped open.

He smiled and pulled her in for a hug.

"Good to see you, Miss Miracle."

THE STORY CONTINUES IN

EDGE OF DIVERGENCE
Book 3 of the Alliance Series

"If judgment is by how I see it, then
I would plunge your world into chaos."

Will they align with the lesser of two evils
or defy fate's relentless demands?

In the epic conclusion of the Alliance series,
one wrong choice will forever alter the
fate of the world.

The Alliance Series

"RARE AND DAZZLING."
- AuthorsReading.com

"A WORLD FULLY IMAGINED."
- PenCraft Book Awards

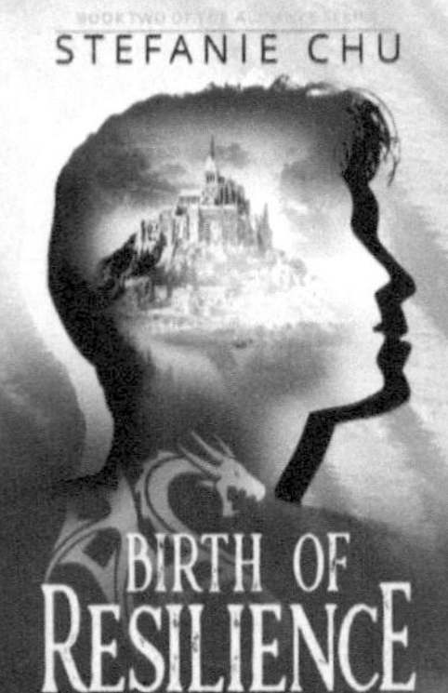

Follow the latest release at

STEFANIECHU.COM/ALLIANCE

Dear Reader,

I am honored that you have made it to this page.

If you enjoyed this read, then please leave
an honest review. Your support
means the world to me.

Love,
Stefanie

Can't wait for the next book? Be the first to
read it when you **become a VIP Member**.
Join today and get free desktop wallpapers.

www.StefanieChu.com/vip

ACKNOWLEDGMENTS

This book was, without a doubt, a true test of my resilience. There were countless moments when I contemplated chucking *Birth of Resilience* into a river. Almost every day, I fought against the overpowering urge to just give up.

The release of the novel was delayed an entire year because beta readers weren't entirely satisfied with the book being solely a prequel. Should I publish a story that isn't the best it could be? It was a tough call, but I made the difficult decision to cut out two-thirds of the story to make it "perfect." My co-habitants watched me become a lunatic as I covered walls in post-it notes, spending weeks upon weeks researching and diving into books like *The Grace of Kings* and rewatching *The Witcher*, all in an attempt to construct a past-present timeline as gracefully as they had done.

In many ways, I felt like Gaven himself—exhausted and beaten down, wondering if it was even worth pushing forward. But deep down, I knew that publishing the Alliance series was my lifelong dream, and the decision to rewrite the book was one I did not regret. I salvaged what I could from this book, and those discarded parts found new life in *Echoes of Enmity*. Looking back now, I'm grateful that the final story unfolded the way it did.

Throughout this journey, I've come to believe that resilience is an extraordinary trait and one we should value over physical strength and intellectual prowess. Life is full of uncertainties and upheavals, but the ability to keep moving forward is what truly makes us the strongest of all.

My editors: Aanchal J., Rick N., Nathanael W.,
and Charisse N. — you are all rock stars.

My imaginative beta readers: Melissa W. and Alex H. —
thanks for reading countless versions of this book.

A big thanks to all my loyal Alliance fans and everyone who has supported me along the way.

APPENDIX

FIGHTER CLASS – Fighters are trained in one of four styles:

Aegis – bow users in touch with nature and animals.

Celta – healers & spellcasters who are masters of *kore*.

Paragon – brawlers & warriors with close-combat weaponry.

Umbra – mixed-weapon fighters with self-defense techniques.

HALE INVENTIONS – The Hale family discovered they could process raw crystals containing energy, known as hāstals, and enhanced them with kore to create new technology.

Aulāce – indestructible shackles made with kore and alloys.

Aulōg – a lock coded with one's aura. Used to secure doors.

Clōve – a hāstal-sewn glove capable of communication.

Comstōne – quartz geodes that direct sounds to other stones.

Kinastōne – a barrel-shaped geode used to generate energy.

Kirinvā Stone – a hāstal rumored to offer protection.

Kōnvoy – a caravan that transports large shipping materials.

Lumastōne – a glowing pebble that replaces candlelight.

Oriōn – a cube that crafts a geometric replica of landscapes.

Renastōne – palm-sized stones that amplify healing abilities.

<u>Visōr</u> – a platform that mirrors images.

RELIGIONS – It is a common belief that all life departs to either the spiritual world of Nagama or Inferna. If the Gods do not deem the soul worthy to join them in Nagama, they are sent to one of the seven flaming gates of Inferna.

Deity of Orism – Orists believe in one deity: Oris, the God of Judgment. He is primarily worshiped by Althaeans and celtas.

Deities of Quintism – Quintists, common among Minettans, worship only the five main Gods and Goddesses.
    <u>Aten</u> – God of Elements
    <u>Cordelia</u> – Goddess of War
    <u>Sarkan</u> – God of Authority
    <u>Taurin</u> – God of Land
    <u>Urabe</u> – Goddess of the Sea

Deities of Plethorism – Plethorists acknowledge the existence of hundreds of Gods and Goddesses, but a tribe in Valenia will often choose to praise one or two deities. The following are only a fraction of all known deities:
    <u>Accolade</u> – God of Reverence
    <u>Candela</u> – Goddess of Purity
    <u>Current</u> – God of Negotiation
    <u>Cygnus</u> – Goddess of Fate
    <u>Erel</u> – Goddess of Mercy
    <u>Kanmor</u> – God of Wealth
    <u>Lachess</u> – Goddess of Devotion
    <u>Mersa</u> – Goddess of Fertility
    <u>Mirari</u> – Goddess of Miracles
    <u>Ophelia</u> – Goddess of Health

<u>Xerxes</u> – God of Power
<u>Verben</u> – God of Wisdom

TERMINOLOGY – These jargons and commercial goods are unique to the land of the three empires.

<u>Aster Spells</u> – an advanced category of spells.

<u>Aura</u> – the spiritual energy unique to each individual.

<u>Bellberry</u> – a bitter, ceremonial juice in Avon.

<u>Bitterworm</u> – an invertebrate good for harvesting vegetables.

<u>Bossle Figs</u> – a fruit that grows underground in a shell.

<u>Buzzbean</u> – a mixture of nuts and herbs used as tea.

<u>Cannonpop</u> – tiny spice berries with intense, fiery flavor.

<u>Cepha Metal</u> – a dense material that blocks psychic energy.

<u>Cryphedeon</u> – a disc-shaped herbal flower used for flavoring.

<u>Featherpit</u> – someone who wears feathers for fashion, directed at insulting Minettan culture.

<u>Flatty/Flat-Faced</u> – a derogatory word comparing two-faced Althaeans with the sides of a flat coin.

<u>Galuchi Seeds</u> – used as hunting bait to beckon wild animals.

<u>Gotchen</u> – a popular card game that often involves a wager.

<u>Gritbear</u> – a large omnivore with stocky legs and shaggy hair.

<u>Hammerhog</u> – an insult to describe someone ugly.

<u>Hueberry</u> – a tart berry with a unique gold color.

<u>Iconel Alloys</u> – materials used to improve durability.

<u>Ilorinae</u> – a territorial plant that can cause fainting spells.

<u>Kamori Powder</u> – pressed ash from the corpse of insects.

<u>Kippin</u> – a type of neutral tea that tastes like water.

<u>Kore</u> – affinity of elemental energy that one is born with.

<u>Lactetara</u> –a tangy, vibrant red berry with refreshing tartness.

<u>Larmender</u> – fortified wine made exclusively by House Tepis.

<u>Lucifera Trees</u> – tall and thin tropical trees with wide leaves.

<u>Lorestone</u> – a yellow sharpening stone.

<u>Lumapetal</u> – a herbal plant that grows in wet caves.

<u>Manchego</u> – a nutty, savory cheese aged thirty-six months.

<u>Mirithium</u> – a common type of ore used to craft armor.

<u>Milark</u> – a tropical leaf containing sweet and spicy flavors.

<u>Milkenkase</u> – a type of fine cheese from Eudoxia.

<u>Muddleberry</u> – a crimson-colored berry used to craft wine.

<u>Muffintail</u> – a fish with a compressed body and round tail.

<u>Norkfruit</u> – a tropical citrus fruit with a purple skin.

<u>Roquefort</u> – a cheese renowned for its rich, complex flavor.

<u>Ruthia</u> – a soft, velvety flower with a gentle fragrance.

<u>Speedspike</u> – plant seeds with a spiky surface.

<u>Swine</u> – a derogatory word used to describe Valenians, who live among nature and are bloated with wealth.

<u>Talla</u> – a symbol or drawing inked into skin.

<u>Torchberry</u> – a sweet jelly glaze used for red meats.

<u>Valkyrie</u> – Obanian women who become fighters.

<u>Yerna Hay</u> – highly flammable grain crops grown in Valenia.

<u>Zotweed</u> – a mind-altering substance made of dried pedals.

ABOUT THE AUTHOR

Meet Stefanie, a bird-obsessed aficionado from the San Francisco Bay Area. Her globetrotting adventures during her MBA degree dragged her from Asia to Europe, but now she's happily grounded in Seattle, Washington. When she is not indulging in Japanese cuisine or something lavender, she subjects herself to cinematic torment.

Learn more at STEFANIECHU.COM

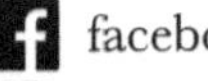 facebook.com/StefanieChu.Author
 instagram.com/StefanieChu.Author

9 781737 712527